"Well, look who survived her own demise."

"What the hell are you doing here, Thane?" And how had he escaped Avari, the hellion Tod had given him to?

"This is all your fault, little Miss Won't-Stay-Dead. You and that blond reaper..."

Chills crawled up my arms. "What's my fault? What's coming?"

A slow, creepy smile spread over his face. "Until next time, little *bean sidhe...*"

"No!" I realized he was about to blink out of the alley, and in my desperation to take the soul he carried before he left, I accidentally unleashed my *bean sidhe* wail at full power.

Top volume.

Praise for the Soul Screamers series
by *New York Times* bestselling author
RACHEL VINCENT

"*Twilight* fans will love it."
—*Kirkus Reviews*

"The story rocks (for teens and adults, I might add)."
—*Book Bitch*

"Fans of those vampires will enjoy this new crop of otherworldly beings."
—*Booklist*

"I'm so excited about this series."
—*The Eclectic Book Lover*

"A must for any reading wish list."
—*Tez Says*

"A book like this is one of the reasons that I add authors to my auto-buy list. This is definitely a keeper."
—*TeensReadToo.com*

Also by
***New York Times* bestselling author**
Rachel Vincent

in reading order

from
Harlequin TEEN

Soul Screamers

"My Soul to Lose"*
"Reaper"
MY SOUL TO TAKE*
MY SOUL TO SAVE*
MY SOUL TO KEEP
MY SOUL TO STEAL
IF I DIE
"Never to Sleep"

*also available in SOUL SCREAMERS VOLUME ONE

from
HARLEQUIN MIRA

The Shifters

STRAY
ROGUE
PRIDE
PREY
SHIFT
ALPHA

Unbound

BLOOD BOUND
SHADOW BOUND
OATH BOUND

RACHEL VINCENT

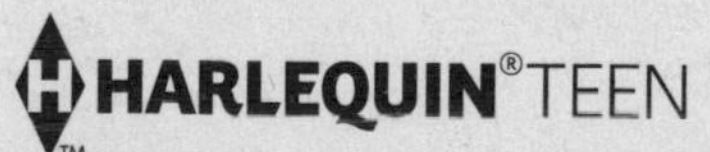

Recycling programs for this product may not exist in your area.

ISBN-13: 978-0-373-21061-9

BEFORE I WAKE

This edition published by arrangement with Harlequin Books S.A.

For questions and comments about the quality of this book please contact us at Customer_eCare@Harlequin.ca.

www.HarlequinTEEN.com

Printed in U.S.A.

This is for every reader who's ever stayed up too late to read just one more chapter. For every reader with a paperback in a purse or backpack or glove compartment. For everyone with an ebook on a phone or tablet or laptop. For everyone listening to an audio book in the car, at the gym, or on the train.

This is for every reader the librarians know by name.

For everyone who's ever said, "You *have* to read this!"

Thank you all so much for making Kaylee and her friends a part of your lives.

I WAS A VIRGIN SACRIFICE. AND YEAH, IT'S JUST as creepy as it sounds. I died on a Thursday, at twenty-seven minutes after midnight, killed by a monster intent on stealing my soul. The good news? He didn't get it. The bad news? Turns out not even death will get you out of high school....

I've always hated Mondays, but this particular Monday, a beautiful day in late April, seemed ready to deliver its very own brand of hell. I stood in front of the bathroom mirror at seven-thirty in the morning, staring at myself, trying to decide exactly how alive I should look. In the movies, people are always faking their own deaths, but I couldn't think of anyone else—real or fictional—who'd faked survival. I'd have to blaze this trail all on my own.

How pale would a person look twenty-nine days after being stabbed to death? That would depend on the severity of the wound, right? On the number of organs injured? On the amount of blood lost? Since no one at school knew any of those details, they wouldn't know if my performance was off. So I could play the part however I wanted. Right?

No one had to know that my pale skin and sweaty palms were really the result of a colossal case of first-day-back nerves.

My stomach churned as I stared at my reflection, wondering how I could possibly feel so different, yet look exactly the same as I had before I died, except for the new scar. Exactly the same as I would look next year, and the year after that, and a decade after that, and for as many centuries as my afterlife lasted.

"Kaylee! Breakfast!" my father called from the kitchen.

"I'm dead, Dad," I called back, dropping my hairbrush into the drawer. "I don't eat anymore."

A minute later, my father appeared in the doorway in a grease-splattered T-shirt and jeans, frowning at me. "You don't *have* to eat. That doesn't mean you shouldn't. I think you'd feel a lot better if you had something warm in your stomach."

I turned and leaned against the counter, crossing my arms over my chest. "That's not really how it works."

"No arguments. I made pancakes and bacon. I want you at the table in five minutes."

I sighed as his footsteps retreated toward the kitchen. He was trying. I wasn't sure *what* he was trying, but he was serious about it.

I crossed the hall into my room for a pair of shoes and blinked in surprise at the empty space at the center of my room, where the bed used to be. It had been four weeks since we'd gotten rid of the ruined mattress and sheets, and I still wasn't used to the new purple quilt that had replaced the blue comforter my psychotic math teacher had bled out on.

After my death, I'd avoided my room for nearly a week until my father figured out what I'd been too embarrassed to tell him—that I couldn't go in there without seeing it all in my head. Reliving my own death.

That night, he and Tod had rearranged every piece of furniture I owned until my room was unrecognizable. That was three weeks ago, and I still couldn't get used to seeing my bed against the wall, my desk slanted across one corner of the room. But this time when I glanced into that corner, I couldn't help but smile.

Tod sat in my desk chair, his curls golden in the glow from my bedside lamp, his eyes as blue as the ocean, the one time I'd seen it. Styx was curled up on my bed, asleep, paying the reaper no attention whatsoever. Half Pomeranian, half Netherworld guard dog, she was the fiercest, most dangerous six pounds of frizzy fur and pointy teeth I'd ever seen, other than her littermates. She was also a living, breathing, growling security system, bred to warn me when danger approached on either side of the world barrier.

It had taken her weeks to understand that growling at Tod wasn't going to get rid of him.

Tod's brother—my ex—was wrestling with that same conclusion.

Tod stood as soon as he saw me, and I couldn't resist a smile, in spite of the nerves still twisting my insides into knots.

My arms slid around his neck and delicious, tiny little sparks shot up my spine as his hand settled at my waist, and I secretly marveled at the fact that I was allowed to touch him whenever I wanted.

This was still new, me and Tod. Our relationship was only a month old, yet somehow, he was the only thing that still seemed to fit, since my death. Going through the motions in the rest of my life—an ironic term, if I'd ever heard one—now felt like trying to fit into clothes I'd outgrown. Everything was uncomfortable, and too tight, and not as bright as I remembered.

But Tod was the same. Only better.

"Aren't you supposed to be at work? Eventually Levi's going to notice that you keep skipping out," I said when I finally had to let him go. Levi, his boss, had a soft spot for Tod, but in their line of work, leniency could only go so far. Tod was a reaper—more than two and a half years dead, but perpetually nearly eighteen. He worked the midnight-to-noon shift at the local hospital, reaping the souls of those scheduled to die on his watch.

Except when he was delivering pizza. And helping me pretend I was still alive.

"I had a break and I thought you might be nervous this morning. So I brought you this." He handed me a paper cup of coffee, and I took a cautious sip. Caramel latte. My favorite, and the only edible thing I still seemed to crave since my unfortunate demise. "And this." He spread his arms, showing off a physique even death couldn't mar, and I wanted to touch him some more. Then some more after that. "I figure one or the other will make you feel better."

"Both. They both make me feel better." I pulled him close for a kiss, then didn't want to let him go. "I don't wanna go back to school today."

"So don't. Come hang out with me at work." Tod dropped back into my desk chair and swiveled to face me while I knelt to grab my sneakers from beneath my bed. "We can play naughty dress up with the hospital gowns and rearrange the supply closets."

"Isn't that dangerous? What if they can't find some important drug or equipment in an emergency?"

Tod shrugged. "Nobody's gonna die without my help, anyway, so what's the harm?"

The harm? Potential brain damage. Paralysis. And all kinds of other nonlethal catastrophes. Fortunately, his grin said he was kidding, so I didn't have to go through with the lecture.

"Kaylee!" my dad shouted, and Tod sniffed in the direction of the hall.

"Is that bacon?"

"And pancakes." I shoved my foot into the sneaker and tugged on the laces to tighten it. "He thinks I should start my first day back at school with a healthy breakfast. I think he's been spending too much time with your mom." In addition to being an amazing amateur baker, Harmony Hudson was the only fellow female *bean sidhe* I knew.

"It's not a bad idea," Tod said. "Breakfast is my third favorite meal of the day."

"Not today." Standing, I tugged him closer so I could slide my hand behind his neck, my fingers playing in the soft curls that ended there. "I think he needs some father-daughter time."

As grateful as my father was for everything Tod had done to try to save my life, he'd had his fill of houseguests for a while. Tod and I had spent nearly every waking moment together since my death, and for two people who didn't need sleep, that was a lot of moments, even with his jobs and my training standing in the way.

"Oh, fine. Enjoy your pancakes and homework."

"Thanks. Enjoy your sick people. Will I see you at lunch?"

The blues in his irises swirled like cobalt flames, and something deep inside me smoldered. "You'll be the only one who sees me. You don't need to eat, anyway, right?"

"Oh, *now* I don't need to eat...."

He pulled me close again, and that kiss was longer, deeper. Hotter. Touching Tod made me feel more alive than anything else had since the moment my heart stopped beating.

"Kaylee, *please* come eat something!" my dad yelled, and Tod groaned in frustration. He held me tighter for just a second, then stepped back and let his hand trail down my arm slowly. Then he was gone, and for a moment, I felt empty.

That was a scary moment, but one I couldn't quite shake. I'd thought that being dead-but-still-there would feel a lot like being alive, but I was wrong. I felt like I was out of sync with the world. Like the planet had kept spinning while I was gone, and now that I was back, I couldn't catch up.

I grabbed my latte and headed for the kitchen, where I dropped into my chair at the card table we'd been meaning to replace with a real one since my dad had moved back to town seven months ago. The plate in front of me held four pancakes and—I swear—half a pound of bacon. Fried, not microwaved, as evidenced by the grease splattered all over the stove and adjacent countertop. My dad was serious about this traditional home-life thing.

It was kinda cute.

My father pulled out his own chair and started to hand me one of the coffee mugs he held, but then he noticed the latte, and his smile slipped a little. "Tod?"

"Yeah, but he's gone. He was just trying to help."

He set both mugs in front of his own plate and picked up his fork. "I'm going to assume the steaming cup of Starbucks means he wasn't here all night?"

Translation: *Your undead boyfriend is supposed to be gone by eleven so you can pretend to sleep.*

"He works nights, Dad." But we both knew that didn't mean anything, when the commute was instantaneous.

For the first couple of days after my death, my father had tried to stay up all night to make sure there were no unauthorized visits, and I didn't bother to point out how futile his efforts were. If Tod and I didn't want to be seen or heard, we wouldn't be. Both reapers and extractors—my official new title with the reclamation department—had selective visibility, audibility, and corporeality. Basically, we could choose who saw and heard us, and whether or not we existed physically on the human plane.

Sounds cool, I know, but it comes with a hell of a price.

My dad set his fork down and I caught a rare glimpse of the concern swirling in his eyes. "I'm worried about you, Kaylee."

"Don't be. Nothing's changed." But that wasn't true, and even if it had been, it wouldn't have set him at ease. My life wasn't exactly normal before I died, and death had done nothing to improve that.

"You don't eat. You hardly ever talk anymore, and I haven't seen you watch TV or pick up a book in days. I walk into your room, and half the time you're not there, even when you're there."

"I'm working on that," I mumbled, swirling a bite of pancake in a puddle of syrup. "Corporeality is harder than it looks. It takes practice." And concentration.

"Are you sure you're ready for school? We could give it another week." But he seemed to regret the words as soon as he'd said them. Another week off would mean another week of me sitting around the house doing nothing when I wasn't training as an extractor, and that's what was worrying him in the first place.

"I need to go. They all know today's the day."

"They" were my teachers, classmates, and the local television stations. I was big news—the girl who'd survived being stabbed by her own math teacher. My father had stopped answering the home phone, and we'd had to change my cell number when someone leaked it to the press. They all wanted to know what it was like to nearly die. To kill the man who'd tried to kill me. They wanted to know how I'd survived.

None of them could ever know the truth—that I hadn't survived. That was part of the deal—allowing me to live my afterlife like my murder had never happened. Protecting my secret meant keeping up with schoolwork and work-work, in addition to my new duties extracting souls from those who shouldn't have them.

"If anything goes wrong, I want you to call me," my father said, and I nodded. I wasn't going to tell him that if anything went wrong, I could blink out of school and into my own room before he could even get to his car in the parking lot at work. He knew that. He was just trying to help and to stay involved, and I loved him for it. For that, and for the pancakes, even if I had no real desire to eat them.

We both sipped our coffee, and I noticed that his appetite seemed to have disappeared, too. Then he set his mug down and picked up a strip of bacon. "You know, I've been thinking about this Friday…." He left the sentence hanging while he took a bite.

"What's this Friday?" I asked, and my father frowned.

"Your birthday, Kaylee."

For a moment, I could only blink at him, mentally denying the possibility, while I counted the days in my head. Time had lost all meaning over the past month. Tod said that was normal—something about absent circadian rhythms—but it didn't seem possible that I could have forgotten my own birthday.

"I'm turning seventeen…" I whispered.

Except that I wasn't. The anniversary of my birth would come and go, but I'd still be sixteen and eleven-twelfths. I'd be sixteen and eleven-twelfths forever—at least physically. I would always look too young to vote. Too young to drink. Too young to drive a rental car, should that urge ever strike.

And none of those limitations had ever seemed more pointless. What did it matter?

What did *any* of it matter, anymore?

"So, who do you want to invite to the party?" My dad picked up his mug and sipped, waiting for my answer.

I frowned. "I don't want a party." Very few people knew I hadn't really lived, and of those, Nash and Sabine—my ex and *his* ex—currently hated me for framing Nash for my murder. I'd had no choice, and I'd accepted the duties of my afterlife mostly to unframe Nash—if I wasn't dead, he couldn't have killed me. But I couldn't blame him for hating me.

Still, even if Nash and Sabine both came, there wouldn't be enough of my real friends to constitute a party, and I didn't want to have to talk to anyone else.

"So, what do you usually do on your birthday?" He didn't know the answer to his own question because he'd left me with my aunt and uncle—his brother—after my mother died. I'd only had him back for seven months.

He regretted leaving me—I knew that for a fact—and that regret was infinitely heavier for him, now that I was dead.

"Em and I usually rent movies and binge on junk food." But that wouldn't work this year. I'd never had a boyfriend on my birthday before, and I'd never had a father on my birthday before. And I'd certainly never been dead on my birthday before.

My dad looked so disappointed I wanted to hug him. So I did the next best thing. "Fine. A party. But a small one. Friends and family only."

He gave me half a smile. "Decorations?"

"No. But you can get a cake. Chocolate, with cream cheese frosting. And I get a corner slice." If my appetite ever came back, I planned to eat whatever the hell I wanted, for the rest of my afterlife. Calories mean nothing to the dead. "And I wouldn't turn down a couple of presents."

"Done." He gave me a real smile that time, and I was relieved to see it. "I'm sorry I missed all the other birthdays, Kay."

I shrugged. "You didn't miss much."

My dad opened his mouth to protest, but before he could speak, a tall woman in a brown suit skirt appeared in the kitchen in sensible low heels, her short brown hair perfectly arranged. "Jeez, Madeline." My dad half choked, then gulped from his mug to clear his throat. "Ever hear of knocking?"

Madeline raised one perfectly arched brow at him. "Mr. Cavanaugh, I'm doing you a courtesy by letting you see and hear me at all. If that isn't good enough for you, I can appear to Kaylee alone."

Madeline was my boss in the reclamation department—she was the one who'd okayed the cover-up that hid my death and kept Nash from going down for my murder. She was also the only department member I'd met so far. My dad didn't like her. She hadn't bothered to form an opinion of him one way or another.

"It's fine. Would you like some coffee?" He held up the untouched mug he'd fixed for me.

"This is not a social visit, Mr. Cavanaugh." Madeline turned to me, arms crossed over her white blouse. "Kaylee, there's some question about whether or not you're ready to begin work on your own as an extractor. Four weeks is a rather short training period, we admit, but the soul thief you were restored to deal with has killed again, and we can't let this continue if there's any chance you're ready to take him or her on now."

A dull knot of fear blossomed deep in my stomach and I fed it with doubts about my own abilities because I knew I should be scared. I *would* be, if not for the pervasive numbness that settled deeper into me with each day of my afterlife.

"Wait a minute—who is this thief, and why does Kaylee

have to be the one to stop him? No one ever bothered to explain that to me. After all, I'm just her father."

Madeline focused her steely stare at him. "We don't know who or what the thief is, Mr. Cavanaugh. That's part of what we need Kaylee to find out. But we've already lost two agents chasing him, and frankly, because she is a *bean sidhe,* Kaylee is our best bet at the moment."

I was far from sure I could actually do what she wanted, but I couldn't find any flaw in her logic. As a female *bean sidhe,* in life, I'd been a death portent. When someone near me was close to death, I got the overwhelming need to wail for the departing soul. But what that wail really did was suspend the soul. Capture it. With the help of a male *bean sidhe*—Tod, Nash, my uncle, and my dad all qualified—I could reinstate that soul and save the life of its owner. But at great cost. To preserve the balance between life and death, when one life was saved, another would be taken.

Madeline had brought me back from the dead and recruited me in hopes that my *bean sidhe* abilities would help me succeed where the other extractors had failed. I desperately hoped she was right, because the alternative was the end to my afterlife. A final rest, as she called it.

"And you want me to do this today? Face this thief?" That fear inside me swelled until I felt cold on the inside, like ice was forming in my stomach.

"No. We don't know the thief's current whereabouts. But we need to know you're ready whenever we find him, so today is a trial run, to see how you perform on your own."

"But the target is real?" my father asked, and I was starting to wonder if I even needed to be here for this discussion of my afterlife.

"Very real." Madeline met my gaze. "Our necromancer has pinpointed a reaper Levi can't identify, which means this reaper isn't from his district." Tod's boss was familiar enough with his own employees to recognize their restored souls from a distance. "We suspect he's a rogue and we think he'll strike very soon. When that happens, I'll come for you, and you will go extract the stolen soul from him. Do you understand?"

"No." In fact, I wanted to curl up in my bed and hide under the covers. "If you know he's there, why not go get him now?"

"Because he hasn't stolen any souls yet."

"So you're just going to let someone die?"

Madeline scowled. "If we were to apprehend him now, we'd never know for sure the reaper is a rogue and we'd lose this opportunity to see you in action, on your own. Whatever life this reaper takes doesn't outweigh our opportunity to stop the thief you were restored to deal with. To put it in terms you'll understand, that's like swatting a fly, but letting the hornet live."

"Those aren't terms I understand! What if yours was the life he was going to take?" I shoved my plate away and stood. I'd found something else that could beat back the numbness—anger. "Who are you to decide what one life is worth?"

"I am your boss." Madeline didn't even raise her voice, and it irritated me to realize she wasn't as upset about this as I was. She wasn't upset at all. "This serial soul thief is much more dangerous than a single rogue reaper, which makes the reaper an ideal trial run for you. Especially considering that we can track the reaper, thanks to our new necromancer."

A necromancer, I'd recently learned, was someone who could see and communicate with the dead. Only *see* isn't a precise term. It's more of a sense than true sight. Though in my case, the literal interpretation also applied—a necromancer could see and hear me, even when I made myself invisible and inaudible to everyone else.

"When am I going to meet this necromancer?"

"Today," Madeline said. "He started class at your school last week, and since it seems likely that the two of you will run into each other, we'd like you to keep an eye on him."

"Your necromancer is a teenager?"

"I believe he's in his junior year."

"Is he alive?" my father asked. He thought the dead-to-living ratio of my friends and coworkers was high enough already.

"Both alive and human, Mr. Cavanaugh. He's also a very polite young man."

"They're gonna eat him alive," I mumbled, and my father chuckled. "Fine, I'll keep an eye out for your necromancer, but I can't promise that associating with me will do him any favors, socially."

"Thank you, Kaylee," Madeline said, and I glanced up in surprise over the courtesy. Not that Madeline was ever truly rude, she just wasn't very…personable. "I'll find you when and if this reaper turns out to be a rogue."

With that Madeline disappeared, and my father sighed. "So much for a normal first day back."

I dipped a strip of bacon in a pool of syrup. "Dad, I can count the number of normal school days I've had this year on one hand."

"I know. I'm sorry about that." He sipped from his mug, and I shrugged, but before I could reply, Madeline appeared in the kitchen again, and this time *I* nearly choked. "Change your mind about the coffee?" my dad asked, but she only shook her head.

"The reaper made a kill. It's time to earn your keep, Kaylee."

I swallowed the bite I'd nearly choked on then stood, nerves buzzing in my stomach like I'd devoured a swarm of flies, even though I knew what to do. I'd been practicing for a month. But… "I have to be in first period in twenty minutes."

"Then work fast." Madeline reached into the pocket of her suit jacket and pulled out what looked like a handful of metal, which she held out for me to take. I lifted what turned out to be a heart-shaped locket on a gold chain. It was pretty, in a sweet, dated kind of way.

"It's heavy." I frowned, trying to slide my fingernail into the edge seam. "And it doesn't open."

"That's because it's not a locket. It's an amphora. This will hold the soul after you capture it. This was designed especially for you, to look like something a young woman would wear."

"A young woman from what era?" I mumbled, slipping the chain over my head.

Madeline frowned. "Bring this back to me when you have the soul. Do not try to apprehend the rogue. It's up to the reapers to police their own—we're only concerned with the stolen soul he carries. Do you understand?"

"Yeah." I wasn't looking to pick a fight on my first day, anyway. "Where is this reaper?"

"He killed someone at the Daylight Donuts shop three minutes ago. If you hurry, he might still be close. If you have trouble finding or identifying him, sing for the soul."

"Okay, but—"

"Go, Kaylee."

I glanced from Madeline to my father, who nodded reluctantly. So I closed my eyes and thought of the doughnut shop—fortunately, I'd been there a million times. When I opened my eyes, I stood in the middle of the small dining area. The shop was open, but empty, and a quick glance around revealed the body of the owner on the floor of the kitchen, still in his long white apron. But there was no reaper.

Panicked, I stepped through the locked back door of the

shop and into an alley, my feet silent on the concrete because I was both invisible and incorporeal at the moment. I expected to have to wail for the stolen soul—hell, I half expected to be too late already—but there the reaper stood, near the Dumpster. Like he was waiting for me.

My breath caught in my throat, which would have been a problem if I'd actually needed to breathe. I recognized the reaper, even in those ridiculous sunglasses. I'd seen Tod give him to a hellion in the Netherworld to keep him from reaping my soul. Yet there he stood, alive and kicking—metaphorically speaking. The reaper who'd wanted me dead since the day he killed my mother, thirteen years ago.

Thane. Back from the dead. Again.

"WELL, LOOK WHO SURVIVED HER OWN DEMISE." Thane had clearly been waiting for someone, but based on the surprise drawn in the arch of his brows, I was obviously not that someone. "This is what happens when they replace an experienced reaper like me with a rookie." Thane shoved both hands into the pockets of the black slacks he'd been wearing the first time I'd seen him, days before I was scheduled to die, and my stomach clenched around nothing. I wasn't sure whether or not I should be personally afraid of him, now that my death date had come and gone, but I had plenty of still-living friends and family he could threaten if he decided he wanted revenge. "That *is* who sucker punched me, then sold me out, right? Your boyfriend's reaper brother?"

"No." Well, yes, but Thane had missed the whole boyfriend/brother drama, and I had no urge to fill him in. "What the hell are you doing here, Thane?" And how had he escaped Avari, the hellion Tod had given him to? "You have some kind of grudge against the doughnut industry? Did they forget to give you sprinkles?"

"Cute." He leaned with one shoulder against the side of the Dumpster and crossed both arms over his chest. "I'm reaping what *you* sowed."

"What *I* sowed?"

"This is all your fault, little miss won't-stay-dead. You and that blond reaper. Normally I hate sharing credit, but that doughnut guy is dead because of the two of you, and everything else that's coming...it's all your fault."

Chills crawled up my arms. "What's my fault? What's coming?"

A slow, creepy smile spread over his face. "Until next time, little *bean sidhe*..."

"No!" I realized he was about to blink out of the alley with less than a second to spare, and in my desperation to take the soul he carried before he left, I accidentally unleashed my *bean sidhe* wail at full power. Top volume.

Thane flinched and slapped his hands over his ears. Glass rattled in the windows of the doughnut shop behind me, and something actually shattered inside the Dumpster. If I hadn't been inaudible to everyone else, anyone within a two-block radius would have wanted to claw their own ears out of their heads.

I'd grown as a *bean sidhe* over the past few months, and death had further strengthened my skills, a fact I'd been kind of horrified to realize during my training.

"What are you?" Thane asked, arms spread for balance as the soul he'd stolen began to leach out of his body like smoke sucked out the only open window in a room. But I had to read his lips, because I couldn't hear him over my own screech, and I certainly couldn't answer.

The soul—a formless foglike shape—began to coalesce

around him, and for a moment, I panicked. I didn't know how to actually get it into the not-a-locket. Desperate, and acutely aware that I was running late for school, I took the locket off and held it by the chain at arm's length. To my immense relief, the soul began to spiral toward the locket, and as I watched, it soaked into the metal, just like Mr. Beck's soul had soaked into the dagger I'd killed him with.

When the soul was completely absorbed, I let my wail die and slid the chain over my head.

"What the hell are you?" Thane demanded again, his eyes wide with fear for the first time since I'd met him. Though the word *met* hardly seemed to do our introduction justice.

"You first. Why aren't you dead?"

"I am. You can't come back from death." His focus narrowed on me. "Which you now know from personal experience, don't you?" But I didn't know how to respond without giving up information he obviously hadn't yet figured out for himself. Thane reached for the amphora around my neck, and I backed away. "I don't know what game you're playing, little girl, but if you think being dead puts you beyond Avari's reach, you're in for quite a shock. He's pissed that he didn't get your soul when you died, and he'll be willing to go through everyone you love to get to you once he finds out you're still… here. So why don't you save them all an eternity of pain and come with me now?"

"Not gonna happen." I backed farther away, one hand clutching the amphora. "He can't get to me, and he can't get to anyone else, either." Because hellions couldn't cross into the human world. That was one of very few things I still knew without a doubt since my death. "Go to hell."

"I'm already there, little dead girl." Thane's voice faded to a whisper. "Soon you will be, too…." Then he blinked out of existence, and I knew he was truly gone, because reapers couldn't make themselves invisible to me anymore. Unfortunately, the opposite was also true.

I took a minute to catch my breath and when the shock wore off, a sharp new fear settled into its place. Avari's threats were nothing new, but Thane was back, and he was reaping again, and that was *very bad.* But I couldn't tell Madeline that I'd identified the rogue reaper or why his presence was a surprise without telling her what Tod had done. If she found out Tod had acted against a fellow reaper without authorization, she'd tell Levi. Levi already suspected what Tod had done, of course, but as long as no one else in a position of authority found out, he was free to keep ignoring what he knew. Because he liked Tod. But if he was notified of the crime through any official channel, he'd have no choice but to fire Tod, and an unemployed reaper was a truly dead reaper.

I couldn't lose Tod. But I couldn't let Thane keep killing people.

Shit!

A glance at the time on my phone threw another layer of trouble over my already-problematic morning. I had five minutes to be in my first-period class.

With a frustrated sigh, I closed my eyes and pictured my own kitchen, and when I opened my eyes again, I was there.

"Here." I shoved the amphora at Madeline and grabbed the backpack slung over my chair at the table. "I gotta go."

"Did you get the soul?" she asked as I threw my bag over my shoulder.

"Yeah. The owner of the doughnut shop. Someone should call the police."

"Did you see the reaper?" my father asked, worry lining his face as I scooped my keys from the empty candy dish on the half wall between the living and dining rooms.

"Yeah. I'll describe him later. I have to be in my chair in

three minutes." With that, I blinked out of the house and left them both staring at the spot I'd just vacated.

When I opened my eyes an instant later, I was in the girls' bathroom, completely incorporeal. Which was good, because two freshmen stood at the sinks, overdoing their lip gloss. I groaned in frustration, then stepped into an empty stall and concentrated on becoming completely corporeal. Then I flushed the toilet and threw the stall door open.

"I hope I'm not behind *her* in the cafeteria," one of the girls said when I rushed past the sinks, and I groaned again, then went back to wash my hands for no reason at all. By the time my hands were dry, I had ninety seconds to be in my chair. I shoved open the bathroom door and ran for my math class, then slid into my seat just as the bell started ringing.

On the bright side, being almost late to school meant that neither the reporters nor the other students had time to mob me with questions. But that didn't stop my classmates from staring at me as a man I'd never seen before started calling roll.

"Hey. I didn't think you were gonna make it," my best friend, Emma Marshall, whispered from her desk next to mine.

"Me, neither." During my convalescence, she'd come to hang out on the afternoons when she didn't have to work and I didn't have to train, and seeing her never failed to make me smile, even when I had to feign interest in school gossip, which had never felt less relevant to my life. She didn't pass on the rumors about me, thank goodness. "I got a surprise visit from Madeline this morning."

Em's eyes widened. "But it's your first day back."

"Also my first day on the job, evidently."

"Kaylee Cavanaugh?" the new math teacher called, and thirty-one heads swiveled my way, thirty-one sets of eyes watching me.

"Here," I said, like I was used to being stared at by the entire class. Before, I'd felt invisible. Now I really could be invisible—if there weren't so many people already watching me. So far, my afterlife seemed *made* of that kind of bitter irony.

"Kaylee, welcome back," the man at the front of the class said. "According to school policy, you have just over a month to complete your makeup work. Please let me know if you need any help at all with the math portion."

I nodded. I'd already finished my makeup work, but I couldn't admit that. Most stab victims aren't concerned with school work during their recovery. I wasn't, either, but without the need for sleep, I'd had hours and hours to kill when neither Tod nor training had kept me busy. During those endless solitary hours, it sometimes felt like homework was the only thing connecting me to the world I was no longer truly a part of.

The new math teacher—Mr. Cumberland—went back to the roll book and Em leaned closer to whisper. "I can't believe they even bothered filling that faculty position again. They might as well rename the class Defense Against the Dark Arts. I mean, seriously, who would answer an ad for this job?"

I shrugged, studying Mr. Cumberland. "Is he…?"

"Criminally dull? Yes. But so far I've seen no sign that he intends to feed from the student body in any way. So? What was the job this morning?"

Normally, no one paid any attention to Em and me whispering in class, but with my unfortunate morbid-celebrity status, I could practically feel the ears all around me perk up, hoping for some juicy bit of gossip about what had happened the night Mr. Beck died. So I concentrated really hard on Emma, to make sure she was the only one who could hear me.

"Rogue reaper," I said, and when no one reacted, I knew

I'd done it right; hopefully anyone else who saw my lips move would think I'd whispered too softly to be heard. "Thane's back," I added, and Em's eyes widened even farther in fear and surprise. But before I could elaborate, Mr. Cumberland started class.

When the bell rang fifty minutes later, only a couple of people headed for the door. Everyone else waited, slowly loading books into their bags or digging through purses, not-quite-surreptitiously watching me. When Em and I headed for the door, suddenly everyone else was ready to go, too.

"Today's gonna suck," I whispered.

As if the crowd of gawkers falling into step behind us wasn't enough, Mr. Cumberland chose that moment to ask Emma to stay after class for a minute. Math had never been her best subject.

She glanced at me apologetically, then veered toward his desk. I started to wait for her, but soon realized I wouldn't be waiting alone. When the second-period students began wandering into the classroom, adding their stares and whispers to the collective, I pushed my way into the hall against the flow of traffic and race-walked toward my locker.

But escape was futile.

Chelsea Simms, reporter for the student newspaper, was the first to take the plunge, falling into step with me as I rounded the corner into the front hall. "Hey, Kaylee, we're so glad you're back."

"Thanks." I walked faster, but she matched my speed.

"So, I heard you died. Like, your heart stopped on the operating table."

"Only for a few minutes." I had to concentrate on remaining corporeal, because my desire to disappear had never been so strong.

"But the news said you were dead. For real. They showed a body bag on a gurney."

Chills traveled down my arms in consecutive waves. Knowing I'd died and hearing about it were two completely different things.

A familiar hazel-eyed gaze met mine from across the hall, and my steps slowed as I passed Nash and Sabine, desperately wishing I could join them. That we could talk, or bicker, or just stand in uncomfortable silence, thinking of everything that had gone wrong between the three of us. Anything to avoid the stares and questions from relative strangers. To escape the crowd following me, a teen-paparazzi mob that felt more like a morbid funeral procession, a month too late.

But Nash and Sabine only watched as the parade of crazy marched by. I wanted to stop and talk, but I had *no* idea where to begin. I hadn't seen Nash since the day I came back from the dead, and "I'm so sorry I dumped you and framed you for my murder" seemed like a really bad way to start a conversation. Or rekindle a friendship. Or ask for forgiveness.

Either way, Em had said the gossip mob only laid off Nash when everyone heard I was coming back to school, and I couldn't suck him back into such a brutal spotlight. Not after what I'd already put him through.

"Kaylee?" Chelsea said, staring at me from inches away, and I was horrified to realize she'd pulled out a pencil and a notepad, and was now taking notes. "The body bag?"

"That was stock footage and a clerical error." I finally spotted my own locker through the sea of heads. "I don't know what else to tell you. The rumors of my death were greatly exaggerated," I said, misquoting Mark Twain. But though she seemed to believe me—after all, I was walking evidence of my own survival—the questions didn't stop.

"Did you see a bright light? Did your life flash before your eyes?"

"If so, it must have been the shortest, most boring recap in history," my cousin Sophie said from her locker. But for once, her insult lacked real bite, which was just as well, because no one seemed to notice she'd spoken.

The crowd parted in front of me as I headed for my locker, several doors down from Sophie's, but before I could enter the combination, a girl from my French class stepped into my private space, leaning with one shoulder on the locker next to mine. I could tell from the bold combination of curiosity and determination in her eyes that someone had finally found the courage to ask what they all really wanted to know.

"Is it true that Mr. Beck died in your bed?"

On my bed. He'd died *on* my bed, not in it. But I knew better than to answer.

I'd known this moment was coming, but knowing you're about to be dunked headfirst into ice-cold water is never enough to prepare you for the shock. And with that one question from the masses, the floodgates opened on all queries personal and inappropriate, and I could only stand there, wishing it all away as voice after voice shouted at me, dissecting my personal trauma and baring my wounds for the world.

"Why was he in your bed?"

"Did you really kill him?"

"Were you sleeping with Mr. Beck?"

"Is that why Nash dumped you?"

"Why was Nash arrested?"

"Why did they let him go?"

"Was he there that night?"

"Did he kill Mr. Beck?"

After all the time and concentration it had taken to reestablish breathing as a habit and convince my heart to beat, my body chose that moment to claim perfect recall of both processes. My heart pounded too hard. Blood rushed through my veins so fast my head swam. Air slid in and out of my lungs so quickly that if I'd had actual need of it, I probably would have passed out.

Panicked, I glanced at Sophie, desperate for help, but she was edging slowly, silently out of the crowd, probably hoping no one knew she'd been there that night so they couldn't assault her with the same questions. When I died, her dad had finally been forced to tell her the truth about our family. I wondered how she was handling it, but I couldn't tell that from watching her back as she fled. I wanted to escape with her, but I couldn't get through the crowd. I couldn't even get my locker open, because there wasn't room.

There wasn't room to move, and there wasn't room to breathe. The world started to close in on me, and the only way I knew to escape was to disappear, and I couldn't do that. No matter what, I couldn't disappear in front of fifty fellow students.

The questions kept coming, but the answers got stuck behind the lump in my throat. They weren't the real answers, anyway, because I couldn't tell them what had really happened, because the truth wouldn't set me free. The truth would get me locked up.

Distantly, I heard a couple of teachers yelling for order, but it was Emma who finally made it stop. "Back off, vultures!" she shouted, and I exhaled in relief as she pushed her way to the center of the crowd. "She just got out of the hospital. Why don't you go gossip behind her back, like decent people?"

I could have kissed her.

Once Emma had achieved near-silence in the hall, the teachers were able to start herding everyone toward their classes again, and through the crowd, I saw Nash and Sabine heading away from us. Without a word.

I don't know what I expected. For all I knew, he might never forgive me, and I couldn't really blame him.

"Are you okay?" Coach Tucker, the girls' softball coach, asked as I finally pulled my locker open.

"Yeah, I'm fine." What else could I say?

"Here." She pulled out a notepad and started scribbling on it, then ripped the top sheet off and handed it to me. It was a late pass, with my name on it. "Take a few minutes and get yourself together," she said, already scribbling on a second pass for Emma.

"Thanks." But all I could think about was that she'd remembered my name for the first time in nearly three years.

"I'm so sorry about what happened to you, Kaylee," Coach Tucker said as she handed Em her pass. "I feel like one of us should have known something was wrong with him. We saw him every day. We talked to him. Ate with him. I'm so sorry we failed you."

I didn't know what to say. The faculty had sent flowers to my house the day after I'd been restored from the dead, but I'd assumed the bouquet was an autoresponse from the secretary. Now I wondered if Coach Tucker had arranged the whole thing.

"Nobody failed me. I'm fine. Really," I said, but she didn't look convinced.

"Let me know if there's anything I can do to help you get readjusted," she said, and I nodded, then started removing books from my backpack and sliding them into my locker. I wasn't trying to be rude. I just didn't know what else to say.

Finally Coach Tucker left to scold a couple kissing in the hall, and I exhaled slowly.

"You okay?" Emma asked, leaning against the locker next to mine.

"Been better. People suck."

Em smiled. "Yeah. People do suck." Her smile died as I stared into my now-empty backpack, trying to remember what I'd been doing. What book I needed.

Second period. Chemistry. Oh, yeah.

"So, Thane's back?" Em said softly as I dropped my chemistry text into my bag again. "How is that even possible?"

"I don't know."

"What does this mean?"

"I don't know."

She frowned. "What are you going to do?"

"I don't know, Em. I don't know anything about it, except that he killed the owner of the doughnut shop around the corner from the school, and you're the only person I've told." But I couldn't tell her what he'd said about Avari coming after my friends and family. That would scare her to death.

"You haven't told Tod?"

"Haven't had a chance." I closed my locker and threw my backpack over one shoulder. "I can't tell Madeline, because she'll tell Levi, and that will force him into making trouble for Tod. Like, *big* trouble. I have to do something, but I have no idea what that is yet. For now—"

The bell rang, and several underclassmen ran past, on their way to class.

"—we're both late for second period," I finished. And Em hadn't been to her locker yet.

"Okay, I know. But one more thing." She laid a hand on my arm and the rare show of nerves in her expression made me stop. "Since you've been gone, Nash and Sabine have been avoiding me, so I've been eating lunch with Jayson."

"Jayson Olivera?"

"Yeah. We've been kind of…going out. For a couple of weeks."

I blinked in surprise. To my knowledge, she hadn't actually dated anyone since Doug died right before Christmas.

"Why didn't you tell me?"

"Because I wasn't sure it would turn into anything—I'm still not sure—and you had enough on your mind without having to worry about censoring yourself in front of my human boyfriend."

My chest ached at the look in her eyes and at the silence, where all the things she wasn't saying should have gone. "I didn't realize you knew Jayson," I said.

Em shrugged. "I didn't, really." She clutched her books to her chest and leaned against my closed locker. "It was really weird here when you were gone. Nash and Sabine were all closed off and unapproachable. Not that I can blame them, with everyone talking about his arrest. And everyone else just wanted to know what really happened that night at your house. Nash wasn't talking, so they came after me. Jayson was the only one who still acted…normal."

And she'd needed normal. I'd tried so hard not to drag Emma into danger, but the Netherworld was like quicksand—the harder I tried to pull her out of it, the harder it sucked her in.

She would have been better off if she'd never met me.

"I'm so sorry, Emma."

"It's okay," Em said. "Really. But I like him, and he was totally there for me when I was…lonely. I just… Is it going to be weird if Jayson sits with us? I'm assuming Tod will be there, and you never know when Nash and Sabine will decide they want to talk. He can't be mad at you forever."

"Yes, he can. So, are Nash and Sabine…together?" Em hadn't said much about that during my month off, and I wasn't sure how I felt about the possibility. The probability. It was officially none of my business who Nash went out with, and I wanted him to be happy, but…just asking the question felt weird.

So much had changed so fast—my head was still spinning.

Em frowned in thought. "I can't tell. You never see one without the other anymore, but they're not all over each other in public or anything. Maybe that was never their style."

But if there'd been a ban on public displays, that was Nash's doing. Sabine would claim him any way she could. Any way he'd let her.

I shrugged and tried to shake the thought off. "I wouldn't worry about Nash and Sabine showing up to make your human boyfriend uncomfortable, and when Tod gets there… we'll make it work." So what if Em's boyfriend wouldn't be able to see or hear mine. "Any boyfriend of yours… You know the rest." I scrounged up a parting smile, then headed for second-period chemistry, where the stares continued for another miserable fifty minutes.

Third period was my free period, so I shoved my backpack into my locker, then headed for the nearest restroom, which was quickly turning into my own personal transit system. But as I passed the front office, the glass door opened and the school's attendance secretary stuck her head out. "Kaylee Cavanaugh?" she said, both her eyebrows and her voice high in question.

I hesitated, almost certain she wouldn't have been able to pick me out of a crowd a month earlier.

"I was just on my way to find you. You're late for your appointment with your guidance counselor."

Well, crap. There'd been a message on my home phone the week before, mentioning an appointment during my free period when I returned to school, but I'd deleted the message and made a mental note to have my dad talk the school out of mandatory trauma counseling.

Obviously I should have left myself an *actual* note…

Reluctantly, I followed the secretary through the main office and into another suite, where several other students sat waiting for the N-Z counselor, whose door was closed. I'd never met my counselor—the A-M counselor—but the moment I entered the waiting room, she stepped out of her office and directed me inside with one outstretched arm while she gave the secretary a thank-you nod.

"Hi Kaylee. I'm Ms. Hirsch. Come in and have a seat, please."

I sat in one of the chairs in front of her desk while she closed the door behind me, then circled the desk to sit in her own chair. My file folder was open on her desk, and when she turned off the computer monitor—though I couldn't see it from my seat—I realized that she'd been reading the local paper online. Or maybe she'd just Googled me in preparation for our appointment. Were school counselors allowed to Google?

"Would you like a bottle of water?" Ms. Hirsch set a small plastic bottle at the front of her desk, next to a bowl full of Jolly Ranchers.

"No, thanks." I set my backpack on the floor between my feet, then realized that left me nothing to do with my hands.

"So, Kaylee, how's your first day back going?"

"Fine." As long as "fine" could be defined as the half-way point between horrible and unbearable.

"What about your classes? Are you having any trouble getting caught up? Did the school set you up with a tutor while you were out?"

They'd tried. But my father had insisted that he could help me with anything I didn't understand. The tutor finally accepted that as the truth—after my father hit him with a heavy dose of verbal Influence, his natural gift as a male *bean sidhe.*

"I'm not that far behind," I said with a shrug.

"Well, if you decide you do want a tutor or need help scheduling any makeup exams, just let me know."

"I'm fine. Really," I insisted, but Ms. Hirsch only frowned like she didn't believe me. And why should she? What sixteen year old is fine four weeks after being stabbed by her math teacher?

Certainly not this one… But that had less to do with what Mr. Beck had done to me than the thought of facing another mob like the one in the hall that morning. Beck was dead and gone, but the vultures were still alive and circling.

"I'm sure it must be very difficult being back here for you," Ms. Hirsch said, and I realized she'd heard about the incident in the hall. "I suspect you're dealing with a lot of unwanted attention today."

"Yeah."

"How do you feel you're coping with that?"

I was *trying* to cope by fleeing school grounds during my free period—until I'd been dragged into the counselor's office. "All I can really do is ignore them, right?"

She nodded slowly. "People, especially teenagers, are curious by nature, they don't always think about how their curiosity affects others. Peers may ask you directly or indirectly about what happened to you. But you have every right to tell them you don't want to talk about it with them. You should never feel guilty about that."

I didn't feel guilty. I didn't feel…much of anything, except for the need—a truly escalating *drive*—to get as far away from school and my "peers" as possible.

I should have been a wreck. People were obviously waiting for me to fall apart at the seams and spill my emotional guts all over the floor, and some small part of me wished I could. I wished things were still simple enough that a good cry could purge all the bad stuff and give me a fresh start. But I'd never felt less like crying, and I was all out of fresh starts. My mother had given me the only one I was allowed when I was three.

"I'm fine. Really," I said, and her frown deepened.

"Kaylee, it's perfectly normal to be upset for a very long time after something like what you've been through. It could be months before you start to feel anything like normal and that is perfectly okay."

Normal? Seriously?

"So, what, there's a timeline for how long it should take me to get over being stabbed by my math teacher? Someone really wrote that? How convenient! Does it happen to mention how long I should be upset about the fact that I had to kill him? Because honestly, with no guidelines in place, I might be tempted to linger in mourning for, like, a solid *week*. Is that too long?"

Ms. Hirsch blinked. Then she pulled open a drawer and took a pamphlet from inside and slid it across the desk to me. "This is the contact information for a group of survivors of violent crimes. I think it would be worth your time to..."

"No, thank you." I pushed the pamphlet back toward her. She was only trying to help. I knew that. But I also knew that through no fault of her own, she was in way over her head. And honestly, she'd probably been there all year, considering how many students and teachers Eastlake had lost under unexplained circumstances since the school year started. "I really have to go," I said, picking up my backpack.

Ms. Hirsch exhaled slowly, then met my gaze again. "Kaylee, this office is a safe space." She spread her arms to take in all four walls, then folded them on top of her desk, rumpling the pamphlet. "You can say anything you need to say in here, and what you tell me is completely confidential. I'm sure you have family and friends you can talk to, but sometimes it helps to talk to someone completely uninvolved. I want you to know that I can be that person for you. If things get too overwhelming at any point during the school day, I want you to come down here. We can talk. Or you can just sit in here and take a break." She placed her hands palms down on the desktop and her gaze intensified. "Safe space. Please remember that."

"Thanks. That's good to know." I threw my backpack over my shoulder and practically ran out the door and through both sets of offices. In the bathroom, I had to take refuge in a stall, waiting for the small mid-third-period crowd to go back to class so I could blink out of the school without anyone seeing me disappear. While I waited, two sophomores whose names I couldn't remember chatted in front of the mirrors, like they had nowhere better to be. As soon as they started talking, I realized they hadn't seen me come in. If there was ever a time to use my new instantaneous method of transportation, this was it. But their conversation froze me in place.

I shouldn't have listened. But I couldn't help it.

"The cops think he tried to…you know. And she fought back."

"How do you know that?"

"My mom works in dispatch."

"Well, I don't believe it. Mr. Beck could have had anyone he wanted, so why go after Kaylee Cavanaugh? And even if he did, it's not like she would have said no. She's a closet slut. She was with Scott Carter the day he was arrested, remember? Cheating on her boyfriend with his best friend—her own sister's boyfriend."

"I think Sophie's her cousin."

"Whatever. She cheats on Nash with Scott, and he ends up in the psych ward. Then she kisses some guy in the middle of the school, and the next day they find Mr. Beck dead on her bed, and Nash gets arrested. She's like King Midas, only everything she touches turns to shit instead of gold."

Anger flared inside me and I threw the stall door open—then realized that's as far as my plan went. "You have no idea what you're talking about," I snapped, glaring at both of them in the mirror. "Is there some broken filter or busted pressure gauge in there that lets every half-formed thought leak out of your mouths?" I demanded, tossing a careless gesture at their heads. "Because if these are the gems you actually intended to share with the world, you should know they don't paint a very flattering picture of your intellect."

I stomped out of the bathroom with them staring after me and ran smack into a tall, dark-haired guy I'd never seen before.

"Whoa, are you okay?" he asked, one hand on my arm to steady me. I nodded, and he frowned down at me, like he suddenly recognized me. "Hey, are you Kaylee Cavanaugh?"

I exhaled, trying to purge my anger, but with it came words I hadn't intended to say. "Yeah. I am. And, yes, I'm glad to be alive. No, I'm not a slut. And, no, you can't see my scar. Does that about cover it?"

He stared at me in surprise and I took off down the hall at a run because I could feel myself fading from physical existence and I couldn't let him—or anyone else—see that happen. My footsteps faded as I rounded the corner, and a girl at the other end of the hall looked up like she'd heard something, but her gaze floated over me like I wasn't even there. And from her perspective, I wasn't.

Dead people have to want to be seen in order to exist on the physical plane, and I'd never wanted to exist less.

"HEY, WHAT ARE YOU DOING HERE?" TOD SAID, taking my hand as I sank into the waiting-room chair next to him. "Rough day at school?"

"Mandatory counseling. And I got mobbed in the hall between first and second period."

He rolled his eyes in mock exasperation. "You'd think they've never seen a murder victim returned from the dead to reclaim the souls of the fallen and grant them eternal rest."

"Well, when you say it like that..."

"Just give them some time, Kaylee. Eventually you'll be old news again, and life will go back to normal." Tod shrugged. "Except you won't actually be living it."

"Not helping." There was a time when I'd thought it would be nice to be noticed. To stand out, like Emma or Sophie. Now I stood out, but for all the wrong reasons. Anonymity was a luxury I'd never expected to miss.

I ran my thumb over the back of Tod's hand. Just touching him made me feel more...real. More *there.* More alive. I pulled him closer for a kiss and my heart beat faster when his lips touched mine. My pulse raced, and I suddenly remembered what it had felt like the first time we'd kissed, not in my head, like a mere memory, but in my entire body. Like I was reliving it. Like I could go back to that moment, the most alive I'd ever felt before or since, and live in it for eternity.

For a second, I almost forgot I was dead. And that he was dead. And that we were surrounded by sick people in the waiting room of the local hospital.

Then someone coughed and a baby started crying. Reality roared back into focus, and it was such a disappointment that my chest ached from the loss of something I hadn't really had in the first place.

Why did I feel so disconnected from everything around me? How could I look the same, but feel so different? Empty, like a shell. A Kaylee-shell, still me on the outside, but hollow on the inside. I'd thought that going back to school—seeing friends and classmates, and even teachers—would help me fill the void. I'd thought that if I could stuff the shell of my former self with the pieces of my former life, everything could go back to the way it was.

I'd thought my death could be just a blip on the radar of my life, over and done with in short order. I should have known better, just from being with Tod. His death wasn't a blip. It was the defining moment of his existence. His death—how, why, and when he'd died—had shaped him. Defined him.

What did my death say about me? That I was a victim? That I wasn't strong enough to protect Nash like I'd protected Emma and Sophie?

"Hey." Tod squeezed my hand to draw me out of my thoughts. "I think death looks good on you." He took my other hand and his fingers wound around mine, my arm stretched over the chair rail between us. "I look forward to the day when I won't have to share you with roving bands of high-school gossip mobs."

"That day could be today," I admitted. "I don't want to go back." But I didn't have any choice. I'd begged and bargained for the chance to pretend I was still alive, and now that I'd gotten that chance, I had to uphold my end of the deal. I had to keep up with appearances.

"It'll get better," Tod said, and his next blink was too long. "So, did you see Nash?"

"Only in passing. I doubt he'll be offering an olive branch anytime soon."

"You could make the first move," Tod suggested, running his thumb over the back of mine.

"Yeah, if I could get him to speak to me. How is he?" During both rounds of recovery from addiction to frost—Demon's Breath, to those in the know—Tod had checked in on his brother regularly, though Nash never saw him.

"I can't get very close to him anymore. That damn dog barks every time I show up, and Nash starts yelling for me to get out."

Nash's dog, Baskerville, was Styx's littermate.

"Nash isn't going to forgive me," Tod said. "Not yet, anyway. But he might forgive you. He still loves you, Kaylee."

Something in his voice made my heart hurt, and I hated that I liked that. Feeling *anything* was so rare lately that even pain had become interesting.

"You're not worried about me and Nash, are you?" I asked, ducking to catch his gaze. "Because—"

"No." He put one finger over my mouth, then replaced it with his lips, and that kiss went deeper and longer than would have been appropriate in a hospital, if anyone could have seen us. And when he finally pulled away, his gaze met mine, and everything that kiss had said was still echoing in his eyes, in fierce cobalt swirls of emotion so bold and confident it couldn't possibly be shaken. "I'm not worried about *you* and Nash. I'm worried about just Nash."

"Me, too."

"Did something happen?"

"Something happened, but not because of Nash. I had my first reclamation this morning," I said, wishing we weren't separated by the arm of the chair between us. "Rogue reaper. Sort of a trial run, before they send me on the job they brought me back for."

"So, did you kick ass?"

I grinned, indulging in a moment of pride over the fact that I'd actually gotten the job done. First time. "There was both the kicking of ass and the taking of names. One name, actually."

Tod's pale brows rose. "I take it this is a name I might know?"

My moment of pride ended in a cold wash of fear and confusion. "Thane."

His brow furrowed. "Thane, the lovable, brand-new reaper I've never met, who means none of us any harm? Please say you mean that Thane…."

"Nope, the other one. Thane, the reaper who killed my mother, then came back for me thirteen years later. He's back, Tod. He killed a doughnut-shop owner this morning, then just kind of hung around waiting to be caught, like he knew someone would come for him. He was surprised to see me, though, and he looked terrified when I took the soul from him."

"Did you tell Madeline?" Tod asked, his irises noticeably still.

"No, I didn't want to get you in trouble."

His frown deepened. "Kaylee, either Avari let Thane go,

or Thane escaped. Either way, something's wrong. You have to tell her."

"No!" That came out louder than I'd intended, and if I'd been audible, everyone in the E.R. waiting room would have been staring at us. "I'm *not* spending eternity here without you. No way."

His fingers tightened around mine. "That's not what I want, either, but we can't just let Thane keep killing."

"I know, but there has to be a way I can get rid of him without losing you. I think we should start at Lakeside." The psychiatric unit attached to the hospital we sat in at that very moment.

"With Scott?" Tod's irises were swirling now, reflecting his emotions as he started to understand my plan.

"Yeah."

Scott Carter, one of Nash's best friends and Sophie's—ex?—boyfriend, had gone insane when addiction to Demon's Breath left him with a hardwired mental connection to Avari, the hellion whose breath he'd huffed. The very same hellion Tod had given Thane to. If anyone knew how and why Thane was back on the human plane, Avari would.

Getting him to tell us would be the hard part.

"Okay," Tod said finally. "We'll go see Scott tonight, but for now, I need to get back to work. These sick people aren't going to kill themselves, you know."

I fought a smile, more relieved than truly amused. "Your sense of humor is so morbid."

"Says the dead girl. See you at lunch?"

"Yeah. It'll probably be you, me, Em, and her human boyfriend, though, so it might be kind of awkward." He could show himself to just me and Em, but it would be easier for Em to pretend not to see him if she actually couldn't see him.

Tod scowled. "Fine. But if I have to stay invisible the whole time, I can't promise to be on my best behavior. There's no telling what I might do… I mean, if no one else can see me, anyway, why bother with clothes at all?"

I laughed, trying to disguise the sudden curious heat settling into my face. "Well, that ought to spice up the lunch period."

"That's a game two can play, you know," he said, his gaze wandering south of my collarbones.

"Except that I won't be invisible," I pointed out as he leaned over the chair arm between us to drop a kiss on my neck, and my heart thumped a little harder, a sensation I'd taken entirely for granted when I was still alive.

Tod groaned against my skin. "Remind me again why we're going to lunch, when neither of us needs food?"

"I'm having trouble remembering at the moment," I whispered when he sat up and the heat in his eyes burned straight through my own. "Something about pretending to be alive…"

"How's that working out?"

"It feels less like pretending at the moment." With my heart beating on its own. My skin tingling from just the possibility that he might touch me again. But that would stop when I went back to school. I'd have to concentrate on the appearance of life—a pulse, regular breaths, physical presence—and everything would suddenly be immeasurably harder.

Everything that came naturally to everyone else would be a constant effort for me. So much to remember. So much to hide. So much to lose.

Suddenly keeping up with appearances didn't seem worth the work.

"You won't have to pretend forever," Tod said. "One more year of high school, and then you can do whatever you want. Universities don't hold students captive, so you could pop on and off campus at will, if you want to go to college. Or we could just…hang out."

"Forever?" The very concept of forever—of time without end—was too daunting to truly contemplate. Doing *nothing* for a millennia of spare time—even nothing with Tod—didn't seem possible. Surely I'd lose my mind.

"What about you? What do you want?" In all the conversations we'd had in the past month—spilling secrets, doubts, wants, and hopes—it had never occurred to me to ask that.

"I have what I want." His hand squeezed mine again, but it felt like he was squeezing my heart. "There's plenty of time to figure the rest out. Hopefully it'll go something like this…."

He leaned in for another kiss, and it took every single bit of willpower I had to pull away from him, when what I really wanted to do was climb into his lap, and bury my hands in his hair, and make a private spectacle of us both. I'd *never* had an urge so strong, and the reasons to resist were suddenly frighteningly vague.

Oh, yeah. Work. And school.

"I thought you had souls to reap…" I whispered, staring into the desire swirling in his eyes, wondering if he could see mine reflected back at him.

"They'll wait."

"I'm trying to do the mature thing here." I groaned when he pulled me close again.

"I'm not."

"Why do I always have to be the one who says 'stop'?" I demanded, my voice little more than a moan.

"You don't. In fact, at this point I'm considering a petition to have that word stricken from the English language." His grin was almost lazy, the gleam in his eyes an effortless challenge. "If I did, would you sign?"

"No fair. If there was a pen in my hand right now, I'd sign whatever you put in front of me."

"Good thing I'm not a hellion."

He was kidding, but thinking about Avari accomplished what I'd lacked the willpower to do on my own. Playtime was over.

"I better get back. But I'll see you at lunch?"

"Yeah, but I might be late. I want to check in at work after my shift and see if anyone else has spotted Thane."

"Okay." I gave him another quick kiss, then blinked out of the hospital and into a bathroom in the food court across the street from school, where I picked up a bag full of burgers and fries. Then, just for fun, I blinked into Emma's third-period art class, careful that no one else could see or hear me, and leaned over her shoulder.

"Lunch is on me."

Em yelped, and when she jumped, she accidentally painted a long yellow line across the canvas she'd been working on. Everyone looked up, and Em apologized, mumbling something about a bee buzzing around her head, then glared at me before turning back to her painting. "Not funny," she breathed, like she was talking to herself.

"Sorry," I said. But it *was* kind of funny, and laughing felt good, even if no one else could share the moment of levity with me. I understood then why Tod had stayed near his family after he died. The living bring out what life remains in the dead. I was drawn to my friends and family, and when I couldn't be with them, the world—my entire afterlife—felt so much emptier in their absence.

I blinked into the empty quad and sat at the picnic table Em and I had shared with Nash and Sabine until the week I'd died, and since no one was watching, I concentrated on pulling myself onto the physical plane right there in the open. Then I munched on fries from my bag until the bell rang.

Unfortunately, I'd failed to factor my new infamy into my lunch plans.

The first few people who entered the quad with lunch trays glanced at me, then sat at their own tables and stared while they ate. The gawking wasn't polite, but it wasn't truly invasive, either, so I could deal. Then the quad started to fill up and more people stared, upping the ante with a little obvious gossip. But before long, people I actually had classes with—the ones who'd known who I was before Beck stabbed me—started asking if they could join me.

Most of them sat without waiting for an answer.

To their credit, they were outwardly polite. Most asked how I was feeling and several offered to help with my makeup work. One idiot even asked me to the prom. I could only stutter in response.

When my table filled up before Em and Jayson arrived, I started to panic again. I was sick of questions, and stares, and friends who hadn't been my friends before. I wanted nothing to do with any of it. I just wanted to disappear.

And as soon as I had that thought, it started to happen. I could feel it—I could feel myself slipping out of the physical plane—and it took all of my concentration to remain visible. I propped my elbows on the table and buried my face in my hands, chanting to myself silently.

I want to be here. I want to be here. Iwanttobehere. But that wasn't true, and it didn't help.

Unfortunately, the rest of the table mistook my concentration for pain and everyone started asking me if I was okay. If there was something they could get me. Someone even tried to pull my hands away from my face to make sure I was still conscious. Evidently I'd stopped breathing.

"All right, back the hell off!" a familiar voice shouted as I jerked my arm free from whoever'd pulled it. I looked up to see Sabine staring down the boldest of my new "friends." I knew by the almost liquid depths of her black, black eyes that she was unleashing their own fears on them, literally scaring them away.

Sabine was a Nightmare. For real. Though the politically correct term was *mara,* the old-fashioned one fit better, in my opinion. She could read people's fears and weave nightmares from them, then feed from her victims in their sleep.

Creepy? Yeah. Especially when she'd tried to use her *mara* abilities and appetite to scare me away from Nash. But in that moment, in the quad, I was more than grateful for the rescue from someone I'd considered my nemesis a few short months earlier.

"Thanks," I said when the last of the vultures was gone, and when I looked up again, Nash stood behind Sabine. Watching me. It killed me that I couldn't tell what he was thinking or feeling, though I completely understood why he would control the telltale swirling in his irises around me now.

"Bastards have no self-respect," Sabine muttered as the last of the crowd dissipated. "Even I don't feed off the weak or the injured."

I decided not to waste my breath telling her I was neither weak nor injured—physically, anyway. "Will you stay and eat with me?" I asked, glancing from Sabine to Nash, who closed his eyes and took a deep breath, then met my gaze again. "I brought burgers."

Free food was usually enough to tempt Sabine, but Nash was another story.

"Is he here?" Nash asked, and I realized that was the first time I'd heard his voice since the day I died.

"He" was Tod, of course.

"Not yet, but you could stay till he gets here. Or you could just stay. You have every right to hate us both, but this doesn't have to be…" Words failed me when the thought behind them trailed into nothing.

"Doesn't have to be what, Kaylee?" Nash demanded softly. "Awkward and painful? Because if you know of some other way for me to view the fact that my brother stole my girlfriend, who then framed me for her murder, I'm willing to listen."

But I didn't. That was all true, and trying to defend either of us would only have made Nash angrier.

He started to turn away, and I stood, hyperaware of all the eyes watching us. "Please, stay," I said, and he stopped. "Please, just… Maybe we could start again?" I said, so that only he and Sabine could hear. "I know we can't erase everything that went wrong between us, but maybe we could kind of turn the page and start on a fresh one. *Tabula rasa.*"

Nash glanced at Sabine, who shrugged, then they both sat. And I realized I had no idea what to say. My plan ended with begging them both to sit with me, because I hadn't really expected that to work.

"Um, Em and her boyfriend will be here any minute, which will probably put an end to genuine conversation, but… How are you?" I asked, pulling burgers from the grease-stained bag. His recovery from frost addiction had suffered a recent relapse and Harmony had said that kicking the habit a second time was even harder, because withdrawal was more severe.

"Do you even eat anymore?" Nash asked, ignoring my question entirely.

"I don't have to, but, yeah, I can." I handed him a burger and a carton of fries, and Sabine helped herself to the bag, impatient as always. "Nash, I'm so sorry."

"You already said that," Sabine said, folding the wrapper back from her burger. "You said it a lot, actually. Which supports my theory that apologies are basically pointless. They don't fix anything, right? That's why I rarely bother."

"An apology isn't a Band-Aid," I insisted. "It's an expression of regret."

"Not that that matters." Nash's voice was deep and angry. He hadn't touched his food. "Half these assholes still think I stabbed you, Kaylee. How is it that I stayed away from you, just like you told me to, yet I still wound up arrested and charged with killing you?"

"I didn't have any choice." That was the truth, and I needed him to believe that worse than I'd ever needed anything from him. "Beck said he'd rape and kill Em and Sophie if I didn't cooperate. I couldn't let that happen. He'd already hurt so many." The memory chilled me, which made it hard to keep my heart beating, in a body that was already reluctant to cooperate. "But I fixed it. I told the police you weren't even there."

"You got the charges dropped, but you can't take back what you did," Nash insisted, and he was right. "I was convicted in the court of public opinion the minute they handcuffed me and threw me in the back of the police car. In front of my *mother.* How are you going to undo that?"

"I don't know." Tears burned at the back of my eyes and I fought to keep them from falling. I hadn't even known I could still cry, but there they were, and suddenly I felt just as powerless in death as I'd been in life. "I'll tell people. I'll say whatever you want. I'll…I'll do an interview for the school paper, if that'll help. Chelsea's been bugging me to—"

"Forget about it." Nash picked up his burger and tore half the wrapper from it, but he looked like the thought of eating made him sick. "Just don't talk about it, and maybe this'll all go away. Eventually."

"Kaylee?"

I jumped, then turned toward the new voice to see the guy I'd collided with in the hall earlier, staring down at me like he was determined to have his say. "Look, I've had a rough day, and I can't handle any more gawkers or gossipmongers, so if that's what—"

"I'm Luca Tedesco. Madeline told me to introduce myself." He smiled and stuck his hand out, and for a moment, I could only stare at it, as what he'd said sank in.

"Oh! I'm so sorry." Instead of taking the hand he offered, I scooted over to make room for him on the bench. "You're the necromancer?" I whispered, unable to hide my surprise. After what Madeline had said, I'd expected small, shy, and awkward, not tall, dark, and gorgeous.

Although, hadn't I once been even more surprised when a certain rookie reaper turned out to be tall, blond, and beautiful?

"The new guy's a necromancer?" Sabine said, and I enjoyed a rare glimpse of her surprise.

"Yeah." Luca sat and glanced around the table, instantly at ease with a group of people he'd never met before. "So, I assume your friends are...?"

It took me a second to realize what he was asking, but Sabine caught on quickly. "I think 'friend' is kind of an iffy descriptor at the moment, but your necro-talk isn't going to freak out a *mara* and a *bean sidhe.* I'm Sabine Campbell and this is Nash Hudson." She placed one hand on her own chest, then gestured toward Nash.

"A *mara* and a *bean sidhe.* Wow." Luca took a fry from the carton I offered him. "Madeline said I'd be in good company here, but I assumed she was just trying to con me into moving."

"Who the hell is Madeline?" Sabine asked as Nash alternately stared at me, then Luca.

"She's my boss in the reclamation department. *Our* boss, I guess," I said with a glance at the new guy. "Luca and I are going to be working together."

"So, how do you know Kaylee?" Luca asked, and I could tell from Sabine's evil grin that I wasn't going to like her answer.

"Oh, Nash used to not-quite-sleep with her, and I hung around to reinforce the 'not quite' part. But I've been relieved of duty on that front, since Kaylee dumped him for his brother in a nasty public spectacle. It was quite the scandal, even for those of us who saw it coming."

Nash frowned, but didn't argue. "Okay, what the hell is a necromancer?"

"He sees dead people," Sabine said, favoring Luca with a rare smile. "Like that kid in the movie, right?"

Luca shrugged. "Sort of. Only without the ghosts. I mostly sense the recently dead and the restored. Like Kaylee. And like that reaper this morning."

Nash stiffened. "Tod?"

Luca shrugged and glanced at me in question, and I winced over the verbal quicksand he had no idea he'd just stepped into. "I don't know. Was the reaper named Tod?"

"Um, no. It was someone else."

Nash relaxed a little, but Sabine frowned at me. As usual, she was too perceptive for her own good. And *way* too perceptive for *my* good. "Someone you know? Do you know another reaper?"

I looked up to find all three of them staring at me, waiting for the answer to a question I desperately didn't want to answer in front of Luca, at least until I could be sure he wouldn't tell Madeline.

"He was a rogue, right?" Luca said. "He killed that guy in the doughnut shop?"

"Yeah, he...wasn't Tod," I finished lamely, while Nash and Sabine stared at me. "I reclaimed the soul, though. Madeline has it."

"Luca?" a familiar voice called from across the quad, and I looked up to see my cousin Sophie crossing the grass toward us, her gaze holding steady on the necromancer. That look was comfortable. Familiar. She didn't even glance at the rest of us. "Did you get lost?"

Luca smiled like he knew her, and another layer of weird settled onto my life. "Nope. I braved the great divide to introduce myself to your cousin." His arm slid around her waist when she stopped at the end of our table, and my mouth actually dropped open. "Turns out we're going to be working together."

"Wait, you two know each other?" My voice sounded kind of funny. Stunned. Sophie knew the necromancer. She knew him well enough to accept his arm around her.

"Yeah," Sabine said, and I realized that neither she nor Nash looked surprised. "If by 'know each other' you're referring to their liberal and frequent exchange of saliva in public, and who knows what other fluids in private."

"You're *dating Sophie?*" I said, gaping at Luca in confusion and disbelief. Could the world get any weirder?

Luca shrugged. "We haven't been on an actual date yet—she's suffered a recent family tragedy, in case you haven't heard," he said, brown eyes sparkling in amusement. "But—"

"You *work* with *Kaylee?*" Sophie demanded, before he could finish his sentence, like she'd just recovered the gift of speech, after our mutual shock.

"We just now officially met, but, yeah."

"I assume you're not talking about scooping popcorn at the Cinemark…."

"My *other* job," I whispered. How much had I missed in just a month? "I don't understand. You hate all things weird and potentially dangerous. No offense—" I glanced at Luca "—but necromancy definitely qualifies."

Sophie's expression frosted over, like it used to when I bought an off-brand pair of shoes or went out without fixing my hair. Like she was thoroughly disappointed in me. "That's specist, Kaylee. Specism is just as bad as racism. Maybe worse. I thought you'd have a little more compassion than that, considering you're neither human nor alive." Her voice dropped into a fierce whisper on the last few words, and I could only stare at her in astonishment as her hand slid into Luca's and she tugged him up from his seat. "Come back over here, where people appreciate you for who and what you are."

"Great to meet you, Kaylee and friends," Luca said, slowly walking backward while Sophie tried to pull him away from us.

When they were gone, I turned back to Nash and Sabine. "Is it just me, or did the earth suddenly do an about-face in its rotation? 'Cause that's what that felt like."

"That was definitely weird," Nash agreed, and the fact that he hadn't argued with me made me unreasonably happy.

"No one over there even *knows* who or what he is," Sabine pointed out, staring at Luca as he sat with Sophie and her friends like he'd known them all his life.

"How does Sophie know?" I asked, and she shrugged.

"They already seemed to know each other when he started school." Sabine leaned closer to me from across the table. "But enough about necro-boy and the dancing queen. You lied about the reaper," she whispered. "You knew him. Spill."

I sighed, then concentrated to make sure they were the only ones who would hear my next words. "I didn't want to say anything in front of Luca, but it was Thane. We thought he was gone, but now he's obviously back."

"Thane, the reaper who killed your mom?" Nash asked. "The reaper who killed *you?* Where did you think he'd gone?"

I blinked at Nash, surprised. I'd assumed someone—Harmony?—had filled him in on how I died, but I was obviously wrong. "Nash, Thane never got the chance to reap my soul. Tod fed him to Avari. Which is why we thought he was gone."

"Tod gave him to the hellion of greed?" Sabine said, and I could hear admiration in her voice. "Bold. Risky. Dramatic. I approve."

Nash scowled, and I could practically feel the progress we'd made toward friendship slipping away. "Why the hell would he do that? It obviously didn't save your life."

"He wasn't trying to save me," I said. "He was trying to make sure Thane wouldn't be the one to end my life, when the time came. Because he was…kind of…stalking me. And threatening my friends and my dad. He was there that day you and I fought about Tod. In my kitchen." I didn't want to remember that. But Nash had a right to know. "He was asking me questions while we were arguing, and it was impossible to hear you both at once. You thought Tod was there. Do you remember?"

He did. I could tell. "Thane was stalking you? He was there with us, and you didn't tell me?" His voice was soft and angry. His irises were too still. "Exactly how long have you been lying to me, Kaylee?"

"I was trying to save your life. He said he'd kill you if I told you he was there."

"Maybe you should have let him. Maybe then—" Nash bit the rest of his sentence off, but I had no trouble finishing it in my head. "I can't do this with you, Kaylee. Not yet." Nash scrubbed his face with both hands. Then he stood and headed for the cafeteria, without another word or a look back. Sabine only hesitated long enough to grab another burger for the road, then she jogged after him, leaving me alone at my table, in the middle of lunch.

"What was that all about?" Em asked, and I looked up to

find my best friend and her new boyfriend, Jayson Olivera, staring after Nash and Sabine.

"History. Secrets. Drama. You know, the usual." I pushed the fast-food bag toward them as they sat. "So, tell me what I missed." Having been abandoned by a necromancer, a *mara,* and an angry male *bean sidhe* in the past five minutes alone, I could sure use a dose of normal. At least until my undead boyfriend showed up.

AFTER SCHOOL, I LAY ON MY STOMACH ON MY bed, with my chemistry text open in front of me. I'd read the assigned chapter three times, but it still hadn't sunk in, so I'd moved on to staring at the not-a-locket Madeline had given me, which I'd found lying on my dresser when I got home.

It didn't look like anything important. But it was the difference between final rest and eternal torture to anyone unlucky enough to have his or her soul stolen at death. Madeline had called it an amphora. I'd looked the word up. An amphora was an ancient Greek style of vase with a skinny neck and two handles.

My heart-thing looked nothing like an amphora. Yet the name seemed oddly appropriate, because like an old jar, my amphora was made to hold things. Specifically, souls.

My phone buzzed in my pocket, and I dropped the necklace into the crack between the pages of the open book, then dug my phone from my pocket. The screen showed a text from Tod.

Incoming in five...four...three...two...

"One," he said, and I looked up to find the reaper standing in the middle of the rug at the end of my bed.

"Cute." I rolled over to make room for him, and Tod stretched out on the bed next to me.

"Shouldn't you be at work?" he asked, glancing at the Cinemark uniform draped over my desk chair.

"Probably," I admitted. "But what's the point? Scooping popcorn and selling tickets for minimum wage feels like a waste of time now."

Tod's brows rose. "It's not like either of us is short on time."

"I know, but I don't want to spend eternity wearing red polyester and smelling like fake butter." Too late, I realized he was doing that very thing, only his uniform shirt was blue and he finished his shifts at the pizza place smelling like grease and pepperoni. Because the reaper gig didn't pay in human currency and without cash, he couldn't pay for his cell phone, or food and clothes he didn't technically need, or the in-public date we kept promising ourselves.

"You obviously don't want to spend eternity doing chemistry homework, either." Tod slid the necklace onto the comforter between us, then flipped the textbook closed and set it on the floor. "I take it your return to class was less than triumphant?"

I rolled onto my back with a sigh. "Today sucked. No way around it. Between the stares, the gossip, and the inappropriate questions, school felt more like a three-ring circus than an institute of learning. Three different people actually asked to see my scar. Can you believe that?"

"Can't say I blame them. As scars go, it's pretty damn sexy." Tod grinned and pushed the hem of my shirt up to expose the straight, pinkish line of raised tissue on my stomach. His fingers traced it slowly and chills gathered just below my navel. Then he lowered his head and followed that line again with a series of soft kisses. I closed my eyes and gripped handfuls of my comforter, and those chills at my center became a fire that burned deep inside me.

Suddenly that scar was my very favorite part of my body.

"No fair," I moaned. "Only you could make me love the wound that killed me."

"Never underestimate the therapeutic power of a few well-placed kisses," he mumbled against my skin.

I laughed and pulled him up until our mouths met. "Mmm… If I'd known the afterlife could be this yummy, I might have tried to expedite the process."

Tod pulled away, frowning. "That's not funny."

"What, you can make death jokes, but I can't?" His morbid sense of humor used to worry me, but now I understood it. Eternity is hard to face when you can't find anything to laugh about. Yet jokes couldn't hide the truth. I was conscious, and warm, and…preserved. But I wasn't alive, and I never would be again. Faking it was the best I could do. He and I had that in common.

"I would have done anything to keep you from dying." Tod slid one hand slowly down my arm, leaving a trail of chills in its wake. "This would have been just as amazing while you were alive."

"That was never part of the plan," I said. "We just didn't know it." Not until he'd seen my name on the list of souls scheduled to be reaped. And because I'd already had my one allowed death-date exchange, there was nothing Tod, or my dad, or anyone else, could do to save me. "Besides, there are advantages to the afterlife. For instance, if I were to do this—" I pushed him gently but firmly onto his back, then I straddled him "—no one could see us unless we wanted them to." And we did not.

"A valid point…" He reached for my hips, and I hated

both layers of clothing between us almost as much as I loved the look in his eyes, part surprise, part heat, and no hint of an objection.

"And if I were to do this—" I leaned forward and kissed the edge of his jaw, and Tod groaned as my shift in position created a delicious friction between us "—and you were to make that sound you just made, no one could hear you unless you wanted to be heard."

His hands tightened on my hips, pressing me tighter into him as my lips trailed down his jaw toward his neck, over the pale, late-night stubble he'd died with. "What happened to the good little girl who blushed and covered her face at the *thought* of what you're doing right now?"

"She died," I whispered into his ear.

That girl had felt alive with every breath she'd taken, even knowing she'd soon breathe her last. This one—the restored me—only felt alive when she experienced very strong emotions, which Madeline had assured me was perfectly normal. And so far the only strong emotions I actually enjoyed were the ones I felt when I was with Tod.

"Why? You like the good girl better?" I asked.

"I *know* her better." Tod's hand slid up my back beneath my shirt. "But this one's certainly making me wish I'd shown up for invisi-lunch." He'd texted me halfway through lunch to say he couldn't make it.

I laughed, then rolled off of him and onto my side, watching his profile from inches away. "What could possibly compete with the lure of cafeteria food, adolescent conversation, and hostile company?"

"I spent two hours trying to question reapers without sounding like I was questioning them. What do you think it says about us as a group, that every reaper I know is either irritable, egotistical, voyeuristic, or some combination of the three?"

"That you fit in well?"

"Ha, ha."

"So, had any of them seen Thane?"

"Not that they told me. But I can't be sure, because I couldn't come right out and ask. It was probably a waste of time that would have been better spent with you. What did I miss at lunch?"

I shrugged with the shoulder not pressed into my mattress. "Nash is still mad. Sabine is still blunt. And I met Madeline's necromancer. His name's Luca."

"A death detector?" Tod made a face. "That's creepy."

"Says the living dead boy."

"I'm serious."

I pretended to study his expression. "So *that's* what that looks like…"

"You know you can't hide from him, right? He'll see you, whether you're corporeal or not, and he'll hear you if he's close enough. Tell me that's not creepy."

"It's a little creepy, but he's the one who found Thane this morning. I'm thinking a necromancer on our side is infinitely less creepy than one working for the bad guys."

"I guess…"

"It gets weirder. He's dating Sophie."

"On purpose?" Tod looked horrified. It takes a lot to scare a reaper.

"Looks like it. She knows what he is and doesn't seem to care. Oh, and we ate with Em's new boyfriend, too."

"These are the days of our lives…" Tod announced in a false baritone, and I smacked his shoulder. "Okay, I'll bite. What's Em's boyfriend like?"

“His name’s Jayson. He’s human. Normal and nice. He’s probably perfect for her.”

“But…?”

“But nothing.” I shrugged. “She’s safer with him than with any of us. She deserves a nice, normal relationship, but—”

“I knew there was a ‘but.’”

“—but I don’t know how to be around her when she’s with him. There’s too much I can’t say. Too much he doesn’t know.”

Tod ran his hand down my arm until he found my hand, and his fingers folded around mine. “Are we still talking about Jayson? ’Cause it kind of sounds like you’re talking about Emma now.”

I sighed. “Maybe.” Em knew a lot about my world—not to mention the Netherworld—but she was still in the dark about a lot of it, too. She didn’t know much about Thane, or that Avari was willing to kill her to get to me. She didn’t know that Mr. Beck—the incubus math teacher who’d murdered me—had planned to kill her, too, but not until after he’d fed from her. She didn’t know that her sister was pregnant with Beck’s incubus fetus, or that Harmony was busy collecting and combining a blend of Netherworld herbs that could end the brand-new pregnancy and save her sister’s life. Though I’d have to tell her most of that very soon, because I was *not* looking forward to explaining the truth to Traci, who could discover her own pregnancy any day.

But mostly, Emma didn’t know how hard it was for me to sit through class after class today, knowing that none of it mattered anymore. I wasn’t going to grow up and go off to college with her. I wasn’t ever going to use the past-perfect conjugation of French verbs, and after finals, I’d probably never again be required to write out a mathematical proof.

The only things still certain in my future were the reclamation of stolen souls and Tod. That’s it. Those were the only things that mattered anymore, and the harder I clung to the plans that were important to the once-living Kaylee, the more I felt like a fraud walking around in her skin.

"I keep forgetting to be, Tod," I whispered, my voice muted by the enormity of what I was admitting.

"Forgetting to be what?"

"To *be.* To be *here.* To exist. If I don't concentrate, I slip right out of the physical plane, and I don't even notice it until I realize people can't see or hear me." That had happened with my dad over and over since I'd died, and if it ever happened at school, I was screwed.

"That's normal."

"That's not normal!" I insisted. "Forgetting to exist is textbook-weird!"

His hand tightened around mine, and his blue irises swirled in sympathy. "It takes a while to get into the routine of taking physical form. I didn't make a habit of it until I met you."

"It's like I don't exist anymore. Like I'm nowhere." I rolled onto my back, and he leaned over me, staring down at me from inches away.

"You're very much here, Kaylee. From my vantage point, you're everywhere." His eyes were all I could see, his irises swirling slowly, confirming everything he was saying and hinting at even more.

"This is the only time I feel real, Tod. Only when I'm touching you. I wish it could be like this forever."

"It can be. It *will* be," he said, and he sounded so sure of that that I could almost believe him.

"What if you get tired of me? Forever's a long time."

"I'm well aware." Tod sat up and pulled me up with him until we faced each other on my bed. "Forever used to feel like a curse. Now it feels like a promise," he said, and my chest ached, and I loved that feeling—that rare pain that came from feeling too much, so different from the emptiness I'd almost gotten used to. "All you have to do is stay here with me."

"That, and eat breakfast for my dad. And reclaim souls for Madeline. And go to school and work to convince everyone that Nash is innocent." I frowned as something ridiculous occurred to me. "In the movies and on TV, there are all these ancient vampires taking math and PE with a bunch of teenagers, and I always thought that was the *stupidest* thing. I mean, if you had eternity to spend however you want—and for the most part, we do—why the hell would you go back to high school? What on earth was I thinking?"

Tod laughed. "I can't speak for ancient, fictional creatures, but *you* were thinking that you wanted to retain what little normalcy still exists in your life. Er, your afterlife. Also, going back to school and work is part of proving you're still alive, and being alive is the only way to prove that Nash didn't kill you."

"Oh, yeah. But I went back for a day, and everyone saw me, so they know I'm alive now. So I don't have to go back, right? Tell me I don't have to go back."

"You don't have to go back." Tod leaned down and kissed me, and my hand slid into his hair, holding him close as my mouth opened beneath his. "If you quit school we could spend every afternoon just…" Kiss. "Like…" Kiss. "This." Another, longer kiss, and this time when he pulled away, he left me gasping for breath.

"Aren't you supposed to tell me to be responsible and stay in school?"

Tod's lips brushed my ear. "I signed on for the role of 'boyfriend,' not 'conscience.' If you want wholesome and ethical, you'll have to look elsewhere. But I promise that won't be half as much fun as this is…."

His hand slid down my side and over my hip, and my heart beat faster.

"That feels so good," I whispered as his lips trailed over my chin and down my neck. "*You* feel good. Real." Solid, like no matter how incorporeal he made himself, I would always be able to touch him. To feel him.

I gasped when his line of kisses skirted my collarbone and dipped into what little cleavage I'd accumulated before death put an end to the possibility of accruing any more.

"You, too," he said, his lips still pressed against my skin. "You make me feel alive. Every time I touch you, I feel like there's some kind of charge flowing between us. Like tiny little bolts of lightning, setting me on fire. Can you feel it here?" He pushed my shirt up and laid one hand on my stomach.

I closed my eyes. "I feel it."

"Can you feel it here?" His hand glided over my skin and around the curve of my ribs until his finger brushed the edge of my bra, and I stopped breathing, just for a second.

"I feel it." I pulled him back up and slid my hands beneath his shirt, feeling my way over his chest as I pulled the material up and over his head. I dropped his shirt on the floor and laid my hand over his heart, and I could feel it beating.

"Does it do that all the time?" I whispered, and he shook his head, his eyes swirling with pale blue twists of need, and hunger, and something deeper, and steadier, and…endless. "Mine doesn't, either."

Tod laid his hand over my heart and I blinked up at him. "It's beating now," he said softly.

"Yeah. It is."

He kissed me, and I didn't realize my legs had wrapped around his hips until he moaned into my mouth and pressed himself into me.

I felt so alive in that moment. So real and—

"Kaylee, are you home?" my father called from the living room, and the front door slammed shut on the tail of the question.

"Shit!" I whispered, before I remembered that he couldn't hear us. He couldn't see us, either, but I couldn't hide the rumpled comforter.

Tod sat up and reached for his shirt while I straightened mine. "Relax," he said as he pulled his T-shirt over his head. "What's he going to do, kill us again?"

"Not me." I ran both hands through my hair to smooth it. "You."

"You're almost seventeen, and you're dead. He has to know that his parental influence is nearing its end stage."

"He does. I think. We're gonna talk about it. Just...not today."

"Kaylee?" My dad's footsteps echoed in the hall, headed our way.

I closed my eyes and concentrated on making myself both visible and audible. "In here." I opened the door and my dad stepped into the doorway as I dropped the amphora around my neck. "Hey, do you wanna go out for..." His words melted into a sigh when he noticed Tod, but then he rallied with a smile. "Hi, Tod, I didn't realize you were here. In my daughter's bedroom. With the door closed."

"Happy to be here," Tod said, and I groaned out loud.

"Kaylee, can I talk to you for a minute, please?" my dad said with a glance at the rumpled comforter.

"Um, yeah." I followed him into the kitchen, where he pulled a soda from the fridge and popped the tab.

"I know things are inevitably going to change, but I'm not going to pretend to be happy that the two of you were here, alone, behind closed doors." I didn't bother to tell him that doors no longer mattered. The only time I didn't feel alone was when Tod was with me.

"I don't really want to have this conversation with you, Dad."

"I don't want to have it, either, but you're kind of forcing my hand."

"No, I'm not." I took a soda from the fridge for myself, and after a moment's consideration, I grabbed one for Tod, too. "If you think about this logically, you have to admit that most of the reasons for me to wait to have sex died when I died."

My dad flinched. "You said it out loud. There's no going back now, is there?"

"Nope."

He was thinking about my mother. Wishing she was here for this conversation. I knew, because I was thinking the same thing. But wishes were worthless, so I launched into logic.

"I can't get pregnant, and I can't catch anything." Not that Tod had anything for me to catch. "And I love him. And he loves me. Shouldn't that be enough?"

"Yes. It should. And it will be." He closed his eyes and gripped the edge of the countertop, like it was the only thing holding him up. Then his eyes opened and his gaze met mine, his swirling with brown twists of regret and nostalgia. "But you're still so young."

"I'm as grown up as I'm going to get, Dad. And hell, I died a virgin. I died *because* I was a virgin. So I hope you can understand why I no longer see the point in preserving something that only served to get me killed."

"Okay." My dad nodded slowly. "Those are valid points. Just promise me you'll think about this before you jump into anything." He flinched again, and met my gaze with what looked like great effort. "You haven't already jumped…right?"

"No. There's been no jumping yet. And I promise that I'm not done thinking. How's that?"

"Is that as good as I'm going to get?"

"It's as good as I have to offer."

"Okay." He didn't look happy, but he didn't look exactly mad, either. He looked…disappointed. And maybe a little scared. "You do understand that if we were to add up all the time we've actually spent together, you'd still only be around five years old to me, right?"

"I know," I said, and his sad smile made me ache. "And you understand that I grew up during those years you missed, right? That's not how I wanted it, but that's how it happened, and I can't go back and fix it. I can't go back and fix anything, Dad."

"I know. And I'm so sorry. So, how 'bout I start making it up to you with Chinese delivery? We got this coupon in the mail…." He set his soda down and started digging through a pile of junk mail on the counter.

"Thanks, but I'm not really hungry, and Tod and I need to do something. Something work-related," I added when his brows arched in suspicion.

"Oh. Okay."

"But maybe we could watch a movie tonight?" I said when his disappointment nearly broke my heart. "Just the two of us?"

He nodded and forced a smile. "I'll be waiting."

Tod caught my gaze from the hallway, where he'd waited, unseen by my father, and when he took my hand so we could blink out together, he leaned close to whisper in my ear. "I'd say he took that pretty well. You know your dad's the coolest dad on the face of the planet, right?"

"I know. One of these days, I may just tell him."

"Do you remember the last time we were here?" Tod asked as we stood on the sidewalk in front of Lakeside, the mental-health unit attached to the hospital where Tod reaped souls and his mother worked the second shift as an R.N.

"How could I forget?" I felt a little queasy just thinking about it. "Feels different this time, though."

"Because you can get in and out on your own?"

"Yeah." That eliminated my fear of being trapped. Caught. Locked up. "Maybe I'll pretend I still have to hold your hand to be invisible."

"Role-playing. I like it." His fingers curled around mine. "Have you heard from Lydia since we broke her out?"

Lydia was a psychic syphon and former psychiatric patient who'd saved both my life and my sanity by taking some of my pain into herself when I was locked up in Lakeside. Tod and I had freed her less than a month ago.

"No." I'd tried two different women's shelters—while I was incorporeal—before I'd realized she might not be allowed to stay without risking being put into foster care. "But I'll keep looking for her." She'd saved my life. I owed her nothing less.

"You ready for this?" Tod asked.

"Let's go." I closed my eyes and concentrated on Scott's room, in the youth wing, on the third floor. Somewhere on the way, I lost Tod's hand and started to panic, but he was there waiting for me when I opened my eyes in Scott's room. "Guess I still need practice doing that in tandem, huh?"

"We have plenty of time to get it right. We have time to get *everything* right." He started to pull me close, but I froze with one glance over his shoulder. Scott lay on his back, on top of his made bed, fully dressed, including laceless sneakers. His hands were folded beneath his head and his eyes were closed. Watching him when he didn't know we were there was a little creepy. I still wasn't used to being incorporeal on purpose.

I glanced around the room and frowned. Scott's clothes were folded neatly on the open shelves bolted to the wall, but all of his other personal items—mostly photos of him, Nash, and Doug, who'd died of the frost addiction that drove Scott insane—were packed into an open box on the floor next to the desk bolted to the wall.

"Maybe they're getting ready to move him," Tod said, squatting to look into the box.

"Why? And where?" I didn't look at his stuff. I didn't want to see pieces of Scott's shattered life and know that they all fit in a single box on the floor. I didn't want to know how close Nash had come to sharing the same fate. I didn't want to remember how I hadn't been fast or perceptive enough to save either of them.

"Is there a way to let him see us without scaring the crap out of him?" I whispered, though my volume had no effect on whether or not Scott could hear me.

"There's the slow fade-in," Tod said, standing again, his hands in the pockets of his jeans. "But I'm a fan of the dramatic sudden appearance." His grin was to lighten the mood, but I had trouble smiling at Lakeside. There was nothing funny about being locked up with only your personal demons for company.

In Scott's case, the demon was real.

"Okay, here goes nothing." I focused on Scott, trying to make sure he was the only one other than Tod who could hear and see me, in case someone else came in while we were there. That's harder than it sounds, and I'd messed it up in practice more times than I cared to admit.

When I was pretty sure I had it right, I cleared my throat.

Scott's eyes opened and his head rolled in our direction. His brows rose, but he didn't look particularly surprised. Maybe because he was accustomed to seeing things that weren't there. Maybe because he was used to seeing me in particular. Avari had been giving him hallucinations of me, a fact that creeped me out almost as badly as the hellion himself did.

"Hi, Scott," I said, and he sat up slowly, feet on the floor, leaning forward with his hands curled around the mattress on either side of his knees. His eyes were clear and focused. He didn't look medicated.

"I heard you were dead. Kinda assumed that meant I wouldn't be seeing you again."

"Sorry." I wasn't sure whether or not I should admit that I had, in fact, died. Scott was officially crazy, so no one would believe him, anyway. But I decided not to mention it. Just in case. "Scott, I need a favor. Could you ask Avari a question for me?"

"Why?" Scott looked straight into my eyes as he spoke, and his gaze was oddly steady.

"Because we can't speak to him directly without crossing over," Tod said.

"What if you could?" His focus narrowed on me, and my skin started to crawl.

"Then we wouldn't be here asking you for help," I said. We'd come prepared for a strange conversation with Scott, but I found this apparent *lack* of strange even stranger than the strange I'd been expecting.

"Why should I help you?" Scott demanded, and his voice had an odd edge to it now. He wasn't confused by either our presence or our questions. "What did you ever do for me?"

Tod glanced at me with both pale brows raised. "Is it just me, or does he seem a little saner than usual?"

"Maybe he's having a good day," I whispered, desperately hoping that was true.

"I'm insane, not deaf," Scott said, and when he stood, I backed away. I was already dead, but because I was corporeal—I had to be, for him to see me—he could do physical damage to me, as both my father and Tod had already demonstrated on Thane.

"Can Avari hear us?" I wasn't sure if Scott served as a sort of amplifier, through which Avari could hear us directly, or if it was more of a messenger service, where Scott had to mentally ask Avari everything we asked him.

"He can hear you, so be careful what you say. He can see you, so be careful what you do." Scott stepped closer, and I backed up as Tod stepped between us. The psych patient peered at me over the reaper's shoulder. "And if you'd come a little closer, he'd be able to taste you, too. Though he'd settle for just a *little whiff.*"

"I don't want to punch a mental patient, but I will," Tod growled.

"So the prince of death has become the white knight. I would not have laid wager on that." In an instant, Scott changed, without changing at all. He stood straighter and suddenly seemed to take up more space in the small room than he should have. His gestures became formal, but didn't seem overstated. He looked older. Scarier. He looked...familiar. "But you know you cannot wear both hats at once, dark prince. Not for long, anyway," the Scott-thing said. "Someday you will have to choose."

Chills raced up my spine "That's not Scott."

"I know," Tod said as I stepped to the side for a better view around his arm. "Avari?"

Scott's mouth smiled, and it was creepy to see the hellion's mannerisms bleeding through the skin of a former classmate. "Human emotion is a handicap to a reaper, Mr. Hudson. She melts your cold heart and softens your hard edges, and she'll keep at it until there's nothing left of you but what beats and bleeds and burns for her. And then the formless lump of a man you'll become won't be capable of reaping souls. What will befall you then?"

"He's possessed," Tod whispered, and I could only nod, trying not to hear what Avari was saying. Trying not to remember that he couldn't lie.

"If you stay with her, neither of you will see eternity." Avari glanced at me through Scott's eyes, and the hunger in them terrified me beyond what I'd thought I could feel in death. "Give her to me, and you will live forever."

"I'm already dead," I said.

"So am I," Tod pointed out.

"But you don't have to be." The hellion focused on Tod, ignoring me completely. "Give her to me, and I'll give you a body. A real one, that breathes and beats on its own. One that can age, and change, and truly feel every proper pleasure and base desire. And when that one wears out, there will be another body, fresh and young. They will stretch into eternity for you, and with them, untold lifetimes in the human world, a part of it again, instead of watching from the fringes. All of that, in exchange for one, insignificant little soul. You will forget about her by the end of your first mortal lifetime. Your second, at the latest. Or I could help you forget her now, if you'd prefer."

Tod glanced at me, both brows raised. "Can a hellion go insane? Because I think this one's lost his fucking mind."

"I'm *dead,* Avari," I repeated. "Doesn't that make this whole stupid obsession kind of pointless?"

Scott clasped his hands at his back like an old man and tried to come closer, but Tod stayed between us, and the hellion didn't seem to like having to look up at him. Or having to look around him to get to me. "Do you still have a soul, Ms. Cavanaugh?"

"Yes..." I said, and I could already see where this was headed.

"That soul is yet unsmudged, and unless I'm mistaken—" he made a show of sniffing the air in my direction, and my chill bumps doubled in size "—you died with other virtues intact. Do you have any idea how rare that is in today's world?"

"So I've heard," I mumbled.

"Now, if a hellion had access to the human plane, to a wealth of even purer souls and younger bodies, you might find your value eroded," he continued. I didn't give a damn about my value in the Netherworld, but I'd never been more relieved that Avari was stuck there. "Or perhaps not. There is something intriguing and rare about your persistent selflessness." His frown was part fascination and part confusion, like he couldn't quite figure out why I drew his interest.

That made two of us.

"Okay, I've had enough of this crap." I stepped around Tod, and when he tried to pull me back, I gave him the warning look I'd perfected on Sabine. He backed off, but stayed close. "What the hell happened with Thane? Why didn't you eat him when you had the chance?"

"What makes you think I didn't?" Avari's words rolled off Scott's tongue with an ease that made me sick to my undead stomach.

"I saw him this morning, so unless you regurgitated him, it looks to me like he escaped your evil clutches. Or something like that."

"No one escapes—"

"I did," I said, before he could even finish his sentence. "Twice, if memory serves."

"Three times," Tod corrected, ticking them off on his fingers. "There was the time in his office, with Addy, then the time at the carnival, then in the cafeteria. Three times."

"Oh, yeah. I forgot about the time with Addy." I turned back to Scott, who looked distinctly unamused. "Three times."

"As loathe as I am to concede the fact, you were never truly captured, so you can't possibly have escaped. And neither has Thane."

I crossed both arms over my chest, frowning. Hellions couldn't outright lie. Possession of a human body didn't change that, right? "Then what was he doing at the doughnut shop this morning?"

"Reaping."

"Why?"

"Because that is what reapers do."

I rolled my eyes and looked up at Tod. "Okay, this is a waste of time. Let's go."

"Not without what we came for," he said, and I'd never heard his voice deeper or angrier. "You have two choices here," Tod said to the hellion. "You can answer some questions, or you can let your boy Scott take a lump to the head." Which would evict Avari from the body he'd possessed and put a temporary end to his playtime on the human plane.

"And how will you get the answers you seek then?" Avari demanded, and neither of us had an answer for that. "Nothing is free, Ms. Cavanaugh. Perhaps if you offered a trade..."

"You're not getting my soul, or any other part of me," I said.

"Information is tonight's currency, is it not?" he said. "You answer two questions for me, and I will answer one for you."

"How is that fair?" Tod demanded, and I realized he'd edged closer to me, like he might have to lunge between me and mortal danger any second. I was beyond the mortal phase of my existence, but his instinct still made me smile.

"Fair is irrelevant. I am a hellion of greed. I won't offer this exchange again."

"Okay," I said, and Tod groaned, but I ignored him. "You

get two questions, but I go first." And as soon as I had my answer, I'd blink out.

Avari clucked Scott's tongue and shook his head. "I haven't succumbed to stupidity since we last spoke, Ms. Cavanaugh. But as a gesture of goodwill, I will allow you the second question."

That was as good as I was going to get. "Fine. Ask."

"What *are* you, little *bean sidhe?* How did you survive your own death?"

"That's two questions," Tod pointed out.

"They are one in spirit," Avari insisted.

"But they were two in…words. So I'll answer one of them," I said. "I am a reclamation agent. I take stolen souls from monsters like you and see that they get their final rest. Now my question." But I had to think about that. If he could possibly answer me without divulging any actual information, he would. I'd have to phrase it carefully.

"Why is Thane on the human plane, if he hasn't wiggled free from your grip?"

"He is doing my bidding, Ms. Cavanaugh. Thane the wayward reaper is now bound by new chains of servitude."

"So you told him to kill the doughnut-shop owner? Why?"

Scott's brows rose, but the expression was all hellion. "Does that mean you'd like to bargain for more information? If not, you still owe me another answer."

"You can settle up with her later." Tod took my hand and reality started to twist and bend around me. The last thing I saw before we appeared in the middle of my bedroom floor was Scott's face, warped in an angry snarl as the hellion peered out at me through his eyes.

"SO, DID THAT CREEP YOU OUT AS MUCH AS IT creeped me out?" I asked, flopping down on my bed on my stomach.

Tod sank into my desk chair and rolled it forward until his knees touched the mattress. "Maybe more. Why would Thane work for Avari, if he's free to leave the Netherworld?"

Styx growled at him from the foot of my bed, then settled into my lap when I clucked my tongue at her and patted my leg. "I think the bigger question is what is he doing for Avari, other than the obvious?" Reaping unauthorized souls.

"What is who doing for Avari?" my father asked, and I looked up in surprise to find him standing in my bedroom doorway. But I could tell from the way his gaze flitted over the room that he couldn't see either of us. "The disembodied voice and the growling guard dog gave you both away, so you might as well show up for real."

"Sorry." I concentrated on the physical plane—on truly

being there—and my father's gaze finally landed on me. "I didn't realize I was only half-there."

"It takes some practice," Tod said, and I knew that he'd become fully corporeal, too.

"So, what's going on with Avari?" My father leaned against the door frame, not truly in my room, but clearly stating his intent to be involved in whatever we were up to. And since he'd overheard part of what I'd thought was a private conversation, we'd have to let him into the loop. Otherwise, he'd ask Madeline next time he saw her, and we'd be screwed.

I glanced at Tod and found just a hint of frustration and fear swirling in the cerulean depths of his eyes. "Thane's back, and Avari appears to be pulling his strings."

My father frowned. "Thane's back? From the dead? Again?"

Tod nodded. "He's like the Rasputin of reapers. He's evidently impossible to get rid of. But don't worry," he said, turning to lay one hand over mine on the edge of the bed. "I'm going to handle this."

My father's forehead furrowed. "And by handle it, you mean…?"

"I'm going to ask Levi for help." Tod met my gaze. "Madeline told you to let the reapers police our own, right?" he asked, and I could only nod. "I'm hoping Levi can deal with Thane before anyone else sees him and reports his return. That way he can't carry out whatever nefarious task Avari put him up to and neither Levi nor I will get in trouble for dealing with him through unsanctioned means like last time."

"How would Levi deal with him?" I asked, and my dad looked just as interested in the answer.

"I assume he'd…end Thane. The only way to do that—that I know of—is to take his soul. I've seen Levi do it several times," Tod said, and my chill bumps were back.

"I've seen it, too," I said, and the memory was enough to

make my hands shake. "I saw him take yours, and he'll do it again, if Madeline forces his hand." I sat up on the end of the bed and met my father's heavy gaze. "You can't tell Madeline about Thane."

My father frowned. But then he nodded.

"I started this, and I'll finish it," Tod said, still watching me. "There's no reason for you to put yourself in any danger."

"I agree," my father said.

"Well, then, it's a good thing I'm not submitting to a vote. I have every reason to get involved in this," I insisted. "First, I am not going to spend eternity alone," I said, glaring Tod into silence when he started to argue. "Second of all, Thane has a grudge against all *three* of us, one of whom he could still kill." I aimed a pointed glance at my father, who looked like he wanted to argue, but couldn't. "And anyway, you and Levi are going to need help finding Thane, and I happen to know someone who can sense the dead."

"The necromancer?" Tod frowned. "How do you know you can trust him?"

I shrugged. "Madeline trusts him."

"But I don't trust *her.*"

"Neither do I," my father added. "She doesn't really care about you, Kaylee. She only cares about what you can do for her and the reclamation department."

"That's because she's my boss, not my guidance counselor." I exhaled slowly in frustration. "Look, we don't have much time and we don't have many resources, and Luca is too great an asset to ignore just because you don't trust Madeline." I focused on Tod. "Come meet him tomorrow at lunch?"

"Okay, but if he brings a Ouija board, I reserve the right to mess with anyone who can't see me."

"Fair enough. You talk to Levi tonight and, in the morning, I'll see if Luca can pinpoint the rogue reaper again—he doesn't even know who Thane is, much less that that's who he spotted yesterday."

"I love a woman with a plan," Tod said, and my father scowled.

"Good, 'cause there's more. Avari and Thane know that the best way to get to us is through our friends and family, and they know where to find everyone we care about. So we need to keep tabs on everyone. Tod, can you keep an eye on Nash and your mom?" I figured Sabine would be wherever Nash was.

Tod nodded, and I turned to my father. "If you can check on Uncle Brendon and Sophie, when she's at home, I'll keep up with Emma and with Sophie while she's at school."

My dad nodded, and I breathed a little easier. Literally. I felt better having a plan, even if that plan was vague and full of holes.

When Tod went to work and my father went to bed, I spent an hour trying to dig up enough interest to get through my chemistry homework, but chemical formulas and equations seemed no more important at one in the morning than they had twelve hours earlier, and every time my mind wandered, I found Scott, or Thane, or Avari, haunting me from my own memories.

After a solid half hour spent tapping my pencil on the page and twisting the amphora heart on its chain around my neck while Styx snored on my pillow, I closed my textbook and admitted defeat. School no longer felt relevant, because I knew for a fact that I wouldn't need most of what I learned there.

Even if I decided to go to college, what would I do with my degree? Assuming someone would be willing to hire a doctor, or a lawyer, or a physical therapist who looked sixteen, I wouldn't be able to hold any one job for very long, because it wouldn't take people long to notice that I wasn't aging. And it would take a very patient boss to overlook all the times I'd have to take a long lunch or an unauthorized hour off to hunt down a stolen soul.

Suddenly my future was looking long and boring. And frustrating beyond reason. And I'd only been dead a month.

What if the boredom and sense of futility got worse? What if I eventually lost my humanity and wound up like Thane, so bored I was willing to hurt people just to entertain myself? To break up the monotony of day after day and night after night of nothing.

If that were to happen, would I know it was happening? Would I even care? Once my friends and family were all gone, would I even have a point of reference for what humanity and normalcy look like? What they feel like? Would Tod and I be enough to keep each other sane and human enough to care about each other? To care about anything?

I closed my eyes and rolled over on my bed, trying to purge the litany of fears and useless questions marching through my brain, but I couldn't get rid of them because I had nothing to replace them with except more fears and useless questions.

What if Luca couldn't find Thane?

What if Levi wouldn't help us deal with him?

How would I protect my friends and family from a hellion willing to use them to get to me?

The questions played through my head like a song list on repeat, but I had no answers, and after a while, the questions themselves stopped making sense. And when I looked up, I realized I'd been staring at the amphora in my hand for forty-seven minutes, without moving. Without breathing. Without even blinking.

My eyes and my throat were dry, but the really weird thing was that I had no urge to stretch or find a new position. Or to move at all. I could easily have sat there doing and thinking nothing for another forty-seven minutes or longer.

The even *weirder* thing was that that thought didn't bother me. It didn't scare me, though I knew it should have. I felt like a bear in hibernation, minus all the sleeping. I'd just... shut down.

That had happened before. Always at night, when I was alone. When there was nothing to do and no one to talk to. It hadn't scared me then, either, but the next day, in retrospect, it always did. And it would again.

I was trying to decide whether or not to get up and find something worth doing, on general principle, when I heard a thud from outside. I froze and listened, and heard it again.

I was on my feet in an instant, racing down the hall in my bare feet. I grabbed a knife from the butcher block in the kitchen and fought memories of sharp metal, warm blood, and excruciating pain as I headed slowly for the door, telling myself I couldn't die twice. Er, three times. I was halfway there before I remembered that I could make sure no one heard my footsteps.

Being dead takes a lot of practice.

At the door, I peered through the peephole, but saw nothing but my empty front yard, damp from a steady drizzle of spring rain. But then I heard another thud, this time followed by a familiar groan. I set the knife on the end table next to my father's recliner and pulled the front door open.

Nash sat on the top step, leaning against the porch railing, a squarish glass bottle loosely held in one hand. His clothes were wet, his hair plastered to his head.

"Nash, what the hell are you doing here?"

He looked up, like he was surprised to see me. At my own house. "I'm drinking on your porch. Care to join me?" He held the bottle of whiskey up and I shook my head, then stepped out of the house and closed the door behind me, so my dad wouldn't hear him. "*Why* are you drinking on my porch?"

"The lawn's too wet to sit on."

"That's because it's raining. Give me that." I pulled the bottle from his grip. "Did you walk here? You're soaked."

He laughed, but the sound was harsh. Half choked. "My mom frowns on driving drunk."

"Your mother frowns on *being* drunk. Come dry off and I'll take you home."

"I don't want to go home."

"You need to go home. Come on." I tried to pull him up but he was too heavy, so he pulled himself up, using the porch railing for balance. Standing, he stared down at me, his eyes half focused in the porch light. He blinked, too drunk to hide the swirls of confusion and longing in his irises. Then he leaned down like he'd kiss me.

I stepped back and put my empty hand on his chest, my heart aching for him. For me. For all four of us, and the ties twisting us together. "No. Don't do this, Nash," I said, and his next exhalation seemed to deflate him.

I stepped over the threshold and held the door open for him, and he trudged inside, dripping on the floor. "Where's your boyfriend?"

"Working." I pushed the door closed and set his whiskey on the half wall between the kitchen and living room, then dug a clean hand towel from a drawer in the kitchen. "Where's your girlfriend?"

"In bed."

"Yours?"

"Yeah," he said, and I caught my breath, surprised by the hollow feeling in my chest—an unexpected residual ache. "That's what you wanted, right? You want me with her, so I can forget about you?"

I handed him the towel and he blotted his face with it, but his gaze never left mine. "I just want you to be happy, Nash." And clean. And stable.

"Yeah, well, that ship's sailed." He stood dripping on the tiled entry, still watching me. "Tell me it hurts, Kaylee. Tell me it hurts, just a little bit."

I exhaled slowly and took the towel when he handed it back. "It hurts. More than a little." It hurt to see him, knowing that I'd played no small part in making him into what he'd become. It hurt a lot. "Go dry off in the bathroom. I'll get you something to wear." My dad's clothes would be big on him, but at least he'd be dry and dressed.

"I don't want to wear your dad's clothes. He hates me."

"You'd rather wear mine?"

Nash scowled, but took off his shoes, stumbled over his own feet, and headed for the bathroom.

I pawed through the dryer for a pair of my dad's drawstring jogging shorts and the smallest T-shirt I could find. When I knocked softly on the bathroom door, Nash opened it wearing only a towel wrapped around his waist.

"Here." I handed him the clothes and he took them, then just stood there, watching me.

"Why did you do it, Kaylee?" he asked, and I put one finger over my lips, warning him to be quiet. I couldn't mute his voice like I could mute mine.

But I didn't know how to answer his question. I wasn't even sure what he was asking—I'd done so many things I wasn't proud of, most of them to him. "Get dressed, and we'll talk. But then you have to go home."

He closed the bathroom door, and I waited in my bedroom doorway, leaning against the frame. A minute later he emerged in my father's shorts, the drawstring cinched around his narrow hips. The T-shirt lay on the closed toilet lid behind him. I stood, blocking the door to my room, and he stepped so close I could smell the rain on his skin. "Aren't you gonna let me in?" he whispered, staring straight into my eyes.

"I don't think that's a good idea." For many reasons. Two of which were Tod and Sabine.

"I just want to understand, Kaylee. Don't you think you at least owe me an explanation, considering you framed me for your murder?"

How the hell was I supposed to say no to that?

I stepped back and let him in, and Nash glanced around my room like he hadn't been there in years. And that's kind of what it felt like. The past month felt like an eternity—so much had changed in such a short period of time that I couldn't even hold all the facts in my head without getting a little dizzy.

"You moved everything," he said, making an obvious effort not to slur the words.

"Yeah. I couldn't… This is where I died. It was…" I swallowed thickly and glanced at the floor. "I needed a change."

He sat on my bed and Styx glanced at him in disinterest, then went back to sleep. Nash stared at his hands while I hovered near the doorway, uncomfortable in my own room. "I've been thinking about everything, trying to make sense out of what happened, but I can't do it. Everything was fine, and then…" He looked up at me, frowning, like something horrible had just occurred to him. "He gets to touch you now?"

"Everything wasn't fine, Nash."

He kept talking, like he hadn't even heard me. "He gets to kiss you, but I don't? I don't understand how we got here, Kaylee."

"Nash—"

"I know the facts. I can sit here and list everything that happened, every mistake either of us made, but when I do the math—I add it all up over and over—it never works out like this in my head."

"I know. The longer I think about any of it, the less sense it makes, and I'm sorry about that." I'd lost count of how many times I'd apologized. "I don't like how we got here, but this is where we're supposed to be." I sat in my desk chair and rolled it closer to the bed. "We're supposed to be friends, Nash. Can't you feel that? We were too close for too long to be anything less, but we can't be anything more. Not anymore."

"Because of Tod."

"No." I shook my head, desperately hoping he'd understand what I was trying to say. "Because of me. Because of you. Because we tried to make it work, but we couldn't. We tried so hard we nearly destroyed each other, and that's not what love is supposed to do, Nash. It's supposed to lift you up and make you feel whole, even if it hurts sometimes."

Nash exhaled slowly, still staring at his hands, then he looked up and met my gaze, and the vulnerability swirling within his nearly killed me. Again. "Tod makes you feel like that? Whole?"

I nodded. "More whole than I've felt since…ever." At least since my mother died and my father left.

Nash's forehead furrowed and his jaw clenched, like he was holding back words he knew better than to say. Then he met my gaze, and I could see the raw pain in his, unshielded, thanks to the whiskey. "I'm sorry I couldn't be that for you, Kaylee. I really wanted to. I wanted to be good enough for you. I wanted to deserve you, and in a way, it was easier after you and he…" His jaw clenched again, then the words tumbled out in an emotionally charged, drunk free fall, and his gaze begged me to understand. "After I saw you with him in the hall. Because you'd messed up, and I thought that if you weren't perfect, you could understand why I wasn't, either, and we could fix things. But that was when I thought it was just one kiss, and—"

Nash stopped and glanced at the floor, and when he looked up at me, there were tears standing in his eyes. "If I hadn't been high that day in the parking lot—if I hadn't started using again—would this have turned out differently? Would you have given us another chance?"

My own tears answered his, and I rolled my chair closer to the bed. "No, Nash. Please don't ever think that. As bad as that afternoon was, you and I had already broken up, and Tod and I were already together." I sucked in a deep breath, then said the only thing I could think of that might help him understand. "He died for me, Nash. He refused to reap my soul, so Levi had to take his." An unemployed reaper was a dead reaper. "That's the way it goes."

Nash's eyes widened, and he frowned. "Then how is he—"

"I had to bargain for his afterlife."

"And for my release…?"

"Yeah." I leaned back in my chair and relaxed a little. "I owed you at least that much, and I'm sorry that Madeline has no pull in the court of public opinion."

Nash huffed, and I could smell the whiskey on his breath. "Yeah, me, too."

"You know, if you didn't openly hate me—if we hung out like we used to—the rumors that you stabbed me would die pretty damn quickly. I'd never hang out with my attempted murderer."

He thought about that for a moment, and when his eyes closed, I thought he'd fallen asleep sitting up, until they opened again. "I could do that. We could try the friendship thing, if that's the best I'm gonna get. But I can't hang out with him."

"Nash—"

"Kaylee, he's my brother, and he stabbed me in the back.

I know you're an only child, so you can't really understand, but I can't… I can't see the two of you together. Not yet."

"Okay." I nodded. "I guess that's fair. But I think you should talk to him, even if I'm not there. You don't understand how much he loves you."

"And stealing my girlfriend was supposed to show me that?"

"He didn't steal me, Nash." And frankly, I was getting tired of being talked about like a car or a piece of jewelry with no free will of its own. Like I'd had no choice in the matter. "I made a decision. I'm sorry about the way it happened, but I'm not going to change my mind."

His eyes closed again. His next words were slurred with both alcohol and sleep, and I wondered if he'd even heard what I'd said. "Can I stay? It's raining…." He laid down on his side without waiting for my answer, and Styx scooted closer to him for warmth.

I sighed. Then I unfolded the blanket at the foot of the bed and pulled it up to Nash's shoulders, and his eyes popped open. He grabbed my arm and his gaze gained coherent focus, just for a second. "I saw Scott tonight," he said, and shock raced through every nerve ending remaining in my undead body.

"What? When did you see him?" But Nash's eyes were closed. "Where did you see Scott?" I shook his shoulder, but he was out cold. "Nash!" I shook him again, and his eyes opened, but didn't truly focus on me. "Where did you see Scott?"

"Out…side…" Then he closed his eyes and started snoring.

"Outside?" Tod said, before I'd even realized he'd arrived. "Outside where?"

"I don't know. Here? His house? Somewhere between?" I pulled two sodas from the fridge and kicked the door shut. "He walked all the way here, so he could have seen Scott anywhere. Assuming he really saw him at all." I shrugged and handed him one of the cans. "I mean, he's drunk. Who knows what he really saw?"

"It was Scott." Tod accepted the can I gave him and popped the top. "I stopped by the hospital on my way here to check, and his room's empty. I guess that's why his stuff was half packed when we were there earlier."

"So, what, they let him out? Can they do that?"

"I don't know." Tod gave me an apologetic shrug. "You're kind of the resident expert."

"Don't remind me." But I couldn't argue. "I got out when Uncle Brendon Influenced my doctor into signing the papers. But I wasn't hearing voices and cowering from every shadow. I can't imagine any doctor worth the paper his degree's printed on letting someone like Scott out of the hospital."

Before Tod could reply, something tapped the front door three times, and I crossed the room to peer through the peephole. "What the hell is he doing here?" Sabine demanded as soon as I pulled the door open. She pushed past me into the living room in a pair of jeans and a snug black tank top, without bothering to wipe her bare feet on the mat.

"The usual," Tod said. "Self-destructing in slow motion."

I shot a frown at him. "Your guess is as good as mine," I said to Sabine, staring out into the dark after her, just in case. But I found nothing out of place except for her car, which was parked on the wrong side of the street, in front of the neighbor's mailbox.

"My guess is probably better." She dropped her keys on the coffee table and headed for the hall, ignoring Tod when he called after her.

"He passed out, Sabine. You may as well let him sleep it off."

"So, what?" I said when she'd disappeared around the corner. "They let Scott out—for no reason I can think of—and he heads straight for Nash's house?"

"Or for yours," Tod said. "We don't know where Nash saw him."

"Do you think he's still possessed?"

"How much did he drink? He's out cold," Sabine said, rounding the corner into the living room again to eyeball the half-empty bottle of whiskey. "Who's possessed?"

"It's a long story." I sank onto the couch next to Tod and folded my legs beneath me.

Sabine shrugged. "It's not like anyone here's missing out on sleep." *Maras* only needed around four hours a night, and Sabine had already gotten nearly that much before I called and woke her up.

"Okay, but hold it down." We were trying not to wake my father up, and I couldn't mute her voice—much to my own frustration. "There's this guy named Scott who used to go to our school—"

"Scott Carter?" Sabine interrupted. "The frost junkie?" When I could only stare at her in surprise, she rolled her eyes. "Nash's my best friend, Kaylee. We talk."

Good to know. I'd assumed they'd skipped straight to body language.

"How much do you know?" Tod asked.

"Nash and two friends got hooked on frost—breath from Avari, the hellion I met in the cafeteria." The time she'd tried to sell me out so she could have Nash to herself. "Doug died, Scott went insane, and because Nash isn't human, he got off with withdrawal and total abandonment from the one person who should have been there for him, no matter what."

"I didn't... That's not..." I gave up trying to explain that I hadn't *abandoned* Nash, and that frost wasn't what broke us up. "What matters now is that Scott's out, and Nash says he saw him tonight."

"Okay, why are the two of you talking about a visit from an old friend like that's worse than Nash being passed out in her bed. Which we're going to discuss later, by the way." Her dark-eyed glare narrowed on me. "You could have at least given him a shirt, Kaylee."

"Like you're an expert on when it's appropriate to wear a shirt," I snapped, thinking of the time she'd pulled hers off and jumped Nash, with me in the next room, and Sabine bristled.

"This seems headed into girl-fight territory," Tod said. "Should I make popcorn?"

I elbowed him in the ribs and glared at the *mara*. "The point is that Scott shouldn't be out of the hospital. He wasn't just a little unbalanced, Sabine. He suffered permanent brain damage from the frost, and Avari sent him enough visual and auditory hallucinations to make sure there was no doubt about his mental instability."

"So, how'd he get out?"

"We're not sure," I admitted. "But he was half packed when we saw him tonight, so it looks like he was actually released."

Sabine frowned. "You saw Scott tonight?"

"Sort of. We went to see if he'd ask Avari some questions for us, but when we got there, he was possessed, so we wound up dealing with Avari directly."

"Well, then, it sounds like you've answered your own question."

Tod glanced at me in question. "Is it just me, or is she making even less sense than usual?"

Sabine rolled her eyes again. "You knew he was possessed because he wasn't acting like himself, right?" she said, and we both nodded. "So couldn't he have been possessed long enough to convince the doctors that he's all cured off the crazy?"

"I don't think so," I said, and I was pleased to see that Tod looked no more convinced.

"He was bat shit when we saw him a couple of months ago," he said.

"Yeah, but for all you know, Avari could have been playing all sane and healthy during his doctors' appointments for a while, right?" Sabine said.

I was far from convinced, but I didn't have any better explanation. "Either way, if Nash saw Scott tonight, chances are good that what he really saw was Avari, wearing a Scott-suit. And if he went after Nash, he could go after anyone else. We need to stick together when we're not at home. Pairs, at the very least," I said.

"I call Nash," Sabine said, glaring at me, and I rolled my eyes.

"I don't want your boyfriend. Not like that." And assuming he remembered anything we'd said before he passed out, Nash and I may have just made major strides toward an actual, healthy friendship.

"He's not my boyfriend," Sabine said, and the thin thread of pain in her voice drew my focus her way.

"But I thought… He said…"

Sabine turned to Tod. "How long does she have to be dead before the naivety wears off?" Before he could answer, she turned back to me. "Only a virgin thinks sex means that much, Kaylee," she said, and Tod's hand tightened around mine before I could argue with her. She was lying. Sex with Nash meant something to her, even if she wouldn't admit it, but Tod didn't want me to call her on it.

Sabine had never lied to me before. Not even when she was trying to break up me and Nash.

She heaved a bitter sigh and scrubbed both hands over her face. "He's sleeping with me, but look where he winds up the minute I fall asleep." Her open-armed gesture took in my entire house.

"That doesn't mean anything," I insisted. "He probably came here on autopilot. Out of habit."

"No, Kaylee," she said as I clung to Tod's hand, feeling awkward and helpless in the face of her obvious angst. "You're his choice. I'm the habit."

TOD HAD TO HEAD BACK TO WORK, BUT SABINE wanted to stay the night with Nash, and I let her, adhering to the whole "strength in numbers" philosophy. Alone, she'd make a much better target for Avari, and I couldn't risk letting her be either possessed, if Cujo—her Netherworld guard dog—fell down on the job, or was hurt, if he warned her and she fought.

I checked on Em and Sophie both twice during the night, and every time I got back to my room, Sabine was just sitting in my desk chair, watching Nash sleep. Not in the creepy way. In the worried way.

"He's going to be okay," I said, perching on the edge of my desk to watch him with her. I tried to say it like I meant it, but the truth was that I held no authority on the subject of Nash.

Or the subject of being okay.

"He wanted to go visit Scott, you know," Sabine said, like we were in the middle of a conversation I couldn't remember starting. "I told him I didn't think that was a good idea."

"Why?"

"Because that's what he needed to hear. He wanted to go see Scott because Scott is a piece of his life from back when his life made sense. He wanted to recapture some of that, and he wanted to apologize for being part of what put Scott in the psych ward. But he was scared that the Scott he knew wouldn't be in there anymore, and if that was true, there'd be nothing left of his life from before. His best friends are either dead or insane, and the rest of them avoid him at school because they don't know how to talk to him anymore. And half of them think he tried to kill you. But..."

Sabine looked up at me, and her dark eyes only hinted at the raw pain her voice laid bare. "But beyond all that, Nash was terrified that being that close to Avari would be too much for him. That he wouldn't be able to resist the temptation, so close to the source." She shrugged. "So I told him he shouldn't go. Not that it mattered. A couple of weeks later, you made out with his brother, and sent him right over the deep end again."

"Neither of us meant for any of that to happen," I said. On the list of conversations I never wanted to have with Sabine, this one was right at the top. "And anyway, you got what you wanted, right?"

Her dark eyes narrowed as she tossed a one-armed gesture at Nash, still passed out on my bed. "Does this *look* like what I wanted?"

"He's having a rough month. We all are."

"A rough month? Kaylee, I spent years trying to find him, and when I finally did, you were standing in my place. So I backed off and let your blatantly ill-fated relationship run its course—"

"You didn't back off, you tried to kill me!" I interjected.

"Well, I had to *try,* didn't I?" she demanded, and I couldn't decide which fallacy in that sentence to address first, so I saved my breath. "But even with me there, waiting almost patiently, doing all the best-friend stuff because I love him, he's moping over the friends he's lost instead of seeing what he's gained. And now you're finally out of the picture—or so I thought—and look where he winds up." She glanced at Nash again, and I flinched, though I'd played no part in his drunken late-night walk. "That's probably the longest he's ever even been in your bed."

"It is."

"What does that mean, Kaylee? Why would he rather be alone in your bed than with me in his?"

Well, damn. Sad Sabine was no easier to deal with than angry Sabine. The last time she'd been distraught over Nash, she'd hijacked both me and my car and tried to make me fix what she'd messed up.

"Okay, look. He didn't come here to climb into my bed, Sabine. He came here because he wanted answers, and it's obviously a lot easier to ask for them when he's drunk. You're just going to have to give him some time. He's lost right now, but he's strong, and he *will* bounce back from this. And when he does, he's going to realize that you were there the whole time."

"You really believe that?"

I'd never seen her so vulnerable. "Yeah. I do." She really loved him. That had to mean something, and when Nash was thinking straight, he *had* to see that.

Sabine glanced at her hands in her lap, like whatever she had to say next required a little bit of a lead-in. Then she met my gaze again. "Thank you." Sabine blinked, and the vulnerability I'd glimpsed was gone. "Now, could we maybe pretend this whole bonding exercise never happened?"

I laughed. "I'd like nothing better."

I started cooking around six-thirty in the morning, my hair still dripping from the shower. I'd never made anything more complicated than microwave pancakes, but with time on my hands, a house full of guests, and a father obsessed with the concept of the "family meal," I thought I'd give it a go.

I microwaved a pound of bacon six strips at a time—turns out the key is good drainage—and made pancakes from a jug of mix-and-pour batter I found in the cabinet. It was only three days past its use-by date, so I figured the chances of it making anyone sick were slim.

The first three pancakes were amorphous blobs—I swear, one looked just like a storm trooper—but by the fourth, I'd figured out how to flip them without making a huge mess.

Nash shuffled into the kitchen as I was putting down a saucer of raw venison for Styx, and she glanced away from her breakfast just long enough to aim a yippy hello his way. She'd always liked Nash, but she still wasn't comfortable with Tod, probably because he was dead. At first, I'd worried that she wouldn't like me after my own death, but apparently our initial bonding transcended the questionable state of my existence.

"Hey," I said as Nash bent to scratch the back of Styx's neck. "I made coffee if you want some."

"Thanks." He sat in a chair at the table—the same chair that had always been "his" when we were together—and accepted the mug I set in front of him.

"Where's Sabine?"

"In the shower." Nash scrubbed his face with both hands. "Kaylee, I'm so sorry for…whatever I said or did last night."

"You don't remember?" I poured coffee for myself and scooped sugar into the mug.

"I remember parts of it," he said, and I wanted to ask which parts those were, but a rehash seemed like a really bad idea.

"You said you saw Scott. Do you remember that?"

Nash's eyes widened in surprise, then lost focus as he nodded, clearly trying to remember. "I thought I was dreaming at the time, but I wasn't. I really saw him. Outside, on the street."

"Where?"

"I don't know. I'm sorry. Somewhere between my house and yours."

"Did he say anything?"

Nash shook his head slowly. "He just looked at me for a minute, then turned around and walked off."

"But you're sure it was him?"

"Yeah."

I sat in the chair next to Nash and sipped from my mug, trying to decide how best to say what needed to be said. "Tod and I saw him last night, too. Earlier. In the hospital. He was possessed, Nash. Which means you probably saw Avari."

Nash frowned. "How do you know? Did he sound like Avari?"

"No, the voice sounded like Scott, but the words sounded like Avari." Normally when a hellion possesses a human, the hellion retains his own voice. But… "He's spent the past few months in Scott's head, so it's entirely possible he learned how to work Scott's vocal chords, just like he did with Alec. When he was possessing Alec, I couldn't tell the difference."

"Hey. Your turn in the shower," Sabine said, padding into the kitchen in my robe.

"Thanks." Nash stood and glanced from her to me, then back, like he wasn't sure what to say with us both listening. Then he made a break for the bathroom while Sabine snagged a piece of bacon from the platter.

"Hi," Sabine said, still chewing as she lifted the card from a vase of wilting mixed blooms on the counter. "The school sent you flowers. I'm sure that totally makes up for the fact that they hired the psychotic, soul-stealing pedophile who murdered you in your own home."

I could only blink at her while she chewed.

With the pancakes warming on a pan in the oven and the last batch of bacon in the microwave, I knocked on my father's bedroom door. "Yeah, Kay, come on in."

I pushed open the door to find him sitting on the edge of his bed in a pair of flannel pajama pants, squinting at the alarm clock on his bedside table. "Guess what? I made breakfast."

"You made…?" But before he could finish that thought, our ancient water heater groaned to life and the sound of running water erupted from down the hall. My dad's eyes widened as he glanced at the closed bathroom door over my shoulder. "Who's in the shower?"

"Nash. We kind of…had an impromptu sleepover."

"You and Nash?" My dad was out of bed in an instant, reaching for the robe tossed over his footboard.

"No! Well, yes. But Sabine stayed the night, too."

"That doesn't sound much better, Kay…."

"Hang on, Pa, don't reach for yer shotgun just yet," I said, grinning over the protective streak I found funny, when there wasn't actually anything to shelter me from. "We were just circlin' the wagons, not having an orgy."

My dad suddenly looked like he might be sick. "Please don't *ever* say that word again."

"Wagons?" I teased, and he actually cracked a smile.

"Yes, you're much too young to be using Wild West analogies." He tied his robe and ran one hand through hair that showed no sign of thinning, well into his one hundred and thirty-second year. "So what happened? Why are we circling the proverbial wagons?"

I sat on the edge of his bed and patted the spot next to me until he sat again. "Scott's out of the hospital. Nash saw him last night, and we're pretty sure that means he actually saw Avari."

"Nash came here because he saw Avari?"

"Actually, he was on his way here when he saw Avari. But he thought it was Scott, and he doesn't remember much of it this morning."

My dad's eyes narrowed. "Why not?"

"Because he was drunk."

"Nash came to see you drunk?" My dad exhaled and rubbed his forehead. "Whatever happened to the good old-fashioned drunk dial?"

"I believe that's now the drunk text, but I think Nash wanted answers in person."

"Okay, so let me get this straight: the reaper who killed my wife and tried to kill my daughter has come back from the dead and is following orders from the hellion obsessed with owning my daughter's soul, and now possesses the body of an escaped mental patient who also tried to kill you. Did I get that right?"

"We think Scott was officially released, but other than that, sounds about right." Why is it that my life can never be summarized in a sentence with fewer than three clauses?

"And you didn't wake me up because…?"

"Because there's nothing you could have done."

My dad scowled. "Kaylee, next time, wake me up."

"We're kind of hoping there won't be a next time."

Footsteps echoed behind me, and we both turned to see Sabine step out of my room, still wearing my robe. "Hey, Mr. Cavanaugh," she said on her way to the front of the house.

"You know this can't be an everyday thing, right, Kaylee?" my dad whispered when she was gone.

"I think it's safe to say none of us wants that. But on the bright side, I made bacon."

Breakfast was a whole new kind of awkward, with me sandwiched at the table by my irritated father and my hungover ex-boyfriend, who still wore my dad's shorts. Sabine seemed oblivious to the unspoken tension—her attention was occupied by a stack of pancakes and a pile of bacon.

After we ate, as I was digging through the hall closet for spare toothbrushes, I heard my father and Nash talking in the kitchen. Alone. The urge to go incorporeal so I could sneak closer and listen was almost too much to resist. In the end, the only thing that stopped me was the fact that I'd spied on Nash once before, with Tod's help, then promised never to do it again.

Instead, I went really still and listened closely, and in retrospect, I was glad I couldn't see either of them.

"Do you have any idea how inappropriate your behavior was last night?" my father demanded in a deep, growly voice.

"I'm sorry, Mr. Cavanaugh. I wasn't thinking."

"No, you weren't. I know you've had a rough time these past few months, and I know that not all of it was your fault. But everyone has it rough sometimes, Nash. What defines us isn't the strikes life throws at us, but how we bear them. I've made my share of mistakes, so it may look like I'm throwing stones from inside a glass house, but my job as a parent is to hurl those stones at *anyone* who puts my daughter in danger. Do you understand that?"

"Yes. Of course." Nash sounded sick and miserable.

"If I ever catch you drinking or not thinking around Kaylee again, you're going to wish they'd never let you out of that jail cell. Are we all clear?"

"Yes, sir."

I couldn't decide whether I was more embarrassed for me or for Nash, but in the end, I considered us both lucky my dad hadn't banned him from the house. Or called his mom.

Sabine had a change of clothes in her car—I was starting to wonder how often she was staying at Nash's and whether or not Harmony knew about the sleepovers—but we had to stop by his house so Nash could change.

In spite of the predawn drama and an awkward start to the day, Tuesday morning was better than the day before. I rode to school with Nash and Sabine to avoid facing the reporters alone, and I was relieved to see that, this time, there were only two, each with a single cameraman. Sabine said they might leave me alone if I gave them a couple of seconds of usable footage to run with the headline Teenage Stab Victim Returns to School! so I let them film me climbing the front steps of the building.

I thought I was prepared for the questions they'd shout at me from the sidewalk—they weren't actually allowed on school property—but instead of asking how I felt or what it was like to be back, the female reporter from the local-news affiliate threw out a question that stopped me midstep, less than a foot from the front door.

"Kaylee, have you heard the news about Scott Carter? Does this latest development represent a setback for your recovery?"

"Don't even look at her," Sabine whispered as Nash said, "Just keep walking."

"How do they even know he's out?" I said when the front doors had closed behind us, careful that only Nash and Sabine could hear me. "What, did Avari hold a press conference?"

"I don't know, but if I see him again, I'm going to expel the hellion by any means necessary," Nash said. So far, the only means we knew of was to knock the host unconscious. "Maybe Scott can stay with me for a few days, so Baskerville can watch out for us both."

Sabine didn't look happy about sharing Nash with another houseguest, but he didn't even notice. "I'll see you both at lunch. I'm gonna go see if the nurse will give me some Tylenol."

"I don't think she treats hangovers," I called after him, and when I turned to glance at Sabine, she was already walking off in the other direction.

At lunch, I went through the line and got a tray, because that's what you do at lunch, and looking and acting normal had become a part of my job. I'd just sat down at my usual table and cracked the cap on my bottle of water when Luca came jogging up to my table. Instead of sitting, he leaned over with both hands flat on the table.

"Hey, I know we just met, but I need to ask you for a favor—" I said, but he interrupted me before I could ask him to find Thane again.

"I just saw Sophie crying, and I tried to find out what's wrong, but she ran into the girls' bathroom in the front hall. Can you go check on her?"

I have to admit, I hesitated. Sophie had turned on me more times than I could count, and even after she'd learned the family secret, she'd abandoned me to the wolves on my first day back at school. And the last time I'd followed my cousin into the bathroom, I'd found her shearing a beauty queen with a pair of pinking shears.

"Please," Luca said, and I was surprised to realize he actually liked her. For real. Even more, he was worried about her.

"Fine. But if a beautiful blond reaper shows up while I'm gone, don't freak out. That's my boyfriend, Tod."

Luca nodded, clearly confused, and I headed through the cafeteria and into the front hall, then pushed open the door to the girls' restroom. The room looked empty, but someone was sniffling in the last stall.

"Sophie?"

The sniffling stopped. "Go away, Kaylee." My cousin's voice had that just-cried nasal quality, but lacked its usual hostile bite.

"What's wrong?" I pushed open the last stall to find her perched on the edge of the toilet seat, her phone cradled in both hands.

"Like you care."

"Why would I be here if I didn't care?"

"I don't know why you do half the things you do, Kaylee."

I crossed both arms over my chest, rapidly losing patience. "Okay, this is your last chance to soak up some free sympathy and attention before I go tell Luca you're throwing a fit over a broken nail."

She blinked when I said Luca's name, then her eyes filled with tears again. "Not that it'll mean anything to you, but I just found out that Scott died yesterday, okay? How's that for a broken nail? *My* ex, whom *you* got arrested, died in the mental hospital yesterday morning."

My hands started to shake, and I had to concentrate to keep my heart from stopping. "That's not possible," I whispered as Scott's face flashed behind my eyes, twisted into a sneer that was all Avari.

"Why? You think you're the only one allowed to die around here? Not everything is about *you,* Kaylee Cavanaugh."

"Are you sure he died at the hospital?"

Sophie set her phone in her lap to blot tears from her eyes with a thin square of toilet paper. "Yes, I'm sure. Where else would he be?"

"And you're sure it was yesterday? Not this morning?" Tod and I had seen Scott since then. So had Nash.

"What is wrong with you?" my cousin demanded, frowning up at me through glittery mascara that had started to streak beneath her eyes. "You're acting even weirder than usual."

I snatched the phone from her lap and ignored her protest while I scanned the article she'd been reading. My horror grew with every word, and when I saw the picture attached to the article, I stopped breathing altogether. It was a shot of me, sitting in my chemistry class, clearly taken through the school window the day before.

The headline read Teen Returns to School the Day Her First Attacker Is Found Dead. The article went on to explain how, months before my math teacher tried to kill me, eighteen-year-old Scott William Carter was arrested and declared unfit to stand trial for attempting to commit the exact same crime. Scott, according to the article, was discovered dead in his bed at Lakeside Mental Health Center on Monday morning, during breakfast.

The article ended with the reporter wondering what it was about me that made people want to kill me. Then he called me a serial survivor.

The irony burned deep, deep inside.

"BUT HOW COULD HE HAVE DIED BEFORE YOU saw him?" Em whispered from across the table. She was trying to get caught up before Jayson arrived and we'd have to either table the discussion or move it elsewhere.

"I don't know," I said, screwing the top back onto my bottle of water.

"The list of things we can't make sense of is extra-long and twisty today," Tod said. He'd shown up with two boxes of pizza while I was still in the bathroom, but if any of the teachers realized he wasn't a student, he'd have to leave. Or at least pretend to leave.

"Are you *sure* you saw him last night?" Em asked, and Nash shook his head, staring at the slice of pizza lying untouched on a napkin in front of him. Tod had brought his favorite—pepperoni and mushrooms—but whatever appetite he'd had and whatever tolerance he'd been willing to extend to his brother had expired the moment he found out Scott was dead.

"I'm *not* sure," Nash said. "I don't remember it very clearly."

"Okay, but we know what *we* saw," Tod pointed out. "Kaylee and I saw and spoke to him in the hospital, more than twelve hours after the newspaper says he died."

"Ohh," I breathed as a piece of the puzzle fell into place. "He wasn't packing to be released. Someone else had started boxing up his things. Because he died."

"Can a hellion possess a dead body?" Sabine asked around a mouthful of pizza

Tod shrugged. "Before today, I would have said no."

Emma frowned and glanced around the quad, on the lookout for Jayson. "Okay, but even if that's possible, are you seriously suggesting that Avari possessed a body in the hospital morgue, dressed it in its own clothes, walked it across the street to the mental-health center, broke into the adolescent ward, then waltzed into Scott's room, and no one noticed?"

Sabine scowled, but before she could defend her theory, Nash pushed the pizza box toward the middle of the table and exhaled. "Can we please stop referring to Scott as a dead body?"

No one bothered to point out that the description was accurate. This was just the latest in a series of losses that had begun shaping Nash's life long before I met him.

"Sorry," Em mumbled, and for about a minute, no one spoke.

Then the silence got the better of Sabine and she turned to Tod. "Okay, then, was he scheduled to die yesterday? Can you ask your boss?"

"Don't have to," Tod said as Luca made his way across the quad toward us. "Lakeside is in my zone, because it's attached to the hospital, and Scott died during my shift. If his death was scheduled, I would have been the one reaping his soul. At the very *least,* I would have known about it."

"Okay, Sophie's calmer now, but they're still sending her

home," Luca said, sliding onto the bench next to Sabine. "She's in the office waiting for her dad, because school policy says that if she's not fit for class, she's not fit to drive, and they won't let me take her home because I'm not a relative."

Emma blinked at him in surprise, then glanced at the rest of us in turn. "Who's this?"

I gestured to her with one hand and him with the other. "Emma Marshall, Luca Tedesco. Em is my best friend. Luca is a necromancer, and my coreclamationist. Or whatever. He's also Sophie's new boyfriend."

"Necro-what?" Emma asked.

Sabine reached across the table to claim a half-eaten crust from Emma's napkin. "He's a metal detector for dead stuff."

Em glanced at Luca, her eyes wide in either interest or fear. "Like ghosts?"

"No, like the undead." He gestured at me and Tod. "And the recently dead. But once someone's been dead for more than a few days or is buried more than a few feet deep, my accuracy suffers."

"That is both creepy and fascinating," Sabine said. Then she gestured to him with the half-eaten crust. "I like him. Not sure why he's wasting his time with the pole dancer, though."

Tod laughed out loud and I groaned. "Sophie takes ballet and jazz. She's not a pole dancer."

"There's more money in pole dancing," Sabine insisted.

"Actually, Sophie takes ballet and lyrical dance. She quit jazz last year," Luca said, and every single one of us glanced at him in surprise. "What?" He shrugged. "She listens to me talk about dead people and soccer."

I shook my head, trying to draw my thoughts back into focus. "Okay, what are the possibilities? About Avari and Scott, not Sophie?"

"Scott's dead, and Avari's possessed his corpse," Nash said, each word short and clipped, as if they actually hurt to pronounce. As far as I could tell, he had yet to actually make eye contact with his brother.

"That possibility should be easy enough to verify or eliminate," Sabine said.

"How?" Em asked.

"Go look in the casket. If the body's there, then Avari obviously doesn't have it," the *mara* said, and she actually looked sorry when Nash flinched.

I glanced at Tod, and he shrugged. "Okay," I said. "One of us should be able to handle that. Other possibilities?"

"He's not really dead?" Em said. "He faked his own death, like on a soap opera."

Sabine's brows rose. "Or he's undead. Something like the two of you." She waved the pizza crust at me and Tod.

I turned to Luca. "If you saw him, you could tell us whether or not he's alive, right?"

Luca nodded. "And if he's close enough, I could sense and track him. But I should probably admit I've never intentionally faced a walking corpse."

Sabine burst into laughter, drawing stares from the surrounding tables.

"You're sitting next to two of them," Nash said, too low for anyone outside our circle to hear.

Luca glanced at me and Tod, whom he'd met while I was with Sophie, then turned back to Nash with a shrug. "Yeah, but they're the good guys, right? I've never picked a fight with anything out to steal my soul."

Nash looked at Tod then, for the first time since he'd sat down, and I knew the fragile peace had met its end, at least for the moment. "*Good* is a relative term, and souls aren't the only things worth stealing."

"Something can't be stolen if it doesn't truly belong to you in the first place," Tod insisted, but Nash stood and walked away from us all without a word, just as Jayson stepped into the quad.

"How come he's always leaving?" Jayson asked, sliding onto the bench seat next to Emma. "I'm starting to take it personally."

"Don't," Sabine said. "He doesn't like you enough to care whether or not you're here."

After school, I blinked into my room—being dead was saving me a fortune in gas—and dropped my backpack on my bed. I scruffed Styx's fur and let her pretend to attack my fingers—if she'd wanted to, she could have bitten them clean off—then headed into the kitchen for a soda.

I wasn't thirsty. But if I hadn't been dead, I would have finished at least one can of Coke before I even considered starting my homework, and lately it felt like observing the old routines was the only way to stay sane.

I was three steps into the living room when I heard Harmony's voice, and when I looked up, I saw her sitting at the kitchen table with my father, cradling a cup of hot tea in one hand. I started to say hi, but then she finished her sentence and I realized they could neither see nor hear me.

"I'm sorry, Aiden. You have my word that he's clean. Sobriety is harder to enforce. But I'm trying, and I think he is, too. He's just having a really hard time right now."

"I know. But that's not the biggest problem involving your sons and my daughter."

Harmony frowned into her mug and closed her eyes for a second, like she was steeling herself for more bad news. "What now?"

"Tod and Kaylee are getting…physical," my dad said, and I could feel my invisible cheeks flame. He'd left work early and called Harmony over just because I'd said the S-word? Seriously?

Harmony burst into laughter, and my father's expression of confusion must have mirrored my own. "They've always been 'physical,' Aiden. That's how this whole thing started, remember? With a kiss?"

My father's frown deepened into a formidable scowl. "No. I mean they're getting *intimate.*" He said the word like it hurt coming out, and the fire behind my face raged on.

Harmony nodded and studied his expression, sipping from her mug, and it looked like she was trying to decide on the right response before she opened her mouth. I'd always admired that about her. "Okay," she said finally. Then she set her mug down. "And you really think that two teenagers contemplating sex is worse than Nash showing up drunk on your doorstep?"

My father blinked. Then he blinked again. "First of all, Tod's not a teenager—"

"And Kaylee's not a child," Harmony pointed out, and I wanted to hug her. Except that would have been the most awkward spyfail in history.

"Doesn't this bother you at all? They've only been together for a month. Doesn't that seem a little…fast?"

Harmony wrapped her hands around her mug on the table, but didn't pick it up. "How long were you and Darby together before you…?"

My father's irritation paled beneath the new flush creeping into his cheeks. I'd rarely seen him embarrassed, and I'd never seen him blush before. Ever. "That's not the point."

"Mmm-hmm." Harmony smiled. "That's what I thought. Yes, Kay and Tod have only been together for a month. And maybe I do think that's too fast, even if that thought could reasonably be considered hypocritical, coming from either of us. But that's not our decision to make."

"The hell it isn't. She's a child."

"No, she's days away from her seventeenth birthday." Which was the age of consent, in Texas. "And she's dead. As is he. I don't think adolescent norms apply here, Aiden. Not anymore."

"We'll have to agree to disagree on that."

"No." Harmony let go of her mug to take my dad's hand, and he looked at her in surprise. She looked…scared. "Aiden, don't chase him away. Please. I know you only want to protect her, and I want the same thing for Tod, but they're good for each other. I promise you that. And if you chase him off because you're afraid of letting your little girl grow up, then what do either of them have left? Eternity alone?"

"Harmony—" he said, but she talked over him and refused to let go of his hand.

"I wish you could have seen him last year. He was a different person. No longer the boy I lost, but not yet the man Kaylee found. He was…indifferent. He was slipping away. Your daughter changed that. He needs her. And she needs him. I don't think you could keep them apart forever, but even a few years alone in the afterlife could be enough to change them both. If you ruin this for them, you'll regret it for the rest of your life. But they'll regret it for eternity."

My father closed his eyes.

"Eternity is a long time to be alone, Aiden."

Finally he squeezed her hand and met her gaze across the table. "What do you want me to do?"

"Nothing," she said. "You don't have to do anything but let them set their own pace. You don't have to condone anything. You don't even have to change your open-bedroom-door policy. Just…let them figure things out for themselves. Please."

I stopped breathing so I wouldn't miss anything. I was too nervous to move closer, even though they couldn't see or hear me.

My dad inhaled deeply. Then, at last, he nodded. And I snuck back to my room, reeling from what I'd just heard.

Checking Scott's coffin turned out to be impossible, because he didn't have one yet. After a little digging in the online versions of the local newspapers, I'd figured out which funeral home his parents had chosen, but after a glance around the place—incorporealty has its advantages—I discovered that the body wasn't scheduled to be picked up until the next day.

Scott was still at the hospital morgue.

That night, I made up for the morning's chaos with a tray of fast-food tacos in front of the TV with my dad. I had to pretend to be surprised by the brownies Harmony had brought over. Fortunately, he seemed no more inclined to discuss her visit than I was to ask about it.

After dinner, I made sure he saw me doing my homework for a couple more hours, then I made sure he *didn't* see that Tod was in my room when he went to bed. My dad had agreed not to stand between us—though I wasn't supposed to know that—but he hadn't changed any of the rules.

"You know what tonight is?" I said when Tod settled into the big bean-bag chair in the corner of my room. That was the only place he could sit without giving away his presence with the loud creak of springs or the squeal of metal.

Tod tugged me down into his lap, facing him, and his hands settled at my waist. "What is tonight? And by the way, whatever it is, it can't top this." He pulled me down for a kiss and I lingered there, enjoying the moment.

"Tonight is take-your-girlfriend-to-work night," I whispered into his ear as his hand slid beneath my shirt and splayed across my back. "So… You should take your girlfriend to work."

"Why would my girlfriend want to spend all night in the company of the sick and dying?"

"She wouldn't." I kissed my way up his neck, and he craned his head to give me better access.

"Should I assume the lure is a certain attractive young dead man?"

"Yup. Scott Carter's in the morgue. But maybe after I've made sure he's resting in peace, I'll come visit you, too."

His hands slid higher and we settled deeper into the bean bag. "Change your mind about playing doctor?"

"No, but I hear candy-striper uniforms are pretty cute."

"We don't have candy stripers." Tod frowned. "*Why* don't we have candy stripers?"

"Emma was a candy *stripper* for Halloween. I thought I might borrow her costume for next year, but I doubt it'll look the same on me as it did on her." I shrugged. "Maybe after we're done in the morgue I could try the costume on, and you could help me decide whether or not it fits…."

Tod's eyes widened, and his irises swirled in tight twists of blue "Well, I don't see that I have much choice, considering that's part of Reaper Law."

"There's a Reaper Law?"

"Of course. 'A reaper is Trustworthy, Loyal, Helpful, Friendly, Courteous…'" He shrugged. "It gets boring after that. But this situation is clearly covered under the 'helpful' category."

I rolled my eyes. "I think that's the Boy Scout law."

"They took it from us. But they left out all the good stuff. The point is that I am both honored and obligated to take an early peek at your Halloween costume. A thorough peek. A good long look, just to be safe. Don't want to be accused of shirking my duties."

I laughed. This wasn't like me. I hadn't even dressed up on Halloween, and now I was considering it for purely recreational purposes, because everything I'd enjoyed before I died—books, movies, music—had lost most of its appeal. It all seemed pointless, and those long hours between the time Tod went to work and the time my alarm clock went off for school had become almost unbearable.

The old wasn't working, so I needed to try something new.

"Tell Em we won't need the costume for very long. And tell her I owe her. And—"

I arched both brows at him in amusement. "I'm not telling her *any* of that. Just come with me to ID the body, and afterward, we'll take a break from all the morbid for a few minutes of teenage normal."

"On what planet is it normal to prance around the hospital in a sexy Halloween costume with your undead boyfriend?"

"I won't be prancing, and I'm only considering trying it on at all because no one else will see me. Besides, normal is a relative term. And I desperately need some normal."

Tod frowned. "What's wrong?"

"It's just… I feel so good when I'm with you. I feel alive, and normal, and real. But then you go to the hospital every night, and my dad goes to bed, and I can't sleep, and I start feeling like I'm all alone, and that feeling gets stronger and stronger. It feels like the air around me is heavy, and it takes too much effort to breathe, much less move. I don't want to do anything. I don't want to watch anything. I don't want to eat anything. I'm alone with my thoughts, and my head feels like a radio playing at top volume, while everything else around me is just…dead. It happens every night, several hours before dawn, and when it's time to go to school in the morning, I've forgotten why I ever wanted to go back in the first place."

"That's pretty normal, Kaylee," Tod insisted. But I could see concern swirling slowly in his eyes. "You're still adjusting to being dead. When I was new at this, I noticed that in the middle of the night, when work got really slow, I kept forgetting to breathe. Which should be no big deal. I don't need the air, anyway, right?" he said, and I nodded. I knew where this was going. "Except it is a big deal, because when I'm not breathing, I feel extra-dead. And the dead don't fit in here." He spread his arms to indicate the entire human world.

"Exactly. But last night, with Nash and Sabine here, none of that happened. I had a problem to think about, and someone to talk to—even if it was Sabine—and that 3:00 a.m. melancholy never came. In the morning, I didn't even think about skipping school. I just got dressed and went, because I felt alive again, and that's what living sixteen-year-olds do. I felt almost normal for the first time since I was brutally stabbed to death in my own bed."

"The first time?" Tod frowned, and I realized what I'd said.

"You don't make me feel normal. You make me feel amazing, like I'm more alive now than I was back when my heart beat on its own." I leaned down to kiss him, and he leaned back in the bean bag until we were almost horizontal.

"This is my very favorite moment."

"Ever?" I said, staring down at him, watching the blues in his irises swirl.

"Ever. Of every moment I've ever not-lived through, this one is the best."

My heart beat faster and the endorphins felt wonderful, yet not as good as Tod felt beneath me, his chest firm under my hand, his fingers warm beneath the hem of my shirt. I leaned down to kiss him and his hand slid farther up my back.

Then my father cleared his throat behind me, and I froze. "Tod, go to work. Kaylee, go to bed."

"He can't see me," Tod whispered against my chin. "Can he see you?"

"Nope. He can't hear me, either." I didn't dare move, for fear of confirming what was surely only a hunch for my father at the moment. And somehow, sharing that moment of stillness and silence with Tod made me feel closer to him than ever.

My father sighed. "It's suspiciously quiet in here, and there's a Tod-shaped dent in the bean bag. For the sake of both my sanity and my temper, I'm going to pretend I can't tell that you're in his lap, so could *you* pretend that this is still my house and you are still my daughter, and I'm within my parental rights to kick your boyfriend out after 11:00 p.m.?"

"Shit," I whispered, and Tod laughed out loud.

I could feel my face flame as I crawled off his lap and stood, and only then did I let my father see me. He may have known what we were doing, but that didn't mean he needed to see it.

"Sorry," I said as Tod stood behind me, and when my dad's gaze focused on him, I knew he was visible, too.

"Sorry, Mr. Cavanaugh," Tod said, and at first, I didn't think my dad was going to answer.

Then he took a deep breath and his gazed narrowed on Tod. "I've been avoiding this conversation for a while now, because considering the circumstances, and the fact that my daughter is technically dead, it seems a little ridiculous for this to even be an issue. But she is still my daughter. So here goes…"

He took another deep breath, and I wanted to interrupt—to somehow stop what we all knew was coming—but I didn't want to make the whole thing any more awkward than it already was.

"I like you, Tod. There was a time when I couldn't have

pictured myself saying that, but I know what you went through for Kaylee, and I can't tell you how much it means to me that you refused to reap her soul, knowing what that would cost you. But none of that changes the fact that if you were still alive you'd be, what? Twenty?"

Tod nodded, and I squirmed.

"That's still a kid, by *bean sidhe* standards, but twenty is considered fully grown in the world we live in, and Kaylee's not even seventeen. Under normal circumstances, I would have already contemplated a dozen different ways to make sure your body never surfaces. Now, I'm not saying I'd kill any other twenty-year-old who touched my daughter. But I'd probably let the fantasy play out in my head. Just food for thought."

I wanted to let myself fade from sight. Permanently.

"She's not a kid anymore, Mr. Cavanaugh," Tod said.

"I know." My father nodded. "But she'll always be my little girl, and I expect you to respect that fact, at least while you're in my house. Okay?"

To his credit, Tod only hesitated for a second. "We didn't mean any disrespect."

"I know that, too." My dad crossed his arms over his chest. "Now please go to work."

Tod nodded and gave me an awkward hug, and neither of us bothered pointing out that his shift didn't start for another half hour. "See you in, what, an hour?"

I nodded, and Tod disappeared.

"Why will he see you in an hour?" My father settled into my desk chair as I sank onto the bed, trying to pretend the past few minutes never happened.

"Because according to the newspaper, Scott Carter died around twelve hours before we saw him possessed by Avari, and even considering all the impossibilities that make up my own afterlife, I can't figure out how that's possible. So I need to go verify that he is indeed dead. By one definition or another."

"Any particular reason you have to be the one to do that?"

I shrugged. "Through no choice of my own, I'm a central figure in this madcap little adventure, and I've got nothing better to do with my time. My homework's all done. See?" I pointed to the stack of books on the desk behind him. "And I'm not gonna let Tod take all the risks by himself. He's already died for me once."

My father sighed. "Being dead doesn't make you invincible, Kaylee."

"I know. It hasn't made Tod invincible, either, which was kind of my point." Death hadn't made me stronger, or smarter, or faster, except for that whole blinking in and out thing. It had also failed to improve my stealth, as we'd all just discovered. "But being dead makes it much easier for me to get in and out of restricted spaces."

"Somehow, that fails to comfort me."

"Sorry. But I'll be fine. I'll be with Tod. He's a good guy, you know." He just hides it under all the sarcasm and curls.

"I know. I also know that he would do anything to be with you, and that kind of limitless devotion tends to snub caution in favor of action, and *that* is enough to scare a poor father to death."

"I don't get it." How could devotion to each other be bad?

"Kaylee, I know what I would be willing to do to protect you, and I see the same kind of commitment in him when he looks at you. There is nothing—no one—he wouldn't be willing to go through for you."

"That's mutual, Dad. I'd do the same for him."

"I know." He blinked, and his eyes stayed closed so long I thought he might be praying. "That's the scariest part of all."

When my dad went back to bed, I texted Emma. One word.

Incoming...

Her response came a minute later—OK—and I blinked into her room just as she turned on her bedside lamp. Toto, another of Styx's littermates, started growling less than a second after I arrived. Evidently being dead made me suspect.

"It's twelve-thirty in the morning, Kay," Emma grumbled, sitting up in the bed in a purple polka-dot pajama top. "Some of us actually have to sleep."

"Sorry. I need to borrow something and I wanted to check on you."

"Why?"

"Because Avari knows who you are and where you live."

"Yeah. That's why Toto's here." She patted the bed and Toto jumped onto it, then curled up in her lap, a fierce little ball of fur with sharp teeth and small, dark eyes that watched me closely.

"Yes, but we don't understand what we saw when we talked to Scott last night, which means we don't know what kind of restrictions Avari has in this form. For all we know, Toto may not even recognize him as a hellion." And even if he did, if Avari had a physical presence in the human plane, what was to stop him from bashing in the poor dog's head just to shut him up? What good was an early warning system when it couldn't prevent the thing it was warning you about?

"Would it creep you out if I pop in a couple of times during the night to check on you?"

Emma frowned. "Yes. But do it, anyway. I'd rather be

creeped out than possessed or dead. No offense to recently departed."

I smiled. "None taken."

"So what did you want to borrow?"

"Okay, promise you won't laugh..."

She threw the covers back and crawled to the end of the bed. "No way. Spill."

"Do you still have your Halloween costume from last year?"

Her brows rose in interest. "The candy stripper? Yeah, I think it's still in there." She was already halfway across the room, headed for the closet. "Why?"

"It's kind of a bribe."

"For Tod?" She glanced at me as she pulled the closet door open, and I nodded. "Not that I don't totally approve of the intent, but I doubt you'd have to bribe Tod into doing anything for you."

"Okay, then, it's a reward."

"Wow. Somebody must have been a very good boy." She dug into the clothes hanging in her closet, all the way at the back, on the right.

"It's probably a stupid idea. I just thought..." But I couldn't explain what I'd thought, and I wasn't sure I should. I didn't want her to know about the emptiness that swelled inside me in the middle of the night, when I was all alone. I didn't want her to know that giving into the emptiness was so much easier than fighting it, and that the only way I'd found to fight it was to keep living. Keep being a student, and a friend, and a daughter, even when sometimes those roles no longer seemed to fit.

Being with Tod was the only thing that still felt natural, and...

"You just thought what?" Emma pulled the costume from the back of the closet and held it up, still on the hanger.

"I just thought that with all the death, and the demon possessions, and the evil teachers, and stuff, we should try to have fun whenever and wherever we can. Even if all we have is a few stolen moments in an empty hospital room. Does that sound stupid?"

"I think it sounds beautiful." She frowned. "What do you think that says about me?"

"That you spend too much time with me." I studied the costume critically, eyeing the short red-and-white-striped skirt and the very low, heart-shaped neckline. "I'm going to look like an idiot in that."

"You're gonna look great. If living dead boy doesn't have a pulse already, he will when he sees you in this."

"Thanks, Em."

"No problem. Now get out of here so I can get some sleep," she said. I took the hanger from her, but before I could blink out, her eyes widened. "Oh, don't forget the tights!" She pulled open the top drawer of her dresser and started rooting in it, and when she turned around again, she held a pair of lacy white costume tights with tiny red crosses embroidered all over. Then she looked at me and frowned. "On second thought, tights get in the way and they're too easy to rip. I'll just keep them."

"Em, your tights are safe. I'm not planning to…go that far. Tonight." Nor was I entirely clear on how that possibility would be a threat to her tights.

She rolled her eyes. "As the poster child for unplanned sex, I wholly recommend spontaneity. As the *product* of unplanned sex, I wholly recommend protection. Not that that's a problem for you. Either way, the tights stay here."

"Wait, does that mean you're *planning* my spontaneous sex?"

"*Someone* has to."

"But if you plan it, how is it spontaneous?"

"You're already overthinking it. You're not supposed to do that until afterward."

"I wish someone would give me a list of the rules..." I mumbled.

"There are no rules. Except the one that says you have to go away so I can get some sleep." She climbed into her bed, rolled onto one side, then pulled the covers over her shoulder. "Tomorrow we'll overthink the whole thing together. In great detail."

"No! No detail. There won't be anything to talk about!" I insisted. But she was already asleep. And for just a second, I envied Emma more than anyone else in the world.

I MET TOD IN THE LOBBY OF THE E.R., WHERE he eyed my button-up pj top and shorts with exaggerated disappointment. "Business first," I said.

"What if my business is love? I could be—"

I put one hand over his mouth. "If you call yourself the love doctor, I'm outta here."

He pulled my hand away and held it. "I was going to say 'Doctor of Love,' but I guess that's close enough."

I rolled my eyes. "Come on, let's get this over with before I chicken out." The last time I was in the morgue, I *was* the body on the table.

We blinked into the viewing area downstairs and chill bumps popped up all over my skin before we even stepped into the back rooms. The morgue is a creepy place to be, even for a dead girl. Maybe especially for a dead girl.

Tod studied a chart on an empty desk in the front office while I hung back, trying not to remember waking up on a cold steel table in the next room, half-covered by only a white sheet. "He's scheduled to be autopsied tomorrow. Drawer three," Tod said. "You sure you want to do this? I could just check for you."

I shook my head. "How am I supposed to walk up to some horrible Netherworld creature I've never faced before and say, 'Hand over your soul,' when I can't even work up the nerve to look at a dead body?"

"You've seen dead people before, Kaylee."

"Yeah." Several of them, including a few who got up and walked around after the fact. "But never here. It seems so much more final here."

"Let's hope that's true for Scott."

There was one employee on duty, so we had to wait for him to take a bathroom break, after I vetoed Tod's alternate plan. He wanted to scare the crap out of the poor man by opening and closing all the refrigerated drawers until he ran out screaming.

When we finally had the place to ourselves, Tod pulled open drawer number three, and I closed my eyes, mentally steeling myself for the worst. "Kaylee, look," he said. So I looked.

It was Scott. And he was really dead. Peacefully, permanently, truly dead.

I exhaled slowly and spent a moment staring at him in profound relief. Scott and I had never been close, but I wouldn't wish what he'd suffered on my worst enemy. Except maybe Avari. And Mr. Beck.

Okay, there were a *couple* of enemies I'd wish insanity, possession, and brain damage on, but Scott wasn't one of them and I was glad his suffering had ended, even if it ended in death.

But then the confusion set in. "So, if he's really dead, what did we see in his room at the hospital?"

"No clue." Tod slid the drawer closed and leaned against it, arms crossed over his chest, like he was perfectly comfortable in the morgue. "Doppelganger? Clone? Bodysnatcher? Name your horror movie cliché."

"You forgot the evil twin."

"What was I thinking? Maybe I'm getting a fever. Why is there never a naughty nurse around when you need one?"

"Naughty nurse? Damn. I brought the wrong costume."

"A candy striper will work in a pinch. Did you really bring it?"

"Yeah." But I hadn't yet convinced myself to actually put it on. "Let's get out of here." I took his hand and blinked us into the empty fourth-floor room I'd already scouted out and stashed the costume in. We were at the end of the hall and around the corner from the nurses' station, to minimize our chances of getting caught.

Tod glanced around the room, his hand warm in mine as his gaze skipped over the armchair, the narrow hospital bed, and Em's costume hanging on the shower rod, visible through the open bathroom door. "What's all this?"

"This is what passes for privacy, in the social disaster that is my afterlife. No parents, no classmates, no E.R. waiting-room patients…"

"They wouldn't be able to see us, anyway."

"I know, but I'm still having trouble controlling my own corporeality, and even if I weren't, it feels like people are watching us, even when they can't possibly be, and I'm not into exhibitionism, so…" I spread my arms to take in the entire unused hospital room. "Privacy."

Instead of glancing around the room, Tod looked straight into my eyes. "You're the best girlfriend ever. Seriously. If I had a trophy, I'd give it to you."

"For appropriating a hospital room and borrowing a Halloween costume?"

He shook his head and pulled me close. "For being here. For saving my afterlife and my sanity. For making me look forward to every single day, instead of dreading eternity. And for the record, I don't care whether you're wearing jeans, or the hottest, most workplace-inappropriate candy-striper uniform to ever grace the sterile white halls of this humble public death trap. I'm just glad you're here."

My stomach flip-flopped, and I let his words play over in my head. "So, no costume?"

Tod shrugged. "Nah. Don't get me wrong—it's hot. But it's hot in an obvious kind of way. It's not really you."

I frowned. "Because I'm not obviously sexy?"

"Because you *are* obviously sexy. Some girls may need costumes to make guys want them, but I couldn't possibly want you more than I do right now, no matter what you were wearing. Or not wearing."

I stared up at him. "How is it possible that every time you open your mouth, I—" *fall more in love with you* "—melt a little more? Seriously. There's nothing in here but mush." I waved one hand over my own torso.

"You don't feel very mushy to me." His hands slid over my waist and up my sides slowly, his fingers whispering against the material of my shirt. "In fact, you feel really good."

"You, too." I tried to say more, then realized I couldn't speak because I didn't have enough air in my lungs. Because I'd stopped breathing. I inhaled, and suddenly I sounded breathless. Which was exactly how I felt. "How long until you have to go…reap?" I whispered as my arms slid around his neck. Like we were dancing. Only we weren't moving, and there was no music.

"Don't know. Don't care."

"Won't you get in trouble if you miss something?"

Tod leaned down until his lips brushed the corner of my mouth. "See my previous answer."

"Mmm…" I said as he walked me backward slowly, arms around me so I couldn't stumble. "But it's not a very good time to get on Levi's bad side."

Tod groaned. "Damn your logic and forethought." He pulled away from me long enough to glance at the time on his phone, and his frown deepened. "I have a dislodged blood clot in eight minutes. Be right back."

"You're going to go kill someone, then come back and kiss me? Is that what forever's going to be like? Making out between corpses?"

"Is that too weird?" He looked worried. Like I might actually say yes. A month earlier, I would have, but now…

"I don't know. It probably should be, but honestly, right now, I just want to be with you, even if that means waiting through the occasional reaping." My frown mirrored his. "How morbid is our relationship?"

"Haven't you seen *Corpse Bride?* We're practically average." Tod grinned, then took a step back. "Nine minutes. I swear."

I nodded, and he disappeared.

I spent the first three seconds after Tod left staring at the space where he'd been. Then I realized I needed to use the restroom, a relative rarity, now that most of the time, I only remembered to drink water when my throat got dry and my voice started to crack.

Afterward, as I washed my hands, I stared at myself in the mirror, trying to see what it was that made Tod's irises swirl when he looked at me, and twist feverishly when he touched me. Whatever it was, I couldn't see it. Except for the scar on my stomach, I looked exactly the same as I had before I died. The same as I would for all of eternity.

That thought was still too big for me to hold in my head

all at once, but occasionally I got a fleeting understanding of eternity—it was like glimpsing a silhouette in your peripheral vision, but being unable to pull the form into focus. Those moments came when I was alone. When everyone else was sleeping. When it was hardest for me to remember why I'd wanted this afterlife in the first place.

I shook those thoughts off as I dried my hands, then froze with a thick brown paper towel clenched in one fist when someone knocked on the bathroom door. I threw away the tissue and opened the door, already smiling at Tod. But it wasn't Tod who looked back at me from inches away.

It was Thane, one hand propped on the doorframe like he was both lounging and blocking my exit, still wearing the same clothes and sunglasses he'd had on behind the doughnut shop. Only this time he didn't look scared of me.

Thane's brows rose as he studied the surprise surely written on my face. "What, you didn't think you were rid of me, did you?"

"Yeah. Kinda." Which was why I'd decided to ask Luca to find him. And why I couldn't just blink out of the room, which seemed like the smart thing to do. Fortunately, Tod would be back any minute.

Being that close to the reaper who'd killed my mother completely creeped me out, but I couldn't back away from him without looking scared. As a reaper, he could theoretically take my soul and end my afterlife. But the reverse was also true, which made this whole encounter feel a bit like a deadly game of chicken—we were waiting to see who would swerve first.

"What are you doing here?" I said.

"The real question is what are *you* doing here?" Thane glanced over my shoulder at the costume hanging on the shower rod. "Is this trick-or-treat, or show-and-tell?"

"It's none of your business. What do you want?" I could

see myself reflected in the lenses of his sunglasses, and that unnerved me. I could see my own eyes, but I couldn't see his.

"I want the soul you stole from me."

"It wasn't yours."

"It wasn't yours, either," Thane said, still blocking the doorway, and I nodded. Then I realized I wasn't stuck in the bathroom. I blinked out, then reappeared in the hospital room behind him, wondering how long it would take for my new afterlife abilities to become second nature.

"Which is why I didn't keep it," I said, and Thane spun to face me, brows furrowed over the rims of those stupid sunglasses. "I turned it in."

"Then I'll take yours instead." He stalked closer and I backed away, the game of chicken forgotten. "And if you don't give it up, I'll take the rest of you, too. The boss will be so pleased." He reached for me and I struck out. He threw an arm up to block my blow, and my ineffectual fist ricocheted off his wrist to graze his temple. His sunglasses fell off and clattered to the floor.

I had a second to stare in shock at solid white orbs where his eyes should have been before he lunged for me. I backpedaled, suddenly terrified to realize that if he was touching me when I blinked out, he'd go with me.

"If I haul you into the Netherworld, your boyfriend will come after you, right?"

Thane reached for me again and missed my arm, but when I took another step back, I bumped into the bed and had nowhere else to go. He grabbed a handful of my shirt, and when I tried to roll away, I felt several little pops as most of the buttons tore free. But he didn't let go, so I kept moving, and the underarm seams of my shirt dug into my flesh. He reached for my arm with his empty hand and I shoved him away with a grunt of effort. More threads popped, and suddenly I was wearing half a shirt.

I backpedaled again, scanning the room for a weapon, and briefly I wondered how long it would be before our noise alerted the nurse on duty.

Then Tod appeared just behind Thane and to his left. His eyes widened, but it took him less than a second to process the scene, and he swung at the side of Thane's head before the rogue reaper even realized he was there. Thane stumbled and started to turn, and Tod swung again. His fist crashed into the other reaper's temple.

Thane crumpled to the floor, and Tod kicked him in the head for good measure.

"You okay?" he said, and I nodded, staring at Thane's unmoving form. Tod stepped around him and lifted a loose flap of material from my torn shirt. "What the hell happened? Why didn't you just blink out?"

"Because we need to deal with him. How can I ask Luca to find him, when I just let him go?"

Tod's irises swirled unevenly in confusion, and it took me a second to realize that meant he didn't know whether to be angry or relieved. "Swear you'll never do that again. Swear to me that next time you'll run."

"No! You broke the rules for me, and I'm not going to let you go down for that just because I'm too scared to face the guy whose existence threatens yours. Besides, I'll be confronting bigger and badder things than Thane soon. I need to learn how to handle myself, not run."

"You need to *survive.* Your friends and family need you to survive. *I* need you to survive."

"Got it. Survival is the prime directive." But surviving didn't always mean running.

"Now that we've established that, would it be completely

inappropriate of me to say that you look *really* hot in half a shirt?"

"Probably." I couldn't resist a smile, and I might have actually been blushing. "But say it, anyway."

"You're beautiful." He stepped over the unconscious reaper and took a long look at me, and to my complete surprise, I had no urge to cover myself. I wanted him to look, and I wanted to know that he liked what he saw.

"He could *not* have picked a worse time to show up," Tod said, and when his hands found my waist, one landed on bare skin, exposed by the torn material. His mouth found mine, and the sense of urgency in that kiss lit me up on the inside.

And suddenly eternity with Tod didn't feel long enough.

"We should…do something with him," I said as Tod's lips trailed down my neck.

"In a minute." His hand slid beneath the back of my torn shirt and I sucked in a deep breath, then closed my eyes. "Near-death experiences release a lot of endorphins, resulting in a natural high," Tod whispered against my collarbone as his mouth trailed lower. "And it's totally true that one passion feeds another."

"You know we're way past 'near-death,' right?"

"My endorphins aren't listening to you."

I laughed and enjoyed the moment for just a little longer. Then I pushed him back gently, and he groaned. "I've never hated anyone else like I hate that bastard *right now.*"

"I know. Did you see his eyes? They're empty."

Tod's brows rose. He knelt next to the unconscious reaper and pulled one of his eyelids up to reveal the clean white orb beneath, absent both iris and pupil. The windows to his soul were empty. Because he didn't have one. "Well, that explains why he's working with Avari."

“Avari has his soul?” I said, and Tod nodded, standing. “So what’s keeping him…here? In his body?”

“My guess would be Demon’s Breath.”

“Just like Addy?”

Another solemn, silent nod.

“I didn’t know that would work with a reaper.”

Tod’s beautiful lips pressed together in a frown. “Me, neither.”

“So, what are we going to do with him?”

“Obviously, we have to call Levi, but I think we should question him first. I’d bet my afterlife he knows what Avari’s up to. But the minute he wakes up, he’ll blink out.”

“Ah, the age-old question: How do you keep a reaper in one place long enough to question him? Too bad he can’t talk in his sleep….” I realized what I’d said the minute the last syllable fell from my tongue. “Sabine. Maybe she could read him while he’s out,” I suggested. “His fears probably won’t tell us exactly what Avari’s up to, but he’d have to be crazy not to be afraid of the hellion, so surely she’ll be able to get *something* from him.”

Tod shrugged. “It’s worth a shot.” He pulled his cell from his pocket and scrolled through the menu for less than a second—a reaper’s contact list can’t be very long—then pressed a button and held the phone to his ear. “Sabine? We need help with something dangerous and probably stupid. You in?”

I couldn’t hear her reply, but it sounded like some variation of “Hell, yes.”

“I assume you’re in my brother’s bed?” he said, and that time I was glad I couldn’t hear the reply. “We’ll be there in a minute.”

“You know, most people don’t ask questions like that,” I said as he knelt to grip Thane beneath his arms.

"That's because most people care what other people think about them. I don't have that problem."

I frowned. "You don't care what I think about you?"

"You're not other people." Tod glanced at my torn shirt, and I realized it no longer covered much. "Why don't you go change, then meet me at Nash's?"

"He's not speaking to you." Not without me there to play mediator. And we didn't know how long Thane would be out. And even if Tod had been willing to leave me alone with the rogue reaper—even unconscious—I wasn't sure I could get him to Nash's on my own. I was still very new at the afterlife. "Damn it. Guess I'm wearing the costume, after all."

In the bathroom, I pulled off the remains of my shirt and pulled Emma's candy-stripper dress over my head, relieved to see that it covered more than my ruined shirt. Barely. But my shorts were hardly visible beneath the short skirt.

"Wow," Tod said when I stepped out of the bathroom.

"Change your mind about the costume?"

He shook his head. "You don't need that to look hot. But it definitely needed you."

I couldn't resist a satisfied smile as Tod hauled Thane up, and I knelt to pick up his feet. "Aim for the living room, unless you want to see Sabine naked."

"Have you seen her naked?"

Tod flinched. "Not on purpose. You ready?" he asked, and I nodded, pulling Thane's legs higher. "In three…two…one."

We blinked out together, and by some miracle we both landed in Nash's living room at the same time. And Thane was in one piece. "What would have happened if you'd gotten here just an instant before me?" I asked, setting the unconscious reaper's feet on the ground.

Tod hauled him over to the only armchair and dropped him into it. "You know how a wishbone works, right?"

"Ew." And I was betting we couldn't get many answers out of half a reaper.

Nash's bedroom door opened down the hall and Sabine came out in a bra, still buttoning her jeans, her shirt tossed over one shoulder. Nash was right behind her, in nothing but boxers.

Sabine burst into laughter the moment she saw me, but Nash stopped cold in the middle of the hall. "What the hell are you wearing?"

"You look like a blow-up doll come to life," Sabine said before I could explain, and I could feel my face flame. She pulled her phone from her pocket. "No one's going to believe this without a picture."

"It's not what it looks like," I said through clenched teeth. "Take your finger off the button, or I swear you will be in the market for a new phone."

"And a new finger," Tod added.

"What are you doing here?" Nash asked. "And please skip the part about your outfit. I don't want to know."

"I do," Sabine said, but we all ignored her. "So, did the costume come with a condom, or is that sold separately?"

"This coming from the half-naked Nightmare who just rolled out of someone else's bed," I snapped, more embarrassed than truly angry. "My shirt got torn in a fight. Yours evidently has a fast-release tab."

"What do you *want,* Kaylee?" Nash demanded again, completely ignoring his brother.

"We need Sabine to read him." I stepped aside so they could see Thane, still passed out in the chair. "Quickly. We're not sure how long he'll be out."

"We?" Nash said, and that's when I realized he couldn't see Tod. "I'm guessing my brother's here somewhere?"

I glanced at Tod with both brows raised, and he shrugged.

"I didn't think he'd want to see me." A second later, Nash stiffened and glanced from me to the brother he could obviously see now.

"Get out," he growled through gritted teeth.

"Nash..." Tod started, and I stepped between them when Nash advanced on him.

"Okay, now, wait a minute," I said, acutely aware that I was still dressed like a naughty candy striper. "I know this is awkward and embarrassing for everyone, but—"

"Not for me," Sabine said.

"—but we wouldn't be here if this wasn't an emergency. So here's what's going to happen. Sabine's going to put her shirt on. I'm going to borrow a shirt. And you two are going to pretend—just for the next fifteen minutes—that you still have something in common beyond DNA."

"Oh, I think you're no-longer-living proof that they share more than that," the *mara* said, and I groaned. "Oh, lighten up. This is funny, and you all know it."

"I'll get you a shirt," Nash grumbled, but before he could even turn toward the hall, Tod pulled his T-shirt off and handed it to me, and I could hear Nash's teeth grind together.

Sabine rolled her eyes. "The three of you are enough to drive a *mara* mad. 'She can wear *my* shirt,'" she growled in imitation of Nash. "'No, she can wear *my* shirt,'" she said, switching to Tod's smoother tone. Then Sabine took off down the hall without a glance at any of us. "I have a spare. Come on, Kaylee, before I choke on testosterone and melodrama."

I followed her into Nash's room reluctantly and she closed the door behind us, then pulled a spare T-shirt from her backpack on the floor. Sabine handed me the shirt, then knelt to look for something beneath the bed.

"Thanks, but I'm not changing in front of you," I said.

"Relax." Her voice was muffled by whatever junk she was

pawing through. "I've got everything you've got, plus a little more on top, and everyone who wants to see you naked is out there. But if you're that uptight, go invisible."

So I did, and when I was sure she couldn't see me, I took off Em's dress and laid it across the foot of Nash's bed.

"*There* they are..." Sabine mumbled, pulling some scrap of black material from beneath the bed. I didn't understand that she'd been looking for her underwear until she started unbuttoning her jeans. "So, what's with the costume?"

"I don't have to explain myself to you," I said, turning my back to her to pull her shirt over my head. And I wasn't sure she'd heard me until she answered.

"You do if you want me to read whoever's passed out in the living room. What am I supposed to think when you show up here alone, wearing that? I know that move. I've *made* that move."

"It wasn't a move, and I wasn't alone." Just because they hadn't seen Tod at first didn't mean he hadn't been there the whole time. "I'm not trying to take Nash from you."

"Good, because we had a deal. You die, I get Nash. You even *try* going back on that, and I don't care how dead you are, I'll make you deader."

"What is *wrong* with you?" I demanded, trying to tug the T-shirt down over my navel. But it wasn't long enough. "You got what you wanted. You and Nash can grow old together and have a whole brood of scary, maladjusted little baby Nightmares, and I'm not going to stop you. I'm dead, and nothing's going to change that. I love Tod, and nothing's going to change that, either. We're facing eternity and the deaths of everyone we've ever cared about, with nothing to cling to but each other. So who the hell are you to tell me where I can't be and what I can't wear? I don't answer to you, Sabine!"

I only noticed she could see me when I realized she was staring straight into my eyes.

"You love him? Tod, I mean?" she asked, finally pulling her own shirt over her head.

"Yes."

"For real? Like, can't-live-without-him love him, complete with all the stupid, dangerous shit love like that makes you willing to do?"

"Yes. My eyes don't want to open when he's not there to look at and my hands feel empty when I'm not touching him. It's the scariest thing I've ever felt."

The *mara* nodded, like she understood.

"He died for me, Sabine. He let Levi kill him, rather than reap my soul, and there's nothing I wouldn't do for him. So you better hope we're never put in the position where I have to choose between you and Tod, because I promise things won't end well for you that day."

She stared into my eyes, and if I didn't know better, I'd swear she was watching my irises swirl. But she wasn't a *bean sidhe,* so she couldn't see that. She was looking for something much simpler. She was looking for the truth. And she must have found it, because she blinked, then nodded, like she was satisfied.

"Good. That's what I needed to hear. Let's go see what scares sleeping beauty."

"Sabine." I put one hand on her arm. "He may be pretty, but I swear he's evil. For real."

She only laughed, like I'd told her water was wet. "All pretty things are, in one way or another."

As I followed her down the hall, I tried to figure out if she'd just called me evil or ugly.

In the living room, Nash and Tod sat in silence on opposite ends of the couch. They both looked miserable. They also looked like they both wanted to say something the other wouldn't want to hear.

Nash stood when Sabine knelt in front of the unconscious reaper. "Who is he?"

"This is Thane," I said. "He showed up at the hospital and tried to drag me into the Netherworld. And he wanted to make sure Tod would follow us, so I'm guessing he wasn't there only for me. We're pretty sure he knows what Avari wants, and hopefully how he possessed Scott twelve hours after he died."

"What happened to him?" Sabine asked, eyeing Thane.

"Tod happened to him," I said. "Again. Could you go ahead, please? We don't know how long he'll be out."

"Don't get pushy," Sabine snapped. "I can't manipulate the fears of the dead, but I should be able to read *something* from him. I haven't had much practice, though. Reapers rarely sleep. This one is actually unconscious, but hopefully that's close enough." She took his hand, then closed her eyes. "He's not dreaming. Could someone...open his eyes?"

The thought gave me chills, but Nash stepped up before I had to admit that.

"Not sure how much good it'll do," Tod said as his brother pulled back on both of Thane's eyelids at once. "He doesn't have a soul."

"Wow." Sabine stared into the plain white in the reaper's eyes. "I've never seen that before."

Nash frowned. "Wish I could say the same."

"You're right, that doesn't help," she said, and he let go of Thane's eyes. "Okay, let's try something else. His conscious mind is asleep, but the subconscious never sleeps. Let's see if we can guide his thoughts, to lead me to his fears."

"How?" Tod asked.

"Um, touch him. We know Avari wants Kaylee's soul, but

we don't know what he wants with you. Even unconscious, Thane'll know it's you touching him, and hopefully he'll think about you, which will lead me to fears related to you."

"Tod's a rookie. He's like a baby reaper. Why would Thane be scared of him?"

"I said fears related to Tod, not fears *of* Tod," Sabine said, and Nash scowled, but kept his mouth shut.

"Okay." Tod pushed Thane's sleeve up and laid his bare hand on the other reaper's arm. "How's that?"

Sabine closed her eyes again and took a long, quiet breath. Then she started to speak, softly, like she was afraid she'd wake up the unconscious reaper. "He's afraid of failing. He's terrified of what Avari will do if he can't bring Tod to him."

What?

"Anything else?" Tod whispered, and Sabine's eyes flew open, her hand still tight around Thane's.

"He heard your voice," she said, and though her eyes didn't close again, they lost focus, like she was looking at something none of the rest of us could see. "He's cold, deep down inside and he's afraid of the cold because it's foreign. It shouldn't be in him, and he wants to get rid of it, but he can't. But as much as he hates the cold, he's even more afraid of losing it, because once his body's gone, he'll truly be at Avari's mercy. And that's what he's afraid will happen if he doesn't bring Tod."

"What cold?" Nash sank onto the couch cushion next to me, like he'd forgotten how mad he was.

"Demon's Breath," I said, then immediately wanted to take the words back. Just saying them couldn't push Nash into relapse, yet I felt guilty for bringing up such a touchy subject. But once I'd started it, I had to finish. "There's Demon's Breath in place of his soul. He wants to get rid of it, but if he does, he'll lose his body, then Avari can do whatever he wants with Thane's soul."

Nash nodded stiffly.

"Is that all?" Tod asked.

Sabine nodded. Then, "Kaylee, you touch him."

Both Tod and Nash looked like they wanted to object, but I grabbed Thane's arm before they could, and Sabine closed her eyes again.

"He's scared of you," she said, almost immediately. "But not scared enough. He's terrified that you can extract his soul, if he ever gets it back, but he knows that if Avari gets you, you'll no longer be a threat. Before, he wanted to take you to Avari because he was scared of Avari. But now he wants to turn you over because he's scared of *you*."

I should have been relieved by that—the big bad reaper was afraid of me. But knowing he was willing to drag me into the Netherworld to eliminate the threat I now represented was enough to wipe out any relief I might otherwise have felt.

"Avari wants us both?" Tod said, and Sabine nodded slowly.

"But for different reasons. He's afraid that if the hellion doesn't get you, he'll never let Thane go free. And based on what little I know of Avari, I'd bet he won't let Thane go even if he *does* get you," she said to Tod. "He's a hellion of greed, right?"

We all nodded, and if we hadn't been looking at Sabine, we might have known Thane was awake before he grabbed her by the throat.

I GASPED AND TOD PULLED ME OUT OF REACH. Nash grabbed for Sabine, but Thane stood and pushed her backward with him. "Who the hell are you?"

"What's the worst thing that's ever happened to you?" Sabine croaked, clutching the hand that held her by the throat at arm's length. "Did your dad beat you? Your mom leave you? Did your girlfriend kick your balls clear up into the back of your throat?"

Thane's eyes widened, and I realized he was surprised into silence for the first time since I'd met him.

"Whatever it is," the *mara* continued, her voice hoarse but audible, "I'm going to top it, if you don't let me go *right now*."

Thane studied her for another second, like he was debating—or maybe waiting for verbal brilliance to strike. Then his eyes narrowed and he frowned at her, and I could see his grip on her loosen a little. "I remember you. You're the feisty little firecracker I saw at Kaylee's house." When he'd been stalking me, in anticipation of reaping my soul.

Sabine frowned—she'd never seen him before—and her eyes darkened. Every lightbulb in the room seemed to dim, and chill bumps rose on my arms. "Know what happens when you hold a lit firecracker?" she said, glaring up at Thane, who didn't answer. "It'll take your hand clean off."

Thane burst into laughter, and Nash edged around the coffee table, closing in on them both.

"Nash..." Tod warned, but he couldn't make himself inaudible to another reaper. Not that it mattered. Thane had already seen Nash.

"Try it, and I'll kill her," he said. "Before you can even blink." The reaper didn't have to hurt her to kill her. All he had to do was remove Sabine's soul, and he could do that in an instant. Much faster than I could retrieve a stolen one.

Nash shuffled backward a few steps, his jaw clenched in fury, hands curled into fists at his sides.

"And how long do you think that would last, in a room full of *bean sidhes?*" Sabine demanded, her voice dark and low, but as fierce as I'd ever heard it. "How far do you think you'd get with my soul?"

"Hmm... Good point," Thane said, and I exhaled slowly. But he kept talking. "Maybe I'll take you whole, and let Avari pick and choose the parts he wants."

"I'll kill you," Nash growled, and Tod edged closer, ready to back his brother up.

Thane laughed. "I'm already dead."

"You could be deader." Nash was so furious he couldn't control the twist of fear in his eyes. I could see disaster coming like an out-of-control train, but I couldn't stop it.

Sabine glanced at him, then at Tod, and something silent passed between them. Tod nodded, then lunged forward and grabbed Nash by one arm. Nash shouted and tried to jerk free, and I stepped in front of him, trying to warn him. Trying to shut him up. He was too scared for Sabine to see the danger he was putting himself in. Thane could kill him just as easily as he could kill Sabine. In fact, that may have been his plan, to draw Nash close enough to take them both at once.

If that happened, Tod and I could only save one of them.

When I finally got Nash to stop shouting and throwing punches that went right through Tod, I realized Sabine was talking. To Thane.

"...more fears than any reaper I've ever met, and I know what they are," she whispered, and Thane stared at her, mesmerized. "You're not afraid of your final rest—you welcome it. You *crave* it. You're afraid of an eternity spent serving Avari. That's the thought that leaves you shaking in your tighty-whities, cowering in the corner late at night. You'd do anything to get free from him, wouldn't you? But taking me won't help. He wants *her*." She let go of his arm to point at me with one hand, and a spark of fear shot up my spine.

Was she selling me out? Again? Or was this a distraction?

"You're right. So let's trade." Thane pivoted with her still in his grip and looked right at Nash. "I'm taking one of them. You decide which."

My breath froze in my lungs for the half second it took Tod to pull me to his chest. "No way in hell." I tried to push him off—I couldn't help Sabine if I couldn't move—but he wouldn't let go, and I didn't know whether to feel loved or underestimated.

"You want her back?" Thane demanded, still focused on Nash—he knew better than to bargain with Tod. "Then give me Kaylee. Just scuttle over there and wrest her from the arms of your brother."

Nash glanced at me and Tod, and the confusion churning slowly in his eyes scared me.

"That's your brother, right? Cain to your Abel?" Thane

asked. "I've pieced a few things together. They betrayed you, didn't they—your brother and your girlfriend? They broke your heart and stomped all over your pride, but you can make all that end, right now. Give her to me, and I'll let this one go. What's it going to be? Which one will you save?"

Nash glanced from me to Sabine, then back, his irises churning with intense green twists of anger and brown swirls of fear, and I could practically read confliction in the frown lines etched into his forehead.

He didn't know what to do.

Sabine could see it, too. She was waiting for his decision. And I saw the exact moment she lost patience. "Oh, for fuck's sake."

The *mara* wrapped both hands around Thane's wrist, then tucked her knees to her stomach and let herself hang from his arm—for the fraction of a second it took for him to lose his balance.

Thane grunted and tried to let go of her, but she clung to him. He tipped over. She hit the floor and Thane fell on top of her, his arm still in her grip. Sabine gave his arm a quick twist and Thane howled as something tore.

He rolled away from her, and Sabine was on her feet in an instant, feet spread for balance, hands curled into fists. "Get the hell out of here before you really get hurt."

Thane stood, holding his wounded arm, staring at all four of us in shock rapidly bleeding into fury. And just before he blinked out of existence, I saw fear closing the gap. He had to go back to Avari empty-handed, with an injured arm.

I almost felt sorry for him.

Almost.

As soon as Thane was gone, Nash wrapped his arms around Sabine. "What the hell were you thinking?" he said into her hair. "He could have killed you in a heartbeat."

Sabine shoved him away. "And you could have saved me just as fast." Her expression said anger, but her eyes said pain, and I knew that the truth was somewhere in between.

"I tried!" Nash insisted.

"Yeah, when you thought I was the only one in danger. But when he told you to choose, you just stood there."

"You wanted me to give him Kaylee?"

Sabine rolled her eyes and glanced at me and Tod. "Neither of them would have let that happen, and I wouldn't, either. I didn't need you to rescue me, Nash. I needed you to *choose* me. Just once." With that, Sabine snatched her keys off the end table by the couch, then stormed out the front door, barefoot and pissed off. And more hurt than I could even comprehend.

"Nash..." I said when she was gone. I wanted to help.

I should have known better.

"Get out. Both of you, just go away." Then Nash stomped down the hall and slammed his door, leaving me and Tod alone in the living room.

Tod had to go back to work, so when I left Nash's, I returned Emma's costume, grateful that she was sleeping when I got there, so I wouldn't have to recount the story that started with me dressing up like an idiot and ended with Nash acting like one. For now. But she'd probably want the details in the morning.

Alone in my room, I knew I should be grateful that the action was over, at least for the moment, but with nothing to do but think and pet Styx while she slept, the night passed slowly. *Excruciatingly* slowly.

I couldn't sleep and I wasn't hungry, and it turns out there's nothing good on television in the middle of the night when you don't subscribe to the movie channels. I considered ordering something On Demand, but my dad had already threatened to kill me—an ironic word choice, for sure—if he got one more bill from the satellite company.

Also, I'd already watched everything that was available.

Around four in the morning, I realized I didn't want to move. The end of my nose itched, but scratching it seemed like too much trouble, so I let the itch continue, because feeling an itch was better than feeling nothing, right?

So I lay there, listening to my own thoughts race through my head so fast I could hardly focus on them. I wondered how long Sabine could stay mad at Nash before she took him back, because we all knew she'd take him back. I wondered why Nash couldn't see what he was doing to her, and how long it would take him to realize that loving her wasn't enough. He had to love her more than anything else in the world. More than he loved me. More than he loved frost. More than he loved his own life. He had to love her like nothing else existed for him, ever, and I wished there was some way for me to tell him that without making him hate me more.

Then I wondered why Avari wanted Tod. Was one reaper not enough for him?

Of course it wasn't. One of anything was never enough for Avari, and asking why a hellion of greed wanted something was pointless. Avari *existed* to want things. He'd probably obsessed over the souls of thousands of people in the eons of his existence. Surely I was just the latest in a long line of obsessions, and I wondered if he'd gotten any of the others.

I wondered if he'd get me.

But by the time the sun came up, even my thoughts had started to slow, and I wasn't sure I even cared if Avari got me. What did it matter? I was already dead. He would make my afterlife hell if he got my soul, but he was clearly prepared to do that, anyway, so maybe it would be easier for everyone if I just…let him.

I couldn't beat him. I couldn't outlive him. I couldn't outrun him. So why fight the inevitable?

My dad came into my room at seven-fifteen—I know, because I'd been staring at my alarm clock for the past fifty-three minutes. "Kaylee, where are you?"

That's when I realized he couldn't see me. Because I had no desire to be seen.

With a sigh, I concentrated just enough to slip into the physical plane, and that took a great deal more effort than rolling over, which I'd been putting off for the past few minutes.

"Why are you still in bed? You have to be at school in half an hour!"

"I'm not going."

"The hell you aren't. Get up. Get in the shower and wash your hair. You look like…"

"Death warmed over?" I blinked when I realized my eyes were dry. "'Cause that's how I feel. Minus the warming over."

"Kaylee, *please.*" My father shoved Styx over and sank onto the side of my bed. "This is normal, but you have to fight it. You're not going to feel alive until you start acting like you're alive. Tod says—"

I rolled onto my back and glared up at him. "You've been talking to Tod behind my back?" A spark of irritation flared deep in my gut and swelled for a moment before sputtering out.

"No, I've been talking to Tod in your absence. I'm worried about you, and he's the resident expert on afterlives. He says you have to want to live—so to speak. That you have to find a reason to be here. I understand that I can't be that reason, but you have to find one. Find something that makes you want to get out of this bed."

"I have plenty of reasons to get out of bed. School just isn't one of them."

"Bullshit," my dad said, and I blinked at him in surprise. "Your life isn't over."

"Um, yeah. Actually, it is. My death kind of coincided with the end of my life. Funny how that works."

"You know what I mean. I know you, Kaylee. I know that a simple change in your state of being isn't enough to make you lose interest in the rest of the world. So *get up.* There are friends at school waiting to see you smile and hear you talk. There are stolen souls out there waiting for you to liberate them. There's even a grim reaper who loves you more than his afterlife itself, and if that's not enough to get you moving, you better close your eyes, because I'm coming back with a bucket of cold water."

I didn't realize my eyes had watered until tears trailed down my face to soak into my pillow. "It's enough," I whispered, pushing myself upright. "You're enough, even without all the rest of that." I wrapped my arms around my dad and laid my head on his shoulder, and more tears soaked into his shirt. "I'm sorry. I just get lost in it, in the middle of the night. It's so quiet, and there's nothing here but my thoughts, and even those start to repeat after a few hours of nothing else, and then they stop making sense."

"But it's better now?" he asked, his arms so tight around me that my ribs ached. I could hear it in his voice, how badly he needed me to say yes. Even if it wasn't true.

"Yes," I lied, and more tears fell. "It's better now."

I still didn't want to go to school. I didn't want to shower, or brush my teeth, or dry my hair, but I did all of that because every time I looked up, I saw my father watching me, and he looked scared. He looked like he wanted to help me, but didn't know how. Like he wanted to save me, but couldn't see the threat.

He looked like he'd already lost me.

I blinked into the bathroom at school to save time, and slid into my desk in Advanced Math just as Mr. Cumberland started calling roll. "Are you okay?" Emma whispered, and I wondered if that "death warmed over" descriptor was more accurate than I'd thought.

"Yeah. I just don't want to be here today."

She gave me a sympathetic smile. "That makes all of us." Her smile faded and her eyes narrowed. "You guys didn't do it, did you?"

"No. Turns out privacy's kind of hard to come by when there's a hellion and his psychotic reaper minion out to steal your soul."

Emma frowned, but before she could demand details, Mr. Cumberland cleared his throat and started class.

Fifteen minutes into the lesson, I would have sworn the clock on the wall was stuck. The hands hadn't moved in ages. I swear, time was deader than I was.

Sure, my previous math teacher was an evil, soul-stealing pedophile, but he'd never once bored anyone to sleep, which was more than I could say for Cumberland and his Bueller-esque monotone.

Halfway through the fifty-minute period, Emma kicked my desk, and I sat upright, startled. "I can see through your arm!" she mouthed, exaggerating each mimed word.

Crap! I'd forgotten to concentrate on being solid—I'd forgotten to concentrate on *anything*—and had nearly disappeared in the middle of class. I narrowed my focus and solidified my form, but it took every bit of willpower I had to make my physical form stick. Seriously, if Mr. Cumberland couldn't summon any enthusiasm for the lesson, how were we supposed to summon the will to be there? Some of us literally…

Sabine was waiting in the hall after class. Alone.

"Hey, have you seen Nash today?" she asked, falling into step beside us.

Em shook her head, and I glanced at Sabine in surprise. "You didn't pick him up this morning?"

"I decided to let him stew a little longer, but how am I supposed to know when he's had enough, if he's not here where I can *see* him stew?"

"Trouble in paradise?" Em asked, and Sabine glowered at her.

"He failed to save her from the clutches of evil," I explained, and Em's brows rose.

Sabine stopped walking and grabbed my arm, pulling us all to a halt in the middle of the hall. "He would have stepped up. Thane just caught him by surprise."

"I *hate* it when evil doesn't send fair warning in advance," Em said, and the hall dimmed as Sabine's eyes grew darker.

"How's this for warning?" the *mara* growled at Emma. "Get lost, or I'm having your pretty little human boyfriend for lunch."

"She doesn't mean that," I said as Em's expression cycled through anger and horror before settling somewhere in between.

"The hell I don't. I haven't had a decent meal in ages, since *someone* insisted I stop feeding at school." She glanced pointedly at me.

"Well, if you'd feed at night, like any normal Nightmare..." But I realized the problem as soon as I'd said it, even if she wouldn't admit it. She couldn't feed most nights because she was watching Nash. Almost twenty-four hours a day, since his relapse the day before I died.

With a heavy sigh, I turned to Em. "Don't worry, I'll make sure she doesn't snack on Jayson. See you both at lunch."

Em headed for class reluctantly, and I turned back to Sabine, but she started talking before I could. "This is your fault, Kaylee. He needs me and he loves me. I can see that in him when we're alone, and he'd see it, too, if you weren't always there, giving him something else to look at. If you'd stayed buried like any decent dead girl, none of this would have happened."

I didn't even know where to start. "I'm not going to apologize for my own existence, Sabine. Besides if I weren't here, Nash wouldn't be, either. He'd be sitting in jail awaiting trial for murder."

"Because you framed him!" she whispered fiercely, dark eyes flashing. "No matter how you look at it, this is all your fault. So take me to him, now, so I can smack some sense into him. Assuming Thane didn't go back for him last night."

Thane. Shit. I hadn't thought of that. And Harmony wouldn't think to tell anyone he was missing, if she thought he was at school.

"I'll go check on him, but I can't take you with me." Blinking all the way to Nash's house was pushing the limit of how far I could go on my own without a layover, and I couldn't get half that far with someone else in tow. "But I'll text you if there's anything wrong. Okay?"

Sabine scowled and grabbed my arm again, and this time she wouldn't let me jerk free. "In case you haven't noticed, Nash is in withdrawal again, but this time the drug is *you*. Don't you think we ought to limit his exposure?"

Seriously? She was classifying me as a controlled substance now?

"I'm just trying to help." And I'd go even without her approval. She didn't own Nash, and he and I were still friends. We'd probably always exist in that weird twilight between friendship and more. We'd been through too much together to ever be any less to each other.

"Fine. But if anything happens to him because of you, I'll..."

"You need some time to work on that one?" I said, pulling my arm free when I realized that for perhaps the first time in her life, she didn't know how to finish a threat. "Threatening to scare me to death has kind of lost its punch, huh?"

"Just go get him. Please."

The rare courtesy told me just how worried she was about him. So I nodded, then ducked into the nearest bathroom and waited until it was empty. Then I blinked into Nash's living room, backpack and all. I set my bag on the floor and started toward the hall, until I heard the clink of glass in the kitchen.

I pushed the swinging door open slowly, expecting to see Nash, but I found his mother instead, and for a moment, I didn't know what to do. Harmony and I hadn't spoken one-on-one since I'd cheated on one of her sons with the other, then framed one for my murder. Since I'd eavesdropped the day before, I knew she thought Tod and I were good for each other, but I wasn't sure if she'd actually forgiven me for what I'd done to Nash. Or if she ever would. And I had no idea how she'd feel about me popping into her house, unannounced.

But then she turned and noticed me in the doorway, and my chance to sneak out expired.

"Kaylee!" She stood and motioned for me to come in, and the minute the door swung shut behind me, she pulled me close in a tight hug. "I've been hoping you'd come see me, but I didn't want to push you, if you weren't ready."

"So... You don't hate me?" And in that moment, I realized that of everything I'd lost when I died, other than my heartbeat, Harmony was what I'd missed the most. She was the closest thing I had to a mother, but with everything that had happened between me and her sons, I'd thought... Well, I hadn't expected open arms.

"Kaylee, I could never hate you." She let go of me and pulled out a second chair at the table, then pushed a plate of cookies toward me when I sat.

Tears burned behind my eyes and I blinked, trying to keep them at bay. "But I got Tod killed and Nash framed for murder." I certainly didn't deserve her sympathy, much less her cookies.

"Honey, I know that was a hell of a crazy week, but you didn't do any of that on purpose. And let's not forget what else you did. You also saved Tod's life and got Nash's name cleared."

"Doesn't matter." I sniffled, in spite of my best effort to hold back tears. "Nash hates me."

"No. Nash *wants* to hate you, but he can't. That's the problem. He just needs time."

"To learn to hate me?"

"No." Harmony arched her brows at me, and I sobbed even as I laughed. "To forgive. To move on."

"Tod and I… We messed up."

She nodded. "Yes, you did."

"But we didn't mean to hurt him."

"I know. Deep down, I think Nash knows. But on the surface, that's harder to understand, and even harder to forgive." She sighed and broke a chunk from her cookie. "I wish I could say I didn't see this coming, but I did." She'd warned me from the very start to be careful with *bean sidhe* brothers. I'd thought I was.

I'd thought wrong.

"Tod told you how he felt?"

She gave me a sad smile. "No. I'm the mother. Neither of them ever willingly tells me anything, but I know how to listen, even to the things they don't say." She sighed again, and this one was heavier. "Still, when Nash comes around, maybe you and Tod could hang out here sometimes. I wouldn't mind seeing the two of you every now and then."

"Sure." Tod checked on his mother regularly, but he rarely let her see him. "For now, can I talk to Nash?"

"I wish you would. He says he's sick, but he's clean, and sober, and has no sign of a fever." She looked worried, but I couldn't help being relieved by the fact that he was still here, instead of suffering in the Netherworld with Avari and Thane.

"I'll see what I can do."

When I knocked on Nash's door, the answer was almost immediate. "Go away, Kaylee." He must have heard me talking to his mother. That's what I get for going completely corporeal, instead of letting only Harmony see and hear me.

"Nope." I pushed his door open and walked in, hoping he was dressed. I got half my wish—jeans only.

"You don't get to just walk in here anymore," he said, stretched out on his bed, hands folded behind his neck. "You gave that up when you started making out with my brother."

"But you get to come to my house in the middle of the night, drunk, and try to kiss me?"

Nash frowned. "I said I was sorry about that."

"No, actually, I don't think you did." Not for that specific offense, anyway. I pulled out his desk chair and sat. "So, are you sorry?"

He sighed, then sat up and met my gaze boldly. "No. You kissed him when you were with me. How was I supposed to know that road doesn't run both ways?"

"Nash..." I hardly knew where to begin. "If you don't love Sabine, you have to tell her. You're all she wants. You're all she thinks about. You're all she has."

"I *do* love her. How could I not?" he said, and I had no idea how to answer that one. "What did you think this was going to be like, Kaylee? Did you think you could dump me, and

I'd bounce back to her and miraculously be happy? I'm not a Ping-Pong ball. You can't just swat me back and forth and expect me to be content wherever I land. If Tod dumped you tomorrow, would you come back to me?"

I shook my head slowly, pushing myself back and forth a couple of inches in his wheeled desk chair. What *had* I thought things would be like between us after the breakup? The truth was that I hadn't given it much thought. I hadn't expected to live past my own death.

"Look. I love Sabine—I probably always will—but that doesn't mean I don't still love you, too. It's not a switch I can just flip off. I wish it was, because I'd flip it in a minute. I don't think I even *like* you anymore, but I can't get you out of my head, and it hurts to see you, Kaylee."

"I'm sorry. I'm *so* sorry. But you still have to come to school, if for no other reason than that our strength is in numbers."

"I'm fine. Baskerville starts barking if anything inhuman or undead gets within twenty feet of the house, in this plane or in the Netherworld. How do you think I knew you were here?"

So he hadn't heard me talking to his mom, after all.

"I'm not worried about you, Nash. But Sabine and Emma are both at school with no Netherworld guard dogs looking after them. Or did you forget that a rogue reaper tried to kill your girlfriend last night?"

"She's not my—"

"Save it." I rolled my eyes and walked the chair closer. "You love her and you're sleeping with her. Do you really think it's worth arguing over how you define your relationship?"

"I don't think that's any of your business."

Okay, he had a point there. But that didn't change anything. "Get dressed. You're going to school."

"I don't feel like it." He lay back on the pillow again, and suddenly I understood how my father had felt when I'd refused to get up that morning.

"No one feels like going to school. Least of all me. But if I have to go, so do you."

Nash shrugged and put one hand behind his head again. "Who says you have to go?"

"My dad. The state of Texas." When that made no difference, my temper flared. "You want to stop loving me? I think I can help you out with that." I snatched the T-shirt slung over his footboard, then sat on the bed and grabbed his free hand. Then I closed my eyes and pictured the alley behind the doughnut shop, where I'd seen Thane the day before. That was as close as I could get to the halfway point between Nash's house and the school—which was as far as I could go with him in tow—and it was the place least likely to be populated.

"What are you—?" Nash tried to jerk free from my grip, but I held on tight, and a second later, I fell onto my butt on rough concrete. "What the hell?"

I opened my eyes to find Nash lying on his back on the ground, propped up on one elbow, one hand still gripped in mine.

"Where are we?"

"Almost there." I closed my eyes again, and pictured the first-floor supply closet, across the hall from the teachers' lounge. An instant later we were there, in the dark, Nash sprawled out on the floor with me sitting beside him.

"What the hell, Kaylee?" He jerked his hand from my grip, and when he tried to sit up, something crashed to the ground with an ominous-sounding slosh.

"Hang on." I stood carefully and felt around on the wall next to the door. When I flipped the switch, dim light flooded the small space from a bare lightbulb overhead, highlighting

Nash's angry face with dramatic shadows. "Here's your shirt. I think second period's almost over."

"*Damn it,* Kaylee!" He jerked the shirt over his head, then shoved his arms through the sleeves. "I don't even have any shoes!"

"Don't you keep cleats in your locker?" I asked as he stood, glaring down at me.

"I can't walk around all day in baseball cleats!"

I shrugged. "Then go barefoot."

"Take me home, Kaylee. Now."

"No." I crossed both arms over my chest. "You can't just stay at home and pout when everyone you care about is at risk. All we have is one another, Nash. You, me, Sabine, Emma, and Tod. You owe it to us—all of us—to look out for us like we look out for you."

"Like you were looking out for me when you kissed my brother?" he demanded. "Or when you framed me for murder?"

"More like when Tod and Sabine kept you from overdosing or hurting yourself when you fell off the wagon. Or when I made a deal with Levi and Madeline to clear your name. Or when Tod got rid of the dealer who supplied you with frost in the first place. Do you even know what he did?" I demanded, and Nash shook his head, brushing dust from the ground off his pants.

"He dropped him in the Netherworld. That's a death sentence for a human. Your brother killed to protect you from yourself. And that's not even…" I had to bite my tongue to keep from saying what else Tod had done for him. That wasn't my secret to tell. "The point is that you're not alone, Nash, and you have to stop acting like you are. We're in this together. All of us. And we need you as badly as you need us. So stop pushing us away, because we're not going anywhere."

Nash blinked at me, surprise shining in his eyes. But that wasn't all. In the low light, I thought I saw something else swirling in his irises. Something serious, and…relieved. "I'm so sorry for what I did to you, Kaylee. In the parking lot. I should have said it before. When I'm thinking straight, I can't blame you for turning to him." Tod, of course. Nash still wouldn't say his name.

"You know it had nothing to do with that."

"But it did," he insisted. "If I'd been the answer to your problems instead of the source of them, you would never have even looked at him. So, I blame myself as much as I blame him."

"Don't." My eyes were watering for the second time in an hour. Three hours earlier, I'd felt so empty I didn't even want to get out of bed, and now I was so full of pain and regret I could hardly make myself breathe. "Don't blame either of you. I did this. I kissed him." I glanced at my feet, then made myself meet his gaze again. "I love him, Nash. I'm sorry, but it's true."

He exhaled slowly. "I know."

The bell for third period rang then, and we both glanced up, startled, even though we'd known it was coming. "I have to go back for my backpack." Which I'd just realized I'd left in his living room. "I can grab some shoes for you, if you want."

"Thanks."

We parted ways in the hall, and I wondered if anyone had seen us coming out of the closet together, him with no shoes. Then I realized I didn't care what anyone else saw, or thought, or said about us. Nash and I had been through more together than any of them could ever imagine, and if they couldn't understand the wounds we'd inflicted, they couldn't understand how long and bumpy the road to forgiveness really was.

I PICKED UP MY BACKPACK AND NASH'S SHOES, then practiced selective corporeality by letting only him see me slide them into his bag during his third-period class. Then I texted Sabine.

Nash is here, and he's fine. And he loves you.

I'd just sat down at my normal table in the quad—invisible, even though there was no one there to see me—and was feeling pretty good about being nice to Sabine for no particular reason when Tod appeared on the grass in front of me. "Hey!" I slid my phone into my pocket, then stood to kiss him, and instead of letting me go, he lifted me onto the end of the picnic table I ate at every day. At least, every day before I'd died.

Since no one could see us, I pulled him closer, and he settled into the space between my thighs, then leaned down for another kiss.

"Mmm... What's the occasion?" I murmured.

"Wednesday."

"My new favorite day."

"No one's scheduled to kick the proverbial bucket in the next hour, so I thought I'd come say hi before I head back for my double shift."

Frowning, I let my hand trail down his chest, wishing there wasn't a layer of cotton between his skin and mine. "Why the double?"

"Mareth didn't pick up the list for the noon-to-midnight shift, and Levi can't find her, so I have to fill in until she shows up." Mareth was the reaper who shared the hospital reaping zone with Tod. She had nearly two decades' seniority over him, but was still considered a rookie, by reaper standards.

"Has she ever flaked before?"

"No, and she's always been cool about trading shifts with me when I need to."

Unease started twisting in my stomach. "It's Thane," I said, and Tod started to shake his head, but I spoke over him. "What if it wasn't you specifically that he needed? What if he just needed a reaper, and he knew he could find one at the hospital? When he couldn't get you, he could easily have gone after Mareth. That way he wouldn't have to go back to Avari empty-handed."

"Why would Avari need a reaper? He already has Thane."

"Yes, but Thane wants out of…whatever he's into. Isn't that what Sabine said?" Or had Thane said that? "Either way, I'm gonna see if Luca can find Mareth. If she's in the local area, on the human plane, he'll know it."

"I still say that's creepy. There's no one out there mentally stalking humans."

"Isn't that what Sabine does?" I said, and Tod laughed. "So, does this mean you're actually working three shifts in a row?" Because there were only two twelve-hour shifts a day.

"Yes, unless Mareth shows up. But I'll have several long breaks. You'll be seeing a lot of me."

"How much of you is a lot?" I asked, sliding my fingers beneath his shirt. The material rose with my hands, exposing smooth, hard abs.

"You can see as much as you want, whenever you want."

"Unless you're working, right?" I teased, but the heat in his eyes when he shook his head was unmistakable.

"Whenever you want. Death itself would wait for you, Kaylee...."

Lunch sucked without Tod, but on the bright side, Nash was acting almost normal again, and Sabine seemed to have forgiven him. Luca sat at Sophie's table, and I couldn't get him away from her long enough to ask him about Mareth, and I didn't really want to get into it with my cousin, even if she did know the truth about the things that went bump in the night.

Jayson seemed hyperaware that he didn't really fit in, so he overcompensated by talking almost nonstop. I tried to participate in the conversation—I really did—but I had very little interest in the baseball team's season standings, especially since Nash had quit the team, and I couldn't care less about senior skip day, because I wasn't a senior, and I wasn't sure I ever would be.

I'd stopped making assumptions about my future more than a month earlier, when I realized that while there are few guarantees in life, there are even fewer in the afterlife.

I was stirring green peas into my mashed potatoes, poking the lumpy concoction aimlessly, when Emma kicked me beneath the table. Or rather, she tried, but her foot when right through my leg and hit the bottom of the bench instead. And that's when I realized I was fading out again.

I blinked in surprise and pulled myself back into focus to

find everyone at our table staring at me. Including Jayson. "You okay?" he said, frowning at me from across the table. "You look kinda pale."

"Yeah, I'm fine." One more second, and I would have looked transparent. "What were we talking about?"

"Prom," Emma said.

"And how thoroughly absent some of us will be," Sabine added.

"You have to go," Em insisted. "It's your senior prom. Why don't you want to go?"

"I don't do dresses."

"Nash." Em leaned forward to see him around Sabine. "Tell her she has to go. Senior prom only happens once."

"Actually, I'm failing three classes right now, so there's a good chance it'll happen twice for me. And it'll probably take me that whole year to talk her into wearing a dress." He grinned, like that was a joke, but only Jayson laughed.

"You're failing three classes?" I couldn't believe it. Nash was an honor student. He'd been ranked twelfth in the senior class at midterms.

He glanced at the table, then met my gaze, his own swirling with some complicated blend of regret and melancholy. "It's been a rough semester."

"He's just behind on a few assignments, but his teachers are all working with him," Sabine said, and I couldn't quite wrap my mind around the fact that she was passing both junior and senior English in one year to graduate on time, but Nash was suddenly failing.

"I can still turn in my history term paper for ninety percent credit, and if I ace that and my final, I'll pull a B for the year," Nash said. He'd lose his ranking, but he'd graduate. Assuming his other teachers were that generous.

"I'm sorry," I whispered, staring at the table.

"Kay, it's not your fault," Nash insisted.

"It's *kind of* her fault," Sabine said, and she was right. When he and I started going out, Nash had been an athlete and an honor student. He'd had several options for college, and scholarships had been a strong possibility. But I'd ruined all that for him. I'd turned him into an addict, then abandoned him, cheated on him, dumped him, and framed him for murder. No wonder he was failing. It was a miracle he hadn't quit school entirely, instead of just the baseball team.

"No, I made my own mess and I can still clean it up," Nash said, and for the first time in a long time, I believed him.

"If there's anything I can do to help, please tell me," I said. And I meant it.

"Thanks," Nash said, and he meant that, too.

I made it through English without disappearing in my chair, and Em and I were just starting a pairs translation exercise in French when Madeline materialized next to my chair and nearly scared me to death. Er, deeper into death. Or whatever.

"Time to go to work," she said, and to keep from looking crazy, I had to direct my response to Em instead of the empty air everyone else would see where Madeline was standing.

"No, it's time to translate conversational French."

"What?" Em frowned. But she didn't look entirely surprised by my random declaration. She was getting used to me talking to people who weren't obviously present.

"Creepy undead employer at three o'clock," I said, so that only Madeline and Em could hear me.

Em stiffened and glanced to the side out of habit, but her gaze passed right over Madeline, who was only visible to me.

"Now," Madeline said, and I exhaled in frustration.

"Sorry to bail on you, Em, but I have to go confiscate a

stolen soul from some horrible Netherworld monster. If I'm not back when the bell rings, could you grab my books?"

Emma's eyes widened, but she nodded, so I grabbed the bathroom pass and mouthed the word *emergency* to Mrs. Brown on my way out of the classroom. Then I faded from the physical plane in the empty hall and followed Madeline to the quad, where Luca waited for us both at our lunch table.

"She got to you, too, huh?" I said, sliding onto the bench seat across from him.

"Actually, I called her." Luca grinned. "I'm vomiting from a possible case of food poisoning. You?"

"Sudden onset menstruation."

He nodded respectfully. "Classic."

"Yeah, but I should have gone for something more long-term. Yours will get you out of the whole afternoon. Ferris Bueller would be proud."

Madeline cleared her throat, bringing all banter to an end. "Luca, if you don't mind?" She gestured toward me.

"Sorry." Luca met my gaze again from across the table, and this time he was appropriately somber. "There's a corpse at the mall. Fresh. Maybe ten minutes dead."

"How do you know that?" I was morbidly fascinated by his abilities.

Luca shrugged. "I can feel dead things from the moment they die until they start to rot or are preserved through artificial means."

"So, you can't feel the bodies in a cemetery?"

"Not usually. Those are either preserved or rotting, or both. But I can feel you, so long as you're within a few miles of me, and when there are two of you, I know Tod's with you."

"I'm gonna try to pretend that's not creepy," I said, and Luca nodded in sympathy, like he agreed with my assessment.

"I've already checked with Levi, and no one was scheduled to die at the mall today," Madeline said. "It's the serial soul thief."

"How do you know? Couldn't it be another rogue reaper? Or the same rogue reaper?" How long could I get away with not telling them about Thane? If I'd given a full disclosure earlier, would I have prevented this latest death? And if so, would this life have been spared at the expense of Tod's?

"It's not a reaper," Luca said. "There's only one corpse at the mall, which means who or whatever the killer is, he's alive. Or at least, he's not dead."

"What does that mean?"

"We're hoping you'll be able to tell us that very soon." Madeline pulled my amphora from her pocket and handed it to me. "But before you go, there's something else you need to know." She sighed and sank onto the bench next to me and the death of her formal manner scared me even worse than knowledge of what I was about to do. "I owe you the truth, Kaylee, and I'm going to give it to you, even though we really don't have time to get into this right now."

"The truth? Have you been lying to me?" *Maybe right before I go face* untold evil *isn't the best time to spring that on me!*

"No, but I've omitted something important, and I apologize for that. I did what I thought was best for all involved, because I believed that if you doubted the strength of the reclamation department, you would doubt your own strength, and there's no reason for you to ever doubt yourself, Kaylee. You were recruited for your strength just as much as for your *bean sidhe* abilities and we are especially grateful to have you right now because…you're the only one left."

I blinked, trying to make sense of words that didn't seem to go together, but she may as well have been speaking Swahili. "What? What does that mean, Madeline?"

"I told you that the serial soul thief has already killed two of our other extractors. Well, two days ago, he killed the third and last. We were a small department in the first place, because under normal circumstances, there isn't much work for extractors—thank goodness. Whatever's been happening in this area in the past few months is almost unheard of. We're not sure what's going on, but it's obvious that something dangerous and powerful has moved into the area."

Avari? His presence had drawn other hellions—and who knew what else—into the area. Did the soul thief have something to do with him? I would have to tell Madeline about Avari and Thane, but there wasn't time to explain it all immediately. Not when she was still confessing her own secrets.

"Levi and I have our hands full trying to keep the human media and authorities out of the way."

The police were suspicious, the media was aggressively speculative, and the parents were worried about the recent rash of mysterious deaths in our small Texas suburb. But Levi and Madeline, and whoever else they were working with, had hidden all the supernatural elements, and since all the recent tragedies had happened months apart, no one in our world had been able to draw any real connections between them.

Still, the community was understandably anxious, and their unfocused fear only further fed Avari.

"New extractors take a while to train, of course," Madeline continued. "And you're the last of them, Kaylee. You're all I have left."

I blinked, then closed my eyes, trying in vain to draw my thoughts into focus. Madeline hadn't been isolating me from the rest of the department because I hadn't proven myself. She wasn't isolating me at all, because there was no one to isolate me from.

"I'm it?" No. It's not possible.

She nodded slowly. "You, and Luca, and me. We *are* the

reclamation department. I've requested additional help from the two closest regions, but they're swamped at the moment. Both of them are reporting an increase in stolen souls and losses similar to ours, and they have no one to spare. And what's worse is that Levi tells me he's now missing a reaper. Something very big is happening, and it seems to have started here. We're the only ones prepared to stop whatever's happening, and the truth is that we don't even know what we're facing. But whatever it is, you have to go face it right now, before the thief disappears again and we've lost another chance, and even more souls."

My hands were shaking again, and my heart was pounding like it hadn't since the night I died. "You're not coming with me?"

Madeline shook her head. "Since you're new, under normal circumstances, I'd go to observe and help out where I can. However, I have a meeting with the head of my old district in five minutes, wherein I plan to beg for some emergency manpower."

I nodded slowly, and a cold numbness blossomed in my stomach, then began to spread. *On my own.* I was going to be on my own. If I died, there'd be no witness to tell my friends and family what happened to me.

"Kaylee, listen to me," Madeline said, and I forced my eyes to bring her back into focus. "If this goes badly, run. We need the thief, but we need you worse. Do you understand?"

"Yeah." Tod had said the same thing the night before. I turned to Luca and could hardly hear the words coming from my own mouth. "Where am I going?"

"Second floor of the mall. East end." He shrugged, and I was relieved to realize he looked as stunned by all of this as I was. "That's where the body is, anyway, though someone may have found it by now."

I nodded. Then I concentrated on the mall and blinked out of the quad before I could lose my nerve.

Three miles was too far for me to go in one shot, at least without more practice, so I had to stop twice on the way, but I still arrived at the east end of the mall just seconds after I'd left school.

The mall was pretty quiet in the middle of a weekday, when most people were still at work and school, but the indoor playground was crowded with toddlers and their mothers, the gossip and giggles floating up to me from the floor below. Two elderly ladies race-walked past without seeing me, their arms pumping, sneakers squeaking on the floor. Other than that, I saw only a handful of shoppers carrying bags, most of them women in their thirties, and the occasional man in a suit, who'd stopped at the mall for lunch.

None of them looked like a murderer, which forced me to admit that I had no idea what a murderer looked like. The police had thought Nash looked like a killer, but he was innocent. Tod killed people for a living—only those whose time was up—and no one would ever know, just from looking at him. If they could've seen him. Mr. Beck could have been a movie star, but he was guilty as hell. And if we were being really nitpicky about the definition, I was a killer, too.

So the only thing I could be certain of as I scanned the faces around me, glad I was incorporeal so no one could see me clutching the heart-shaped amphora hanging from a chain around my neck, was that no one had found the body yet. There wasn't a security guard or an EMT in sight.

As I walked, heading toward the department store at the very end of the mall, I let a thin ribbon of my *bean sidhe* wail leak from my lips, satisfied that no one else could hear it when a Sears employee walked right past me with a large fountain drink in hand. Any disembodied soul should have been pulled toward the sound, and I, in return, should have been pulled toward the soul. But I felt nothing.

Was I too late? Had the thief already taken his stolen soul and fled?

Frustrated, I stopped at the end of the mall, in front of the cornerstone department store, and crossed both arms over my chest, scanning the few shoppers for something—anything—that stood out. I was just about to admit defeat and return to Madeline empty-handed—secretly relieved at not having found the monster that would most likely have stolen my soul and ended my afterlife—when someone stepped out of the back hall that housed restrooms, storage, and the mall's security office.

My gaze probably wouldn't have snagged on the girl for very long, if hers hadn't already snagged on me. She shouldn't have been able to see me, yet she was looking right at me. And she looked familiar. Eerily, thoroughly familiar—every single part of her, including her short, sparkly dress, sequined sandals, and her long, reddish blond hair.

Familiarity bled into recognition, and chills shot through me, settling into my fingers and toes, reverberating the length of my spine. I'd never actually met her, and I'd only seen her once, but I would have recognized her anytime, anywhere, even if she weren't still wearing the clothes she'd had on the night I saw her. The night I predicted her death. The night she died on the floor of the bathroom at Taboo, the eighteen-and-over dance club where Emma's sister worked.

Heidi Anderson. Her death was the very first prediction I'd ever been able to verify, and that led to my discovery of my *bean sidhe* heritage, which threw me and Nash together as a couple and brought my father home from Ireland. Heidi's death had changed my life and set into motion the events that had led to my death. Which was how I knew for a fact that I couldn't *possibly* be seeing what I was seeing.

Heidi was dead, yet there she stood. Then she started walking. Toward me. She could clearly see me, even though I was *sure* I'd done the invisibility thing right this time.

I backed up, eyes wide, still clenching the heart around my neck, and still she came, smiling that creepy dead-girl smile, long hair swishing behind her with every step. I retreated until my spine hit the wall and there was nowhere left to go unless I blinked out of the mall. But I couldn't do that. Someone was dead, and a soul had been stolen, and Heidi's presence couldn't be a coincidence.

Was she a ghost? Was there any such thing? I made a mental note to ask Tod or Luca when this was over and I wasn't staring into the eyes of a dead girl. It takes one to know one, right? So was she like me? Was she undead? If so, where had she been for the past seven months? She wasn't a reaper. Not a local one, anyway—Tod would have told me if she were. And she *definitely* didn't work for reclamation.

"Kaylee, right?" Heidi said, and her voice wasn't familiar, because I'd never heard her speak. "We almost met once. Do you remember?"

I nodded, my insides cold from shock, my hands shaking at my sides.

"Oh, you're trembling!" Her smile brightened, but her gaze was cold. "Is that fear or guilt?"

It was actually confusion and terror, but admitting that seemed unwise, so I started with something more basic. "Are you real?"

"As real as you are." She reached for my right hand, then held it in both of hers. Her hands were warm around mine, and undeniably solid.

"How…?" She was dead. I *knew* she was dead. Was she the

corpse Luca had sensed? If so, what was she doing here? Was this a trap?

I couldn't make sense out of all the possibilities, and I couldn't make sense out of her.

"You're asking the wrong question. How doesn't matter," Heidi said, and she laughed when I pulled my hand from her warm grasp. "What should matter to you is *why*. Ask me why."

I blinked, but no words came out. I was drowning in shock and horror, followed closely by a devastating confusion.

"Okay, I'll say your lines, but just this once." Heidi cleared her throat and closed her eyes, and when they opened again, she frowned at me in a mask of bewilderment obviously meant to mimic my own. "Why are you here, Heidi, when we both know you died months ago?" she said in a falsetto that sounded nothing like me.

"I'm so glad you asked," she continued in her normal voice. "I'm here because of you, Kaylee. Also, not coincidentally, I'm dead because of you. I wasn't supposed to die, and you failed to save me, just like you failed to save all those other girls. Just like you failed to save the woman propped up on a toilet in the bathroom. I left the stall open. Someone will find her soon, and they may never know her death was your fault, but I'll know it. And *you'll* know."

I was breathing too fast, and I wasn't even sure how that was possible, but I couldn't make it stop. Luca had only sensed one corpse, and if there was a dead woman in the bathroom, she *had* to be what he'd felt. Which meant Heidi wasn't dead.

How could she not be dead?

"You can't hyperventilate anymore, but I appreciate the drama. Very angsty. But even if you could pass out, this would all be here waiting for you when you wake up. Me. The woman in the bathroom—a random, innocent soul, plucked in its prime. And she's only the start. Every life I take will be on your shoulders. You couldn't stop it then, and you can't stop it now. All you can do is squeeze your eyes shut and scream for their souls. Isn't that right, little *bean sidhe?*"

I don't know if it was the way she called me a "little *bean sidhe*" or the way her gaze narrowed on me, her mouth open slightly, like she could taste my fear on the air. Either way, in that moment, I realized I wasn't talking to Heidi Anderson.

I never had been.

"Avari," I whispered. "You're the soul thief?"

Heidi threw her head back and laughed. She sounded like a girl, but that look in her eyes, that brutal mirth in response to my pain—that was all hellion. "That shall be my new epithet," he said, abandoning the borrowed teen-speech pattern altogether. "Avari, thief of souls. I like it. Although, 'devourer' has more of a menacing undertone. But we can work on the details later."

I blinked, resisting the urge to shake my head in denial. This made no sense. But then, neither did my existence.

"What is this? First Scott and now Heidi? How are you possessing dead bodies?" I demanded, trying to find even one connection between the jumble of mismatched puzzle pieces in my head.

Had he taken Scott's corpse, then returned it to the morgue? Why didn't Luca sense Heidi as a walking corpse? And how could Heidi possibly look exactly as I remembered her, seven months after she'd died? How was she still dressed the same?

"You haven't figured it out yet," the Heidi-thing taunted. She put one hand on my shoulder and circled me slowly, trailing her hand across my back, then down my arm, and I could only shudder in revulsion. "The dead can't be possessed, and even if they could, the real Heidi Anderson would not be fit for public viewing. She has long since started to decompose."

"Then what is this? How are you here?" Was this some kind

of illusion? Was I dreaming? Sabine could design one hell of a nightmare, but she couldn't manipulate the fears of the dead, so this couldn't be her work.

"I've learned a new trick. And I have a new toy." Avari spread his borrowed arms and turned Heidi slowly, for my appraisal. "Isn't she pretty?"

"She's not a toy."

"You're right. She's more like a pawn, and pawns exist to be sacrificed. Fortunately, your world is full of pawns." Avari waved one arm at the shoppers ambling from store to store, but the gesture had greater meaning. Greater horror. His chessboard wasn't the mall; it was the world. *My* world. "And I will use as many of them as it takes."

"They're not pawns, they're people," I said through gritted teeth.

"And you want to save them?" he asked. I didn't bother to answer. "You can't save them all, Ms. Cavanaugh. Even in your new state of being, you don't have that kind of power. But you can save one. I will gladly accept your soul in exchange for the one I now carry—the woman in the restroom."

The dead woman was bait, chosen at random, to bring me to Avari. But why? "You want to trade my soul for hers?"

"Precisely." The Heidi-thing leaned forward until her cheek brushed mine, and my heart stuttered to a stop. "I'll tell you a secret," she whispered into my ear, and I wondered what the shoppers would see, if one glanced at her then. Could they see her, and her malicious invasion of my personal space? Because they couldn't see me. "I don't think your noble streak runs that deep. I don't think you're willing to save a stranger's soul at the expense of your own. Am I wrong?" She stepped back to look into my eyes, and hers were alight with vicious pleasure at my pain. "Will you suffer eternal torment in exchange for her peace?"

My chest tightened painfully. "You say that like it's the only option, but we both know there's another way." My hand curled around the amphora hanging from my neck and I clutched it, wondering how my predecessors had met their true end. Had their souls been stolen? Were they now suffering in the Netherworld?

"Ah, the inevitable plan B." Avari glanced at my fist, closed around the gold heart, and shook Heidi's head slowly. "Like those who came before you, you are ill-equipped for the job. This isn't as simple as taking a soul from a reaper. You're going to need something more like this."

The Heidi-thing held her hand between us. Lying across her palm was a very familiar double-bladed dagger. I gasped, so shocked it didn't occur to me to run, and I only survived the next few seconds because Avari made no move to kill me.

I'd never carried a weapon before, and I'd only used one once. The night I killed my math teacher in self-defense. I knew that dagger by heart—after I was resurrected, it sat on my dresser for more than a month. Had he taken it from my room? When had he been in my room?

Chills ran the length of my spine and settled into my bones. "This is mine," I whispered in shock.

The hellion in Heidi's body looked distinctly amused. "That depends on how you define the concept of ownership."

"I killed the incubus who killed me with this," I insisted. "That makes it mine."

The hellion's manicured eyebrows rose. "I wrenched the metal from the ground and shaped it with my own hands, several of your human centuries ago, and it has been wielded by many other hands for many purposes since. But it always finds its way back to me eventually. Had I known yours was the soul that incubus intended to capture, I would never have sold him the blade."

Because Avari wanted my soul for himself.

"Take it," the hellion said with Heidi's voice.

I picked up the dagger in a horrified mental fog, vaguely aware that Avari could kill me anytime he wanted, dagger or no dagger. Was I supposed to use it against him? If so, why would he give it to me?

The blood—both mine and Mr. Beck's—had been scrubbed clean, but the hilt hummed in my palm with a familiar resonance, like a whispered echo of my own *bean sidhe* wail. Beck's soul was still trapped inside, and it called to me every time I touched the hellion-forged steel.

"I don't understand..." I said, and my voice sounded hollow.

"Yes, you do. You now hold the instrument that could have saved your predecessors' lives. Surely you must have known this little confrontation could only end in violence." Avari spread Heidi's arms, offering her up for sacrifice. "Have it done, then. Slaughter the girl you failed to save."

He wanted me to stab her. Him. Them—or whatever. He *wanted* me to shove my knife through flesh he'd proven to be solid and warm.

The dagger shook in my hand.

Heidi was already dead. I wouldn't be killing her. Intellectually, I knew that. But this wasn't self-defense. This wasn't even a fair fight, because for no reason I could understand, Avari wasn't trying to kill me.

"Ticktock, little *bean sidhe.* Kill me now, or the next blood I spill is on your hands. It might be her blood." The Heidi-hellion glanced to the left, where a woman in a mall cop's uniform walked past us in blissful ignorance. "Or his." She nodded toward a boy not much older than me, in a fast-food restaurant uniform.

"Why would you let me kill you?" I whispered, tightening

my grip on the dagger. I had no choice. I couldn't let Avari kill again, nor could I let him leave with an innocent soul.

"Because you will suffer from this far more than I will," Heidi whispered, and suddenly I understood. The hellion wouldn't die just because his physical form did, but he *would* feed from my trauma. "Do it now, or I will take the small one."

I followed his gaze and horror swallowed me whole when I found a toddler holding her mother's hand, clutching a star-shaped Mylar balloon in the other.

"How many souls do you intend to reclaim today, Ms. Cavanaugh?" the Heidi-thing said, already inching toward the mother and child. "The choice is yours."

Stab Avari and capture the soul he'd stolen in the dagger he'd forged, or abandon that soul and let an innocent child die.

There was really no choice at all.

I sucked in a deep breath and swallowed a sob, tightening my grip on the dagger. I tore my gaze from the toddler and stared into Heidi's eyes, trying to see Avari staring back at me. Tears rolled down my cheeks. I shoved the double blades deep into Heidi's stomach. Warm blood leaked sluggishly onto my hand, slower than what had flowed from Beck's chest, but just as warm, and red, and gruesome.

Her eyes widened and she made a strangled sound of pain. "That truly hurts," the hellion whispered, with a rare note of surprise. A silver bracelet slid down her arm as she grasped my shoulder for balance, hunched over my knife. "How extraordinary."

I couldn't hold her up, so we both fell, and distantly I noticed that no one rushed to help her. As solid and real as she was, they couldn't see her, just like they couldn't see me.

Heidi sprawled on the floor beneath me, her jaw clenched

in pain, her gaze glued to mine as the hellion swallowed my agony, along with his own.

I didn't want to spill blood. I didn't want to fight hellions. I didn't want to watch people die.

As I blinked through my own horrified tears, a colorless, shapeless haze leaked from Heidi and curled around the dagger, soaking into the hellion-forged steel like water pulled up into a sponge dropped into a puddle.

Her soul. Or maybe the soul of the woman Avari killed.

"Until we meet again," the demon whispered with a dead girl's voice. "And, Ms. Cavanaugh, next time it won't be a stranger."

His words sent fresh terror through me as I watched, paralyzed by the true pain racking the hellion's borrowed features. The last of the soul soaked into the dagger and Heidi began to fade from existence, like a shadow dying slowly with the rising of the sun. When she was gone, I still held the double-bladed knife, on my knees on the second floor of the mall.

All that remained of Heidi Anderson was the blood on my knife and a dark bit of smoke where she'd lain, like the Nether-fog that constantly churned between worlds. And as I watched, breathing slowly through my own horror, that dark smudge of…something…began to fade into nothing, just like Heidi's body had.

On the floor, where she'd been, lay the bracelet she'd been wearing moments earlier. And on the night she'd died.

11

"KAYLEE?" TOD RACED ACROSS THE E.R. WAITING room toward me, dodging chairs but running right through patients. "What happened? Are you okay?"

The dagger slipped from my grip and clattered to the floor as he reached me, and several people turned to stare at the strange, bloody knife that had appeared out of nowhere, from their perspective.

Tod bent to snatch it, and the onlookers' eyes widened as the dagger disappeared from their sight. Several blinked and shuffled slowly toward the drops of blood still on the floor, the only evidence that they hadn't imagined the whole thing. Several looked scared. Several more looked confused.

Tod led me toward an empty hall without even a glance at them.

"Kaylee. Are you hurt?" He took a step back to look me over, but I couldn't see anything except my own right hand, still trembling and covered in blood. And Heidi's bracelet, clenched in my left fist.

"I'm fine," I whispered, only vaguely frightened by the pitiful sound of my own voice, like a mere echo of my thoughts. "It's not my blood. I killed her."

"Who? Who did you kill, Kaylee?"

"Heidi," I said as he led me down the hall toward an empty grouping of chairs near the radiology department. "Only she was already dead, so it wasn't really her. It was Avari. But he didn't really die. I don't think he can, but I killed him, and now she's gone but he's not, and her blood is literally on my hands." I held my hand out to show him, and that's when I noticed that my shirt was soaked in it, too. "And there was this bracelet on the floor."

"Okay, you're not making any sense, but you *are* covered in blood. Let's get you home."

Before I could pull together enough focus to blink myself out of the hospital, Tod did the work for us both. We appeared in my living room, and he tugged me toward the hall and into the bathroom. He lowered the toilet lid and turned on the sink faucet. "Sit down, and let's get you cleaned up."

"I'm sorry," I said as he set the bloody dagger on the countertop and rummaged beneath the sink for a clean rag. "I didn't mean to go to the hospital. I was just standing in the mall, holding a bloody knife, wishing you were there, and the next thing I knew, I was in the E.R."

"No better place to be, when you're covered in blood," he said, running tap water over his fingers in the sink, to check the temperature.

"This is better." I glanced around the bathroom, but my gaze was drawn to him as my hands turned the bracelet in aimless circles.

When the water was warm enough, he held the rag beneath it, then turned the faucet off and wrung the rag out. It steamed from the hot water.

Tod sat on the edge of the tub and turned me by my knees to face him. I closed my eyes, and more tears fell. Behind my eyelids, I saw Heidi as she'd been in the club seven months ago. Right before she'd died. She'd danced and people had watched her. She'd glowed with youth and beauty—the very vitality that had nominated her for death by the rogue reaper who'd killed her and stolen her soul.

"What happened?" Tod asked, and I gasped when I felt the warm rag on my cheek.

I opened my eyes as he wiped away my tears, and his blue-eyed gaze chased away thoughts of blood, and death, and the horrible, visceral resistance Heidi's very solid flesh had presented against my dagger. The images were still there, but they were memories now instead of moments extracted from time, playing over and over in my head and behind my eyelids.

"The soul thief killed again." I set the bracelet on the edge of the tub, then cradled my bloody hand in my clean one, resting on my leg. "Madeline said I had to go get the soul. It had to be me, because there's no one else left. I'm the last one." I could hear the uplift of panic in my voice on the last word.

Tod picked up my bloodied right hand and began to wipe my palm clean, slowly. And the panic eased again. The chaos raging inside my head and my heart couldn't survive the calm, rhythmic strokes of the warm rag as it cleaned away all evidence of what I'd done. What I'd had to do.

"What happened to the other extractors?" he asked, and his voice was like his hands. Steady. Too strong and measured to give in to confusion.

"Avari killed them. He's the soul thief, but I don't know what he's doing. Or how he's doing it. Or why he didn't kill me."

"How could he steal souls from the Netherworld? How would he have killed you from across the barrier? Please tell me you didn't cross over...?" he said, rotating my hand to wipe my knuckles clean.

"No. I was at the mall—the version in our world. But he was there, wearing a dead girl's skin like he wore Scott's. It's not possession, Tod. He was really there, in the flesh. Just, not his own flesh."

Tod set my hand back in my lap and frowned at me, and the twists of color in his irises deepened in hue as his concern grew. "Could people see him?"

"Not when I was there, but he killed a woman in the bathroom. Like, physically killed her. And I touched him. He was solid. Flesh and blood." I held my hand up for emphasis, though most of the evidence was now on the rag, which he was rinsing in the sink again. "He said that if I didn't kill him—he called it sacrificing the pawn—he'd kill this little girl who was there with her mother. And it would be my fault. So I had to stab him. I had to kill Heidi...."

The tears were back, and I couldn't stop them.

"Who's Heidi?"

"The dead girl. She's been dead for months, but he looked just like her. Clothes and all, just like the night she died. But when I stabbed her and she disappeared, that didn't." I glanced at the bracelet on the counter.

Tod studied it, then laid it on the edge of the sink again. "I have no idea what that means."

"Me, neither."

"And you're sure she's not just undead?" He sat on the tub again and started wiping the remaining blood from my hand.

"I'm sure. He said she was rotting in her grave, and hellions can't lie. They can't possess the dead, either, right?" Which was the only real bright side to my new state of being.

"Right." Tod frowned and draped the rag over the edge of the tub to his left. "So, he took a corporeal form that looked and felt like a girl who's been dead for months. And the other day he took a corporeal form that looked like Scott, at least twelve hours after he died."

"Yeah. It makes no sense. It's like he's cloning dead people and possessing them, but that's not possible, is it?"

The reaper shrugged. "I'm not ready to call anything truly impossible at this point, but that doesn't sound very likely, does it?"

"No. He's killing people, Tod. He says people are his pawns, and the world is full of them, and he'll kill as many as it takes."

"As many as it takes for what?"

"I don't know. All I know is that he acted like Avari, but he looked and sounded like a girl I saw once, and I had to kill her. He *made* me kill her, and he wouldn't do that unless he knew he could come back. He's found a way into the human world and the only way to get rid of him—even temporarily—is to kill his physical form. Even if it looks like someone you know." I sucked in a deep breath. "I'm going to have to do it again, Tod. I'm going to have to kill him over and over, and every time, it's going to feel like murder."

I couldn't do it. I couldn't keep killing people, even if they weren't really people, because killing not-Heidi had felt like murder. And Avari knew that.

Tod took my hands and looked straight into my eyes. "It's not murder, Kaylee. You didn't kill a person, you killed a demon. And you saved a little girl's life in the process."

"I know." But it didn't feel like I'd saved anything. The woman in the bathroom was still dead, and she'd suffer the postmortem indignity of being found propped up on a public toilet. It was hard to feel like I'd done anything right at all, knowing that.

"Let's get your shirt off," he said. "I think we're going to have to call this one a total loss."

I glanced down in surprise. I'd forgotten about the blood drying stiff on my clothes. That was two ruined shirts in two days.

"How can there be blood?" I demanded, staring down at the evidence of what I'd done. "Do hellions bleed?" Their breath was toxic and addictive. There's no telling what random evil properties their blood had.

"I don't think this is hellion blood," Tod said, staring at my top button. "A hellion can't physically cross the world barrier, so whatever flesh he was wearing wasn't his own. It wasn't Netherworld in origin. Which means the blood isn't, either."

"Then what did I kill?" My words lacked volume because I hadn't taken in enough air to give them voice. Because I could hardly comprehend the question I'd just asked. That was the root of the problem. How could it not be murder, if there was blood? And if it was murder, what did I kill?

"I don't know what you killed," Tod admitted, and that cold horror began to unfurl within me again. "But I know it was evil. You did what had to be done, Kaylee, and you saved lives."

I nodded, but I felt like there was still blood on my hands, and no matter how hard I scrubbed, they'd never come clean.

Tod's gaze met mine again, and his irises swirled with a single tight burst of color, then went still as he got control over them. "Do you want me to…?" His focus shifted to my shirt again, and I realized that it would have to come off. "I can step outside if you want."

"Stay," I said, and his irises swirled again. "Stay with me, please. I don't want to be alone."

Tod's gaze met mine. "You'll never be alone again, Kaylee."

My hands shook as I pushed the first button through the hole, and that burst of color was back in his eyes. The second button slid free and Tod's gaze never left mine, but he was breathing harder. It took me a moment to realize I was breathing again, too. And that my inhalations had matched the rhythm of his.

His gaze burned into mine, like he could see past my eyes into parts of me no one had ever seen, and I knew I was seeing the same in him. No one else had ever seen him so vulnerable before, like if I pushed him away, he might crumble into pieces that could never be put together again. Yet there was strength, too. He was strong beneath that fragile need, and I knew that I could never fall with him next to me. If I tripped, he would catch me. If I lost my balance, he would find it.

I wanted to be those things for him, too. His strength. His balance.

I found the third button and flinched. It was sticky and cold with drying blood. I didn't want to touch it.

"Do you want me to get it?" Tod asked, and that complicated mix of strength and vulnerability echoed in his voice, deeper than it should have been, like his question meant more than what his words actually asked.

I nodded. "Take it off. Get rid of it. Please."

He reached for me, and his gaze held mine until the last possible moment before his focus shifted to his fingers on my shirt. To the button, as he slid it through the hole, then moved on to the next. His fingers brushed my skin as he worked his way lower, and I sucked in a deep breath. My eyes closed again, and I let my head fall back against the shelf above the tank.

I didn't realize he was finished until he whispered, "Lean forward." So I did, and his hands slid over my shoulders, pushing the material down slowly until I could pull my arms from the short sleeves.

Then my shirt was gone, and so were his hands. I opened my eyes just as he turned the hot water on again and rinsed the rag beneath it. He wrung the cloth out, then took my hand in his warm, damp one. "Stand up."

I stood, and he knelt in front of me. The cloth was scratchy on my skin, and each stroke was torturously short and deliciously hot as he worked his way across my stomach. When he was finished, he laid the rag across the tub again and his hands found my hips. He kissed the dimple above my navel, and his hair brushed my stomach, so soft I had to touch it.

His grip on my hips tightened and he exhaled against my stomach. "Every time I see you, I want to touch you, and I'm still a little stunned every time you let me."

"Why?" I whispered. If anything, *I* was the lucky one.

"Because this feels too good to be true, so I keep expecting something to ruin it. When I saw you covered in blood, I thought it was happening again, the way it was supposed to last time. I thought Thane got to you."

"I'm fine." Physically, anyway.

"Not much scares me anymore, but I'm terrified of losing you, Kaylee." His lips skimmed my stomach again, and I closed my eyes as my hands curled in his hair. "I don't want to let you go long enough for that to happen."

"Then don't. Nothing else feels right," I confessed. I couldn't tell anyone else what I was telling him, because no one else would understand. They were worried enough about me already. "Everything that isn't *us* is pain, and blood, and death. Or nothing at all. Everything that doesn't hurt is just… emptiness. It closes in on me when I'm alone, and I hate it, but I can't fight it. Food doesn't taste right. Music sounds flat and tinny. Colors look dull and faded. Why? What's wrong with me?"

"Nothing. It won't be like this forever, Kaylee," he promised, his lips brushing my skin with each word, his breath hot on my stomach. "Your body and your mind are still adjusting to the afterlife. You have to give your senses time to readjust."

"*You* feel good." I lifted his chin and his gaze met mine again. "Why are you the only thing in the world that feels good right now?"

"I don't know." He stood, and his hands trailed slowly up my sides. "But I'm not gonna question it."

"I know why," I said as his lips met mine and he reminded me that he tasted as good as he felt. My hands slid beneath his shirt and my mouth fed from his. When he kissed his way along my jaw, I let my head fall back. "It's because I love you," I whispered, and I could feel his heartbeat speed up. I'd never actually told him. I'd been scared to, because it was too fast, and too crazy, and…

"I love you, too," he said, his lips brushing my ear. "Eternity isn't long enough."

My heartbeat raced to match his, and I pushed him back just enough that I could see his eyes. "I want to feel something good. Something real. Something that isn't bitter, or cold, or ugly." I stood on my toes to whisper the rest in his ear. "I want to feel alive again, Tod. Make me feel alive."

When I dropped onto my heels, his gaze searched mine, tight spirals of cobalt twisting in and out of the darker blues in his irises. "Are you sure?"

"I've never been more sure of anything." I took his hand and pulled him across the hall into my room, then closed the door behind us and leaned against it.

The heat in his eyes threatened to devour me.

I pulled his shirt off and dropped it on the floor. Then I had to touch him. "You're beautiful," I whispered, running my hands over his chest and down his stomach. My heart beat so hard I could almost hear it.

He laughed, and the sound was deep, like it got caught in his throat. "That's my line."

"You already said it." And I could still see it in his eyes. "So why don't you show me instead?"

Tod groaned. "If you don't mean that, please tell me now."

I stepped back and unhooked my bra. "I mean it." I let the material fall to the floor between us, and his gaze smoldered. "Show me."

I closed my eyes, and waited for him, my entire body buzzing in anticipation.

His fingers brushed mine first and the sparks started there, then followed his touch as it skimmed slowly over my knuckles and up the back of my arm. I could hardly breathe. How could such little contact—innocent, yet scorchingly intimate—bring my entire world grinding to a halt, like the planet had suddenly stopped spinning?

His hand rested on my shoulder, warm for just an instant, then trailed up my neck to cup the back of my head. He brushed a strand of hair behind my ear, and my mouth fell open.

Tod's mouth met mine and he sucked my lower lip between his. I reached for him and when my hands brushed the hard ridges of his stomach, he moaned into my mouth. His hand tightened behind my head and that kiss deepened until I was glad I didn't need to breathe.

"You are so beautiful…" he whispered against the corner of my lips, when that kiss finally ended.

My eyes opened, and I started to deny it, but he pulled away just far enough that he could look into my eyes. "No. You are. You are selfless on the inside and beautiful on the outside, and I am the luckiest man who has ever walked this earth, alive or dead."

I had no idea what to say. I didn't feel worthy of the things he was saying, yet I felt the same way about him. So would everyone else, if they could see the parts of himself he kept hidden from the rest of the world.

"Kaylee, this means something to me." His hands trailed down my arms to cup my elbows, and his gaze held mine. "With any luck, we're going to have millions of moments over the course of eternity, and I plan to love every one of them. But we'll never have *this* moment again, and this is very important to me." The twists of blue in his eyes coiled so tightly the color was almost gone, lost among pale shades of a need so deep it couldn't possibly be captured in a kiss, or a touch. "I need to know that this is important to you, too. I need to know that this isn't like last time. That you're not doing this just so you can say you've done it. Because that's not good enough for me. That's not good enough for *us*."

The ache in his voice echoed throughout every part of me. I hated the doubt in his eyes, but more than that, I hated that I was the one who'd put it there.

I laid my palm on his chest so I could feel his heart beating. "This is *nothing* like last time." The last time I'd been down this road, I'd been with Nash, and we'd been traveling for all the wrong reasons. I had no regret that we never finished the trip. "This is important to me, Tod. *You* are important to me."

He stared into my eyes for another moment, searching. Reading. Then his irises burst with colors so bright they hurt to see, blues jumping and flickering like the flames at the center of a fire. And that's what it felt like. Like his eyes reflected the blaze burning deep inside him, and I could feel the heat within me answering in return. That heat built, spiraling tighter and hotter in the narrow inches of space separating us until I knew that if I touched him, I might actually see the spark jump from my skin to his.

Then, suddenly, the anticipation was too much.

Tod lifted me, and I wrapped my legs around his waist. My mouth found his, and I couldn't taste enough of him. He was warm, when everything else was cold. He was sweet, when the world tasted bitter. He was mine, and I wanted to be his, in every sense possible.

I'm not sure how we wound up on the bed, but suddenly my pillow was beneath my head, and Tod was over me, and I could touch him without having to hang on for balance. His mouth fed from mine, desperately, hungrily, then suddenly his lips were gone, and mine were left open. Empty and lonely.

But then he kissed my neck, and I gasped as he worked his way lower, my fingers tangled in his hair, my body alive with possibility, on fire from every touch.

My jeans came off slowly, his fingers trailing over my hips, then down my legs along with the material.

His jeans came off in an instant, and briefly I wondered if there was some kind of quick-release trigger built into his zipper.

Then my underwear was gone, and his was gone, and he settled onto the bed next to me on his side, one hand at my hip, splayed out like he couldn't touch enough of me with only the two hands he was born with.

"I love you, Kaylee. More than I've ever loved anyone. More than I will ever love anyone. If I could freeze this moment in time and never have to let you go, I would do it without a second thought."

"I love you, too." I pulled him down for a kiss. "But maybe we could freeze the next moment instead," I whispered against his cheek when he settled over me.

He laughed, and the sound rumbled through me, triggering fiery anticipation all over my body. "Does that mean you're ready? You really want this?"

"That means I really want *you.*"

"I'm yours," he said, guiding my leg around his hips. I gasped, then bit my lip and stared up at him. "Forever."

"YOU KNOW, IF WE'D DONE THAT A FEW WEEKS ago, I wouldn't have been a very good candidate for a virgin sacrifice."

Tod rolled onto his side facing me, and that one stubborn curl fell over his forehead. "I always *knew* my sexual prowess has the power to save lives."

"You can turn anything into an ego boost, can't you?"

"I have a healthy sense of my own worth. But I have an even better sense of yours."

"Aww…" I pulled him down for another kiss and chose to ignore what neither of us was saying. Losing my virginity earlier might have saved me from Mr. Beck, my incubus math teacher, but it wouldn't have saved me from death. My time was up.

The irony there was that Tod's wasn't. Nash was living out his brother's lifeline, and he had no idea what Tod had given up for him.

"Well, as much as I hate to leave—and I *truly* hate to leave—

I have a fatal aneurism scheduled for 3:14—" He started to sit up, and I pulled him back down.

"No, don't go...."

"I'll be back, I swear. Not even death could keep us apart." He grinned over his joke and I rolled my eyes.

"Do you take anything seriously?"

"Only you. I take you seriously. Everything else goes down better with a joke—the verbal equivalent of a spoon full of sugar." He gave me another kiss, then sat up and started pulling his clothes on. "You should get dressed, too. How much longer do you think Madeline's going to wait for a report?"

Crap. I glanced at the clock to see that it was just past three in the afternoon. School was out, which meant Em would be coming with my books. And Tod was right about Madeline. "Come back when you get a break?" I said, stepping into my underwear.

Tod pulled me up and wrapped his arms around my bare waist. "I'll be back as soon as I can." His grin faded and the colors in his irises went still. "Kay, you have to tell Madeline what happened at the mall. All of it. There's no way any of us can fight Avari in the human plane if we don't all know exactly what we're up against."

"But Levi..."

"Things have changed, Kaylee. This isn't just about reaper-on-reaper violence anymore, and he'll understand that he can't afford to lose anyone who's been up against Avari before." But the doubt I saw in his eyes worried me. "Call Madeline. And you should spend as much time with Emma as you can. Avari's gone after her before, so she'll probably be high on his list this time."

"So will Nash. Fortunately, he and Sabine made up, so she won't let him out of her sight."

"Good. I'll check on them, too, just in case." Tod kissed

me one last time, then he disappeared and I was alone in my room, in my underwear.

I grabbed my jeans from the floor and dug my phone from the pocket as I sank onto the edge of the bed. Instead of calling Madeline, I texted her, both because I didn't really want to hear her voice and because if she was going to not-live in the twenty-first century, she might as well learn to use the technology.

I'm fine. Got the soul. We need 2 talk. My house. 1 hr.

After that, I pulled my jeans on, then slid my phone back into my pocket, and I was buttoning a clean shirt when the doorbell rang. Styx followed me to the front of the house, where Em stood on my porch, holding my backpack. I opened the door and she marched inside, then dropped my bag into a chair.

"I was worried about you. Why didn't you come back to school?" Her eyes narrowed and I could practically hear her focus zoom in on me like a long-range camera. "Why is your hair all tangled? And why is your shirt buttoned wrong?"

Was it? *Crap.*

I looked down and started fixing the buttons, and when I headed for the kitchen, Em followed me. "*And*...now you're blushing and running away...!" She cornered me next to the fridge, and her grin was huge. "You weren't working! You skipped school to sleep with Tod!"

"I *was* working." I squeezed past her and pulled two bottles of water from the fridge. "I had to stab someone and that really freaked me out, and he was trying to make me feel better, and I wanted to feel something that wasn't scary, and painful, so..."

Her brows rose in amusement. "And losing your virginity wasn't scary or painful?"

"Well, there was a little pain, but that's a whole different—"

I stopped and scowled when I realized she was kidding. "Why do they call it losing your virginity, anyway? It's not like I don't know where I left it."

Em's brows rose. "You'd be surprised how many people don't. So? Details?" She hopped onto the counter and cracked the lid on her bottle.

I shrugged. "There was a hellion, and a dead woman, and a knife, and a triple helping of trauma."

Em frowned. "Sex, Kaylee. Details about you and Tod, not the demon slaying."

"So glad you're keeping things in perspective." I leaned against the fridge and sipped from my bottle. It worried me that she didn't seem surprised or bothered by the hellion part of the story. That was probably a sign she was spending too much time with me.

"You're gonna be around long enough to slay hundreds of demons—" the thought of which made me sick "—but you only lose your virginity once. So, spill."

But I didn't want to. I wasn't done going over it in my head and I didn't feel like sharing the memory just yet. Even with my best friend. "It's kind of private, Em."

"Bullshit. I told you everything about my first time."

"Yeah, but you may remember that I didn't actually ask you to."

Emma frowned, and I realized I'd hurt her feelings. "Fine. Forget it." She set her bottle down and hopped off the counter, and I had to chase her across the living room.

"Em, wait. I'm sorry." I grabbed her arm and she stopped and turned to face me. "I want to tell you. I just… I don't want to spoil the memory by talking about it. If that makes any sense."

Her eyes widened and she studied my face. Then she smiled.

"Wow. I didn't think talking about my first time could possibly make it worse than it already was."

"What do you mean?"

She laughed, but there was a bitter edge to the sound. "There's not much you can do to further ruin a memory consisting of staticky radio music, the backseat of a Camry, and a three-minute mistake."

"Oh. I'm sorry, Em...."

She waved my apology off. "Forget about mine. I want to hear about yours. Whatever you want to tell me." She reclaimed her water from the kitchen and we sank onto the couch facing each other, and I realized that she'd been waiting for this for more than a year. Since the night of the Camry and the boy who'd barely spoken to her afterward.

I made a mental note to tell Tod how wonderful he was every single time I saw him, for the rest of our afterlives.

"So...?" she prompted, leaving the details up to me.

"So...he's beautiful." I couldn't stop smiling, and my stomach was doing flip-flops over just the memory of the past hour of my life, so blessedly different from the hour before that.

Em rolled her eyes. "I know. Everyone who's ever seen him knows. The Hudsons have freakishly good genes. What else?"

"I love him. Like, to-the-end-of-*time* love him. Is that silly? Because I've truly lost all perspective. Is it naive of me to think he'll be the only one. Like, *ever?*"

Em laughed. "Could you have imagined this moment a year ago? You're up to the hilt of your magical dagger in demon guts one minute, then ready to vow forever to an angel swinging a scythe the next."

"He doesn't actually have a scythe, you know."

"My point stands."

"So, have I lost it? Am I crazy for even mentioning forever?"

Emma shrugged. "Normally I'd say that's the postcoital euphoria talking, but considering that the two of you are facing eternity together, I think you're feeling exactly what you're supposed to be feeling." Emma shrugged. "That said, I don't think you understand how this is supposed to work. Your details are adorable and sweet. Like, *diabetic-coma* sweet. But I'd really appreciate anything in the neighborhood of time, place, or position."

"Position?" I could feel my face flame.

"Never mind. Time and place, then."

"Um, right before you got here. My room."

Em glanced around, suddenly paranoid. "Is he still here?"

"No, he had to go back to work, and I still have to meet with Madeline, so…"

"You want me to go?"

"No, I want you to stay. I told you Thane's back, right?" I said, already hating the change in subject, and she nodded. "Well, he's not alone. Avari's here, Em."

"Here, as in…?"

"In the human world. I don't know how he's doing it, but he killed a woman at the mall, and—" My phone beeped from my pocket, and I pulled it out to find an incomprehensible text from Madeline.

T&# at you3.

I was still frowning at the screen when she materialized in my living room, and Styx started growling from his perch in my father's chair. "I apologize, Kaylee, but there doesn't appear to be enough buttons on my phone to actually type a complete sentence, and I don't see the point of text messaging, when we could just as easily speak on the phone or in person." She stopped when she noticed Emma, who obviously could neither see nor hear her. But she could see me staring at an empty spot in my living room, and she'd been around long enough to know what that meant.

"Tell her to leave," Madeline said, crossing both arms over her chest, phone still clutched in one hand. "We have business to discuss."

"Emma's involved in that business, so she stays."

"This is not up for negotiation, Ms. Cavanaugh." Madeline always used my last name when she was frustrated with me. Which was most of the time.

"Unless you've recruited a new extractor in the past couple of hours, I don't see that you have much of a choice. You need me. We need each other. And Emma is involved, so she gets to hear everything I get to hear." Until and unless I decided that knowing too much would put her in more danger than she was already in.

Madeline scowled, and a week ago, that alone would have made me give in. But not anymore. Not now that I understood just how many people's lives were at stake.

Finally, she nodded and perched on the edge of an armchair, and I knew Em could see her when she jumped a little. "Madeline, this is Emma Marshall. Em, Madeline."

"Pleased to meet you," Madeline said, though she sounded anything but.

Em nodded. "Thanks for letting me join your reindeer games."

"Excuse me?" Madeline said, but before I could explain, the doorbell rang.

I peeked through the window to find Nash and Sabine on my porch, and Luca on the sidewalk behind them. "Great. The gang's all here," I said, pulling the door open.

The necromancer followed Nash and Sabine inside, and suddenly my living room was crowded. Styx decided we'd exceeded the maximum capacity defined by the fire code and started growling at everyone, so I had to put her in the backyard.

"Luca told us you left for an extraction, then never came back," Nash said, eyeing me like I might be secretly broken as I closed the back door.

"I told them you were here with Tod, and that you were fine," Luca added.

"You didn't answer your phone," Nash said. Sabine groaned and pushed my front door shut. "What?" he demanded, scowling at her. "This morning she insists that all we have is one another, but this afternoon she won't answer my calls. How am I supposed to take that?"

"I didn't get any calls," I said, pulling my phone from my pocket again. But there they were. Three missed calls and two voice mails. All from Nash. All between twenty-five and thirty-two minutes earlier. When I was otherwise occupied, and wouldn't have noticed an explosion in the living room, much less my phone buzzing from the pocket of my pants. On my bedroom floor.

I flushed, and Sabine's gaze narrowed on me. "Sorry," I said. "It was on silent. I didn't hear it ring."

"This is not a high-school social," Madeline said. "Your friends will have to leave."

"They don't call them that anymore, Aunt Madeline," Luca said, and it was obvious that only he and Emma could see and hear her.

Madeline frowned. "Friends?"

Luca laughed. "No, socials. They're called dances now."

"Wait a minute, *aunt?*" I said. "You're his aunt?"

"What the hell is going on here?" Sabine demanded, glancing at those of us she could see.

"Okay, that's it!" I stood in the middle of the room and glanced around until I was sure I had everyone's attention.

"We are now operating under a full-disclosure policy. Everyone in this room knows who and what I am, and they all have experiences or skills that could come in handy. So, Madeline, show yourself."

"Ms. Cavanaugh, this is completely inappropriate...."

I turned on her, and my temper got the better of me. "I'm an eleventh-grade girl who was murdered in her own bed by a mystical dagger-wielding incubus posing as a math teacher, about an hour before I was resurrected in order to extract stolen souls from monsters for the rest of my unnatural life. What part of that led you to assume anything I do or say will be appropriate by traditional standards?"

Madeline gaped at me for a second. Then she blinked and nodded. "A valid point."

"Good. Then make yourself visible and introduce yourself to the rest of your crew."

"My crew?"

"What crew? What the hell is going on here, Kaylee?" Nash asked.

I could tell the minute Madeline appeared to the room in general, because both Nash and Sabine focused on her instantly. "Madeline, this is Nash Hudson. You saved him from going down for my murder. And this is Sabine Campbell, his...Nightmare." I wasn't sure how else to explain their relationship. "Madeline is my boss in the reclamation department. And evidently Luca's aunt. That part's new to me."

"Great-great-aunt," Madeline supplied. "I was originally recruited for my own abilities as a necromancer, but they turned out not to extend into the afterlife—evidently being dead interferes with one's ability to detect the dead. When I realized we would need the skills I lost, I brought my nephew on board, because his mother didn't inherit the gift. It seems to skip random generations."

"My parents think I'm at some fancy boarding school, on a soccer scholarship," Luca added with a conspiratorial smile.

"So, what kind of crew is this, and why do you need us on it?" Sabine asked.

"It's the reclamation department," I said, just as Madeline said, "I don't need you."

"The hell you don't," I snapped. "Luca and I are all you have left, and we're not going to be enough against Avari, especially now that he's figured out how to cross over. You're going to need everyone you can get, and everyone in this room except for you and Luca has survived an encounter with Avari, which puts them at the top of a very short list of people who can help you."

And that's when the room exploded into chaos and questions.

"Who and what is Avari?" Madeline asked.

"What do you mean, he can cross over?" Nash demanded, looking more scared than I'd seen him in a long time.

From Sabine: "Why are you and Luca all she has left?"

Em said, "What about Tod? Can't he help? And his boss? What's his name?"

"Okay, one thing at a time." I wanted to bury my head in my hands. Or curl up in bed and pull the covers over my head. Instead, I took a deep breath and sat on the arm of my father's chair. "I don't want to have to repeat this, so everyone get comfortable and listen up."

"Em's right," Sabine said from the kitchen as she helped herself to a soda from the fridge. "If we're looking for people who've survived run-ins with Avari, shouldn't we wait for Tod? And Alec. He'll be more help than anyone else, right?"

"You're right. Call Alec." I nodded to Emma and she started scrolling through the contacts on her phone. "Tod already knows. Madeline can talk to Levi after we're done here, and

I'll hit up my dad and my uncle when they get home from work."

Madeline made a stuffy humphing sound. "Ms. Cavanaugh, this isn't how we at the reclamation department operate."

I raised one brow and eyed her boldly. "As of right now, we *are* the reclamation department, and if you don't jump on board, we'll carry on without you. Frankly, at this point, you're the one with the least to offer."

Madeline fumed visibly, and Sabine laughed out loud. "Damn. Death looks good on you, Kay!"

I ignored her and crossed the room to speak to Madeline in semiprivacy while Emma spoke to Alec on the phone and Nash and Sabine filled Luca in on some basics of dealing with hellions—most of which were no longer relevant, now that Avari could cross over. "Look, I don't mean to be disrespectful, but I think we need to face facts here. Your people are dead because they didn't know what they were up against. We do, and that still may not be enough to protect us, but we're the best shot you have at saving more lives than you can even imagine. Including your nephew's."

Madeline stared into my face, studying me. Looking for something worth putting her trust in. I don't know if she found what she was looking for or just finally truly understood that we were all she had. Either way, she nodded, hesitantly. Then she blinked, and I saw a new fortitude building on her face. And this time when she nodded, she meant it.

While we waited for Alec, Emma and Sabine filled Madeline and Luca in on Avari—all stuff Alec already knew—while Nash and I listened in growing discomfort. It was an odd conversation, at best.

"He's kind of obsessed with Kaylee," Em said, by way of an opener.

"With her soul," Sabine corrected. "Because it's all purer-than-thou, with her being both a martyr *and* a virgin."

I flinched, and Sabine noticed Emma's sudden silence. The *mara*'s focus narrowed on me and her brows rose. I groaned inwardly. She knew. Why did she have to be bitchy *and* perceptive?

"But, um..." Em said when Nash glanced from Sabine to me and frowned. "Avari likes to spread the pain around. He's possessed me and Sabine, and Nash was addicted to his breath for a while. Then again for another while..." Her words faded into uncomfortable silence when Nash tried to obliterate her with only the power of his glare.

"Alec was his servant in the Netherworld for a quarter of a century," Sabine said. "And Tod did this whole drug-trafficking gig for him—"

Madeline frowned, like she was trying to keep it all straight. "Tod is the undead boyfriend?"

"He had no idea what he was carrying," I interjected. "And he had a really good reason."

"A mule should *always* know what he's carrying," Sabine insisted, and I wanted to smack her a little more than usual.

"Okay, clearly you all have very complicated relationships," Madeline said, effectively calling a truce for us all. "But the point seems to be that the hellion in question has had quite a bit of contact with you. I appreciate your willingness to help us deal with him."

"What happened to the others?" Nash asked. "The rest of the department?"

"I suppose the truth is the least that I owe you all." Madeline sighed and glanced at her hands before meeting his gaze again. "Until a couple of months ago, the reclamation department had no real presence in this district, because we weren't needed. But then we got word of an incubus in the area. That happens from time to time. They tend to frequent the same haunts, and we knew that if he was breeding, he'd need a soul for his son. So I was transferred here along with three extractors. As you probably all know, we didn't have a chance to deal with the incubus—Kaylee did that for us. But by then, we'd discovered another problem. Something else had settled into the area and was making unscheduled kills and collecting the souls."

"Avari?" Emma said.

Madeline nodded. "Evidently. But we didn't know that at the time. I sent my extractors after him one at a time, and none of them ever returned. We lost two men before Kaylee died, and I started to panic. That's why we needed her so badly."

"Because she's a *bean sidhe?*" Nash asked.

"Yes. When I found out that a female *bean sidhe* had killed the incubus but lost her own life in the process, I...made some emergency phone calls and arranged to have her restored so I could ask her to join us. We were hoping her unique abilities would give her the edge my other extractors obviously lacked. I only had one left by then, and even though the soul thief kept killing, I held my last extractor back, so he could help run things while I trained Kaylee. Then she proved herself in a dry run—" when I'd been sent to the doughnut shop after Thane "—so I sent my last man after the serial soul thief two days ago. He never came back. Now Kaylee and Luca are all I have left."

"No, you have all of us," Nash said. "There's no way we'd let Kaylee do this alone. Neither will Alec or...my brother."

Em nodded eagerly, and Sabine rolled her eyes at the room in general. "Yeah. I'm all about the greater good. But it's gonna cost you some snacks. I'm starving." She got up to help herself to my kitchen, and I followed to keep her from making a mess I'd get stuck cleaning up.

"There's popcorn in the cabinet over the bar," I said, pointing. "And there's fruit in the fridge." But Sabine didn't even glance in either direction.

"So, was it all you hoped it would be?" she asked, soft enough that no one in the living room could hear.

"What are you talking about?" But I knew. And she knew I knew.

She stepped so close I wanted to back up, but I was already leaning against the counter. "You know, the only thing worse than a self-righteous virgin is a self-righteous *fake* virgin."

"I'm not faking anything." I pulled a bag of popcorn from the cabinet and unwrapped it, then practically threw it into the microwave and pressed some buttons so the noise would cover yet another discussion I really didn't want to have with Sabine. "I'm saying it's none of your business."

"Does Nash know?"

I sighed heavily, wondering if it was too late to take the fifth. "You know he doesn't. And you can't tell him." I took a large salad bowl from the dish drainer and set it next to the microwave.

"He needs to know, Kaylee."

"The hell he does! Are you *trying* to hurt him?"

She exhaled slowly, like *she* was the one fighting for patience. "I'm trying to pull off the Band-Aid and expose the wound so it can heal."

"I don't even know what that means."

"Yes, you do. You ripped Nash's heart out, and instead of dealing with the gaping hole in his chest, he just slapped a bandage over it, so he wouldn't have to see the wound."

"A bandage?"

"Denial. He was avoiding both of you, so he wouldn't have to think about it, and now he thinks he can pretend to be happy with your friendship, and if he plays his cards right and stays clean, you'll realize Tod was just a temporary comfort and everything will go back to the way it was. You and I both know that's not going to happen, but he refuses to see it. But he won't have any choice if he knows that after all those months when you barely let him touch you, you gave it up to his brother after a month."

Anger clouded my judgment and defeated my determination not to have this conversation with her. "Why do you have to make it sound like that? And who the hell are you to question my timing or my relationship with Tod? You can't possibly understand what he and I have been through or what he means to me."

"I'm not questioning anything," Sabine insisted. "And maybe I can't understand all the specifics of your weird-ass, undead relationship, but I *do* understand what he means to you. And Nash needs to understand that, too. Which is why you have to tell him."

"Are you *insane?*" I demanded, and when the microwave beeped, I pulled out the full bag and threw another one in, then pressed more buttons, again for the noise. "Nash is only a month past a relapse, and he's just now speaking to me again. He still won't be in the same room as Tod. And you want to tell him I slept with his brother. Which is none of your business *or* his, for the record."

"Yes, it is. Whether you like it or not, the four of us are all tangled up, Kaylee. And we always will be. Nash loves me, but he loves you, too, even though you're in love with his brother. Whom he currently hates, but can't get rid of. And you're the first girlfriend I've ever had. Can you see those threads, all tied in a knot?"

"I'm not your friend, Sabine." How could I be, after she'd stalked my dreams and given me nightmares, then tried to sell me to Avari so she could have Nash for herself?

She looked hurt for a second, then that familiar obstinacy was back. "Then why did you try to help me with Thane the other night? Nash loves me, and he just stood there, at first, but you tried to come to my rescue. Tod had to hold you back."

"I..." I had no good answer for that. "Fine. I didn't want you to get hurt. But if you want to call yourself my friend, you should know that position comes with boundaries."

Sabine frowned. "I'm no good with boundaries."

"Yes, and the ocean is damp. Can we be done with the understatements now?"

"I'm just trying to help Nash move on."

"Bullshit. You're not thinking about what's good for him. You're thinking about what's good for *you*."

"I *am* what's good for him!" The microwave dinged, then went silent, and she lowered her voice, but not the intensity of her argument. "I'm the only good thing he has left until he starts speaking to his brother and trusting his mother again. But he won't see that as long as he thinks there's a chance for the two of you. He knows you were waiting for the 'right' time to break the world's most damage-resistant hymen and if he finds out that time came and went without him, he'll know the two of you are truly over. And he really needs to know that, Kaylee."

I hate it when she's right.

"He does need to understand that we won't be getting back together," I finally admitted. "But what Tod and I do in private is not up for discussion. I'll think of some other way to show Nash. And, Sabine, if you really want to be my friend, you'll respect that." I dumped both bags of popcorn into the bowl and left her in the kitchen to think about that.

Alec knocked on the door as I set the bowl on the coffee table, and four different people yelled for him to come in. To my house.

"Hey, Kaylee," he said, pulling me into a hug as Luca closed the door behind him. "How's Death treating you?"

"No better than life did." I hugged him back, treasuring one of the few uncomplicated relationships I had. Alec was my friend, and that line was blessedly unblurred by attraction, jealousy, or any feelings of neglect or betrayal. Alec was a drama-free safe zone.

He laughed. "I meant Tod. You know, death with a capital *D*?"

"Ah. More death humor. Never gets old." I let him go and grabbed a handful of popcorn. "Tod's great." I wanted to say more, but Nash was listening, and I didn't want him to think I was rubbing anything in his face.

"Who're they?" Alec whispered, less-than-subtly tossing his head toward Madeline and Luca.

I reached up and turned him by his shoulders to face them both, then cleared my throat to catch everyone's attention. "Madeline is my boss at the reclamation department. She helped me cover up my own murder and clear Nash's name. And Luca is her great-great-nephew. He's a necromancer, which means he sees dead people."

Alec frowned. "Like that kid in the movie?"

"Not really. But close enough," Luca said, crossing the room to shake Alec's hand. "No ghosts, but I see the undead, even when no one else does, and I can sense corpses until they're preserved or start to rot."

Alec shook his hand. "No offense, man, but that's creepy."

I rolled my eyes. "This, coming from a psychic parasite."

"Half," Alec insisted. "*Half*-psychic parasite. My mother was human."

"Okay, so everyone knows everyone else now, right?" I said, and heads all over the room nodded.

"Don't you wanna call in Tod before we get started?" Alec said.

"He's filling in for a missing reaper at the hospital, but he'll be here when he can. He already knows all this, anyway."

"Missing reaper? Is that what this is about?" Alec sank onto the couch and I sat between him and Emma.

"No," Madeline said, just as I said, "Yeah, in part."

"Maybe start from the beginning?" Alec suggested. "For those of us just joining the party?"

"Okay." I took a deep breath and did a mental search for the beginning of the story. "For those who may not know this, Madeline recruited me specifically to help hunt and take out a serial soul thief—"

"I call him Cap'n Crunch," Luca interrupted, and was rewarded with a roomful of frowns. "You know. Because he's a *cereal* thief?"

"Wouldn't that make him more like the Cookie Crook?" Alec said, then shrugged at all the blank stares. "Am I the only one who remembers breakfast food from the eighties?"

"You're the only one who remembers *anything* from the eighties," Nash said, and Madeline frowned.

"That's the wrong kind of 'serial' entirely, and we do not have time for anecdotal tangents. Kaylee, please continue."

Sabine muttered something bitter and profane beneath her breath, and Nash laughed.

"Anyway…" I said. "The serial soul thief turned out to be Avari. Also, he is now officially a serial *killer,* which is how he comes by the souls ready to be stolen."

"So, how's he getting them into the Netherworld?" Alec asked. "Sounds like you're actually looking for whoever's working for him."

"Nope. You know how they say old dogs can't learn new tricks? Well, they're wrong. Avari's figured out how to cross over."

"THAT'S IMPOSSIBLE," ALEC SAID. "HE DOESN'T have a soul. He can't cross over."

"Yeah." Emma tucked her feet beneath her, like she did during scary movies, so nothing evil could grab her ankles from beneath the couch. "The only reason I get any sleep at all anymore is because you told me he couldn't cross over. No way, no how. That's the rule. How is he breaking it now?"

"Kaylee," Madeline said, before I could even try to answer Em. "I've been dead for more than half a century, and my superiors have been here even longer, and in all that time, I've never heard of a hellion crossing through the fog. It can't be done. If it could, they would have taken over the human realm centuries ago."

"The realm? The *whole* realm?" Em was close to panic.

"Stop saying the word *realm*," Sabine said. "I'm having sci-fi convention flashbacks."

"When were you at a sci-fi convention?" Alec asked, and the *mara* shrugged.

"Nerds give good nightmare. They're afraid of everything."

"Could we focus, please!" I snapped. Then I turned to Alec. "If a soul is all that's keeping hellions from crossing over, why has it taken them this long to make the trip? I can think of half a dozen souls Avari's stolen this school year alone."

"It's not that easy," Alec explained. "Devouring a soul isn't the same as having one of your own. He's been trying to make that work for centuries, but once he eats the soul, it's gone, and he can't make it past the fog. To cross over, he'd have to be able to sort of…install a soul in his own body. And that's impossible."

"Well, he's figured something out. I spoke to him here, on the human plane, twice in two days, and both times he was wearing the skin of a dead person. First Scott Carter, then Heidi Anderson."

Em shrugged. "So maybe he's just possessing them, and not really crossing over. Not that that is any less terrifying."

"What's the difference, in practical application?" Luca asked, and I nodded to Alec, tossing the question his way.

"Hellions can only possess the sleeping and unconscious, and even then, only those who have some link to the Netherworld. Possession victims have to have died—even if just for a minute—or have traveled across the fog at least once. And since possession is merely borrowing someone else's body, his abilities would be limited to those his victim already has."

"Like when he possessed Sabine and gave you nightmares?" Em asked, and I nodded, while the *mara* scowled over the reminder that she'd lost control of her own body, even briefly.

"But none of that is applicable here," Alec insisted. "Because he can't possess the dead. No one can. It can't be done. Period."

"Are you sure about that?" Nash asked, and Alec nodded firmly. So Nash turned to me. "Are you sure Scott was already dead when you talked to him? No chance there was a misprint in the obituary?"

I shrugged. "I seriously doubt it. But even if Scott was still alive and Avari was possessing him, that doesn't explain how he showed up as Heidi Anderson. She died seven months ago. No misprint can explain that away."

"Okay, so what do Scott and Heidi have in common?" Sabine asked, glancing at each of us in turn.

"You've never met them?" Nash said.

Sabine gave an exaggerated nod. "And I never will. Because they're both dead."

"Which means they're no longer using their souls..." I said, starting to catch on. Then I turned to Alec. "He's figured it out. Somehow, Avari's figured out how to install a soul in his body. Or whatever."

"Not possible," Alec said again, but no one was listening to him.

"And that makes him look like the person the soul belongs to?" Em asked.

"More likely—assuming any of this is true—it makes him take the form that soul last took," Madeline said. "Souls don't really belong to anyone, once they've departed their most recent bodies. They'll be recycled, and they've been recycled before. But until that happens, they retain the psychic memory of the life they just lived, including perfect recall of the physical form."

"It's much more than that," Alec insisted. "Disembodied souls retain much more than a psychic memory. If they didn't, how would hellions be able to torture them for all of eternity? Life has two parts," Alec said, leaning forward on the couch, and I was both amused and relieved to realize that everyone else leaned toward him a little, ready and willing to hear the wisdom that could save us all.

"There's the physical body, and the soul—the life force that supports it. When the body dies, a reaper takes the soul to be recycled, but that process isn't death like we understand it. The soul doesn't cease to exist. It's just wiped clean of the existence it supported most recently. Until then, the soul still thinks and feels, and it can be tortured for a hellion's pleasure or nutrition. So if Avari has figured out how to install a soul in his body, what he's actually discovered is how to absorb a human life force, something he, as a hellion, lacks entirely. And if he's really figured that out, we are all—all seven billion of us—in very big trouble."

"Okay, you're really starting to freak me out," Em said, and her voice trembled.

"Good." Alec reached over my lap to squeeze her hand, but his tone of voice lacked any comforting qualities. "If Kaylee's right, we should all be very freaked out. And we should be willing to do whatever it takes to stop Avari from crossing over, much less handing out tickets to the rest of his hellion garden club."

"Okay, let's talk strategy," Madeline said, and I couldn't help noticing that no one had touched the popcorn. "But first, Kaylee, where is the soul you extracted?"

"Um, the dagger's in the bathroom. I'll get it."

"The dagger?" Madeline frowned, and I realized I hadn't actually made my report to her yet.

"Yeah. Avari had it when I got there. He said my amphora wouldn't work on him—maybe because of whatever method he's found of crossing over?—and that the other extractors died because they didn't have my dagger."

"How did *he* get it?" Alec asked, his forehead deeply furrowed in concern.

"I'm assuming he took it from my room." And that was one of the scarier parts of this whole thing. "He obviously has at least some of the standard undead abilities when he crosses over."

"Let me see this dagger, please," Madeline said, and I stood, but Nash was already up.

"I got it," he said. "I'm headed that way, anyway."

"Thanks," I said as he crossed the living room toward the hall. "If we're right about Avari figuring out how to harness a human soul, there should be two in the dagger. Heidi Anderson's, and the soul of the woman Avari killed in the restroom." I frowned with another realization. "Well, make that three, with Beck's." And I couldn't help wondering how many souls the dagger could hold.

"So, tell us everything you remember about both encounters with him," Madeline said, and to my amusement, she pulled a small leather-bound notebook from an inside pocket of her jacket and started taking notes. "Did he have a physical form that you could tell? Or was he more of a specter?"

"There's no such thing as ghosts, Aunt Madeline," Luca said.

"Yes, but most varieties of the undead have a spectral form," she insisted, and a lightbulb went off in my head.

"That's what that's called?" I wasn't invisible; I was *spectral.* "Anyway, he was truly physically there, in both cases. I touched him. But no one else in the mall could see either of us."

"Kaylee, what the hell happened?" Nash asked, and I looked up to find him standing in the living-room doorway with my dagger in one hand, my bloody shirt in the other.

I shrugged. "Turns out extracting a soul from a hellion involves actually stabbing it to death. It was totally traumatic."

Madeline stood and took the dagger by the hilt, then held it up to the light as she examined it. "Hellion-forged steel..." she muttered, turning the blade over. "It's inscribed, but I don't recognize the language." Finally she lowered the dagger and met my gaze. "It appears to function as an amphora in a basic, rather barbaric fashion."

"Yeah. I gathered that when I barbarically stabbed a girl-shaped demon with it. Thus the trauma."

"There was actual blood?" She set the dagger on the coffee table, then took my shirt from Nash and held it up for a better view.

"Yup. Blood. Melodrama. Threats. He said that if I didn't stab him, he was going to kill this little girl carrying a balloon. Why would he do that? Why would he volunteer to die?"

"Because he knew it would traumatize you, and your trauma is like his chocolate-fudge brownie," Alec said. "It's yummy."

Sabine shrugged. "That, and as a message."

"What's the message?" Em asked.

"That we're nothing to him. We're ants on the sidewalk, so small compared to his foot that he can't even squish us one at a time. By making you banish him from one stolen body, he's pointing out that he can get another one anytime, anywhere," the *mara* said, and for about the billionth time, her insight scared me. More than ever, in fact, because this time she was demonstrating understanding of a hellion's thought process.

"Well, the souls in the dagger should verify some of this for us," Madeline said, exchanging the knife on the coffee table for my shirt. "And if this Heidi Anderson's soul is among them, I'd call that fairly conclusive proof that Avari has in fact discovered how to wear the souls of the dead on the human plane."

"The real question is how he got her soul in the first place," Nash said. "Scott's, I can understand. He could have sent Thane to kill him, or Avari might have done his own dirty work, if he was already on the human plane by then. But Heidi died months ago, and Avari didn't get her soul."

"How do you know that?" Madeline asked, and the unease churning deep in my stomach swelled.

He shrugged. "Because Belphegore got it."

"Who is Belphegore?" Madeline and her nephew asked in unison, and even Alec looked confused.

"She's the hellion of vanity my aunt made a deal with. Aunt Val hired a rogue reaper named Marg to collect the souls of five innocent, beautiful young women to trade in exchange for her own eternal youth and beauty. Heidi was the first of them. Marg tried to take my cousin Sophie's soul as the fifth, and my aunt traded herself for her daughter. Belphegore got all five souls, including my aunt's."

"Sophie's mom died to save her?" Luca said.

"Yeah, and she's only known that for a few weeks." Since the night I'd died and her father had come clean about the family secret.

"So, Belphegore is involved in this, too?" Emma had all but curled into a ball. Hers had been one of the souls Marg tried to take, and the minute and a half she was dead had made her eligible for possession by Avari, or any other hellion who decided to try.

"Sounds like it. How else would Avari get Heidi's soul?" I said. Em had tears in her eyes. I gave her a hug, but that was the best I could do until someone invented a Band-Aid for pure terror. "I think we need to face the fact that Avari will be back, but we have no way of knowing where, when, or in what form."

My dad got home from work shortly after Madeline left to extract and identify the souls in my dagger. She promised to fill Levi in and ask for his help.

When my dad heard what was going on, he immediately called both Harmony Hudson and my uncle Brendon, who showed up twenty minutes later with Sophie in tow. Our poor little house had never been so full, but everyone agreed that we had strength in numbers.

Everyone except Styx, who barked to be let back in, then walked around growling at everyone she didn't know until I finally closed her in my bedroom to keep everyone from being bitten by a nervous half Nether-hound.

Sophie was sullen and uncooperative until Luca emerged from the bathroom, at which point she recruited him to help her take dinner orders and make a run to my dad's favorite Chinese restaurant.

For the next hour, everything we'd already discussed was dissected ad nauseam over cardboard cartons of rice and noodles, and at some point, I realized I'd rather pull my hair out and spend eternity bald than have to explain one more time that I didn't *know* how Avari had done what he'd done, or what he was up to.

After dinner, my uncle Brendon took Luca for a drive around town—Sophie insisted on going—to see if he could sense either Thane or Mareth, who had yet to turn up. We were pretty sure Thane had snatched her and taken her to Avari, but no one wanted to admit defeat on that front. Not yet, anyway. And we still had no idea why Avari wanted another reaper.

Tod turned up as they were leaving and took one look around at the chaos and the mess, then tugged me toward my room to escape the noise. "There are several advantages to invisibility," he said, closing the door at his back.

"The word of the day is *spectral,*" I said as my arms slid around his neck. "We're not invisible right now, we're *spectral.*"

"I don't care what you call it, so long as it's just the two of us. It's crazy in there."

"Yeah, but it could be worse. I, um, wasn't able to keep this afternoon a total secret."

"This afternoon?" He glanced at the bed for confirmation, and I could feel myself flush as I nodded. "Em, right?" he said, and I nodded again. "Kaylee, I don't care who knows, as long as you're comfortable with it. Assuming you made me sound good."

I laughed. "She didn't get the details she was hoping for." I sat on the edge of my desk and pulled him closer, one hand on his chest as I looked into his eyes. "That's between us."

"I'm good with that...." He leaned in for a kiss, but I stopped him.

"Sabine knows, too."

Tod's brows rose, and he leaned back for a better look into my eyes. "I didn't think you two were that close."

"We're not. She's crazy perceptive and psychotically honest."

"Meaning...?"

"She wants to tell Nash."

Tod frowned. "I don't see how that could possibly be good for his ego. Especially if you told the story the way *I* remember it." He grinned, trying to lighten the mood, but I couldn't even summon a smile.

"I don't want to hurt him any more than we already have. I told her that if she values our friendship, she'll keep her mouth shut."

"You're friends now?"

"If that'll keep her from spewing our personal business in front of the entire world, then, yes. We're friends."

"Sophie?" I set my backpack on the ground next to my usual lunch table, surprised to find my cousin sitting on it. I was almost always the first to reach the quad—a benefit of having no third-period class—but even when someone beat me there, it wasn't Sophie. My cousin had never once sat at my table. In two years, she'd rarely even glanced our way without throwing an insult at me.

This time she just blinked at me and brushed blond hair behind her shoulder. "Hey."

My frown deepened. If she hadn't spoken with her own voice, I'd assume she'd been possessed—that had certainly happened before. "Is something wrong?"

"No." She frowned and reconsidered. "Well, yes. Everything's wrong. But no one would know that better than you, I guess."

"I meant, why are you here?"

She shrugged. "I'm meeting Luca. I have yet to convince him that he doesn't have to sit in the social wasteland."

"And you honestly think he'd be more comfortable in the intellectual wasteland?" I tossed a pointed glance at the table where she and her jock friends had been sitting every day of the two years she'd been at Eastlake.

Sophie exhaled and nodded, and I waited for verbal venom that never came. "I guess I deserve that. I just..." She hesitated, glancing at the grass for a moment before meeting my gaze again. "I never got a chance to tell you that I'm sorry for what happened to you that night. With Mr. Beck."

Except that she'd had plenty of chances. She just hadn't taken any of them.

"Oh." I crossed my arms over my chest. "You mean the night I was brutally murdered in my own bed?"

Sophie flinched. "You don't have to make it sound so..."

"So what? True? Because it's true."

"So...*ugly*." Her face scrunched up, like she found the word personally offensive. Or maybe it was the truth that offended her. "You don't have to go for the shock factor with every weird-ass sentence that comes out of your mouth. Especially considering that you got a happy ending."

"Happy ending?" I couldn't pile enough disbelief into my voice to accurately express how much of it I was dealing with. "What part of 'walking corpse' sounds like a happy ending to you? The part where I'll never reach the age of consent or the legal drinking age?" Not that either of those really mattered anymore. "Or the part where there's still a demon from another dimension out to get my soul, and willing to go through everyone I love to get to me? I understand that there's a discrepancy between the way the world really looks and the way you see it, but I think you need to open your eyes a little wider."

Irritation flared behind her gaze. "I'm trying to apologize, Kaylee, and you're not making that very easy."

"So sorry to have inconvenienced you with the truth. Go ahead. I'm listening."

Yes, I was being hard on her. But life would be even harder on her, assuming she survived long enough to graduate. And with Avari on the warpath, there was no guarantee of that at all.

"Look. My dad said you saved my life that night," Sophie said, and I shrugged. I'd actually saved her life several times, but who was counting? "So I wanted to say thank you, and tell you I'm sorry for all the mean things I said about you being a crazy freak before. I swear I had no idea those weren't personal life choices."

I didn't know whether to pity her or smack her. Fortunately, the decision was taken out of my hands when the bell rang and students started pouring into the quad with lunch trays.

Nash and Sabine arrived first, but Luca was only a minute behind, and one glance at what passed for chili on their trays was enough to make me grateful that I didn't have to eat ever again, if I chose.

"Is my brother here?" Nash asked, sliding onto the bench seat across from me and next to Sabine. Sophie sat on his other side, so she could stare across the table at Luca.

"No, and I don't know if he will be. He has to cover all the hospital shifts, with Mareth gone. Levi's filling in for him tonight, though, so he can do a shift at the pizza place."

"Because delivering pizza is more important than reaping souls?" Sophie's brows rose as she took a carrot from Luca's tray.

"Spoken like someone who doesn't have to cover her own cell-phone bill. Or make her own car payment. Or buy her own clothes," Sabine said, and I realized it would be hard for me to choose sides in a Sophie/Sabine cage match.

"So who pays *your* cell bill?" Sophie asked.

"It's a prepaid phone," Nash supplied, and from the look on his face, I could tell he regretted sitting between them.

"And how does she prepay for it?"

Sabine leaned around Nash to glare at Sophie, and I swear a cloud rolled across the sun and the whole quad got darker. "Don't ask questions you don't want answers to."

"Okay, truce!" Luca threw his arms out across the table, like an umpire declaring the batter safe. "Let's talk business before Jayson gets here." Em had been holding him back at the beginning of every lunch period—I could only guess her method of distraction—to give us a chance to talk about something more important than prom and postgraduation parties.

"Was your aunt able to ID the souls in the dagger?" I asked. The knife had been on my desk when I got out of the shower that morning, but Madeline hadn't waited around to talk to me.

"Yeah. You were right. Other than the incubus, there were

two souls, and one of them has been missing for seven months. It was last reported in the possession of a rogue reaper Levi says he killed." Marg, of course. "They have no reason to doubt that Belphegore ended up with the soul, and as for how Avari got it from her... Their guess is as good as ours."

Which meant we had yet to uncover the connection between Avari and Belphegore, or figure out what Avari wanted with the reapers.

"Did you find Thane?" I asked. Thanks to Tod, I already knew Mareth was still missing. Tod was pretending that didn't worry him, but how could it not?

"No." Luca exhaled heavily. "Either he's left town, or he's left the human realm altogether."

"My money's on the latter," Sabine said, and Sophie laughed so hard she nearly choked on a carrot.

"What money?"

Sabine stood, fists clenched, and Nash pulled her back down.

"Sophie, Sabine beat up a reaper two nights ago," I said. "And it's entirely possible that she may one day be the only thing standing between you and a hellion ready to rip your head off and suck out your soul. Do you really think it's wise to piss her off?"

Sophie glanced from me to Sabine, then back, scowling. "I'm not scared of her. I can handle myself."

"Yeah, and hissing kittens think they're badass, too," Sabine said.

"Okay, listen," I said, and I couldn't quite shake the discomfort of having all four sets of eyes turned my way. I wasn't used to being the center of attention, and the recent media coverage of my so-called attempted murder had done nothing to change that. But someone had to say what needed to be said. "Everyone here has some reason to dislike everyone else at this table. Except for Luca," I added when he started to object. "But we don't have the time or energy to waste hating one another, so from here on out, everyone gets a clean slate. No more grudges. Got it?"

"You know that's a lot easier said than done, Kaylee," Nash said softly, and we all knew he was thinking about Tod. About a betrayal he didn't think he could forgive. But he was wrong about that.

"Yeah, I know. But I'm willing to—" The rest of that sentence died on my tongue as my gaze snagged on something behind him. A girl in a green-and-white-letter jacket, watching me from the edge of the quad, half-hidden by the brick wall of the building.

"Kaylee?" Nash twisted to see what I was looking at.

I stood and the girl smiled at me. My heart stopped beating.

No. It couldn't be.

But it was.

Meredith Cole. Sophie's fellow dance-team member, who'd died last September, here in the quad. I'd screamed for her soul. Which Marg the reaper had then given to Belphegore, the hellion of vanity.

Meredith was back, and that could only mean one thing.

"Shit," Luca mumbled, and in my peripheral vision—I didn't dare let Meredith out of my sight—I saw him scrub one hand over his face and through his hair. "There's a body. In the parking lot, I think."

I grabbed my backpack and climbed over the bench seat as Meredith disappeared around the building. I took off after her, dodging tables and kids with trays, and I ran right past Emma and Jayson, who stared after me in surprise.

"Kaylee!" Nash shouted, and footsteps pounded on the ground behind me, but I couldn't tell how many of my friends were following me. And I could only hope the rest of the student body hadn't decided to come watch whatever drama they imagined we were playing out.

I chased Meredith around the corner of the building and she stopped halfway to the parking lot and turned to face me. I slowed to a walk and my grip tightened around the strap of my bag as I pulled the zipper open with my free hand.

"Avari?" I said so softly I could barely hear myself.

"Who else?" the hellion said in Meredith's voice. "I thought this ensemble most appropriate for a visit during school hours. However, I'm not sure I got the smile quite right. How does she look on me?" He spread Meredith's arms, inviting me to inspect her. She looked exactly like she had the day she'd died. Letter jacket. Skirt that barely passed the dress code. Too-thin legs. Honey-brown ponytail. This was beyond creepy. I was being haunted by everyone I'd ever failed to save—all the ghosts of my past.

Dickens was probably rolling over in his grave.

"Who'd you kill?" I demanded as several sets of footsteps slowed to a stop behind me.

Meredith cocked her head to one side. "I didn't ask his name. I only asked if he knew you, and when he was finished soiling himself—evidently he recognized my disguise—he managed to say that he shares a class with you."

My backpack shook in my grip. Another death laid at my doorstep. Another classmate dead for no reason. Who would be next? One of my friends? A member of my family? I could hardly see through the horror clouding my vision. I couldn't let this go on.

"I warned you, Ms. Cavanaugh, yet you greedily cling to your soul, when you could have spared your friends and classmates another loss."

"Meredith?" Sophie's voice was a shocked whisper as she slowed to a stop at my side, and I glanced back just long enough to make sure no one else—no one human—had followed us out of the quad. They hadn't, but that couldn't last long.

I tried to step in front of my cousin, but she shoved me away, her eyes wide and filled with tears.

"Get her out of here," I said to Luca. He tried to lead her away, but she wouldn't go.

"Meredith?" she said again, and I could hear the tears in her voice.

To my horror, the hellion answered, in Meredith's voice. "Don't let them hurt me, Sophie. Your crazy cousin wants to kill me."

"Kaylee?" Sophie demanded, and on the edge of my vision, I saw Nash move to help Luca with her. "No! Get off me!" She shoved their hands away. "Kaylee, is that Meredith?"

"No. Meredith is dead." I didn't dare look away from the hellion as he watched her, a quiet smile turning up one corner of his stolen mouth, enjoying her confusion and pain.

"So are you!" Sophie hissed, pushing Nash away. If she threw a fit, people would come running. We had to keep her quiet and get her away from the hellion. "Is Meredith back? You can't kill her! I won't let you!"

"Sophie, get out of here and let me do my job." I desperately didn't want her to be there when I had to stab a monster who looked like one of her friends.

Luca stepped in front of Sophie, blocking her view of the hellion, and when she tried to step around him, he wrapped both arms around her—more hug than restrictive hold. He spoke into her ear, so softly I could hardly hear him. "I don't know who Meredith is, but if Kaylee says that's not her, then that's not her. That's not even her corpse—you have my word."

"Then what is that? What the hell *is* that?" Her voice went shrill and terrified, and for the first time I thought I heard a little of her mixed-blood *bean sidhe* heritage leaking through. "What's going on? What does it want?"

"I came back for you, Sophie," the Meredith-thing said. "Come with me. You belong in hell. That's where all snotty little bitches wind up eventually, anyway." The hellion's lips curled up into a creepy smile, and Sophie screamed.

Luca and Nash tried to cover her mouth, but her lungs were powerful and her voice was shrill.

I reached into my backpack and pulled the dagger from an inside pocket. I'd had to blink straight into the school building to get it past the metal detectors, and now I was glad I'd gone to the extra trouble.

The hellion was drinking up Sophie's trauma, but Meredith's eyes narrowed on me when she saw the blade, and she spread her arms. "This is my favorite part," Avari said with Meredith's voice. "Until next time..."

I drove the dagger through her stomach and up into her chest.

"SOPHIE." I KNELT IN FRONT OF MY COUSIN AND Luca on the spring grass, but she wouldn't look at me. She wouldn't look at anything. She just clung to Luca, staring at the letter jacket that had remained after Meredith disappeared. Her name was on the back and several dance-themed pins were attached to the green letter *E*. "Sophie, I need you to focus."

Finally she blinked and started to look up. But then her gaze snagged on the bloody dagger still in my hand—I couldn't put it in my backpack until I'd cleaned it—and she turned away from me and buried her face in Luca's shoulder.

"Was that him?" she said, her words muffled by the material of his shirt. "Was that the hellion we saw in the Netherworld?"

I thought I'd heard her wrong until Luca answered, stroking her hair with one hand. "I couldn't swear to it, but my guess would be yes."

"What? When were you two in the Netherworld?" I asked, and Luca shrugged.

"The day we met. That's kind of...how we got together. She's stronger than you think she is, you know."

I certainly hoped he was right. "I'm gonna want to hear that story when things calm down. But for now, Sophie, Sabine's going to take you to Nash's house and I want you to stay there with her. We'll tell the school you went home sick." Nash could make them believe it without question, at least long enough to excuse her absence, and Avari would be less likely to look for her at his house than at mine. "I'll drive your car home later. Okay?"

Sophie shook her head sluggishly, but her eyes were clearer. "I'm not going anywhere with her." Her gaze flicked up to where Sabine watched her over my shoulder.

"You're not my idea of a good time, either," Sabine snapped. Then she glared at the rest of us. "You guys need me here."

"No, I need you to stay with Sophie in case Avari goes after her." I needed someone who could fight, if necessary. Luca had volunteered for the job, but we needed him to take us to the corpse in the parking lot.

"If she makes one snotty comment, you won't have to worry about the hellion killing her. I'll save him the trouble."

"Sabine!" I stood and turned on her, but she only shrugged and held her ground, not the least bit intimidated by the bloody dagger in my hand or the fact that I'd just killed Avari. Again.

"I'm a Nightmare, Kaylee. You want me to scare someone to death? I'm your girl. But I'm not cut out to be a babysitter."

"Just don't let anyone kill her. It's not that complicated," I snapped, and Sabine scowled at me. "Look, lunch will be over in a few minutes, and I need to get her out of here. Just take her to Nash's, and I'll be there as soon as I can. If you're really my friend, you'll do this."

The *mara*'s scowl deepened. "You know, you were much less work as a nemesis." Then she stomped off toward her car with my cousin in tow, and too late I realized I should have specified that she wasn't allowed to feed on my traumatized cousin's fears.

While Nash went to the office to influence the attendance secretary into signing Sophie out, I blinked into the teachers' restroom and locked the door, then cleaned the dagger and put on the letter jacket Nash had lent me to cover the blood on my shirt.

At my current rate of consumption, I wouldn't have a shirt left in my closet by the end of the next week.

When I was fit to be seen again—just in case—I met Nash in the parking lot and Luca led us to a dusty blue compact car, where Brant Williams was slumped behind the wheel.

"No!" Nash reached for the door handle, but I stepped in front of him and refused to move when he tried to reach around me. "Kaylee, get the hell out of my way!" He and Brant had been teammates in both football and baseball since Nash transferred to Eastlake. There were tears in his eyes, and even more half-choking his voice, but I stood my ground.

"No fingerprints, Nash."

"I'll say I found him," he insisted. "They'd expect me to try to help him."

"You can't be the one to find him." I waited for understanding to surface among the agonized twists of brown and green in his eyes, and when it didn't, I said what I'd been trying to avoid. "You were arrested as a suspect in a double homicide a month ago. You don't need to pop up on the police department's radar again this soon. The line between witness and suspect can get really thin."

Nash flinched like I'd slapped him, and he couldn't quite

hide the twist of resentment in his eyes. It was my fault he was on their radar in the first place. "How long am I going to be paying for the fact that I didn't kill you, Kaylee?"

Before I could even make sense of what he was asking, the bell rang, and all three of us jumped, and when I tried to make Nash go to class, he refused. I couldn't really blame him.

A glance into Brant's car told me the doors were locked and he wasn't breathing, but I blinked into the car to check his pulse just in case, careful not to touch anything else.

He was dead. And I wanted to throw up. We'd never been close, but I'd known Brant since the third grade. He was one of the basketball team captains and one of few Eastlake baseball players other than Nash that I'd ever spoken to outside of school. He was a nice guy. And now he was dead. Because of me.

My hands were shaking when I rejoined Luca and Nash next to the car. "I'm sorry, Luca, but you have to find the body." I couldn't do it. My shirt was covered in blood.

Luca looked sick. But he nodded. "What do I say about why I was in the parking lot?"

"Do you have a license?" I asked, and he nodded again. "Tell them you told Sophie you'd drive her car home, and you found Brant just like this."

"Okay." He pulled his phone from his pocket, ready to call either 9-1-1 or the front office. I didn't ask which.

"You sure you're good with this?" Nash asked, his voice grim, his forehead deeply furrowed.

"Yeah." Luca started pressing buttons. "You two get out of here. And call my aunt."

I promised him I would, then I took my backpack in one hand and Nash's hand in the other and blinked us into his living room, after a stop behind a convenience store about halfway between.

Sophie sat on the couch in tears, and she nearly jumped out of her own skin when we appeared right in front of her. "Where's Luca?" she said, frowning when he didn't appear with us.

"At school discovering Brant's body."

"Brant Williams?" More tears filled her eyes. "Brant's dead? How? What happened?"

"That hellion you saw? That's Avari. He tortures and kills people for fun. Which is why he pretended to be Meredith—to hurt you." I couldn't tell how much of that she'd actually heard over her own sniffling, but she had enough to process already. "Where's Sabine?" I asked when a cursory glance into the kitchen revealed no disgruntled *mara*.

"Back there somewhere." Sophie gave a tearful glance down the hall, and I turned to look just as Sabine stepped out of Nash's room with a half-full bottle of tequila.

"Hell, no." I grabbed for the bottle as she stepped into the living room, but she pulled it out of my reach. "The last thing we need right now is a drunk Nightmare."

"In case you haven't noticed, your cousin's a bit of a delicate flower." Sabine gestured toward Sophie, who still sat curled up on one end of the couch, in spite of Nash's best efforts to comfort her. "So you can give her a shot, and hope that makes her a little easier for me to stomach, or you can give *me* a shot and hope *that* makes her a little easier for me to stomach. Otherwise, I'm outta here." The *mara* shrugged. "Your call."

I sighed, digging my phone out of my pocket. "Fine. Give her a shot. *One*." Was that really any worse than the pills her mother had given her when Meredith died the first time? At least you don't need a prescription for tequila.

Sabine produced a shot glass from her pocket, and while I texted Tod, I tried not to worry about the fact that Nash had a bottle of tequila in his room and Sabine carried a shot glass in her pocket.

@ Nash's. Can u come?

Tod appeared in front of the television just as Sabine handed the full shot glass to Sophie. "What's going on?"

"Nothing new," Sabine said as my cousin took a sip from the shot glass, then grimaced. "Just getting a cheerleader drunk."

"She's not a cheerleader. She's a dancer," I said, sliding my phone into my pocket.

"Wow. Look how much of a damn I don't give." Sabine pushed the shot glass back at Sophie. "What, you're too precious to drink it straight?" She twisted to glance around the room. "Anybody got some lime and a cute little paper umbrella?"

"I'll get her a chaser." Nash headed for the kitchen without a word to his brother.

Tod glanced at me with one brow raised, and I sighed. "Avari showed up at school as Meredith Cole, another one of the girls Marg killed for Belphegore. Meredith was on Sophie's dance team, and we all saw her die last September."

"Seeing a classmate return from the dead would freak anyone out," Tod said as we both watched Sabine try to get my cousin to drink.

"Yeah, but he made an effort to upset Sophie specifically. I'm worried he'll go after her next."

"What's with the jacket?" Tod asked as Nash crossed the room with a glass of soda.

"Oh." I'd forgotten I was wearing it. "I ruined another shirt." I unsnapped Nash's letter jacket and pulled it off, then laid it over the arm of the nearest chair.

"You know, there's a much easier, simpler way to sedate her," Tod whispered as Sophie downed half the shot, then gulped the soda Nash handed her.

I rolled my eyes. "No, you can't knock her out. She's traumatized, but she'll come around." She'd evidently survived a trip to the Netherworld, which told me that as upset as she was about Meredith, Luca was right. She was stronger than she looked. She had to be. "I have to text Madeline." I sank into the chair, typing with both thumbs, and Tod sat on the arm opposite Nash's jacket.

"I get that that was a hellion." Sophie leaned back on the couch, clutching the glass of soda as she stared at the shot glass standing empty on the coffee table. "But why did it look like Meredith? Why did it *sound* like Meredith?"

Sabine picked up the shot glass and refilled it. "It looked and sounded like your dancing chick because it was wearing her soul like a raincoat."

"We don't know that for sure," I insisted as Sabine tossed the shot back.

"Sure we do. But on the bright side, Kaylee freed her soul, so she's no longer being tortured in the Netherworld."

"Tortured?" Sophie's chin quivered, and Sabine nodded, pouring another shot.

I stood and grabbed the bottle from her, and tequila splashed onto the coffee table. "We can't afford for you to be at less than your best right now."

"Kaylee, we just watched you stab the undead cheerleader who threatened to drag your cousin into hell. I think we could all use a drink."

"You just had one."

Sophie was sniffling again. "Why would a demon want to torture Meredith? Or send me to hell?"

"Can't imagine," Tod said. "Got any sins you wanna confess? Something in the vein of narcissism and cruelty?"

"It's not hell," I said, elbowing him. "It's the Netherworld."

"What's the difference?" Sophie wiped her nose, glaring at Tod.

Sophie's question was rhetorical, but Sabine huffed in reply anyway. "Hellions vacation in hell to cool off."

"Not helping, Bina." Nash sank onto the couch next to Sophie and took her hand. "It has nothing to do with you, personally. This particular hellion has been around for thousands of years and has been directly or indirectly responsible for more deaths than any of us can even imagine. His breath killed Doug Fuller. He killed Mr. Wesner, Mr. Wells, and Mrs. Bennigan at school. This afternoon, he killed Brant Williams in his own car. And even if he didn't personally kill Scott, he's ultimately responsible for his death."

"Why?" Snot dripped from Sophie's nose and she wiped it with the back of one hand. "He tried to lock me up in the Netherworld and now he's killing everyone I know. Why is this happening to me?"

Sabine rolled her eyes. "Because you're the beautiful fairy princess and the evil Lord of Hell can't secure his kingdom until he's feasted from your flesh and slaked his thirst with tea brewed from the ashes of your incinerated bones."

Nash groaned, and Tod laughed out loud.

Sophie hiccuped and turned to me, frowning. "Is she serious?"

"This isn't happening to *you,* princess," Sabine snapped before I could do more than shake my head. "This is happening to *us.* While you spent the past few months prancing around in ignorant bliss, we were all being possessed, or kidnapped, or stalked by this hellion. So dry your tears and take off the tiara, because this is a call to arms, not a pity party. You're not going to find any sympathy here."

"Okay, that's enough," I said. "She's still new to the horror." And the truth was that she'd been involved in most of this from the very beginning. She just hadn't known it.

"I'm only showing her the bigger picture," Sabine insisted. "She needs to understand what's really going on."

"I understand." Sophie reached for the shot glass and held it out to me with one shaky hand. "So I'm gonna need one more of those."

I hesitated, until I noticed that Sophie's eyes were already glazed with shock. "Fine." I poured one more shot for her, then screwed the lid on the bottle. "But that's it. I'm not putting my life in the hands of a bunch of drunks."

My phone buzzed in my pocket so I handed the bottle to Tod and dug my cell out so I could answer it. "Hello?"

Luca's number was on the screen, but I couldn't understand whatever he whispered into my ear, so I had to shush the rest of the room so I could hear him. "Sorry. I'm in the office, so this'll have to be quick. Is Tod with you?"

"Yeah. Why?"

His voice dropped even lower, and I glared at Sabine, who was still talking to Nash. "There's someone at your house. Someone *like you,* and it's not Aunt Madeline. If it's not Tod, either, my guess is Thane…."

"Shit. Okay, thanks."

"How's Sophie?" he asked, before I could hang up.

"Shaken. But she's dealing."

"What's up?" Tod asked as I pocketed my phone.

"Luca says there's a walking corpse at my house. His guess is Thane."

I stood already heading for the door before I remembered

that I hadn't driven, and that walking would be a ridiculous waste of time. I held my hand out and Tod took it. "Ready?"

Nash stood. "I'm coming, too."

"No way." Sabine scowled. "You are not leaving me here with Ballerina Barbie."

"Call her dad," I said. "But if she's drunk when he gets here, *you* can explain how that happened." I glanced at Nash, holding up the half-empty bottle. "Any more where this came from?"

He shook his head. "You still have my whiskey." Because he'd left it at my house the night he showed up on my porch, and my dad had confiscated it.

"Good. Let's go." I took Nash's hand and glanced at Tod. "See you on the other side." Then I blinked us both into my living room, which I could only do over short distances. Fortunately, Nash only lived a few blocks from my house.

Tod appeared in my living room as I let go of Nash's hand and set the tequila on the coffee table.

"Good thinking," Thane said, and I whirled around to find him standing in my kitchen, holding an open bag of my dad's favorite tortilla chips. "I was getting thirsty." His empty white eyes made it impossible to tell what he was looking at, and my skin crawled as I stared at him.

Nash and Tod started across the living room toward him, and their combined rage made the hairs on my arms stand up. In that moment, watching them face a mutual enemy, I caught a glimpse of just how powerful a force they could be together—if I could keep Nash busy fighting someone other than his brother.

But Thane held up one hand. "I'll be gone before you get halfway here, and then you'll never know what I came to tell you."

"Did Avari send you?" Tod stopped and hauled his brother

back by one arm when Nash didn't stop on his own. Nash jerked free of his grip, but stayed put.

"Where's the other one? That feisty little *mara?*" Thane said. "Is she going to jump out of a closet somewhere and yell 'boo'?"

"Are you going to deliver whatever threat Avari sent you with, or are we going to have to start guessing?" Tod said. "I gotta warn you, I'm insanely good at charades."

"There's no message. I'm jumping ship. But I need your help."

"Why the hell would we help you?" Nash demanded as I edged around them for a better view.

"Because I know what Avari's doing, and how he's doing it."

"And, what?" I said. "You've reached the limit on how many secret evil schemes you can keep a lid on? We're supposed to trust you because you conveniently show up with answers when we need them most?"

Thane set the chip bag on the counter behind him and shrugged. "You're going to trust me because I'm all you have. Unless you want Avari to keep picking off your friends and family one by one until he gets what he wants."

"Start talking," Nash growled, but Thane shook his head slowly.

"I'm not saying a word until you swear you'll help me."

"Help you with what?" I asked, arms crossed over my chest. I wasn't convinced he wasn't just playing another of Avari's games. But I believed that he hated the hellion as much as we did, and that gave us a common goal. Potentially.

"He has my soul. I want you to swear you'll get it back for me."

"Why would you trust us to do that?" Nash said.

"I wouldn't trust the two of you to hit the pot when you

piss. I trust *her.*" He pointed at me, and they both turned to follow his blank-eyed gaze. "If she gives me her word, she won't break it."

"How do you know that?" I asked.

"Because you're trustworthy and you have a hero complex. That's why Avari wants you—you're everything he's not, and he doesn't understand that. You protect people with lies, and he manipulates people with the truth. You keep saving those who've hurt you—" his empty eyes rolled in Nash's direction briefly "—and he hurts people who've done him no harm. Avari wants to dissect you, physically, mentally, emotionally." Thane shrugged. "I just want to offer you a fair exchange of services. My information for your help getting my soul back."

"He's lying, Kay," Nash said, fists clenched at his sides. "Hellions can't lie, but we all know reapers can."

"Careful, pot," Tod said. "Someone might notice your resemblance to the kettle."

Tod only shrugged when I tried to scold him with a frown. "He started it. As for *this* clown—" he glanced at Thane, then back at me "—I'm with you, whatever you decide."

I didn't want to rescue Thane—or his soul—from Avari. There was a large part of me that thought he deserved to be tortured for all of eternity for all the poor souls he'd condemned to that very fate. And for killing my mother when it wasn't her time. But Thane was our best shot—maybe our only shot—at stopping Avari from going through everyone I knew or loved to get to me.

"Okay," I said at last, and Nash groaned. "I'll help get your soul away from Avari. But there are conditions. The first is that you have to help yourself, too. I'm not doing it on my own."

Thane nodded eagerly. Maybe a little too eagerly.

"Second, you tell us everything you know first. Right now."

He shook his head and leaned against the end of the short kitchen peninsula. "That's not how this works. You give a little, I give a little."

"I can't give you a little of your soul, and I'm not going after it until I know exactly what'll be waiting for me. So start talking now, or we'll take our chances without you."

Thane's brows rose. "Someone woke up on the wrong side of the grave."

I shrugged, afraid to admit that I wasn't sure I'd woken up yet at all—most of the past month felt like a nightmare. "What's it gonna be?"

"Fine. But I have a couple of conditions of my own."

"Hell, no. You don't get to make up the rules," Nash said.

Thane ignored him. "First of all, keep your assorted collection of authority figures out of it. Levi will kill me the minute he sees me, and I don't trust Madeline. There's something in her eyes..."

"I believe that's integrity and dedication to her job."

"Yeah. It's disturbing."

"What about my dad?"

"I don't know how much help he'll be in the Netherworld, but sure, bring him along." Thane shrugged. "If he gets hurt, that's all on you."

I had no plans to take my dad to the Netherworld, but he and my uncle could be helpful on this side of the world barrier. If I could keep them from tattling to Levi and Madeline.

"Second—and you're gonna want to pay attention here," Thane said. "If you go back on your word and I'm stuck with that hellion bastard, I *will* help him torture and kill everyone you've ever even said hello to."

"That's a big threat," Tod said. "Someone's compensating for inadequacies."

"Do we have a deal?"

"No." I sank onto the arm of my father's recliner. "We have an agreement and a bunch of pointless threats. If you're going to talk, start now. I have no idea how long it'll be before Madeline checks in."

"So, should I just make myself at home, like company?" Thane started toward the living room, but Nash stepped into his path.

"No, you should stay right where you are, or my estranged brother and I will settle our differences by seeing who can break more of your bones."

Tod glanced at him, brows raised. "You want to settle our differences?"

Nash frowned. "No, I want to break every bone in his body, and I didn't think you'd let me do it alone."

Tod nodded. "Good call."

Thane glanced at me, brows arched over empty white eyes. "Are they always like this?"

I shrugged. "Sometimes they're less subtle. Let's get this thing moving."

Thane nodded. "What do you want to know?"

"Who killed Scott?" Nash demanded. That wasn't where I would have started, but I couldn't blame him for jumping in, and honestly, I was glad to see him participating in something other than his own self-destruction.

"That was me, but I was under orders," Thane said, leaning against the kitchen counter with his arms crossed over his chest. Like he was comfortable. "Avari needed a form that would traumatize her, and psycho-boy fit the bill."

"How'd he know we'd go see Scott?" I asked.

"He didn't. He was going to bring the party to you, but Scott died with no shoes on, so Avari went looking for some in his room. Then you two showed up and saved him the trouble of hunting you down."

"So it *was* a possession, then? Is that why he needed the shoes?" I asked.

"No. Hellions can't possess the dead. Avari figured out how to cross over. But that comes with both requirements and limitations."

"Requirements?" Tod said.

"Souls," Thane said. "A pair of them, specifically. One is to get him through the fog, like a ticket for a train ride. The other provides his physical form on the human plane. But here's the catch. That first one—the one that lets him cross over—has to be a resurrected soul."

"A RESURRECTED SOUL? RESTORED? LIKE MINE?" My chills were so strong I was starting to feel more like a corpse in refrigerated storage than a warm-blooded member of the undead.

"Yes, or a reaper's soul. Or anyone else whose soul has been restored. It has something to do with that process. I tried to find out more from the reanimation department, but those are the most closed-lipped sons of bitches you'll ever meet. They just kept repeating the same line about proprietary processes and—"

"So that's why he sent you after me and Mareth?" Tod's voice was deep, almost shaking with rage.

Thane nodded. "He's using my restored soul as we speak, but eventually he'll use it up—I get weaker every day he has it—and he'll have to replace it. But right now, he's just collecting them. Trying to corner the market before anyone else realizes there's a profit to be made. He's an enterprising hellion who knows big business when he sees it."

By "enterprising," of course he meant greedy.

"He's selling restored souls?" Like a train-station ticket booth in the Netherworld.

"Only a couple so far. I bet you can guess who the first one went to…."

"No, I—" But then suddenly I did. "Belphegore. That's how he got Heidi's soul. And Meredith's. He traded a resurrected soul for them."

"For those two, and for several more. He can charge whatever he wants. That's the beauty of a monopoly."

"Where's Mareth?" Tod demanded.

"I don't know," Thane said, and Nash huffed.

"This isn't a good time to start lying, reaper."

"There's never a bad time to start lying, but I'm telling the truth. I turned her over to Avari, but I didn't stick around to see what he did with her. He could have her in cold storage, with the rest of the collection, but if I had to guess, I'd say he sold her. At a huge profit."

"Who would he sell her to?" I asked, trying not to think about the fact that Tod could have easily been taken instead of Mareth. As could I.

Thane shrugged again. "Could be anyone. There are hundreds of other hellions in the Netherworld, and every one of them would pay anything for a single day spent on this plane. Avari has what they need to cross over. The prize goes to the highest bidder. And the demand *far* exceeds the supply."

"And every time Madeline sent an extractor after Avari, she was just giving him another ticket to sell," I said, unable to purge horror from my voice.

"He found that irony especially satisfying."

"So, why hasn't he taken me?" I asked, and Thane frowned like he didn't understand the question. "I'm not a fighter. If he could take the other extractors so easily, why hasn't he done the same with me?"

"He will. You're part of the long game," Thane said. "Until then, he's playing with you. I think he wants to see just how deep your noble streak runs. He wants to see if you'll really turn yourself in to save everyone else you love. While you resist, he feeds from your guilt and angst over the deaths you could have prevented. Once you give in, he'll be able to feed from you directly." Thane shrugged. "He can't lose."

"Bullshit," Nash spat. "He's not going to stop killing just because Kaylee turns herself in. I don't care what he says. He'll never stop killing."

"True. Avari has never been in a better position to slaughter at will. But he can't go back on his word. If she turns herself in, he'll stop choosing his victims from the Kaylee Cavanaugh friends-and-family plan."

Stunned and a little nauseated, I sank into my father's chair and shoved hair back from my face. "What's the long game? What is he doing, Thane?"

The reaper shrugged. "That, I don't know. But he's obsessed with it. Everything he's doing plays into it. And you have a central role."

"Okay, let's go back to the basics." Because if I thought any more about the people I could have saved—and the people I would have been damning in their place—I was going to lose what was left of my mind. "He's using your resurrected soul to cross through the fog into our world. What about this second soul? The one that gives him a physical form. How does that work?"

"I don't know all the details. He figured that part out himself, by accident, so—"

"Whoa, what does that mean?" Tod demanded. "Who figured out the first part?"

Thane shrugged. "Not to give myself too much credit, but… I did. Decades ago."

"And you told Avari that he could use your soul to cross over?" I frowned, watching him through narrowed eyes. "Why would you do that? Why would you give him a reason to need your soul?"

"Your boyfriend didn't give me much of a choice!" Thane shouted, pushing away from the countertop to gesture angrily at Tod. "One sucker punch from a rookie, and I'm staring at the business end of a hellion!"

"Yeah, he's all about the sucker punches," Nash mumbled.

"As long as Avari needs my soul, he'll keep me alive. More or less. Anyway, it shouldn't have mattered." The rogue reaper shrugged. "What I showed him let him cross over, but gave him no physical form. Like a visitor's pass, where you can't touch anything. He figured the rest of it out on his own, when he was playing around with another soul."

"Okay, so back to the part where Avari shows up in the guise of the dearly departed. What *do* you know about that?" My head was already spinning from everything he'd told us, but we had to get it all down now—there was no telling when Avari would call him back or Madeline would show up.

"I know that it's a one-way trip. He needs a human soul and something that belonged to the deceased. He crosses over with both of those in his possession and takes the form that soul had when it died. Down to the clothes it was wearing."

"The bracelet…" I said, and Tod nodded. "How did Avari get Heidi Anderson's bracelet?"

"How the hell do you think? He sent me after it. But you're missing the point. Once he crosses back into the Netherworld, that nonresurrected soul is useless. Gone. Poof." He made an exploding gesture with both hands. "It can't be worn again."

"Disposable packaging," Tod said. "It works for bottled water, why not for hellions?"

"I don't understand." And I wasn't sure I really wanted to. "How does wearing a human soul give him a physical body?"

"I truly don't know how it works. But his physical restrictions seem to be the same as mine, maybe because he's using my soul as his passport. Selective corporeality and audibility. Transportation. But no hellion superpowers."

"So he's vulnerable when he's here?"

Thane shrugged again. "As vulnerable as I am. But as you may have noticed, killing him doesn't really kill him. When his physical body dies, he just gets sucked back into the Netherworld, along with my soul."

"So, is there any chance we can get your soul back without having to cross over?" I asked.

"I don't know. And I don't really care. How you fulfill your end of the deal is up to you."

"You said you'd help," I reminded him.

Thane nodded. "But I've told you everything I know, so I don't know how much more help I can be."

"You can find out why my amphora doesn't capture your soul from him when I take the others," I said, picturing the two human souls that last sank into the hilt of my dagger. "And find out how to fix that."

"How am I supposed to do that?"

I shrugged and enjoyed throwing his own words back at him. "How you fulfill your end of the deal is up to you."

"So, let me get this straight," Nash said, before Thane could blink out in anger. "Avari's going to keep showing up disguised as dead people, and while he's here, he's going to kill even more of them? Just for fun?"

Thane nodded. "At the moment, human souls are easy for him to come by, so he doesn't mind losing them every time she stabs him, because her trauma is worth more than the lost soul."

I shoved more hair back from my face and rubbed my forehead. Can dead people get headaches? "And since he's sold a resurrected soul to Belphegore, we can expect her to show up any day, but we have no idea when, or what she'll look like. Right?"

Another nod. "Though you may never see her. I can't imagine she's as obsessed with your shiny little soul as Avari is." He glanced at Tod then—as near as I could tell, considering his eyes were featureless white orbs. "Just think. None of this would have happened if Avari and I had never met."

Tod looked sick. "This is my fault. Avari would never have figured all this out if I hadn't thrown Thane at him," he mumbled beneath his breath.

The only comfort I had to offer him was my hand intertwined with his.

"That's right, lover boy." Thane obviously enjoyed Tod's self-torment. "No good deed goes unpunished."

"So, how do we stop him?" I said, fighting the overwhelming, numbing lure of despair.

"Stop him?" Thane shrugged. "I have no idea how to stop him, and I don't really care."

"But we had a deal!" I stood, furious. "I snatch your soul from the grip of a demon and you tell us how to stop him."

"Uh-oh. Someone wasn't paying attention. I only promised to tell you what I know, and I've done that. What you do with the knowledge is up to you. And if you even think about defaulting on your end of the bargain, keep in mind that your little 'circle the wagons' routine can't last forever. I spent days following you around in advance of your death, and just because there were times you didn't see me doesn't mean I wasn't there. I know everyone you know. I know where all your friends and family live. If you don't produce my soul in very short order, you won't have to worry about Avari killing everyone you love. I'll save him the trouble."

"You can't tell Madeline!" I cried, chasing my father down the hall as he went for his cell phone. He'd left work the minute I'd called him, as soon as Thane left.

"Oh, yes, I can. I can't believe you're even thinking about keeping this from her."

"I didn't have to tell you, either, you know." I grabbed his arm, and he finally turned to face me, forehead deeply furrowed, irises stubbornly still so I couldn't see how scared he really was. But I knew. He was almost as scared as I was.

"Kaylee, I'm glad you told me, but I can't reward your good decision with a poor one of my own. Madeline knows much better than either of us how to deal with rogue reapers and runaway hellions," he insisted, already on the move again, and I shouted after him.

"If that were true, she wouldn't have lost all three of her other extractors!"

My father stopped cold in the hall, then turned to face me. "I'm not Madeline's biggest fan, but even I know that wasn't her fault. She did the best she could with the information she had, and you'll only be making her job more difficult and dangerous by withholding more information from her."

"There's nothing she could do with this information, even if we gave it to her!" I insisted. "She doesn't have any other extractors to put at risk—I'm the only one left. The ones Avari took are trapped in the Netherworld in cold storage—whatever that means—and I have no idea what state they're in. Thane still has a body, but that could be because he's useful. For all I know, Avari's already disposed of the extractors' bodies, so their souls can't escape. And that's assuming he hasn't already sold them."

"Sold them?"

"Yeah. To other hellions. Thane says there are hundreds of them, and once they know what Avari's up to, they're all gonna want in on the fun, and no matter how bad you're thinking that's gonna be, I promise it'll be worse. Mass-slaughter of the human race. Bodies dead and defiled. Souls enslaved and tortured. The end of existence, as we know it."

My father stared at me without speaking for close to half a minute, and I could practically see the rapid succession of thoughts and fears as they raced across his expression. Then he scrubbed his face with both hands and met my gaze again. "Is there any chance at all that this is some massive misunderstanding, or the product of an overactive teenage imagination?"

"Nope," Tod said, and I turned to find him in the hall. "Nash and I heard the whole thing."

"Okay, then, what are the chances that Thane made it all up and Avari's feeding off of our panic?"

"That's not impossible," I admitted. "But everything Thane said lines up with what we already knew. Missing reapers and extractors. Avari haunting the human plane in the guise of the dead."

"Mr. Cavanaugh, I think all hell really is breaking loose," Tod said.

"And if I tell Madeline…?"

"She'll tell Levi, who may or may not hunt Thane down and kill him by removing the Demon's Breath keeping his body functioning in the absence of his soul." And then we'd have lost our source of inside information and any chance of more help from the only person in either world who had free access to Avari and his evil scheme.

"Look, no one wants to kill Thane worse than I want to

kill Thane," my dad said. "But Levi—much like me—will understand that there are bigger problems at hand. He won't act rashly at the expense of so much human life."

"Doesn't matter," I said. "Thane knows Levi would never let me return his soul, so if he finds out we involved Levi or Madeline, he'll consider our deal broken and he'll go after everyone we care about on his own, without waiting for Avari to give the orders. Emma. Sophie. Harmony. Who knows how many other souls he'll be able to reap before someone catches him?"

My father sighed so heavily I wondered if he had any air left in his lungs at all. "We're all *already* in danger, and so long as you, Tod, or Luca are around, Thane can't sneak up on anyone." Because he couldn't hide from the three of us. "Levi and Madeline need to know, Kaylee. You have to be willing to compromise here."

I exhaled, my thoughts racing. "Fine. We tell everyone—including Levi and Madeline—what Thane told us, but we make it sound like we pounded the information out of him, and we don't mention my promise to get his soul back from Avari. I don't think we can keep Sabine from finding out, for obvious reasons—"

"I can keep a secret!" Nash shouted from the living room.

"We all know how good you are at keeping secrets," Tod said, and I elbowed him. "What, he can take shots at me, but I can't return fire?"

"Exactly," I said.

"Why?"

"Because you won the war, and he's still nursing his wounds," my father said softly, glancing pointedly at Tod's hand, which was wrapped around my own.

"There was no war," Tod insisted, and I knew from the intimate resonance of his voice that Nash wouldn't have been able to hear it even if he'd been standing right next to us. "We didn't fight over Kaylee. She made a choice. And no one feels worse about how that happened than she and I do."

"Oh, I don't know about that..." my father whispered, glancing down the hall toward the living room to drive home his point.

"You know, just because I can't hear you doesn't mean I don't know you're talking about me," Nash snapped.

I swallowed another upsurge of guilt. Then I pulled us back on track. "So, you're not going to tell Madeline about our deal with Thane?" I said, where everyone could hear me.

My dad only hesitated a moment, then shook his head. "No, but I reserve the right to change my mind, at my own discretion."

I nodded. That was the best we were going to get.

"Sabine's bringing Sophie over," Nash said when we rejoined him in the living room. "And Emma's bringing Luca straight from school." They'd cut the school day short because of Brant's death—a hauntingly surreal déjà vu for a student body that had already lost several members since the start of the school year—but Luca'd had to stay to talk to the police and school officials. "My mom's dropping by before her shift starts at eleven."

"I expect to hear from Madeline any minute, and I'm about to text Alec," I said.

My father sighed, resigned, already heading for the home phone. "Another full house. I'll order a giant sub."

"Okay, here's what we know," I said, leaning against the half wall separating the kitchen from the living room, where six of my closest friends—plus Sophie—watched me, listening, and for just a second, the surrealism threatened to overwhelm me. What qualified me for the position I'd somehow assumed? Nash, Sabine, and Tod were all better fighters. My father had way more life experience. So why were they all looking to me? What if their trust was misplaced?

What if I got us all killed?

I glanced at Tod, suddenly unsure of myself, and he smiled and nodded for me to continue. There was no doubt in his eyes. None at all. He had more confidence in me than I'd ever had in myself.

"Um, Avari will be back, and he may not be alone. We don't know how many other hellions currently have the ability to cross over, but we know that when they show up, they'll look like…well, like the person whose soul they're wearing. And since you can't fight an enemy you can't see, I'm thinking the best way to start is by familiarizing ourselves with what the enemy might look like."

"What does that even mean?" Sophie asked. Her face was still swollen and her eyes red from crying.

"The hellion you saw this afternoon is named Avari. Avari looked like Meredith Cole because he was wearing her soul, kind of like a costume. So what we're going to do is make a list of souls—potential costumes—Avari and his demon buddies could be wearing."

Behind me, cellophane crackled in the kitchen as my dad unwrapped a massive sub sandwich and set a stack of paper plates on the island. He'd set several six-packs of soda into a chest of ice. But I'd caught him eyeing the whiskey he'd confiscated from Nash.

He'd had a rough month, too.

"And how do we do that?" Em asked. "Wander through the cemetery playing 'knock-knock, who's there' on the headstones?"

She was upset. Maybe as upset as Sophie was. She'd known Brant as long as I had, and she knew firsthand what kind of damage a single hellion could do, even without crossing into the human plane. The thought of several of them turned loose in our world was almost too much for her to think about.

I could totally sympathize. Her life would have been so much safer if she'd never met me.

"I thought we'd start with the obituaries instead," I said at last. "That seems less disrespectful of the dead. Levi sent over this list…." I glanced at Tod, and he held up a stack of printed pages Madeline had brought when she'd come to pick up the dagger. "It contains everyone in the local area who died on schedule in the past month. We're going to compare this list with the local obituaries covering the same time period. What we're looking for are people who died but are not on Levi's list."

"Why?" Sophie asked, but Sabine beat me to the answer.

"Because those are the people who weren't supposed to die. And if they weren't supposed to die, their souls weren't turned into the proper authority by your friendly neighborhood reaper. Which means their souls are MIA. You see where I'm going with this…?"

Sophie nodded. "Any missing soul could be worn like a costume by a hellion like the bastard who killed Meredith."

Meredith was killed by a reaper, not a hellion, but… "Close enough," I said. She was catching on pretty quickly for a traumatized human. "Okay, everybody grab a sandwich and pick a partner. Each partner gets a laptop and you'll go through the online obituaries in pairs." Tod and I had already made lists of the local papers and paired them as best we could with sections of the list Levi had sent, which was organized by geographical zones.

Nash and Sabine settled onto the couch with his laptop, their portion of the reaper list, and a plate piled high with food. Sophie and Luca took her laptop and claimed the kitchen table.

Tod sat between me and Em and our laptops at the bar, checking off names as we read them to him, while Em munched on her sandwich and I picked at mine with no real interest.

"You know, it's amazing how much of this Netherworld creepy demon crap winds up involving a bunch of teenagers armed with laptops and a wireless connection," Em mumbled as she scrolled.

Tod chuckled. "We're the twenty-first century's Mystery Inc."

"Well, that's comforting, right?" I said, summoning a grin in spite of the circumstances. "Scooby always gets his man…."

My phone buzzed in my pocket and I pulled it out to find Alec's name and number on the display. I accepted the call and held the phone up to my ear, swiveling on my bar stool to face away from most of the talking at my back. "Hey, shouldn't you be at work?"

"Yeah." The tension in that one syllable rang sympathetic notes of fear down the length of my spine. "We have a problem, Kaylee."

I excused myself with a glance at Tod, then blinked into my room and closed the door. "What's wrong, Alec?"

"I need your help. Now."

My chills became icicles growing in place of my bones, freezing me from the inside out. "Where are you?"

"My place. And, Kaylee? Bring your dagger."

"DID HE SAY WHO IT IS?" TOD PACED AT THE END of my bed while I typed furiously on my phone with both thumbs.

"No. He just said to bring my dagger, which I can't do until Madeline brings it back." I hit Send on the text to my boss.

My room. Need dagger. Now.

"Who do you think it looks like? It has to be someone you know." Tod stopped pacing and the fear in his eyes no doubt mirrored my own. "Someone you both know. How else would Alec know it's actually a hellion?"

My phone slid through my grip and thumped to the floor at his feet. I hadn't thought of that. Alec would have to know whomever he'd seen well enough to know that person was acting strange. "There are only a few people on that list, and most of them are in this house," I said, grasping at that fact for what little hope I still clung to.

Tod knelt for my phone, then handed it back to me. "So who's not here? Your uncle?"

I nodded slowly and squeezed his hand when it slid into mine. "And your mom."

"No." His denial surfaced as a furious burst of pale, pale blue, churning within the brighter cobalt in his irises. "I'll kill the bastard myself if he's touched my mother."

"You won't have to." I'd do it. That was my job. I'd thought I was being resurrected to save souls, but so far I felt more like a murderer than a savior, even though I knew in my head that I was only doing what had to be done.

Tod pulled his own phone from his pocket and started to dial his mother's number, but before he could place the call, Madeline appeared on the rug behind him, holding my dagger. I was off the bed in an instant and took the knife from her so fast I almost grabbed the blades instead of the hilt.

"Thanks. Don't tell anyone where we're going. We'll explain to everyone all at once, when we get back."

"Where *are* you going?" Madeline demanded as Tod stood and took my hand.

"Be back soon." I squeezed his hand, then blinked us both into the living room of Alec's apartment, about half a mile away.

I'd only been there a couple of times, but the minute my feet touched the carpet, I knew something was different. Everything looked the same, but felt…wrong.

The TV was off. Alec left the TV on all the time when he was home, and I'd always assumed that was part of his ongoing quest to integrate with the twenty-first century, after having missed a quarter of the previous one. Sports, cartoons, infomercials—he'd watch anything. But this silence was new. And creepy.

"Alec?" I called, then immediately wished I hadn't. I couldn't limit my audibility to him if I didn't know where he was, and I really didn't want to alert the hellion to our presence.

The tiny galley-style kitchen was empty, but an open bottle of beer stood on the counter, next to a half-eaten chocolate cupcake—Alec's favorite snack food.

A second later, I realized that television sounds weren't the only things missing. "Where's Falkor?" I whispered as Tod headed across the living room toward the short hall. Alec's half Nether-hound—another littermate of Styx's—was named after a flying dog-creature he'd loved in some movie from his childhood in the eighties. And like Toto, Cujo, and Baskerville, he'd growled every time he saw me since my unfortunate demise.

But now Falkor was silent.

"Stay here," Tod said, and I could tell from his bold volume that no one but me could hear him. "I'll check the back rooms." Which included the only bedroom, the bathroom, and a single small storage closet.

I stomped after him. "This is *my* job! I'm not gonna stay behind while you—"

"Kaylee, wait!" Tod tried to hold me back from the bedroom doorway, but it was too late. I saw it over his shoulder as he wrapped his arms around me and tried to walk us back into the living room. I saw it all. Blood streaking the walls and Alec's unmade bed. A small lump of bloody fur on the floor, too mangled to recognize.

"Falkor..." I buried my face in Tod's shoulder and he led me toward the living room, holding me up when I backed over my own foot and nearly tripped. "Who did this?" I whispered, blinking back tears I didn't want to let fall.

"It was him or me," a familiar voice said from behind me, and Tod stopped walking as I twisted in his arms.

Alec stood in the middle of his own living room, a bloodied, broken broom handle in his right fist while his left arm dripped blood onto the floor from the jagged, gaping wound on his forearm. Only it wasn't really Alec. It couldn't be.

Avari couldn't take Alec's shape unless he already had Alec's soul.

Alec was dead.

"No..." I whispered, and this time I couldn't stop the tears. "No, not Alec," I said through teeth clenched against an agony I couldn't possibly express in mere words.

Alec, who'd helped me rescue my father and Nash from the Netherworld. Alec, who'd made me tie him to a chair so he couldn't hurt me if Avari possessed him in the middle of the night. Alec, who'd proofread my history term paper, and listened to my French recitation, and shared the last chocolate-chip pancake with me, even though he'd called dibs fair and square.

Tears pooled in my eyes until I couldn't see clearly, mercifully blurring a face Avari had no right to wear. They poured down my cheeks, scalding against the cold of my own shock and denial.

Alec couldn't be gone. Not after everything he'd already suffered at Avari's hands. Lost youth. Dead parents. Avari had used him to kill three teachers just a couple of months earlier.

Alec was supposed to be okay now. He was living the life he'd missed out on. He was supposed to get a happy ending, not death at the hands of a hellion who stole his soul and wore it like a costume.

Then Avari smiled coldly at me with Alec's beautiful mouth, displaying malice where there had only ever been kindness before. His dark eyes shined with greed as he drank up my pain and abused the memory of my good friend.

I choked on sobs, trying to collect myself and my thoughts so I could do what needed to be done. The only thing I could still do for Alec—reclaim his soul from the monster who'd stolen it.

"Alec..." Just saying his name brought more tears to my eyes, and I blinked them away. "You soul-stealing bastard," I hissed, and the Alec-monster shrugged.

"Is this about the dog? He was a ferocious little beast—tougher than his size would indicate. He reminded me of you, and I didn't want to kill him, either. Not that quickly, anyway. But he gave me no choice." Avari held up his injured left arm. Both his sleeve and his flesh were shredded, and still dripping blood. "Your true death will last much longer. I've given the matter serious thought, yet I can only imagine it one way. Your pain will be elegant and beautiful, your screams crystalline and fragile in tone, but robust in volume. I have always wanted to hear a *bean sidhe* scream in pain. I'm positively glowing with anticipation."

"Kaylee, give me the dagger," Tod said, his voice low and dangerous, threaded throughout with a thin ribbon of fear. But I pulled the knife out of his reach.

"No." This was *my* job. Alec was *my* friend. The least I could do was give his soul some peace.

"You shouldn't have to do this. He was your friend, and I can't watch you do this."

"Then close your eyes." I stepped away from him, and he let me go, but I could feel how badly he wanted to pull me back again. To protect me from what I was about to do.

"I warned you," Avari said with Alec's voice. He stood his ground as I advanced, knife gripped tightly, eyes still wet. "You could have prevented this."

"Don't listen to him," Tod said at my back, and I realized he was closer. Within arm's reach. He wouldn't interfere with my job, but he wouldn't let me assume the risk on my own, either.

"A stranger in the mall. Then a boy from your class. Now a personal friend. Can you see the progression at work here?" Avari lifted one of Alec's dark brows at me in question. "It's a crescendo of death, all building toward that powerful note at the finale that makes the audience gasp and hold its collective breath. You are that last note, Kaylee. You are my finale, and the symphony of pain we create together will echo throughout eternity before finally fading into an agonized silence. Much like the *bean sidhe*'s wail itself. Unless you'd like to cut this whole production short and skip to the end." The hellion shrugged with Alec's shoulders, still holding his injured arm. "Normally I'm fairly patient—I suppose I have eternity to thank for that—but there *is* something to be said for instant gratification."

"I'm gonna be gratified the instant she shoves that knife into your gut," Tod said at my back. "And if you even look like you're gonna touch her, I'll take your head off myself."

"I have no intention of stopping her, but that has nothing to do with your useless threat." Avari's focus shifted to me then. "Eliminate this form, and I will see you again soon, in another, even more treasured one. Or you can come with me now and spare the life of someone you love. What will it be, little *bean sidhe?*"

My teeth ground together and my fists curled around the handle of the knife in my grasp. My free hand wiped tears from my face. He'd already killed someone I loved—Alec was the closest thing to a brother I'd ever had. The closest I would *ever* have.

My mouth opened, and a bellow of rage burst from me, lower and more raw than any sound my *bean sidhe* lungs had ever produced. I lunged forward and shoved the double-bladed knife into his stomach and up beneath his sternum, going for the heart—for the quick kill—out of some instinct I hadn't known I possessed.

Avari's eyes widened. A sound of pain caught in his throat, like he was choking on it. He swallowed thickly, then smiled at me in spite of obvious pain. Blood poured over my hand, gruesomely warm and wet. Avari fell forward, one hand grasping weakly for my shoulder, and I stumbled beneath his weight.

Tod was there in an instant, trying to pull him off me, and cold horror unfurled deep inside my stomach. This wasn't right. None of the others had died like this, with weight, and staggering pain, and blood gushing over my hand and onto my clothes, pooling on the floor between us.

Tod pulled, but Avari clung to me with what had to be the last of his strength, and whispered into my ear. "I didn't kill Alec, Ms. Cavanaugh. You did that yourself. And it was magnificent..."

Then he let go, and Tod shoved him to the floor.

Avari sucked in a shocked gasp and stared up at me, blinking in confusion, dark skin waxy with pain and blood loss. "Kaylee?"

And that's when I understood. Avari wasn't wearing Alec's soul. He was wearing Alec's *body.* Alec had only been possessed. And I'd just killed him.

"No!" I dropped to my knees next to him, and my hands shook over the hilt of the knife. I didn't know whether to pull it out or leave it in. Which would be worse? Did it even matter? He couldn't survive this. No one could.

I hadn't.

"Alec!"

"What happened?" His lips moved, but there was no sound, other than the wheezy breaths he pulled in slowly, and exhaled even more slowly.

"Avari." I couldn't see through my tears. "I'm so sorry. Oh, Alec, I'm so sorry!"

"Kay." Tod tried to pull me away, but I wouldn't go. "Kaylee, let him go."

"No! We can save him. Just... Just don't take his soul. Then he can't die, right?" With no reaper there to end his life and take his soul, he'd be okay. The doctors could still work their miracles. I stood and took his hand, staring at him through my tears. "Call an ambulance. No, take him to the hospital yourself. Please, Tod!"

"Kaylee, it's too late." He turned my head gently so that I had to look. So that I had to see Alec's soul, pale and clean, already wrapping around the hilt of the blade still in his stomach. "He doesn't need a reaper—the dagger took his soul. He's already gone."

"No." I closed my eyes, so I wouldn't have to see Alec staring at the ceiling, his eyes empty. Dead. "No! This wasn't supposed to happen. This isn't how it works! I don't kill people. I rescue souls. This can't be..."

I dropped onto my knees again, sitting on my feet. My hands fell into my lap and left dark, sticky smears of blood on my jeans. The world started to lose focus.

"Kay, look at me." Tod tried to pull me up with one hand, but I wouldn't stand. I couldn't. So he lifted me by both arms. "This is not your fault. Avari did this. He fooled us both. Alec's fate was sealed the minute Avari possessed him, and you saved his soul from eternal torture."

"No." I shook my head, blinking through tears. "My knife. I stabbed him."

"Kaylee, don't do this to yourself."

"How can I...?" I couldn't finish the sentence. I didn't have the words. How could I live with myself, knowing what I'd done?

I couldn't. I wasn't living, anyway. But I wouldn't even be unliving when Madeline found out. She'd kill me for real, which was no less than I deserved, but my father would be devastated. Em would be devastated. Tod would be...

And it was all my fault.

Tod started to let me go, but my legs buckled beneath me. "Kaylee, hold it together. I need you to stand up."

I stood, and distantly I saw him pull the dagger from Alec's stomach and wipe the blades on his pants, where they left dark smears. "Come on." He wrapped one arm around my waist and slid his hand beneath my shirt so that his skin connected with mine. "I'm going to take you some place safe, so you can get yourself together. So we can deal with this. I need to think." He squeezed me so tight my ribs ached, and as the world dissolved around us, his last words echoed in my ears. "I won't let them take you away…."

The world pulled itself into focus around me again and when Tod let go of me, my skin felt cold without his touch. Everything felt cold.

"I'm freezing," I whispered, and my teeth started to chatter on the last syllable, drawing it out.

"I think you're in shock. Here. Sit down." Tod led me by the elbow to a chair in one corner of the room. I thought the elbow thing was kind of weird—until I realized my hands were still covered in blood.

"How can I be in shock, if I'm dead?" I sank into the chair and laid my hands in my lap, palms up. And when I remembered why my hands were messy, the chattering got worse.

"That's actually a really good sign. It means that you're still tapped into your humanity. If you weren't upset right now, I'd be worried. Well, *more* worried."

I should have been glad to hear that I wasn't turning into an emotionless undead monster—like Thane—but I couldn't think past the blood on my hands and the memory of Alec staring up at me in agony as he died. "This doesn't feel like a good sign." And for the first time since I'd been restored to my body, I understood that it might actually be easier to let my humanity go—to divorce myself from emotion entirely—than to watch loved one after loved one die, or to live with the guilt of what I'd done to Alec.

Was that what had gone wrong with Thane? Had he given

up his humanity to avoid suffering guilt and loss? If I took the easy way out, would I turn out just like he had?

"You've only been dead for a month," Tod said, drawing me out of the most terrifying temptation I'd ever experienced. "Your emotions are going to be inconsistent for a while." His voice sounded kind of distant, muffled by the sound of running water. "Sometimes it's hard to feel anything, then suddenly you feel everything all at once, and I honestly couldn't tell you which of those is harder to deal with."

"This." My voice sounded hollow. Why did my voice sound hollow? "This is the hardest to deal with." The numbness I'd been resisting for weeks was suddenly the most appealing thought in the world.

But Tod had made it. He'd held on to his humanity in spite of the pain, and if he could do it, I could do it.

"Come here." Tod stepped into the doorway, and that's when I realized he'd left the room in the first place.

I stood and took two steps toward him. Then I stopped and glanced around. The room was tiny—space only for the twin bed, armchair, and a small television on a cart. "Where are we?"

He tugged me into the other room with him and I realized it was a bathroom. A tiny bathroom, with a shorter-than-standard shower/tub combo, a toilet, and a pedestal sink, with hardly any room between them. Water was running in the tub. Steaming water.

"This is my place." Tod slid his hands beneath the sides of my shirt, and his skin was *so warm.* I closed my eyes and just felt him for a moment, blocking everything else out. Because everything else hurt. Then his hands moved, pulling my shirt up, and the way the cotton clung to my skin, sticky with blood, made me gag. "Arms up," he ordered softly, and I couldn't comply fast enough.

"You have a place?" *Think about the place. Tod's place.*

Don't think about Alec.

Don't think about the knife.

Don't think about the blood.

"It was supposed to be a surprise. Everyone gets a locker, but there aren't enough rooms for all the reapers, and I'm kinda low on seniority," he said, and I wondered if he was talking just so I'd have something to listen to. To keep my mind off things I shouldn't think. "That never mattered before, though—I always just hung out at my mom's house when I wasn't working, whether they could see me or not. But after you died…" He shrugged, then tugged the sticky material over my head, careful not to let it touch my face. "I put my name on the waiting list the next day. This spot opened up yesterday."

"Yesterday?" That was good timing. Too good. "Because of Mareth…" My eyes closed, denying this new layer of pain when I had yet to deal with the others. They were too heavy. I could hardly move. "This was Mareth's room?"

"I don't know. Maybe." He dropped my shirt on the floor, in the corner, then turned me by my shoulders and unhooked my bra. "But she's not the only one missing. Two more reapers have disappeared in the past few days. One before her. One after her."

"And you inherited a room."

"Yeah." He reached for the button on my jeans, but I brushed his hand away. I could do it. I wasn't a baby.

"Because Levi doesn't think they're coming back." I slid my jeans over my hips and stepped out of them one leg at a time.

"Yeah." Tod reached over to turn the water off while I stepped out of my underwear, and I was already calf-deep in the water before I realized I was naked. In front of him. I should have been embarrassed, or at least nervous. I'd been naked with him before, obviously, but last time there'd been more touching than looking.

But he wasn't looking now. He was very obviously not-looking, which was good, because I couldn't think about being naked. Not until the blood was gone. The water was pink with it.

There was so much blood.

Tod set a bottle of guy-shampoo on the edge of the tub, along with a bottle of guy-body wash. "I'm going to go…take care of things. I'll bring some clean clothes, too."

I caught his hand, and finally he looked at me. At my eyes, which were wet again, and I wondered if we could both pretend I'd gotten bathwater in them. "Don't leave."

Please don't leave….

"I'll be back. You're safe here. No one else can get in. There's no door."

"No door?" I hadn't noticed, but now that he'd mentioned it, I realized he was right. The other room had no door, except the one leading to the bathroom.

"Reapers don't need them," he explained. "I'll be back. If the water gets cold, run some more. Here's a towel." He laid one hand on a folded towel on the shelf above the toilet—one of only two. "Sorry, I don't have a robe."

"It's okay."

"Just…stay here. I'll be back as soon as I can."

Then he was gone.

I lay back in the tub, but it was short, so I had to bend my knees, and they got cold. I opened the guy-shampoo and sniffed the bottle. It smelled like Tod's hair, and for some reason, that made me cry.

I tried not to think, but that got harder with each second of silence. So I slid beneath the surface. I didn't even have to hold my breath. I just…stopped breathing. I don't know how long I stayed under, blinking up at the world through hazy pink water. Minutes, maybe. Or maybe an hour. I didn't have to come up, so I didn't.

Until someone shouted my name. "Kaylee!"

Nash? No. Nash couldn't get into Tod's special reaper room. The water was messing with my hearing.

"Give her some privacy," Tod said, and I blinked. Then I frowned.

"She's not coming up!" Nash insisted. And it *was* Nash.

Water sloshed around me as I sat up with my arms crossed over my chest, to find Tod blocking the bathroom doorway with his back to me, one hand on Nash's chest, holding him back. "She doesn't have to breathe, remember?"

Careful to keep myself covered, I scrubbed water from my eyes with one hand and blinked at Nash just as Tod shoved him into the bedroom. It wasn't a hard push. But it wasn't a push that would be misunderstood, either.

"I brought you some clothes, but I couldn't get your robe out of the bathroom without having to explain something to your dad." Tod set a stack of clothes on the closed toilet seat, because there was nowhere else to put them.

"Thanks."

"How do you feel?"

"Lost. I feel lost." I was supposed to save souls, not take lives. I was supposed to protect my friends, not kill them. How had this happened? This *couldn't* have happened.

Tod sank to his knees next to the tub and put one hand on my bare back. "You're not lost, Kaylee. You can't ever be lost, because I'll always know where you are. And if I'm not there with you, I'm on my way, and nothing standing between us will be standing for very long."

Tears blurred my vision again, but he was still beautiful, even out of focus. "Promise?"

"I swear on my very existence."

I believed him. I'd never believed in anything more.

Tod stepped out of the room and pulled the door closed, but didn't latch it, and while I lathered my hair on autopilot, I listened. I couldn't hear all of it, but I heard enough.

"What am I doing here?" Nash demanded in a fierce whisper. "Listening to the two of you is like having spikes driven through my ears."

"I think actual victims of impalement would disagree with you there."

"She's naked," Nash hissed.

"That's how a bath works."

"You're sleeping with her, aren't you?" Nash made a horrible choking sound, and I flinched. "Is that why you brought me here? To rub it in my face?"

Tod exhaled, and I knew that whatever came out of his mouth would only be half of what he wanted to say. "I'm gonna have to take a rain check on the part where you get all angry and morose, but if you want, you can threaten to kick my ass again when I get back."

"Where are you going?"

"I have to deal with Alec, but I don't want to leave her alone. So could you hate me quietly for now and be there for her?"

"You want me to be your understudy? I'm not sure I have the dark wit to pull that off."

"Nor the tragic backstory. Don't be my substitute. Be her friend. This hasn't truly hit her yet, but when it does, it'll be bad, and I don't want her to be alone when that happens. Do you?"

"No." Nash sighed.

I slid beneath the water again and considered never coming up.

I WOKE UP IN A COLD SWEAT, WITH THE SHEETS tangled around my legs, the pillow squeezed so tightly in my arms that feathers threatened to burst from the seam. But they weren't my sheets. It wasn't my pillow.

I rolled over to find Nash watching me from the armchair in the corner. The room was so small that his right knee touched the end of the mattress and his left was pressed against the TV cart. But this wasn't Nash's room, either. It was Tod's. Tod had a room—really more of a big closet—and I was in his bed. Alone with his brother. Drowning in remorse and grief too thick to breathe through.

"You didn't have to stay," I said, sitting up to pull the pillow into my lap. My voice was hoarse from crying.

"Yeah, I did. There's no door."

"Oh, yeah." I pushed damp, tangled hair back from my face. "Sorry. You want me to take you home?"

Nash shook his head slowly. "If you leave, you won't be

able to get back." Because I had no idea where I was. "Are you okay?"

I stared at my hands in my lap, my legs crossed beneath me, bare beneath my short pj shorts. "Did Tod tell you what happened?"

"He said Alec died and you reclaimed his soul."

I looked up in surprise, fighting flashbacks so vivid I could still feel Alec's blood on my hands, warm, and sticky, and horrible. "Is that all he said?"

Nash's eyes narrowed. "Is there more?"

"The dog. Falkor was dead, too. Butchered." My eyes watered. Why hadn't Tod told him what really happened?

"I'm so sorry, Kaylee."

"Me, too." But sorry didn't cover it. Sorry didn't even come close.

"It wasn't your fault."

"Yes, it was." The blood. The knife. The look in Alec's eyes. "It's all my fault. All of it."

Nash exhaled and leaned forward with his elbows on his knees, and when he looked at me, the unease and discomfort in his eyes echoed deep inside me, striking similar chords in my own heart. He didn't know how to be there, in Tod's room, with me, and I didn't know how to be there, in the land of the living, with everyone else.

"Kaylee, I don't know how to do this," Nash said finally, and there was a fragile note in his voice. A delicate hesitance that made me want to apply a Band-Aid or spray on some disinfectant. But his wounds were too big for that.

So were mine.

"I don't know how to talk to you anymore," he continued. "I don't know what you want to hear or what I'm allowed to say. But I do know *you.* You can sit there and tell me how much has changed, and how different you are now, but it's not true. Death didn't change you. It couldn't. You're still the girl I fell in love with the moment I first heard you laugh, and I still know exactly who you are."

"Nash..."

"You would never hurt anyone," he said, still watching me with that bruised look in his eyes.

"I hurt you."

"Yeah. But not on purpose, and not as badly as I hurt you. That's how I know that whatever happened, this isn't your fault."

"I killed him, Nash," I said, and he blinked, then sat up slowly, staring at me in disbelief. "I stabbed him." Then I burst into tears.

Nash circled the bed and sat on the edge of the mattress, then pulled me into a hug. "What happened?"

"I thought it was Avari." More tears fell, and I half choked on them. "I thought he'd killed Alec and was wearing his soul. I thought I was freeing his soul, but... I killed him." I could hardly form words around the sobs shaking my entire body, but Nash understood. His arms tightened around me, and I cried harder. I'd thought saying it out loud—admitting my guilt—would make me feel better. Like releasing the pressure behind a dam. But I felt worse for having said it out loud. Worse, knowing that Nash knew what I'd done.

I felt guiltier than ever for thinking I deserved relief from that guilt in the first place.

"What happened?" Tod asked, and I looked up to find him standing in the middle of the little available floor space. Nash stood and shoved his hands in his pockets, and I threw my arms around Tod. He squeezed me and I laid my head on his shoulder.

"Nothing," Nash said, and my guilt thickened when I saw

him watching me over his brother's shoulder. "I was trying to convince her that this isn't her fault. Avari tricked her."

Tod pulled away so he could look at me. "You told him? Kaylee, you weren't supposed to tell him. I spent the past two hours cleaning everything up so no one would know."

"Cleaning it up?" A sick feeling bubbled deep in my stomach. "What did you do?"

"I did what had to be done to keep you out of this." His gaze held mine. He was unashamed of whatever he'd done. "But that won't work if you're not on board."

"Then maybe you should have told me what you were doing."

"I didn't think you'd let me." He sank onto the bed and pulled me down to sit next to him. "Besides, I kind of felt like 'don't confess to murder' goes without saying."

"It's not murder. It was an accident," Nash said, and he looked even more out of place, since he was the only one standing.

"We know that, but what are the police going to think? How likely are they to believe that she *accidentally* stabbed a good friend in the stomach, a month after she killed her math teacher the same way?"

"But that was self-defense." Shock echoed inside me, ricocheting from one terrifying thought to the next. "Beck stabbed me first."

Tod took my hand, and his fingers wrapped around mine. "And right now they believe that. But since we can't tell the police you're doing battle with a demon who can possess your friends and wear the souls of the dead, we have to start thinking about what conclusions they're going to draw if they find out you were in that apartment. Two stabbing deaths in a month aren't going to be labeled 'coincidence.'"

He was right. I didn't want him to be right, but what I wanted had never mattered less. "So what did you do?"

"I buried the dog and got rid of any evidence that he ever existed."

"Why?"

"Because Alec's apartment is now the scene of an open homicide investigation, and they're going to test every blood sample they find. But Falkor's DNA isn't anything their lab geeks will recognize. I also busted in the front door and took his TV and stereo, so it'd look more like a robbery."

"Did you report it?" I asked, blinking more tears from my eyes at the thought of Alec lying all alone in a pool of his own blood.

Tod shook his head. "An anonymous call would look suspicious, but I left the door open. One of his neighbors will find him and report it."

I shook my head slowly. "It doesn't feel right. He deserves better than to be found by a stranger."

Tod tucked one arm around me, his fingers curling over my hip. "Kaylee, there's nothing more we can do for Alec, so I did what needed to be done for *you*. And I'd do it again in a heartbeat."

"Thank you." I wrapped my arms around him again and he held me so tight breathing wasn't an option. "But maybe you could not alter any more crime scenes on my behalf? At least, not until I've had a fair chance to talk you out of it? The whole 'ask for forgiveness rather than permission' approach to our relationship doesn't really work for me."

"So, what? I'm just supposed to let you get arrested, which would force you into hiding, which means you wouldn't see your friends and family, and the two of us would be all alone together…?" Tod faked a frown. "Hmm… Maybe I should have thought that one through a little more."

"That's not the conclusion I was headed toward, but if it works..." I kissed him, desperately trying to see through the dark to the light at the end of the tunnel.

"Okay, seriously, it was bad enough the first time. I don't need the instant replay," Nash said, and I pulled away from Tod reluctantly.

"Sorry."

"Someone take me back. Now."

Tod stood. "I'll take you both. Kaylee's dad's going to call in the cavalry if she's not back in half an hour, and since I can only assume that when he says 'the cavalry,' he means Levi and Madeline... We should probably all go."

"I don't want to go yet." I still hadn't figured out how to tell my dad what had happened—I didn't want him to look at me and see a murderer. "I'll call him and tell him I'm staying here. Unless you want me to go...?"

"I want you to stay forever. But if you want to stay here tonight, you need to tell him that in person. If he doesn't see you in the flesh very soon, he's going to lose it. He's worried, Kaylee."

I nodded reluctantly, and Tod turned to Nash. "You can't tell anyone what she told you," he said, and Nash bristled under the command.

"I'm not going to tell anyone because it wasn't her fault and I don't want to ruin her life. Not because of anything you say. But I can't promise Sabine won't find out." Because her fear-reading ability was often eerily like mind reading.

"Then make sure she won't say anything," Tod said.

"Wait, I'm not going to lie to everyone, guys. Not to my friends and family. They deserve to know how Alec really died. *He* deserves that."

"No," Tod said, and behind him, Nash was shaking his head.

"Now how is that fair? The only thing you both agree on is disagreeing with me."

"We agree about protecting you," Nash clarified.

"Well, that's not your call to make, and I don't need to be protected."

"Yes, you do." Tod crossed his arms over his chest. "And don't try to turn this around and call us sexist. This isn't a damsel-in-distress moment. We all need to protect one another, and you've done your fair share of that."

"Yeah. We protect one another from Avari and Thane, and anything else that goes bump in the Netherworld. Not from our own friends and family."

"He's not worried about Em and your dad," Nash said. "He's worried about Levi and Madeline."

"There are *rules* in the afterlife, Kaylee." Tod looked scared. "And killing innocent people is against most of them."

"You were there. You know it was an accident!"

He took both of my hands and looked right into my eyes. "And I will die shouting it from the rooftops, if I have to. But at the end of the day, the bottom line is that you couldn't tell the difference between a hellion wearing a human soul and a hellion wearing a human body, and it's *your job* to know the difference. And if you're not competent in your job, they have no reason to keep you...alive."

"You think I'm incompetent?" My chest felt sore. Bruised. I knew Alec's death was my fault, but it hurt to think that he agreed with me.

"No. I think Madeline would have done the same thing you did. The same thing I would have done in your position. But if you tell them what really happened, there will be incident reports, and inquisitions, and eventually a hearing. Madeline can't afford to lose you right now, but once all this is over and they've recovered from a massive personnel shortage, someone will have to be held accountable for a mistake that cost the life of an innocent man. And when Madeline comes to take you, we'll have to run, and we'll be on the run for the rest of forever with only each other, and nothing to do but explore the youthful perfection eternity has blessed us with, and…" Tod frowned. "Okay, that makes it sound better than it will actually be."

"Don't you think that's a bit overblown?" I asked.

"Well, I guess we could skip straight to the young lovers on the run part, but do you really want to leave all your friends and family behind?"

He was joking—hopefully—but his point was as serious as the fear in his eyes. Fear for me.

"I'm not going to lose you, Kaylee. No matter what I have to do, or whom I have to fight. Even if that means quashing your vexing tendencies toward self-sacrifice."

"Did you just say 'vexing'?" Nash asked.

Tod scowled. "Nothing else seemed to fit. I stand by my word choice."

"Are you going to be like this for eternity?" I demanded, trying to resist when he pulled me close again.

"If you mean protective, and devoted, and perfectly preserved, then, yes. That is the burden I bear."

"I mean stubborn. I mean unrelentingly, infuriatingly stubborn."

"That, too. But have you looked in the mirror lately, because we happen to share that particular personality flaw."

"I'm not going to lie to my dad, Tod. Not again. Not about this. He won't tell anyone."

The reaper exhaled slowly. "I guess I can't argue with that."

Nash huffed. "Never thought I'd hear those words come out of your mouth…."

"Wanna hear some really colorful ones?" Tod started to

turn to Nash, but I swiveled his face back in my direction with one hand on his cheek.

"Play nice or go home."

Tod lifted one brow and glanced pointedly around the room. His room.

"Oh. Well, then, take me home."

"WHY CAN'T EVERYONE STAY AT OUR HOUSE?" Sophie's voice greeted me from the direction of the living room the moment Tod, Nash, and I appeared in my empty bedroom. "We have more space and better accommodations, and squinting at this tiny television is giving me a migraine."

"You're not going to be watching TV, you're going to be sleeping," my uncle Brendon said, and I realized the party had grown since I'd left.

"Or you could be unconscious," Sabine said. "I could make that happen."

"What the hell?" I muttered on my way down the hall, with Tod and Nash right behind me.

"Kaylee..." My dad pulled me into a hug as soon as I stepped into the living room. "Are you okay?"

"No." That question was starting to sound pointless. Would any of us ever be okay again? "What's going on?"

"We're circling the wagons a little more thoroughly. If Avari can get to Alec, he can get to anyone else."

"So we're just going to camp out in Kaylee's living room until…? Until what?" Sophie demanded, glaring at the room in general from the center cushion of the couch. "Hellions are immortal, remember? He's not going to be done screwing with us until we're all dead. Permanently," she added with a contemptuous glance at me and Tod.

"This is just until we figure out how to keep hellions from crossing over," my uncle said from the kitchen doorway. "And you're not all going to stay here. The guys will stay at Nash's. Harmony already okayed it."

The barrage of objections was loud and unanimous.

"What are we, twelve?" Sabine scowled and crossed her arms over her chest. "This isn't a junior-high dance, and frankly, dividing us down the gender line reeks of sexism. And if that isn't enough to change your minds, I'll be forced to point out that Nash is of age, and I have my legal guardian's permission to stay at his house."

"But you don't have Harmony's," my dad said, and Sabine's glower seemed to dim the whole room.

"I think we should all stay together," Sophie said, glancing less than subtly at Luca, who heartily agreed with her. "If our strength is in numbers, why would we divide?"

"To keep us from grouping into pairs, right?" Sabine said, glancing from my father to my uncle, then back. "But let me point out that if you separate the guys from the girls, you'll be awake all night trying to make sure no one sneaks in or out. Whereas if you let us all stay here, we have no reason to go anywhere else. And it's not like anything's going to happen with us all stuck in one room, anyway," she pointed out. And in the end, it was Sabine's unprecedented show of logic that won the case.

My dad glanced at Sophie's dad, who shrugged. Then my father sighed. "Fine. But this is a strategic maneuver, not a slumber party. Everyone will be fully dressed in modest nightclothes. And there will be no ingesting anything that didn't come from my kitchen, no sharing sleeping bags, and no complaining when at least seven of us have to share the shower in the morning. Speaking of which, I call the first shower."

No one argued.

Luca and Sophie followed her dad back to their house to grab extra air mattresses and sleeping bags, then came back without him. Having never died or been to the Netherworld, Uncle Brendon didn't qualify for hellion possession and he had to be at work at eight in the morning. Sophie was happy to leave him behind.

I was happy that staring at Luca distracted her from complaining about my small house, small TV, and small bathtub.

While they were gone, Tod went to check in at the hospital—he'd missed the last third of another of Mareth's shifts to help me with Alec—and Em closed my bedroom door and plopped onto the bed next to me. "Is it true about Alec?" she asked, her eyes shiny with unshed tears. "Avari got to him?"

I nodded. That much was true.

"How? What about Falkor?"

"Avari killed him. I don't have the details. All I know is that hellions being able to cross over changes everything. No one's safe." And the people I knew and loved were practically walking around with targets on their backs.

"I have a really bad feeling, Kay. Like I should be looking over my shoulder. But that's pointless, because suddenly evil looks like our friends. How can we fight it if we don't even know it's there?" But I had no answer for her. She picked at a thread on my comforter for several seconds, then finally looked up. "Is it going to be like this forever? I mean, now that they know how to cross over, what's to stop them from doing it any time they want?"

"Us, Em. *We're* what's going to stop them. I don't know how yet, short of reclaiming every resurrected soul they have. That may be what this comes down to, and if so, this will be an ongoing battle. But it's not *your* battle. I'll do everything I can to keep you out of it." She'd suffered enough, just because she was my friend.

"It *is* my battle." She blinked, and the first two tears rolled down her cheeks. "Avari made it my battle when he possessed me, and poisoned my boyfriend." Doug had died of a frost overdose back in December, just days after Scott was arrested and hospitalized. "He made it my battle when he killed my friend." She sniffled, and I had to brush away more tears of my own. "Alec. Do you think…?" She blinked again and wiped mascara from beneath her eyes with both hands. "Do you think he suffered?"

"I think he was caught by surprise, and it was over quickly. I think that's the only way it could go down." His eyes had only focused on me for a second. And as grateful as I was that Alec didn't suffer for long, I hated it that the last thing he saw and knew—his very last thought—was that he'd been murdered by a friend.

By midnight, Sabine, Nash, Emma, Luca, and Sophie were all sprawled out in my living room, taking up every bit of available floor space as well as the couch and my dad's recliner. I stood in the hall for a minute, listening to them whisper to one another like they were camping out under the stars. Their whispers were sad, and angry, and scared, but those were things they shared, even in the worst of times—and this night definitely qualified. But I couldn't share those with them. Even if I were to clear a place for myself on the floor next to Em, I wouldn't be one of them. Not anymore. Not knowing what I'd done.

"You okay?" Tod asked, and I looked up to find him leaning against the wall next to me, his light features shadowed in the dark hallway.

"I don't know if I'm ever going to be okay again," I said, and when his arms wrapped around me, I laid my chin on his shoulder and whispered into his ear. "I'm not like them anymore."

"No, you're not," he said, rubbing my back with one hand. "But you can still be *with* them."

"How? How am I supposed to pretend that prom, and graduation, and college are still the most important things in the world when I can't close my eyes without seeing Alec on the floor in a pool of his own blood?"

"You aren't. You're not supposed to pretend with anyone in there, and you're not supposed to pretend with me. I know it doesn't feel like it right now, but you're the luckiest dead person I've ever met. You have so many people who love you and know what you're going through."

"They don't know. How could they?"

"They may not understand everything you're feeling, but they know about your job and your afterlife, and they want to be there for you. Which means you can be yourself with them, whether being yourself means sitting through classes you hate, or ranting over the injustice of the afterlife in general. The point is that you have people to talk to."

He was right. "What do you have?"

"I have you. That's all I need." He tugged gently on my arm and I let him pull me into my bedroom, where we stretched out side by side on the bed. Fully clothed, on top of the covers, to keep my father from having a meltdown.

"Thank you for what you did for me today."

Tod shrugged. "What's a little crime-scene tampering between immortal lovers?"

"Not that. I'm still not sure that protecting me is a valid reason to cover up a crime—"

"We'll agree to disagree on that...."

"—but it means the world to me that you were willing to go to such lengths to protect me. But I'm talking about your room. The bath. A place to crash. Clean clothes. You even picked out my underwear—"

"*Truly* my pleasure." He dared a naughty grin.

"—and what you said..." I didn't have the words to tell him how grateful I was. So I kissed him. It was a sad kiss, more comfort than heat, but there was strength in it. There was strength in *him,* and when I was with him, I felt like I was stronger, too. Like I might actually get through this.

"Thank you. I didn't think I'd ever fall asleep again, but evidently I needed that nap."

"That was less sleep than shock-induced shutdown. Your head needed time to catch up with your heart, and you needed someplace private to let that happen. I've been there."

"Kaylee?" my dad said, and I glanced up to see him standing in the doorway, his gaze aimed at us, but unfocused. "It worries me when I can see body-shaped dents on your bed, but can't see the bodies making them."

"Sorry." I sat up, then concentrated on making myself corporeal as Tod sat up next to me. "Fully clothed. As per orders."

"Thanks for doing your part to keep your father sane." He came in and sank into my desk chair. "I think you need some more furniture. More places to sit that aren't the bed." He was kidding—mostly—but when I couldn't make myself smile or remind him that I was as grown as I was going to get, his focus narrowed on me in concern. "Are you okay? About Alec?"

"No," I said, and fresh tears filled my eyes as Tod rubbed

my back. "Can you close the door, Dad? I need to tell you something." I could make sure that only he and Tod heard me, but my confession still wouldn't feel private with the door standing wide open.

My dad closed the door, then sank onto the bed next to me, and his eyes swirled with concern. "What's wrong, Kaylee?"

"I killed him." The words burst from my mouth on the front edge of a sob, like they'd been waiting there all along. The room lost focus beneath my tears and as I stared at my hands in my lap, sniffling, trying to get myself under control, drops trailed down my cheeks to fall on my jeans.

My dad pulled me into a hug, and more of my tears soaked into his shirt. "No, Kaylee, you freed his soul and stopped Avari from wearing him like a costume." He ran one hand over my hair, smoothing it against the back of my shirt. "You did your job, and I know it was hard, but if Alec were here, he'd thank you."

"No." I sniffled and blinked tears from my eyes, but more came to replace them. "Avari wasn't wearing his soul, he was wearing Alec's *skin*." My words came out in staccato bursts, punctuated by half-choked sobs. "Alec was just possessed, and I killed him."

"She didn't know," Tod said as my father reached for the box of tissues on my nightstand without letting go of me. "Neither of us did. He manipulated her. It wasn't her fault."

I shook my head, drowning in guilt. Choking on grief. "I should have known." My fist clenched around a handful of my father's shirt, and I couldn't let it go. "He was my friend. I should have been able to tell the difference between my friend and a demon."

"No, Kaylee, don't do this to yourself." My dad pulled away from me so he could see my face, and when I tried to wipe my cheeks with my bare fingers, he pressed a tissue into my hand. "This is what he wants." My father's whole face was twisted with pain, for me. For Alec. For all of us caught up in Avari's carnival of lies and torment. "He wants you to suffer."

"*I* want me to suffer." I blotted my face with the tissue, then wadded it into a ball I couldn't stop squeezing. "I should have known better, Dad. With hellions, the truth hides in what they *don't* say." Since they couldn't outright lie, they'd become masters of implication and manipulation. "He never actually said Alec was dead." I'd gone over everything Avari had said a dozen times since I'd woken up in Tod's bed. "I should have known better."

"Kaylee, Avari has spent hundreds—maybe *thousands*—of years perfecting the art of misdirection. And he had more than a quarter of a century to learn how to imitate Alec in particular." My dad ducked to catch my gaze. "There's no way you could have known. There's no way *anyone* could have known."

But that didn't help. As badly as I wanted to let them comfort me, their words held no weight. I'd killed him. I should have known better. The guilt was mine to bear, and neither of them had the power to absolve me of that.

"Kaylee." Tod looked blurry through my tears, and I wanted to touch him, but that wouldn't be fair. Alec would never touch anyone again, and that was my fault, so I didn't deserve comfort. "Alec wouldn't blame you for this, so you have no right to blame yourself. Give credit where it's due. Avari did this. He used you and your dagger just like he used Alec's body. I understand why you feel guilty, and I know that's going to be hard to overcome. But what you should feel is *anger.* This wasn't a tragic accident. It was a crime, committed not by you, but by Avari. I don't know about you, but I'm ready to make him pay for that."

I nodded. I was ready. "How? How do you hurt a hellion?"

It was the age-old question, without answer for who knew how many thousands of years.

"Let's start by starving him," Tod said. "He feeds from pain, and yours is his favorite flavor. So cut him off. Turn your pain into anger, and he can't feed from it. You have a responsibility to make sure that Avari's not profiting from his crime." He shrugged and summoned a small, crooked smile. "Anger's more productive, anyway."

I couldn't help but notice my father's look of surprise. And respect. And a tiny ray of hope shined through the clouds thick on my emotional horizon. I wanted my dad to love Tod as much as I did. Just not in the same way.

"Okay?" Tod said, and I nodded. Letting go of the pain would be much harder than embracing the anger, but he was right. Avari didn't deserve even a *taste* of my grief over Alec.

I took another tissue and wiped my face, and my father looked at Tod, fresh worry twisting in his irises. "How much trouble are we looking at from the police?"

"None, hopefully." Tod met my dad's gaze boldly. "I took care of it. They'll never know she was there."

"Thank you."

I tossed both tissues in the trash and glanced at the time on my alarm clock. It was after midnight. "You're late for work," I said, and Tod shrugged.

"Levi's taking this shift for me, to give me a break."

I had no words to express my relief. I didn't want to be awake all night, alone, even for the few hours Sabine would actually sleep. "Will you stay?" I turned to my dad. "Can he stay the night? Please? We'll leave the door open, I swear."

My dad actually chuckled. "Considering everything that's conspired to take my little girl away from me in the past few weeks, I have to admit I'm thankful that you'd actually ask for permission. Of course he can stay. But I'm going to hold you to that open-door promise." He was looking at Tod then, not me.

Tod nodded.

A few minutes later, I went to the bathroom to brush my teeth and froze in surprise when I heard my dad and Tod talking in the hall. Curious, I pressed my ear against the crack between the door and its frame, careful not to let the wood creak.

"I hate it when she cries," my father said, his voice low and soft, and difficult to hear.

"Me, too," Tod said. "Nothing makes me feel more helpless. I'd kill anyone who tries to hurt her, but I can't save her from herself."

"You'd kill for her?" My father's voice was still. Deliberate. This was a test, and I didn't know the right answer. But Tod didn't hesitate.

"In a heartbeat." There was a moment of silence, and I peered through the crack, desperately trying to see them, but I couldn't even see their shadows. "Mr. Cavanaugh, I know this isn't the future you wanted for Kaylee, and I know I'm not who you wanted for her. And I'm not even going to pretend to think I'm good enough—I know I've made mistakes, and I'm probably going to make more. But I love her with every single cell in my body. She's the reason my heart beats—literally. There's nothing I wouldn't do for her. There's no one I'd put ahead of her. And I will never, ever leave her, as long as she wants me. Kaylee's the strongest person I've ever met. She can make it through eternity on her own. But I swear on my soul that as long as I'm here, she'll never have to."

Fresh tears filled my eyes, and my heart ached like it no longer fit inside my chest. I wanted to throw open the door and tell him I felt the same way. Exactly the same. But those words weren't meant for my ears. He was talking to my dad, and as hard as it was to respect his intent instead of rushing into the hall to kiss him harder and longer than he'd ever been kissed, in either his life or his afterlife, I took a deep breath instead.

But I wasn't noble enough to stop eavesdropping.

"Tod…" my dad began, and my breath caught in my throat. *Please don't ruin it, Dad….*

"I don't need your acceptance to be with her," Tod said, like he'd read my mind. "She wants me, and that's enough for me. But if you don't disapprove of the two of us together, it would be really nice to hear that someday."

My dad cleared his throat. "The world lost something when you died, Tod, and I know that wasn't easy for your family. But the world's loss was Kaylee's gain. I hope the two of you have the forever her mother and I never got."

"I will do my damnedest to make sure of that."

"I know you will."

My tears spilled over, and when I sniffled, the sudden silence from the hall made my heart jump. I turned on the faucet to hide my sniffles and remind them that I was only a door away. Then I finished brushing, and when I emerged from the bathroom, the hall was empty and my dad's bedroom door was closed.

Tod was in my desk chair when I shuffled into my room in my Grinch slippers. "How much of that did you hear?"

"Enough. You were cute."

He scowled. "I am not cute. I am the dreaded Grim Reaper. People fear me, you know. There's a whole song about it."

"Only because they don't know about the dimples. People don't fear a man with dimples."

"Levi's a nine-year-old with red hair and freckles, and you'd have to be crazy not to fear him."

"I have been called crazy a few times."

"Seriously. What did you hear?"

I turned and gave him a secretive smile. "I heard you ask my dad for his blessing to be with me, in your own way."

Tod covered his embarrassment with a heated glance at the tank top and shorts I slept in. Back when I used to sleep. "You should have heard the things I *didn't* ask his blessing for...."

"What things would those be?"

"Things we're not allowed to do under his roof." He stood and I let him pull me close, and little sparks shot through my stomach, like they had the very first time we'd kissed, and I hoped that it would always be like this. That every time either of us lost something or someone, we'd still have each other, and that would be enough to make forever worth shooting for.

"Is that why you got a roof of your own?" I teased, watching the lazy swirls of contentment in his eyes, and beneath those, the tighter, faster coils of blue that said how badly he wanted me, in every possible sense of the word.

"Well, that, and so I'd have somewhere safe to plug in my cell phone. Someone turned it in to the lost-and-found at the hospital last week."

"Mr. Hudson, if you can't keep up with your own cell phone, how is my father supposed to trust you not to lose his only daughter?"

"Are you suggesting I clip you to my waistband, like a phone?"

"I don't think I'd fit."

"Let's give it a try." He lifted me, and I wrapped my legs around him, glad no one else could hear us, because we needed this. This one moment of happiness in the midst of so much pain and fear. "Feels like a good fit to me," he said, and the heat in his eyes made me burn inside, all over, but instead of putting out the fires, I wanted to stoke the flames.

I kissed him, feeding from his mouth as he walked us toward the bed, and I knew in that moment that I would never need another sustenance. Tod was more than enough, and he was all I wanted. And I wanted all of him.

He lowered me to the bed, and my heart raced, and only when he stood to pull his shirt off did I realize we were no longer in my room. Or anywhere else in my house. I propped myself up on my elbows and lifted both brows in question, and Tod shrugged with a wicked smile. "I respect your dad too much to do this under his roof, but I love you too much not to continue this under my own."

"We promised not to…" I started, but then he crawled onto the bed with me and I ran my hands over his stomach. I couldn't help it.

"*You* promised. I never promised. Besides, I told him I'd probably make more mistakes. But my hands are in the right place."

"Heart," I corrected. "Your heart's in the right place."

"Yeah, but my hands are in an even better place."

And so they were.

19

BY SOME MIRACLE, NO ONE NOTICED US MISSING, and when we blinked back into my room an hour later, everyone else was sound asleep. So Tod and I borrowed some of my dad's DVDs and we watched a *Predators* marathon on my laptop, curled up together on my bed.

In the morning, my dad made good on his threat to take the first shower, then he started frying bacon. I pitched in with the pancakes while Tod fried eggs, and the morning was off to a surreal start.

Em woke up at a quarter to eight and started to panic over the late hour. She'd woken up both Nash and Sophie before my dad could explain that no one had to go to school. Which was news to me, too.

"We're taking the day off," he announced from the kitchen doorway, wielding a greasy spatula and wearing the apron I'd given him for his birthday. "Since Avari showed up at school, I'm deeming the campus unsafe—at least for the moment." He, Uncle Brendon, Harmony, and Madeline had called in sick for me, Sophie, Nash, and Luca. Then my dad had used his Influence over the phone to get the attendance secretary to write in medical absences for both Sabine and Emma.

"Today, we're spending the day at the lake," my father said. "All together, for safety in numbers, to make sure that what happened to Alec won't happen to any of the rest of us."

Tod's hand slipped into my grip and squeezed. He was reminding me not to blame myself—not to let Avari benefit from what he'd done—but that was hard, because Avari hadn't done it alone. I'd helped.

"Doesn't that seem kind of…cold?" Em asked. "Taking a day off to go to the lake when Alec hasn't even been buried yet?"

My father nodded and set his spatula on the counter. When he turned to face us again, I read confliction in his frown lines and determination in the smooth swirls of color in his eyes. "I know most of you are probably very upset over Alec's death. As am I. That's how I know that the temptation to mourn him is overwhelming, and that's normal."

"I never even met him," Sophie mumbled, and Sabine shoved her in the shoulder, a wordless warning to shut the hell up and respect the dead.

"But today should be about celebrating his life and remembering what he meant to those of us who knew him. That's what he'd want, and that's exactly what Avari and his hellion pals will *not* want, and this is a really good chance to piss them off." My father glanced at me then, and I was surprised to see a hint of a smile haunting the corners of his mouth. "Also, today is Kaylee's birthday."

"Oh, shit!" I said, and my dad frowned at me. Seventeen and dead, and I still wasn't allowed to cuss in front of him. "I forgot about my birthday." Again.

"Well, *I* didn't. I rented one of the picnic areas at the lake.

Harmony's going to meet us there at eleven with burgers and hot dogs, cupcakes, and enough brownies to exhaust the world's supply of cocoa powder for a month. We're bringing chips, soda, buns, and this very spatula." He picked up the spatula on the counter for emphasis. "So, everybody get up, deflate your air mattresses and roll up your sleeping bags, take showers—one at a time, please—and get dressed. Food's on the bar. Serve yourselves."

"Can I invite Jayson?" Emma asked, and my father glanced at me, deferring to my judgment. Because it was my party. Evidently.

I shrugged. "Sure." There'd be plenty of room at the lake to avoid the one human who wasn't supposed to hear about the basket of crazy trauma my life had become.

While Sabine, Em, and Sophie argued over bathroom access, Tod snagged a slice of bacon and pulled me aside. "I'm gonna go shower at my place to save time," he said. "I'll be right back." He kissed me, and I took a bite of his bacon. "Happy birthday."

But instead of blinking out of the kitchen, he dropped onto the couch next to Nash, and I had to strain to hear them over the three-way girl-squabble in the hall. "Did you know it was her birthday?"

"Of course, I knew," Nash said, meeting the reaper's gaze boldly.

"Why didn't you tell me?"

"Why didn't you not-steal my girlfriend the day before she died?"

I sighed and went into the kitchen for another slice of bacon. Some things were just going to take a while.

We didn't actually make it to the lake until nearly noon, and by the time we got there, Harmony already had charcoal stacked like a pyramid in the grill attached to the covered picnic area my dad had reserved. "This is how my husband used to do it," she said when my dad approached wielding a spatula and a set of tongs. "But that's as far as I go. The grill's all yours."

"Is Brendon coming?" my dad asked softly, and I glanced at them in surprise. Why would he need to ask her if his own brother was coming to the lake? Had he and my uncle had an argument?

"He said he'd swing by after work," Harmony said, and the slight flush to her cheeks said much more than her words had.

"What's wrong?" Tod asked, snatching a chip from the open bag on the table in front of me.

I pulled him close enough to whisper, though no one else could hear me, anyway. "I think your mom's going out with my uncle."

Tod laughed. "Yeah. For a couple of months now. Do *not* ask me how I know."

"See something you didn't want to see?"

"Occupational hazard."

"Is that why he left Sophie at my house last night?"

"He left at, what, nine?" Tod asked, and I nodded. "Mom doesn't have to be at work till eleven." He scowled. "Great. Now I need something more pleasant to purge the unwanted visual. Kittens on fire should do the trick."

"Does Sophie know?" I asked, and Tod shrugged, but I knew the answer before I'd even finished the question. She didn't know. Nash didn't, either. If either of them knew, we'd have heard about it during the sleepover.

While my dad and Harmony talked over the grill, Tod, Em, and I sat at the end of the dock with our feet dangling over the water, staring out at the lake while we waited for the burgers to cook. "This is weird," Em said. "I can't believe he's gone." She pushed her hair behind her shoulders and pulled her knees up to her chest. "If Alec were here, what do you think he'd be doing?"

"Sitting on the picnic table, eating all the cupcakes," Tod said.

"Telling us how, in the Netherworld, cupcakes are stuffed with entrails and bile instead of cream," I added, and I could see him saying that so clearly in my head I didn't know whether to laugh or cry.

"That's kinda true, though," Tod said with a sad smile. "Over there, we are the cupcakes. Human cupcakes."

And Alec would have been able to make us laugh about even such a horrific truth—if I hadn't cut him open and spilled his bloody filling all over us both.

Fresh tears filled my eyes and I was trying to wipe them away without looking like I was wiping them away when a dark blue sedan squealed into the parking lot, spitting gravel beneath its wheels before swinging into the space between my car and my dad's. Em stood and took off down the dock. "Jayson's here!" she called over her shoulder, and I was glad, because now there was someone to comfort her, too, even though Jayson had never met Alec.

"What do you think the appeal is?" Tod said as we watched Jayson get out of his car, grinning like he'd just ridden his first roller coaster. Evidently skipping school was a new thrill for him.

Emma threw her arms around him and kissed him, and he looked surprised by the enthusiasm of her greeting. I wasn't, though. She'd felt like a fifth wheel—or maybe a seventh wheel—for the past eighteen hours.

"I don't know, but I hope the appeal is that he's normal. Both human and alive. I've dragged her into enough weird and dangerous crap this year."

"She would have come willingly, if you hadn't dragged her," Tod insisted. "She's your best friend. Is there anything you wouldn't do for her?"

"No..."

"Well, that's obviously mutual."

When I looked up, I found Emma dragging Jayson down the pier, their footsteps shaking the boards beneath us. Em dropped onto the end of the dock next to me, and Jayson sat on her other side with a nod and a "Hey" to Tod.

Tod returned the casual greeting, and I almost laughed out loud. His regular-guy act was good enough to fool anyone who didn't know him, but I couldn't think of him as a regular guy. Yes, I knew he'd gone to a regular high school before he died, and he'd played regular-guy football, just like Nash. And he'd probably done regular-guy stuff like watch sports, and break curfew, and kiss girls—one of my least favorite visuals *ever.* But I couldn't see him like that. Tod was anything but normal to me.

"Happy birthday, Kaylee," Jayson said, leaning around Emma to look at me. "I brought you a gift, but I didn't see any others, so I left it in my car...."

"Oh, you didn't have to bring anything!" I could hear surprise in my own voice. "This is a gift-free party, except for my dad. Because he's my dad."

Jayson shrugged. "Well, if you don't want it, maybe Emma will."

"Yes. Kaylee's rejected birthday present. *That's* what I want." She laughed, then pushed him playfully, and Tod pulled me up by one hand.

"Let's give them some privacy," he said.

"What about our privacy?" I asked as he tugged me down the pier.

"We can make our own privacy." His fingers slid between

mine, his hand warm in contrast to the cool breeze coming off the lake. "You weren't serious about the no-presents rule, were you?" he asked.

"Why? Did you get me something? You didn't have to get me anything."

"Well, it's not a present in the traditional sense. But it's something I've never given anyone else, and I want you to be the first."

"We're not talking about your virginity, are we? Because I happen to know that ship has sailed." Long before I'd been seaworthy.

"Ha, ha." We stepped off the dock and onto the sand, and Tod let go of my hand to slide his into his pocket. "Please excuse the lack of wrapping and girlie ribbons...." He handed me a folded scrap of paper, and the nervous twists of bright blue in his eyes said this gift—whatever it was—was worth as much to him as he obviously hoped it would be to me. In spite of its modest appearance.

My hands shook as I unfolded the paper. It held an address, written in pencil, in Tod's handwriting. "What is this?"

"This is my place. This is the local reaper headquarters. No one other than my coworkers is supposed to have this address, and I could get into a lot of trouble for giving it to you. But my room is in this building, and I want it to be your room, too, for whenever you need it, whether I'm there or not. If you need to rest, or hide, or cry, or scream, or just want to be by yourself for a little while, you can go there, day or night. No one else can get there. Not even Levi—he doesn't know which room is mine."

I felt dizzy, for the first time since I'd died. My stomach was twisting in knots, but they were good knots. "This is like the key to your apartment...." Only there was no key, because there was no door.

"Yeah. Only more secure. This is a safe place. This is a place no one else can find us. Later tonight, I'll show you how to find my room inside the building, but for now… Just know it's your room, too. Our room."

"You gave me privacy. For my birthday."

"Um, yeah. Did I mess this up? You're not really the flowers and jewelry type."

"It's perfect. It's so far beyond perfect it gives all other presents a bad name." I stood on my toes to kiss him—in public, for the first time since the kiss that had started all the trouble—but my birthday kiss was cut short when someone cursed on my left.

"Well, shit, that can't be good," Sabine said.

I dropped onto the balls of my feet, ready to snap at her to leave me and Tod alone. But neither she nor Nash was even looking at us. I turned to see what they were staring at and found an unfamiliar car parked next to Emma's at the end of the row, a too-thin woman in jeans and a faded T-shirt stepping out of the driver's seat.

"Who is that?" I asked, and Sabine scowled.

"Tina. My foster mother," she said through gritted teeth, already stomping toward the woman, leaving me, Tod, and Nash to catch up.

We jogged after her, and were still shouting-distance away when the woman propped skinny hands on bony hips and tossed short brown hair over one shoulder. "Sabine, I *specifically* forbade you from coming here today," she said, and Sabine stopped walking so suddenly I almost plowed into her.

"Kaylee, please tell me you brought that magic knife," she whispered, throwing one arm around my waist like we were good friends.

"It's a hellion-forged steel dagger," I said, squinting at the woman now glaring across the grass at us. Beneath the pavilion, my dad handed his spatula to Harmony, took off his apron, and started across the grass toward the new arrival, obviously ready to make introductions.

"Whatever it's called, go get it. *Now,*" Sabine whispered fiercely.

I couldn't remember when I'd last eaten, but my stomach seemed intent on tossing the food back up. "Why?" I asked, sliding Tod's address into my pocket, but I was pretty sure I already knew the answer.

"That's not Tina."

"Not again…" I groaned. We'd had too much death already. Too much vicious, personal, life-wrecking death. "Not on my birthday."

"Are you sure?" Nash asked.

Sabine nodded. "Beyond sure. Get the damn knife."

I let go of Tod's hand and shrugged out from under Sabine's arm, then headed for my car. When my father reached Tina and offered her a hand to shake, she turned to look at him and I blinked across the grass and into the driver's seat of my car, where I pulled the dagger from its sheath on the passenger's side floorboard. I hadn't touched it since Alec's apartment. I didn't want to touch it now. But I wanted to lose another friend even less, so I blinked back into step between Tod and Sabine, the dagger at my side, hidden from sight by my leg.

We were feet from my dad and Tina when Sabine tried to take the knife from me. "No," I said, so that only she and Tod could hear me. "We have to be sure." What happened to Alec couldn't happen to anyone else. I couldn't let it.

"I *am* sure," the *mara* hissed as we stopped feet from my dad and her foster mother.

"Sure about what?" My dad frowned with one look at our faces.

Before any of us could come up with an answer, Tina

pulled something from her pocket and swung low at my dad. He backpedaled, but her fist connected with his thigh, and he screamed and collapsed to the ground.

Nash tried to tackle Tina, but she dodged him, then laughed when he hit the ground rolling. I raced for my father, still clutching the dagger, and dropped to my knees at his side, staring in shock at the pocket knife sticking out of his thigh.

Harmony screamed and her footsteps pounded toward us. My dad grabbed my hand. "Run," he said as Sabine pulled the dagger from my other hand. When I only shook my head, he looked past me to Tod. "Get her out of here."

But when Tod reached for me, I shot him a warning look. "Help me with him." I wasn't leaving my father, or the rest of our group. So we each took one of my dad's arms and pulled him away from the demon in the foster-mom suit.

Tina laughed as the *mara* faced off against her, feet spread wide, double-bladed dagger held ready. "One down," the imposter said, glancing at my dad. "One to go." Her gaze flicked up to focus on Harmony, who'd almost reached us. "I find the adults just get in the way, don't you?"

"Nash!" Tod tossed his head toward his mother as we pulled my dad toward the nearest car, in spite of his protests. Nash rolled onto his feet and ran to intercept Harmony.

"How did you know?" Tina asked as Tod joined Sabine and they herded the hellion away from me and my father, who was still bleeding on the ground.

Sabine shrugged. "You knew stuff Tina would never know. Like my name and whereabouts. Also, FYI, very few twenty-first-century foster parents use the word *forbade*."

The demon nodded, like she was actually interested. "I shall keep that in mind."

"Tod!" Harmony shouted, and I twisted to see Nash physically holding his mother back from the action, while she watched her other son help confront a hellion who'd already stabbed my dad.

My father pushed me back and started to get to his feet, knife and all. I could see where this was headed—more blood loss and heroics—so I grabbed his hand and blinked us both to the other side of the pavilion, then blinked myself back to Tod and Sabine before my dad could even wrap his head around what had happened.

"Kaylee!" he shouted, but we all ignored him.

Sabine rushed the imposter, and fake Tina kicked her in the chest, with more strength and speed than any normal foster mother would have. Sabine flew backward—her feet actually left the ground—and crashed to the earth several feet away. A grunt of pain exploded from her throat with the impact and the dagger fell from her hand.

"Bitch broke my arm!" she shouted.

I grabbed the dagger and blinked onto the grass at Tina's back while Tod held her attention in the other direction. On my periphery, Harmony knelt next to Sabine to examine her arm and Nash raced to a halt at my side, irises twisting with fear and fury. Before I realized what he meant to do, he took the knife from me and grabbed Tina's left shoulder from behind. Then he shoved my dagger into her right side.

Tina collapsed to the ground and rolled awkwardly onto her back, her eyes wide with shock, one hand hovering uselessly over the knife still protruding from her side. Nash dropped onto her legs and shoved the heel of his palm against the hilt of the dagger, driving it deeper, and I realized that with the hellion-forged steel still inside her, she couldn't just disappear. She was trapped with us, until her borrowed form died.

"Who are you?" he demanded through clenched teeth, while I watched in shock.

Tod pulled him off Tina and the imposter's mouth widened in a cruel smile when Sabine stopped at her side. The *mara* clutched her left arm to her chest as foggy wisps of her foster mother's soul curled around the hilt of the knife still in the monster's side. "You're a clever one…" the demon said. Then her body melted into nothing, leaving my bloody dagger on the ground.

On the grass where Tina's head had been a moment earlier lay the eighties' vintage banana clip that had secured her thick hair on one side of her skull.

"What the hell just happened?" Harmony demanded, one arm around my dad, who was limping toward us from the pavilion, a stack of paper napkins pressed to the wound in his leg.

"Hellion sneak attack," Tod said.

"Who do you think it was?" Nash asked, studying Sabine's injured arm, and she shrugged, her jaw clenched in pain.

"Has to be someone who knows a little about me. Avari or Invidia."

"Or anyone they're working with," Tod said.

My father limped to a stop next to me, one arm around Harmony's shoulders. "I assume you all know what this means."

"Other than the fact that my foster mother is dead and I'm homeless?" Sabine handed me the bloody dagger, and I took it between my thumb and forefinger, reluctant to get yet more blood on my hands.

"She was trying to get rid of the adults," I said, staring at the place where the demon had died on the ground. "That means Avari's finally finished setting up whatever game this has all been leading to. Now he's ready to play."

"OKAY." I TOOK A DEEP BREATH, TRYING TO gather my thoughts, and sank onto a picnic bench beneath the pavilion. "Whoever that was impersonating Tina, he's down now, but not out. He'll be back, and there's no telling what he'll look like." Or she. The hellion could have been female.

"So, what's the plan?" Sabine asked, her face lined in pain as she laid her injured arm on the picnic table in front of her.

"Well..." my father said from the opposite side of the table. He was naked from the waist up, his leg stretched out straight on the bench beneath him, pressing his shirt to the wound, like Harmony had shown him. "I'm sorry about your birthday party, Kaylee, but I think we all need to go. Now."

"Agreed." I scanned the shoreline, looking for Em and Jayson, and Sophie and Luca. They'd paired up on opposite sides of the lake—no doubt for privacy—and were out of earshot. Fortunately, they'd missed the demon slaying. "Harmony, can you drive Sabine and my dad to the hospital? We'll get the others and follow you."

"No..." my dad started to object. But I cut him off.

"You're bleeding all over the place. We'll be right behind you, I swear. I'm not looking for any more hellion interaction today, of all days."

"You *are* still losing blood..." Harmony said, and my father sighed.

"You swear you'll be right behind us?"

I nodded. "You'll probably be able to see us in the rearview mirror." When my father finally gave in, Tod and I helped Harmony get him into her car while Nash helped Sabine buckle her seat belt beneath her broken—and now swollen—arm. Then Nash headed to the pavilion to pack up the lunch stuff. Tod and I were about to blink to opposite sides of the lake to gather the rest of the troops when Luca came running toward us from the shore.

"Kaylee!" he shouted, and all three of us turned. An instant later, and Tod and I would have been gone.

"What's wrong?"

"Dead guy. Or dead girl," Luca said. "Either way, someone here is deader than either of you."

A jolt of fear shot up my spine, followed by an echoing bolt of anger. *Not again...*

"It's probably Tina's body," Tod said, while Nash filled Luca in on what had happened, and I was almost ashamed by how relieved that thought made me. As awful as it was to think that Sabine's foster mother had been hauled around in her own car by the demon who'd killed her and stolen her soul, that was better than the alternative—yet another death. "Where?" I asked.

"Over there somewhere." Luca nodded toward the parking lot, and my relief swelled. If Tina's body had arrived with her car, that would explain why Luca hadn't sensed it before.

"Show us," I said, and we followed him away from the covered eating area toward the parking lot, with spaces for just six vehicles. Four of the spaces were occupied by cars we'd driven: mine, my dad's, Tina's, and Jayson's.

Luca stopped in front of our row of cars, then veered to the right, past my car, like he was being physically tugged that way. "Here." He started down the aisle between Tina's car and Jayson's, and my heart pounded so hard my chest ached. I didn't want to think about Sabine's foster mother lying dead in her own car. I didn't want to think about anything. I wanted this moment to be over, before it had even begun.

At the end of the aisle, Luca turned to the right—away from Tina's car. He stepped slowly, hesitantly toward Jayson's trunk, his eyes narrowed in concentration, and I could feel my own brow wrinkle in confusion. "It's in there. Dead. Not rotting yet, so it's very recent."

"What? No," I said, frustrated by the fact that logic and the truth didn't seem to line up. "Why would someone put a body in Jayson's car? He doesn't know anything about any of this."

"No, but his trunk obviously made a convenient delivery system." Tod peered over the roof, and I followed his gaze to the shore, where Em and Jayson were two indistinct forms near the edge of the water, enjoying their normal day, and their normal lives, with no idea how much macabre horror had hitched a ride in Jayson's normal car. "He's not looking. I'm going to pop the trunk."

Tod disappeared, and an instant later he reappeared in Jayson's driver's seat.

My hands shook and my mind raced. Who was in the trunk? It had to be someone I knew. Someone close to me. The pattern was escalating—Avari had said that himself. A stranger. A classmate. A friend.

This time it was a relative. It had to be. Except that all of my relatives were alive and accounted for.

Except for Uncle Brendon.

"No..."

My uncle had cared for me like a father when my own father hadn't been able to deal with my mother's death. Uncle Brendon had been there on every first day of school and every trip to the doctor. He'd turned on the bathroom light when I was scared of the dark and thrown away the steamed broccoli I hated, when Aunt Val wasn't looking.

But whatever he'd been to me, he was more to Sophie. He was all she had left. And no matter what she'd said and done to me in the past, she didn't deserve this.

Tod leaned forward in the driver's seat and something popped inside the car. The trunk lid rose a couple of inches, but I only stared at it. I couldn't look. I didn't want to see.

"Kaylee?" Luca said, but I shook my head.

"I need a minute." How was I going to tell my dad that his brother was gone? How was I going to tell Sophie that her father was dead? And that it was my fault?

"Kay?" Tod appeared at my side and his arm wrapped around me from behind.

"I can't do it. It's Uncle Brendon. Am I a total coward if I don't look?"

He squeezed me, then let me go and lifted the trunk. I turned my head. I didn't want to see my uncle dead, and I especially didn't want to see him dead in the trunk of Emma's boyfriend's car.

Luca made a sound, deep in his throat, and for a second, I thought he'd choked on horror. I'd come close myself, several times. "What the hell?" the necromancer said. "I don't understand."

"Kaylee," Tod said, and something in his voice set off alarms in my head. He seemed to be calling me forward and warning me back at the same time. "It's not your uncle."

Chill bumps sprouted all over my arms, and finally I looked, because I had no other choice. But at first, I couldn't process what I was seeing.

Tod was right; it wasn't my uncle. This man was younger, thinner, with unruly brown hair and…

My hands clenched around the edge of the trunk and I looked up at Tod, my eyes wide. He nodded in response to the question I couldn't voice. "He said he brought you a gift."

Yes, that's exactly what Jayson had said. Except it couldn't really have been Jayson speaking, because Jayson was dead in the trunk of his own car.

"So, who's that with Emma?" Luca asked, and I glanced up in horror, searching the shoreline for her and for not-Jayson. I had to squint to see them clearly. They were a quarter of the way around the lake, standing in the sand. Em's shoes dangled from the fingers of one hand. And she was kissing…him. She was kissing not-Jayson.

My best friend was kissing the demon wearing her boyfriend's stolen soul.

"That son of a bitch played us." And now he had Emma within his grasp. Literally.

Tod saw my intent before it could possibly have surfaced in my eyes. "Kaylee, wait!"

But I couldn't wait. I couldn't let him have her.

Frantic with rage and impatience, I turned and stomped toward the picnic table, where my dagger lay, still smeared with blood. "Kaylee." Tod followed me. "We need a plan."

"I have one: kill him, before he lays another hand on Emma."

"That's not a plan, it's a goal. Plans have steps, and forethought, and—"

I grabbed the dagger, but Tod stood his ground, blocking me in between the table and the grill. "Step one. Kill him. Step two. Repeat as necessary." I turned to Nash and Luca.

"Will you guys go get Sophie?" When they nodded, I turned back to Tod. "You comin'?"

Then I blinked out, without waiting for his reply. An instant later, I stood on the sand behind the Jayson-thing. Over his shoulder, Em saw my knife and gasped.

Jayson turned and laughed out loud. "I wondered how long that would take."

"About this long." I swung the knife at him, but he turned at the same time, with Emma in his grip. Em screamed. I tried to abort my swing, but the dagger sliced through the side of her blouse as he swung her around like a human shield. The blade scored her skin in an arc, just above her right hip.

She screamed again, and I gasped, almost frozen by my own horror and regret. "Em, I'm so sorry!"

"Ow, shit! What the *hell,* Kaylee?" Em slapped one hand over the wound, but Jayson nearly pulled her off balance when he dragged her backward, away from me.

"Let her go," I said, trying to divide my focus between his face and the blood seeping between her fingers.

"Kaylee, put the knife down," the Jayson-thing said. His voice was full of trepidation and fear, but his expression didn't match. His grin was creepy and irrepressible, but Emma couldn't see that with him at her back. He leaned down to speak directly into her ear. "I always heard she was crazy, but I didn't think she was *violent.*"

And that's when I understood the game—the hellion was still playing his role.

"Kaylee?" Emma's face was white with pain, and her hands were red and slick with her own blood. She was breathing too hard. Too fast.

"I'm so sorry, Em. I was aiming for him." My focus shifted to his eyes, sparkling with new pleasure over her head. "Let her go. This isn't about her."

"What is she talking about?" Jayson's voice asked, practically shaking with fake fear, while his eyes shined in malicious pleasure. "And why is she armed?" He pulled her farther away from me, pretending to protect her, when he was really shielding himself.

"What's going on?" Em demanded, and the strength in her voice gave me hope. Surely if the wound was very bad, she'd weaken quickly. Right?

"Don't mean to scare you, Em," Tod said, appearing on the left edge of my peripheral vision. "But there's a better than average chance you may be dating a demon."

She glanced at him, then back to me. "What the hell is he talking about?"

"That's not Jayson. Jayson's dead in his own trunk."

"What does that mean?" the Jayson-thing said. "They're crazy, Em. How could I be standing here right now, if I were dead?"

Tod made an exasperated sound. "Oh, let me count the ways...."

"Emma, listen to me, please." I stepped forward, but he dragged her back again. "Jayson is dead. He's in the trunk of his own car, in the parking lot. The thing holding you is Avari, and he's not protecting you from me, he's using you as a human shield."

"No..." Em flinched and pressed her hand harder against her wound. But she'd seen and survived too much to let fear and disbelief—or even pain—blind her to the dangerous truth. That was one of the things I liked best about her. "Jayson's dead?"

"The word *doornail* comes to mind," Tod said.

I nodded and gestured toward the thing still clutching Emma to its chest. "Ask him. Hellions can't lie."

Tears spilled from Emma's eyes and trailed down her cheeks,

and I couldn't tell which hurt her worse: her bleeding cut or the thought that her new human boyfriend—innocent, and ignorant of the danger he'd walked into—had been killed by a monster. "Are you Avari?" Her words were halting, half choked with her own tears. "Did you kill Jayson?"

The Jayson-monster's brows rose at me over Emma's head. "No, to both questions." He was challenging me. Daring me to prove him wrong.

But… Hellions couldn't lie. Of course, they weren't supposed to be able to cross over, either. What was I missing?

"Okay. I believe you," Em said, holding my gaze with a teary one of her own. She was talking to me, but he was supposed to think she was talking to him. "But I'm hurt, Jayson. Let me go, so they can take me to the hospital."

"I will." He glanced over my shoulder toward the pavilion, probably making sure no one else had noticed the trouble yet. "As soon as she puts the knife down."

But I couldn't do that.

"Who are you?" I demanded. "Obviously you're a hellion. Someone working with Avari." But no self-respecting hellion would help out another without something to gain from the favor. Was Emma the payment? If so, why not just take her? Why would the Jayson-thing practically *tell* me he'd left something in his car for me, then walk down the shore with Em in plain sight, instead of just crossing over with her? "Belphegore?" I said. "Invidia?"

"Oh, now you're just guessing," the hellion said. And with that, the charade was over.

"Let me go," Em said, her voice deep with hatred, haggard with pain. "Let go of me, you murdering, soul-stealing demon bastard!"

Jayson laughed. "I like this one. Easy on the eyes and even better on the tongue." He bent toward her ear again. "Do you think they'll save you?" he stage-whispered loud enough for me and Tod to hear. "If she has to kill you to get to me, do you think she'll even hesitate?"

Fresh rage blossomed inside me, fire shooting up my spine. He was playing on old fears that I would let her die. On doubt that I would be able to save her a second time.

"Kaylee would never hurt me. On purpose," she amended as blood continued to seep slowly between her fingers.

"Tell her what really happened to Alec," the hellion said, and my rage was drenched in a cold wash of dread as he met my gaze again. "Don't your friends deserve the truth?"

"I don't want the truth." Emma's voice was weaker now from blood loss, and fear, and maybe from confusion. "I just want to go to the hospital. Please..."

"She killed him," the hellion whispered. "Kaylee stabbed Alec, and it wasn't an accident, like the scratch she just gave you, which smells so deliciously painful." The Jayson-thing pushed Emma's hand aside and pressed his fingers into her wound. She gasped in pain. He lifted his hand and licked a smear of blood from it, his hungry gaze holding mine the whole time. "She stabbed him on purpose. It's true. I can't lie."

Em looked at me through tear-filled eyes, asking me for the truth without actually asking for anything.

"That's not how it happened," Tod insisted when I made no attempt to defend myself. "He was possessed, but we thought Alec was already dead. We thought Avari was wearing his soul."

"Let her go," I demanded.

Jayson laughed and licked another smear of blood from his hand, his other arm tight around Emma's waist. "Drop the knife, or I'll take a real bite out of her, right here. I do *love* a picnic at the lake."

Emma's breathing sped up and her face paled even more.

My fist tightened around the hilt of the knife. I glanced at Tod, and he nodded. I blinked, sure I'd seen wrong. But he was still nodding, telling me to drop the knife.

"Drop it and distract him," Tod said, his lip barely moving, and I knew from Em's lack of reaction that I was the only one who could hear him.

I held up the knife, blade down, to catch Jayson's attention. Then I dropped it. The knife speared the sand in front of my feet, stuck hilt up. "Now let her go. You said you would, when I put the knife down."

Jayson's head cocked to the side, like he was thinking back over everything he'd said. "True..." He let her go, and Emma stumbled toward me, one hand clutching her bloodied side, relief and fear mixing in her features only to be overshadowed by pain. I reached for her, but the second her hand touched mine, the hellion snatched her back.

Emma screamed, and he laughed. "I never said I wouldn't take her back."

I looked around for Tod, but he was gone. I glanced toward the pavilion and saw several human shapes, but we were too far away for me to tell who I was looking at. Had they heard her scream? Why was no one running to help?

"Distract him and move away from the knife," Tod said from behind me and I realized no one else could see or hear him now.

Distract him? How? What would distract a hellion who already had what he wanted? But then, he'd had what he wanted the whole time. So why were he and Em still there? Unless he *didn't* have what he wanted...

"Take me instead," I said, stepping to my left. "You need me to go willingly, don't you?" Because I was already dead, stealing my soul wasn't as simple as just killing me for it.

The hellion shrugged. "Willing, or unconscious. Similar to

mating rituals here on the human plane, isn't it?" He laughed at his joke, and my stomach churned.

"Keep moving..." Tod said, and I stepped to my left again. This time the hellion had to turn Emma to keep me in sight. But in turning, he stepped closer to the dagger.

"Fine. I'm willing. Let her go."

"Prove it." The Jayson-monster lifted one foot and deliberately stomped on the hellion-forged dagger. The hilt broke off with less than two inches of blade, and a scream of despair rose up inside me, like a mockery of my *bean sidhe* wail. "Cross over."

"Shit!" Tod swore.

"What?" I'd heard Jayson, but I couldn't make sense of what he was saying. I couldn't drag my gaze from the ruined dagger, and the loss it represented.

"Cross into the Netherworld, and I will let her go," Jayson said. "You have my word."

"No!" Tod said, and I glanced at him. The hellion followed my gaze, but he couldn't focus on what he couldn't see. "Kaylee, do *not* cross over."

"Cross. Now. Or I'll chew her throat out, slurp up her blood, and keep her soul."

"Kaylee..." Emma was terrified.

"Kaylee..." Tod was terrified.

In the Netherworld, I wouldn't have any of my undead advantages, except for the ability to cross back into the human world. But if I didn't go, he'd kill Emma, and I'd have to chase him into the Netherworld to retrieve her soul, anyway—there was no way I'd let Em's soul be tortured or worn like a costume.

"I cross, and you let Emma go? Alive?"

Jayson nodded. "That's the deal."

I looked straight at Tod. "Take her to the hospital. I'll be right back." Then I crossed over.

In the Netherworld, I stood alone next to the lake. Except I wasn't really alone. I couldn't be.

Everything looked the same, only different. The sand was too pale. White. More like salt than like sand. The trees were skeletal, as if they were caught out of season, and the few leaves still hanging had shapes I didn't recognize.

The lake was…not made of water. I don't know what the Netherworld version of our lake was filled with, but it was thick, and dark, and it stank to high hell. Things slithered just beneath the surface, leaving ripples in the thin, foul membrane that had formed on top. I gagged just from looking at it, and without the ability to teleport, I couldn't get far enough from the stagnant body of…fluid to avoid the smell.

I'd done my part. I'd crossed over. I closed my eyes, preparing to cross back into the human world to make sure Em had been released, when someone shouted my name.

I spun around to find Emma limping toward me from only feet away, leaving small drops of bright red blood on the sand. Behind her, long, black, multilegged creatures—carnivorous caterpillars?—crawled out of the sand and gathered around each new drop, fighting over her blood, scratching, clawing, and devouring until each stained grain was gone.

Invidia stood at Emma's back, stuck in her own form now that the Jayson-costume had expired with her trip back into the Netherworld. The hellion of envy looked just like I remembered. Thin hands sticking out of the long sleeves of her black dress. Gaunt cheeks. Dark circles beneath featureless black-orb eyes staring out at everything. Or at nothing.

With a hellion you never could tell.

Invidia's long, ever-flowing rivulets of black hair dripped

down her back and over one shoulder, shining with a green tint in the anemic light of the Netherworld sun. Each drop sizzled on the sand at her feet, but instead of gathering for a bite, the caterpillars scurried away from the noxious fluid. Except for one unlucky creature, who suffered a direct hit and was consumed alive by the acidic drop of liquid hair.

"Em…" I threw my arm around her waist while hers went around my neck, and in the process, I stepped on several of the creepy little bugs still following the source of Em's human blood. "You were supposed to let her go in the human plane!" I snapped at Invidia, then flinched over my own volume. Shouting in the Netherworld was like ringing a dinner bell in the Old West.

"I don't recall saying *where* I would release her," Invidia said, and her cackle of laughter grated against my bones like nails on a chalkboard. "You should take her home while you still have a chance. They've had a taste of her, and they'll want more." Her grand, skinny-handed gesture took in the army of tiny cater-creatures marching around the threat of Invidia's toxic hair drops on a steady path toward me and Em. "I've seen them strip slabs of meat twice your size to the bone in under a single of your human minutes."

I frowned in confusion, carefully backing Emma and myself away from the growing mass of bugs crawling over one another to get to us. "You're letting us go?" It was a trick. It had to be.

"If she is still here in ten seconds, I won't leave enough scraps of that pretty little body to feed a single one of the bugs…."

She didn't have to tell me twice—er, three times. I grabbed Em's hand and closed my eyes. A second later, we stood on the lakeshore in the human world, where the sand was brown and nothing crawled out of it ready to devour us.

Emma sagged against me, her breathing ragged, her grip

on my shoulder weakening with every second. "Is that it? She just let us go?"

"That's what it looks like..." But my nerve endings were on fire, and every hair on my arms was standing straight up. Why would she let us cross over? It was almost like Invidia *wanted* us in the human world. "Something's wrong. That was too easy."

"Speak for yourself."

"Oh, Em..." I lowered her to the ground carefully and she removed her hand from the wound long enough for me to take a look. But I couldn't even tell what I was looking at, much less how bad it was. I only saw blood. "We're going to get you to a hospital. They'll fix you up."

"It's going to be okay, though, right?" she asked, staring up into my eyes, her entire face lined in pain and fear. "I can't die if I'm not on the list, right? And Tod would have told us if I were on the list?"

"Yeah, if he saw your name, he'd definitely tell us. But..." *Damn,* I didn't want to have to tell her this. "That knife—it's actually a dagger made of hellion-forged steel."

"What does that mean?"

"Supernatural events trump the list. Which means..."

"I could die," she finished for me, and her gaze dropped in shock. "Again."

"Yeah." Of a wound I'd inflicted. "But we're not going to let that happen. We're going to get you to the hospital." I couldn't take her that far in one jump, but maybe Tod could.

Where *was* Tod? Why hadn't he crossed into the Netherworld with us? He was gone, and so was the broken dagger.

"Shit. Give me your hand." I reached down, and Em placed her bloody left hand in mine, still clutching her wound with the other. I closed my eyes and blinked us to the pavilion my father had rented, then helped Em onto one of the picnic table benches.

"Where is everyone?" she asked, and I glanced around, wondering the same thing.

"Harmony took my dad and Sabine to the hospital. Nash and Luca went to find Sophie, but I don't see any of them."

"What about Tod?"

"I don't know." The chill bumps on my arms grew even fatter.

The fire was still going in the grill, burning the burgers and charring the already-burned hot dogs. My dad's spatula lay on the grass a few feet away. The soda cans he and Harmony had been drinking from still sat on the table nearest the grill. Nash hadn't packed anything up yet, which meant they'd been gone since I went to confront Jayson/Invidia.

"Kaylee!" Nash shouted, and I looked up to see him and Luca running around the curve of the lake toward us, from the shore opposite where Em had been taken hostage. I exhaled in relief—until I realized they were alone.

"Hey, Emma's hurt!" I said as they stopped beneath the pavilion, winded from their run. "Where are Tod and Sophie?"

"We couldn't find Sophie," Nash said. "There were several sets of footprints in the sand—some of them ours—and hers seemed to head into the woods. But we couldn't tell for sure."

"Didn't know we were supposed to be looking for Tod," Luca added, still trying to catch his breath from the sprint.

"What happened?" Nash dropped to his knees in front of Em before I could pull another word out of him. She moved her hand so he could look at her wound, and her nose and forehead wrinkled in pain.

"I accidentally cut her. I was aiming for Jayson, who turned out to be Invidia."

"Invidia?" Luca said.

"The hellion of envy who turned Sabine and Kaylee against each other," Em explained.

"It wasn't just us!" I insisted. "The whole school went crazy because of her!"

"Emma needs a hospital," Nash said.

"I know, but I can't blink her that far, and we can't leave Sophie and Tod." I dug my keys from my pocket. "Why don't you take Em to the hospital, and Luca and I will stay here and find them."

Nash shook his head and refused the keys when I tried to hand them to him. "I'm not leaving you here."

"But, Em…"

"I'm fine for a little while," she insisted, but I found that hard to believe. "Besides, if you find Tod, he can get me there faster than driving, right?"

I nodded. "In theory."

Em's gaze focused on something behind me, and her frown deepened. "Shit. We have company." She grabbed my hand and squeezed it before I could turn and look. "I don't know what's going on, but you guys have to make it stop," she said, glancing from Nash to Luca, then back to me. "Before some-one else gets caught in this like Jayson did."

And like Emma had. And Sophie. And Brant. And Scott. And countless others.

She was right.

I turned to follow her line of sight and froze, blinking in disbelief. A thin woman in designer jeans was rounding the corner of the jogging trail, where it disappeared into a thickly wooded area of the park. I knew that blond hair, perfectly cut and styled, and I knew that her eyes were blue, though I wasn't close enough to see that for myself.

"Oh, no…" I whispered, not surprised to hear the hollow, shocked quality of my own voice. "Aunt Val."

"OH, SHIT," NASH BREATHED, AND EMMA STIFFened in my peripheral vision.

"That's Sophie's mom?" Luca said.

"Yeah. She traded her life for Sophie's last September," Nash said, and I have to admit, I bristled.

"But it was Val's fault Sophie died in the first place." I didn't want my aunt's last-minute attempt to abort her own evil scheme to be confused with my mother's genuine sacrifice on my behalf. They were two *entirely* different women. "And, no, that's not Sophie's mom. That's a demon wearing her soul."

"Speaking of..." Em said, and I glanced up again to see Sophie round the corner of the trail, calling after her mother.

"Sophie, *no!*" I glanced at Nash. "Stay with Em. Please." Then I took off with Luca, headed for my cousin. "Sophie, that's not your mom!" I yelled again, and Sophie stopped, startled, wiping tears from her shell-shocked, tear-reddened face.

"I know, but..."

Aunt Val crossed her arms over her chest and studied me without even looking back at Sophie. "You must be Kaylee."

I slowed to a stop ten feet away, but Luca ran past the hellion and hugged Sophie so tight he actually lifted her from the ground as he pulled her away from the hellion.

"And you would be…?" I couldn't tear my gaze from my aunt's imposter. She wasn't Sophie's mom. Intellectually, I knew that. But there was something about the way she moved Aunt Val's body, like she *knew* it. Like she truly identified with the soul she wore. And suddenly I understood. "Belphegore." The hellion of vanity who'd offered my aunt eternal youth and beauty.

"Who else?" Aunt Val's mouth smiled, not too wide, not too much teeth. Just like she'd smiled in real life, to maximize the illusion of kindness and minimize wrinkles.

"She has my mom's soul," Sophie sobbed, clinging to Luca's hand when he finally let her go. "Don't let her cross over."

I frowned at the hellion in confusion.

"The younger Miss Cavanaugh has just been informed that when I cross back into the Netherworld, her mother's soul will dissipate into the ether, scattered throughout both worlds for as long as it takes the soul to pull itself back together again. And that could take centuries."

"What does that mean?"

"It's like purgatory," Tod said, and I whirled around to find him standing on my left. I started to reach for him, then stopped when I saw who stood next to him, her arm linked possessively through his.

Addison Page. She looked just like she had the day she'd died. Beautiful long blond hair and bright blue eyes. She had everything my aunt had ever wanted and gave it all up for fame and fortune in exchange for eternity at Avari's mercy.

Whatever your weakness, there's a hellion to exploit it.

"Is that…?" I said, and Tod nodded stiffly, his jaw clenched in fury. He was angrier than I'd ever seen him. "Avari," I said, but my greeting felt more like a curse.

"Always a pleasure, Miss Cavanaugh," the hellion said with Addy's voice, and seeing him wear Addison bothered me more than any other form he'd ever taken—except for Alec's. Avari glanced around at the rest of us through Addy's wide blue eyes. "We appear to be missing a couple of guests…."

"Guests?" I asked, but instead of answering, Avari disappeared. "What the hell is going on?" I demanded, but the only one who could have answered—Val/Belphegore—only smiled.

"Kaylee, I am so sorry," Tod said as I stepped into the embrace he offered. "She—*he*—showed up the second you, Em, and Jayson crossed over, and he said you'd be fine. He gave his word." And hellions couldn't lie. "But he said if I went after you, he'd cross over, too, and Addy's soul would…dissipate."

Before I could ask what the hell that meant, or what the somehow-unified hoard of demons wanted, Emma shrieked behind us, and Nash's shout of outrage echoed hers. I turned toward the pavilion just in time to see Addison grab Emma's arm and disappear with her. Before I could even think to run toward them—not that that would have helped—Addison/Avari reappeared next to Val/Belphegore, Emma's arm gripped tightly in her fist.

Em was crying, one hand pressed to her still-bleeding stomach. "What—?" she started, begging me with her gaze to explain.

A second later, Sophie squealed as Belphegore jerked her out of Luca's grip with a single brutal tug. Then she shoved Luca closer to me and Tod. "You three stay put," she said with my aunt's voice. "One move from any of you while we're waiting for the last player in this little game, and the humans will die in a great deal of pain."

Sophie whimpered and Emma moaned, in both pain and fear, as behind us, Nash's footsteps thumped to a stop next to Tod. "What the *hell?*" he demanded, but I was just as confused and horrified as he was by the parade of demons wearing faces from our past.

Belphegore ignored him and focused on Luca. "I can see what you're thinking, necromancer. You think you can bring them back if they die, but they won't be the same, will they? Do you really think either of them would appreciate your particular talents?"

Luca shook his head slowly, eyes narrowed in anger while most of the rest of us looked on in confusion.

"What's up with all the dead people?" Nash stage-whispered.

"Aunt Val is Belphegore and Addison is Avari," I said. "And when they cross over, the stolen souls will dissipate, doomed to wander both worlds for centuries, trying to coalesce. Or something like that."

My explanation didn't seem to help. "I'm assuming Kaylee didn't invite the hellions to her birthday party, so the object of this little gathering would be…?"

"We're still waiting for the big reveal," Tod said. And as much as I hated waiting in ignorance, the alternative—*suffering* in ignorance—seemed infinitely worse.

"Sorry I'm late," Thane said as he appeared in our midst, sunglasses sliding down the end of his nose. Before I could yell at him for what was obviously a betrayal of the deal we'd struck, he tugged on the hand he held and a waif of a girl with stringy blond hair stumbled forward.

"Lydia?"

"Kaylee?" Lydia's eyes were wide and scared. Her clothes

were dirty and her skin was pale. Where had Thane found her? Had she been living on the street?

"What the hell does this have to do with Lydia?" I demanded, but instead of answering, Avari looked around through Addison's eyes at the group he'd assembled, then nodded his approval.

"If you want answers, you know how to get them," he said with Addy's voice. At her nod, Thane disappeared with Lydia in tow, and Belphegore disappeared with Sophie. And just like that, Aunt Val's soul was gone, disintegrated and distributed across both worlds like dust scattered in an explosion for however long it would take all the bits to coalesce so she could be given a final rest. Or doomed to torture once again.

"Wait!" Tod shouted, and Avari turned to him with Addison's wide-eyed look of expectance. "You said you wouldn't cross if I didn't go after Kaylee! You can't go back on your word!" That no-lie rule was to hellions in the Netherworld what physics was to humans in our world—a law that could not be broken.

"No, what I said was that if you went after Kaylee, I *would* cross over. And that was no lie." With that, the Addison-monster disappeared with Emma, and Em's scream echoed even after her body was gone.

Tod shouted, a wordless expression of rage and despair. Addison was gone. We'd failed to save her. Again.

Then, for a single, tense second, Tod, Nash, Luca, and I stared at one another in shocked silence. Luca was the first to break it. "We're going after them, right? We have to go after them!" But he couldn't cross on his own, and neither could Nash.

"Yes, of course," I said, closing my eyes. Trying to think. "But rushing in would be suicidal."

"It's not like we have any choice!" Luca cried. "They have Sophie and Emma. And…that other girl."

"It's a trap," Nash said, running one hand through his mussed brown hair. He looked like he wanted to hit something, but all the bad guys had disappeared.

"How do you know?" Luca demanded.

"Because *everything* Avari does is a trap, and I've been caught in a couple of them."

"They took our friends so we'd follow them into the Netherworld. Right where they want us," Tod explained. "They're looking for resurrected souls, like me and Kaylee."

"You don't know that," Nash said. "Maybe this time they want Sophie and Emma and…"

"Lydia," I supplied.

"Right," he said. "Why would they bring Lydia here, when Sophie and Emma would have been plenty of bait on their own? The hellions brought them here for more than that."

Tod and Nash started to argue, but I cut them off, beyond grateful that Nash was clean and sober. I'd almost forgotten how smart he could be. "Nash has a point," I said. "Any one of them would have been enough bait. And if the hellions just wanted us in the Netherworld, Invidia would have kept me there earlier, and Avari would have let you cross after me."

Tod nodded, grudgingly conceding the point.

"It doesn't matter whether they want us here, or there, or in the next damn galaxy. *They. Have. Sophie.* Take me, or I'll find my own way to cross," Luca said, brown eyes blazing in fury and fear. I had no idea how he'd get himself there, but I didn't doubt he could do it.

And his determination to save my spoiled, bitchy cousin was *so* damn sweet I almost wondered if I'd judged her too harshly all my life. Almost.

I glanced at Tod, and he nodded. Then Nash nodded. We were in agreement.

"Okay," I said. "But we can't cross here—this is where

they'll be expecting us. And don't forget that Tod and I don't have any undead abilities in the Netherworld. We can cross back over, and I assume we can function as *bean sidhes,* but no invisibility, inaudibility, or blinking from one place to the next. Understand? No shortcuts." That thought terrified me beyond reason, especially considering that I'd been to the Netherworld a dozen times before I even *had* any undead abilities.

"I don't care." Luca glanced around the clearing. "Where should we cross?"

I looked around, thinking of my brief visit to the Nether minutes earlier. "Away from the water and out of the sand. Um… Over there. Beneath the trees."

"You guys meet us there," Tod said, one hand on my arm to catch my attention. Nash scowled, but when I didn't object, he led Luca out of earshot. Tod stared down at me, his eyes swirling with nerves. "Kaylee, this isn't going to end well. It could be worse than what happened with Alec, and I need you to promise me that if this goes bad, you'll run. Just get the hell out of the Netherworld. I'll be right behind you with Nash and anyone else I can reach to cross over with."

"No. This is all or nothing, Tod. I'm not coming back without everyone." What good would my afterlife be if I had to live it knowing I'd let my best friends die?

Tod exhaled slowly, obviously frustrated. "Fine. But I had to try."

"And I love you for it." I took his hand, and we blinked over to the trees just as Nash and Luca got there. "Ready?" Tod asked, and everyone nodded.

I sucked in one last deep lungful of human-world air and took Luca's hand while Tod took Nash's forearm. Then we crossed.

The Netherworld version of the tree limbs we stood beneath

were heavily laden with fat, knobby purple fruit and long, thin leaves with serrated edges. Luca reached up like he'd touch one, then thought better of it. He was smarter than I'd been during my first trip to the Netherworld. Then I remembered that he'd been there before, with Sophie. Which was good. Experience counts for a lot in the Netherworld.

Uncommon sense counts for even more.

"Over there," Tod said, and I followed his gaze to see Sophie, Lydia, and Emma, obviously terrified and in tears, sitting in a row on a concrete picnic bench that had bled through intact from the human world. Nothing else from the human park still stood in the Netherworld, except for the pavilion, its canvas covering ripped and flapping in a breeze that smelled faintly of the rot from the lake. The park wasn't frequently or highly populated enough to bleed through in much detail.

In front of the bench, the three hellions stood arguing. I couldn't make out every word, but the gist was clear. They were arguing over which hellion would get which girl. Belphegore wanted the pretty one—not sure if she meant Emma or Sophie—Invidia was jealous of whichever one Belphegore wanted, and Avari insisted that he would get the first choice, because he'd pulled the entire plan together.

But that was bullshit. He wanted first choice because he was a hellion of greed, and if he could possibly get away with taking all three of them, he would.

They argued like cartoon bad guys, but the hellions were omnipotent, damn near omnipresent, and immortal, as far as we could tell. Their only weaknesses were the character flaws they embodied and fed from. They couldn't be hurt with anything originating from our world, and as far as I knew, they were impervious to most of the dangers the Netherworld had to offer.

We were in *way* over our heads.

I'd never seen Belphegore in her own skin before, but I wasn't surprised to see that she was unspeakably beautiful, as a hellion of vanity ought to be. What *did* surprise me was that the moment I turned away from her, I couldn't remember what she looked like. Not because she wasn't beautiful—she was—but because she was so generically flawless that no one feature stood out enough to be remembered. She was average height, with skin that could have belonged to any human ethnicity. Her hair was neither short nor long, and neither light nor dark, but seemed to change slightly every time my gaze returned to her.

Was beauty so impossible to define? So pointless that it couldn't be accurately remembered? What must it feel like to be the most beautiful creature in all of existence, but be forgotten the moment you leave the room?

Was that how Aunt Val had felt?

Luca was the first to ask the obvious question, pulling me from my own thoughts. "What do the demons want them for?"

The moment he spoke, all three hellions turned to look at us, like they'd been expecting us all along. And, of course, they had been. Avari disappeared, then reappeared close enough to whisper in Luca's ear. "Why don't you join us and find out?"

Before we could answer—or think, or plan, or run—he grabbed Luca and disappeared again, then reappeared beneath the pavilion, where he shoved Luca onto the bench next to Emma.

"Okay, *plan?*" I whispered, glancing from one Hudson brother to the other.

Nash huffed. "We probably should have come up with one before we crossed over."

"It's not like we had notice or anything," Tod said.

"Only two of us can cross," I said, eyeing our friends on the bench. "Even if we could get to them, I don't know how many I can take at once." And the hellions could probably hear every word we were saying.

"Maybe you should go get help?" Tod whispered.

"Your mom?"

"No!" both Hudson brothers said.

"Levi, or Madeline," Tod suggested.

"The more, the merrier," Avari said, and somehow, his voice came from right next to me, though he hadn't left the pavilion. "Bring Madeline. I haven't yet made her acquaintance."

"No!" Emma shouted, with what may have been the last of her strength. "Don't bring Madeline. Avari needs her."

Tod and Nash both glanced at me, and I knew what they were thinking. What could unite three hellions who hated one another, and why the hell would they want Madeline?

Thane slapped Emma, and she gasped, then kicked him in the shin, still holding her side with one hand. He pulled his hand back to hit her again, but Luca stood and shoved Thane back, glaring silently, and the reaper actually stayed back. Tod wasn't the only member of the undead unnerved by the necromancer.

Sophie was sniffling quietly. Lydia looked paralyzed with fear and pain, and I realized she was syphoning some of Emma's pain. Neither of them would last long like that.

"Come on." I wasn't sure what the hellions were up to, but we couldn't help anyone from fifty feet away. I marched down the slight incline toward the pavilion and both Tod and Nash followed me.

"—don't need Madeline," Thane was saying when we got within earshot. "I told you, she can do it." He looked pointedly at me.

"I can do what?" I asked.

"You lying, traitorous bastard," Tod spat, but Thane only shrugged.

"We do what we have to do to survive. You promised to try to recover my soul if I helped you. Avari promised to give it back if I helped him. The difference is that he can't lie, and you can. I had to go with the sure thing."

"Is this a trade?" I asked Avari. "You want me? Fine. I'm here. I'll trade myself for all four of them," I said, glancing at my friends lined up on the bench.

"Oh, we're way beyond a simple trade," Belphegore said. "Avari can no longer afford to keep you for himself, and these four meat sacks are all necessary for our little project." She waved one hand at the bench and its occupants.

"But we are not unreasonable," Invidia said. "If you do what we ask, we will let both of your little men go free." She gestured at Nash and Tod.

"Hell, no," Tod spat, just as Nash said, "No way."

"We don't even know what they want yet," I said, without taking my attention away from the hellions. And Thane.

"Doesn't matter," Tod growled. "They don't get you."

"They don't get *any* of us. What do you want?" I asked Avari again.

"You may have noticed that we've learned how to cross into your world," he began, and I nodded. They'd gone to great pains to make sure I knew that. "The problem is that our current method of transportation requires a new human soul for each trip. We would like a more efficient way to utilize our resources. You help us, and both Hudsons will go free. You have my word."

"What about them?" I asked, glancing at the full bench again.

"Unfortunately, they are all part of the permanent solution. As are you."

"No." Tod grabbed my hand and started to haul me backward, and when I pulled free, he stood at my back, quietly fuming, strung so tight I could hear his teeth grinding.

"What do you want?"

"You and the *necroanima* will bind my life force with a resurrected soul already in my possession."

One of the reapers he'd snatched? And what the hell was a *necroanima?* Were they talking about Luca?

"Then you will install both in the body of this young woman—" Avari gestured to Lydia "—so that I can come and go from your world at will. There is one for each of us."

"What?" I frowned at the hellion. "I don't even know what that means. You want to live in Lydia's body? Forever?"

"Of course not." He frowned like my guess was preposterous. "Only until her body wears out. Then I will select another."

"What the *hell* is he talking about?" Nash asked. But no one had an answer.

"You will do as I instructed," Avari said. "I will have a reusable body to use in the human world, and your men will go free. Or… I will kill every single one of you and feast on your souls for eternity."

"That's not possible!" I insisted. "And even if it were, I can't do that. I *reclaim* souls, not reinstall them."

"You can do both," Invidia insisted. "Just like Madeline."

"Madeline?" I asked, and Luca's gaze fell to the ground and stayed there. I was missing something.

"Madeline reinstalled your soul," Avari said. "After her nephew reanimated your body."

"What? Luca can't reanimate dead people! He just finds them."

"Of course he can." Belphegore laughed out loud. "What did you think the *anima* part of *necroanima* meant?"

"I don't know what any of that means! He's a necromancer. Right? Luca?" I demanded, and finally he met my gaze.

"Over here, they call me a *necroanima*. Which is technically more accurate. Madeline was afraid that knowing too much would put you in danger, so she wouldn't let me tell you what I can really do. Or what *you* can do."

"I can install souls? Into *corpses?*" As a *bean sidhe,* I'd only been able to help put them back into their own not-yet-truly-dead bodies.

He nodded. "All extractors can."

"But you're more special than that, aren't you?" Avari reached out to touch my cheek, and Tod pulled me out of reach. After that, I didn't want to let his hand go. But I did, because I couldn't afford to look weak.

"How? How am I more special?" And why the hell was I the last to know?

"It takes the combined skills of both an extractor and a *bean sidhe* to bind a human soul to a non-human life force," Avari said. "There hasn't been one of those—one of *you*—in nearly a century, by the human calendar."

"What does that mean? It's actually possible?" I asked Luca, because even though Avari couldn't lie, I didn't trust him.

"In theory," Luca said. "It's never been done with a hellion, but it was done once with a lesser Nether-creature, so he could cross over and give testimony. The binding was done by a restored female *bean sidhe*. Just like you."

No. *No.* Where the hell was my copy of *History of the Nether?* Shouldn't that have been issued to me upon my death?

"That is the only reason I let your *necroanima* leave the Nether when he and your cousin crossed over by mistake," Avari said. "So that he could reanimate you. If you'd stayed dead, I would have lost your soul."

"You…?" Avari had planned this. Probably from the moment Thane showed him how to cross into the human world.

"Okay." I turned back to Avari, fighting to maintain focus. "But even if I wanted to help you—" and I didn't "—I can't do it. I don't know how."

"I think you'll figure it out. Let's practice the installation first. All you need is the proper…motivation." Belphegore hauled Emma off the bench and shoved Luca down when he tried to pull her back. "This one is your… What is the word? The one you care about. Your friend?"

Em was sniffling, tears pouring down her face, but her chin was stiff. Resolute. She was *so* much braver than I'd ever suspected. Braver than I'd ever *been*.

My hands curled into fists. "Don't touch her!"

"Pay attention, now," Belphegore said, her featureless, black-orb eyes trained on me. "We're going to play a game. All you have to do is catch the soul. Then we'll move on to the bonding."

"No!" I shouted when she reached for Emma. Em screamed.

Invidia snapped her neck with one hand.

Em crumpled to the ground and the scream that tore from my throat had no equal. Sophie, Lydia, and Luca slapped their hands over their ears. Even the hellions winced. The canvas overhead flapped, stirred by the power of my voice. Tree branches shook in the distance, and several fat purple fruits dropped to the ground.

Still screaming, I fell to my knees at Emma's side. I checked for a pulse, but there was none. I felt for breath, but she wasn't breathing. Her beautiful brown eyes stared up at the yellowish Netherworld sky through the ripped canvas, but they had no focus.

Emma was dead. Not *un*dead, like me. She was *gone,* her life stolen, her lifeline aborted without a second thought from the hellion who'd ended it. And with her, I'd lost a part of myself that could never be replaced. Emma was my other half. The sister I'd never had. The cousin I'd always wanted. We'd shared every triumph, every failure, and every secret.

I'd promised I would protect her. Instead, I'd gotten her killed.

I held Emma's head in my lap and screamed, and screamed, and screamed. Tears filled my eyes and poured over. Inside my head was a maelstrom of grief and fury that couldn't be expressed by either thought or word. I was *made* of pain and loss.

Luca let go of one ear to stare at his hand, and distantly I noticed that it was smeared with blood, more of which dripped from his ear.

Jaw clenched in fury, Tod took something from his pocket and handed it to Nash, but I couldn't see what it was through my tears, and I doubted Nash could, either. Neither of them were bothered by the female *bean sidhe*'s wail. They heard only the song I sang for my best friend's soul.

I would have screamed for Emma forever. I would have screamed for her soul until the earth crumbled beneath us both, just to keep from losing her. But Belphegore knelt in front of me and clamped her smooth, hard hand over my mouth.

"Nicely done," she said in the sudden, deafening silence. "But you cannot install what hasn't yet left the corpse."

In my grief and outrage, it took me a minute to understand. I'd screamed so fast and so loud for Emma that her soul didn't have a chance to leave her body. I'd suspended it in place, still inside her.

But the moment my scream ended, her soul began to rise. Belphegore opened her mouth and inhaled, and Em's soul began to float toward her.

My heart hurt. My head hurt. My throat hurt. My entire existence was pain and bleak darkness. Em could *not* die.

But it was too late. She was already dead. And even if the hellions would let me put her soul back in her body, there was no guarantee she'd ever regain consciousness. Her neck would still be broken, her body irreparably damaged.

So this time I screamed for her soul. Belphegore wouldn't get it. Neither would Avari or Invidia. No part of the Netherworld would have Emma, or any of the rest of my friends.

I sang for Emma's soul, and when I held my amphora out, her soul slid into the heart around my neck like it was always meant to be there. It wasn't. But at least she was safe there. Even if they took the amphora, they couldn't destroy it, and they couldn't remove her soul from it.

"Wonderful!" Belphegore clapped her flawless hands, her perfect lips curled into a forgettable smile. "Now bind her soul to me. Pull her out of your little heart and—"

"No." I laid Emma's body gently on the ground and stood, clutching the amphora in my fist, glaring at the world through fresh, furious tears. "*Hell,* no. You're not getting her. You're not getting any of us. You can kill every single one of them, and I'll put every single soul in here, where you can't touch it."

Sophie and Lydia cried harder behind me, and Luca tried to comfort them both through his own shock.

"And if we kill you?" Avari demanded. The hellions stood in front of me now, all in a row, united in their shared rage. In power so strong it radiated from them in waves that stung my skin.

"If you kill me, you will never, *ever* get what you want."

Avari opened his mouth to make another threat, and Tod shouted over him. A single word that approached the power and volume of my own voice.

"Now!"

He charged Avari, and from the other side, Nash charged Belphegore. Both hellions screamed, then bent at odd angles, reaching for something behind them. When they turned, still reaching in vain, I understood. The hilt end of my broken dagger protruded from the center of Avari's back, where he couldn't reach it. The blade end was stuck in Belphegore, where she couldn't reach it.

Only Invidia remained unhurt, and she was so confused by the chaos and competing demands from Avari and Belphegore for her help that for a moment she turned in circles, paralyzed by indecision.

Nash rushed around Belphegore and pulled Luca off the bench. I held Emma's arm while each of the boys grabbed one of my wrists, and right before I blinked us into the human world, I realized that Thane was gone, but I had no idea when he'd left.

A minute later, Tod appeared next to us beneath the human-world pavilion, with both Lydia and Sophie.

I dropped onto the ground with Emma's hand clutched in mine, and though the others stood around me, I saw nothing but Em. Until Nash picked her body up and her hand slid from my grip. He carried her toward the cars, while Luca herded the other girls and Tod pulled me to my feet. I walked, but I didn't see where I was going.

I didn't care.

After only a few steps, Lydia collapsed and I blinked, jarred out of my own shock. Tod and I knelt next to her. She was still breathing. She still had a pulse. But her eyes were closed and she wasn't moving.

"We have to go," Tod said, sliding one arm behind her shoulders to pick her up. "They'll cross over as soon as they get the blades out and heal."

"No, they won't," Thane said, and I jumped, startled, to find him behind us. "I cleaned out their stockpile, during your convenient distraction."

"Their stockpile?"

"The restored souls. I took them all. Including mine." He took off his glasses, and I was oddly relieved to see that he had both pupils and irises again. "Can't have them coming after me, now can I? And the restored souls will fetch one hell of a price somewhere else. *Anywhere* else."

Before I could demand that he turn the souls over to the proper authority, his gaze fell to Lydia, lying motionless on the ground. "I couldn't get hers, though."

"What? Her soul? Where is it?"

"In the Nether. Here. Everywhere. She was syphoning Emma's pain when Emma died, and part of her soul went with Emma's."

"Part?" I wrapped my hand around the heart hanging against my sternum. It was unnaturally warm.

"The rest dissipated."

"So she's…empty?" Tod said, staring at Lydia, and his hand curled around mine, around the amphora, like he would help me protect it.

Thane nodded. "I've only seen that a couple of times—a living body with no soul. She'll be dead in minutes."

"If she doesn't get a soul…" Tod said, his gaze holding mine. Challenging it. There was a choice to be made, and I had to make it.

I nodded. I understood.

I could save Emma. Part of her, anyway. And I could save part of Lydia. Nothing would be the same. But at least life would go on. I owed it to them both to try.

Nash laid Emma on the ground next to Lydia.

I closed my eyes, but I could still see them in my head and I could feel everyone watching me. Sophie was still sniffling, clutching Luca's arm. Nash held Emma's limp hand. Tod was waiting, and he was ready, too. Once I withdrew Em's soul from the amphora, I'd need a male *bean sidhe* to help guide it into another body.

I sang out to Emma's soul, and when it came out of the amphora, Tod helped me guide it into Lydia's body. Then we waited.

At first, nothing happened, and I didn't know whether to be horrified or relieved by the thought that I'd done it wrong. That Emma's suffering would end with her life.

Then Lydia opened her eyes. They weren't blue, like they should have been. They were brown. Emma-brown.

"Kaylee?" Emma said with Lydia's voice, blinking those familiar brown eyes at me. "What happened? Where are we?" She sat up, and everyone moved back to give her space. "Why do I sound weird? Why am I so pale?" she demanded, staring at Lydia's forearm, stretched out in front of her.

"I couldn't save you," I whispered, and those four words held more shame than I'd known I could feel. I'd promised I wouldn't let her die. Then I'd failed her. "This was the best I could do. But I swear on my afterlife that they'll pay, Em. All three of them."

Avari wanted my soul, but he was going to get a hell of a lot more than that. He was going to get pain. And loss. And justice. He was going to get vengeance in kind for every soul he'd stolen. For every friend he'd taken from me. This time I would feed from *his* pain, and with any luck, it would hurt worse knowing that he'd put into motion his own downfall.

Avari had woken me up and given my afterlife purpose. He'd awakened my rage.

Emma had given me reason to use it.

★ ★ ★ ★ ★

Kaylee's revenge is coming.
Don't miss the final story!

A special treat from Rachel Vincent
A Day in the Afterlife of Tod
(pre-IF I DIE)

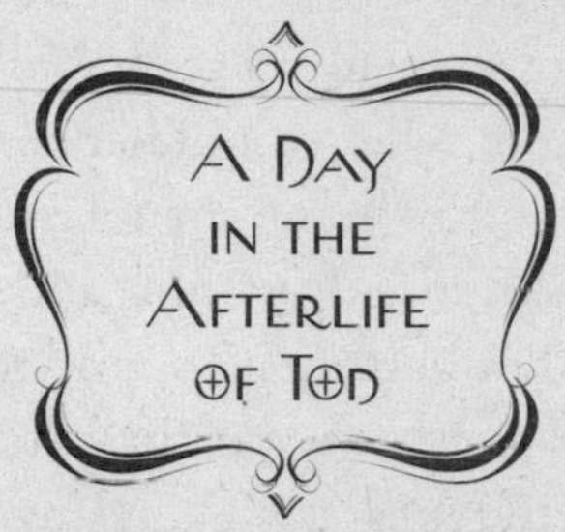
A DAY
IN THE
AFTERLIFE
OF TOD

8:00 a.m.—Another cup of coffee. Pecan caramel, this time. I've tried every flavor of creamer the cafeteria has. The coffee still sucks.

8:54 a.m.—These E.R. chairs were manufactured in the seventies. I swear cave men were more comfortable sitting on logs and rocks. That's it. I'm filing that requisition form today. Eight months of practicing the attending physician's signature is about to pay off....

9:47 a.m.—Rush-hour traffic collision. Crushed sternum. Splinters of bone sticking through his skin. Two punctured lungs. Death is a mercy. Hey, is that coffee on his shirt? Smells good. Wonder what kind of creamer he uses?

10:38 a.m.—Third period. Kaylee has no class this period. I have no one to kill. Coincidence, or fate?

11:54 a.m.—Six minutes left on my shift. *I will not go to the school after work. I will not go to the school after work. I will not go to the school after—*

12:22 p.m.—Lunch in the quad. Nash is having pizza. I

don't care if I never see another slice of pizza. Kaylee's wearing that blue shirt again. That one that matches her eyes. She looks tired. *I will not show myself to her at lunch. I will not show myself to her at lunch. I will not show—*

12:24 p.m.—Nash's pizza tastes as bland as it looks. But since I already took a bite, he said I should just take the rest of it. Wonder what would happen if I took a nibble on Kaylee…?

1:48 p.m.—Wonder what would happen if I switch the labels on some of the bottles in the chemistry lab's storage closet? Ooh! Or I could test the acidity of the toilet-bowl water with these litmus strips. I'm betting it's acidic….

2:36 p.m.—Seriously, *why* do they still teach history in school? If it's going to repeat itself, anyway, can't we just catch it the next time around?

3:02 p.m.—School's out. Only nine more hours to kill until there will be actual people to kill. Er, reap.

4:22 p.m.—Large pepperoni and sausage. There in thirty minutes, or your money back. Minus the fifty-second commute, and the actual delivery leaves me twenty-five minutes to pop over to Mom's house for a brownie.

4:26 p.m.—Kaylee and Nash are trying to swallow each other whole. I suggested they eat the brownies instead. Nash threw one at me. My appetite is gone.

4:40 p.m.—There's never anything good on TV. At the hospital, they only play news and cartoons. And not the good cartoons. The ones where animals dance around and some little girl with a big head counts in Spanish. *Ayúdame!*

4:41 p.m.—If Nash and Kaylee are going to make out instead of watching the movie, they should just hand over the remote.

4:42 p.m.—The remote slid down between them on the couch, and I am *not* going after it.

4:43 p.m.—I wonder if there's any reasonable way to reinterpret the phrase "Get the hell out of here, Tod" to mean "Please stay and help us maintain the PG rating on this hormonal train wreck." Maybe if I rearrange the letters…

5:58 p.m.—Dude. Do NOT answer the door in your underwear. No two-dollar tip is worth that. Now I'm going to have to find something prettier to purge that mental image. Mangled bunny roadkill should do the trick.

7:00 p.m.—Is it time to reap souls yet?

7:01 p.m.—Seriously, has time stopped moving? Is this what eternity feels like?

9:10 p.m.—Kaylee's practicing conjugating irregular verbs for a French test tomorrow. I said I'd check the verb chart for her, but this stupid language has more sounds than letters, and I'm not sure I even remember how to conjugate English verbs.

9:24 p.m.—I have no idea what she's saying, but it's hot.

11:05 p.m.—Sabine suggests we play Guess Whose Life Sucks Worse. I can't lose this one. I'm not even alive.

11:14 p.m.—New game. Guess Whose *Love* Life Sucks Worse. It's a tie. A big, pathetic tie.

1:00 a.m.—An hour into my shift, and no one's died yet. Is it possible to be bored to death if you're already dead?

3:42 a.m.—Massive cranial and spinal trauma from head-on collision. A cause of death near and dear to my heart. *Now* we're talkin'…

5:19 a.m.—The guy in room 434 looks tired. He looks *done.* We both know this is the last room he'll ever see, and he's ready to end it. He deserves a merciful, peaceful death in his sleep. But he's not scheduled to go for another four days. Poor guy. Sometimes I wish I was the boss.

7:43 a.m.—Hit-and-run at an elementary school crosswalk. She can't be more than eight years old. I hate my job.

8:00 a.m.—Parents crying in the waiting room. They don't know yet. I wish I didn't know. I wish I didn't have to see her last moments. I wish I didn't have to *be* her last moments. I'm sick of white walls and endings. The only thing that doesn't end in this place is me. I don't end. I just go on, and on, swinging that scythe glued to my hand. There's no rhythm to the strokes. Few see death coming, and even those who do see death don't see *me.* Because there is no me. Not anymore. Always the reaper, never the reaped. Soon that won't bother me. Soon I won't care. Emotional death follows physical death at a different pace for each reaper. I've put it off for more than two years, but it's inevitable.

It would take a miracle to keep me alive on the inside.

When I was a kid, my mom said that everyone gets one miracle. She said the trick is recognizing your miracle from a distance, so you're ready when it arrives. I'm watching. I'm waiting.

I'm ready for my miracle.

•

Acknowledgments

Thanks first of all to my husband, who puts up with the mental fog I walk around in midbook.

Thanks to my editor, Mary-Theresa Hussey, for endless advice and patience.

Thanks to everyone at Harlequin Teen, for everything done behind the scenes to make this book happen. That is truly an enormous list.

Thanks to my agent, Merrilee Heifetz, who made this book possible.

And a special thanks to Karen Shangraw, who brought Kaylee's guidance counselor to life.

The Spellbound Novels

In this contemporary series of spells and magic, curses and love, new-girl Emma Connor faces snobs and bullies at her elite Manhattan prep school. When the hottest boy in school inexplicably becomes her protector, Emma finds her ordinary world changing and a new life opening to her, filled with surprising friendships, deadly enemies and a witchy heritage she never suspected.

AVAILABLE WHEREVER BOOKS ARE SOLD!

HTSPELTR2